Ver Sacrum

_or_

"Heaven Help Us All"

A novel

_by_

W. E. SMITH

_A poignant mediation on the emotional wages of war . . .
deftly told . . . often strikes a poetic note._
Kirkus Reviews

This novel is dedicated to

the Vietnam Generation

the People of Vietnam

Gail, love giver

my brothers Henry Albert Smith III and Timothy Neal Smith,

&

my father, Henry Albert Smith
First Lieutenant, Maryland National Guard

PEACE!

&

The term *ver sacrum* (sacred springtime) was used by Roman authors to designate an Italic rite that was attested several times by sources dealing with the origins and history of peoples classified today in the Sabellian-Umbrian linguistic branch. As far back as the time of the very first settlements by people known as the Aborigines, there was a custom of consecrating to the god the entire generation born in a given year after wars, famines, or even overpopulation. Young men old enough to bear arms were compelled to leave their country and found 'colonies' in new lands.

Doniger and Bonnefoy, *Dictionary of Mythology*

VER SACRUM

or

"Heaven Help Us All"

A note from Caroline Curtis, literary agent

All agents have their anecdotes, strange, quaint, or startling, about how manuscripts come into our hands. We're flooded with the written word, thousands upon thousands of pages a week, sent by desperate graduate students hoping a stunning literary success will spare them the indignity of getting a job. These efforts run the gamut from not being worth the paper they're printed on; through efforts showing glimmers of real talent—even, in some cases, genius!—but lacking the integrity of design needed to reach the zone of art; to masterful works of literature—the last of these being by far the most rare. Where the following effort resides on that continuum I'll leave to you to decide. Having taken on the project, it should be clear that I think it not without merit.

In any case, the purpose of this preface is not to critique the work, but to relate the unusual way in which the manuscript came to my attention. The young man whose letter follows called me one day at my office. His story of a binder buried in a closet for fifteen years hardly whetted my literary appetite; but there was in his demeanor a joyful openness (which I seldom find in the young these days) and a truly touching admiration for his mother, so I decided to take a look. To wit the following:

September 18, 2006

Dear Ms. Curtis:

Here's that stuff I said I'd send. I hope you like it. I find it pretty fascinating, but I realize that may just be because it's about my own family. My mother, Marjorie Llewellyn, wrote it years ago when she worked as a therapist in Washington, DC. People didn't have internet or even cell phones back then. One thing was the same, though. We were having a war with Iraq. I was still just a tot and didn't know Mom yet. I know that sounds strange, but I'm adopted.

When I was growing up, I used to look around her room. I would even go in the closet and check out her stuff. Just curious, like any kid. Sometimes I'd come across this binder with the words *Heaven Help Us All* written across the spine in black magic marker. I especially liked to look at the photos stuffed in the back—photos of Mom and Dad, my grandma and grandfather, Uncle Bob, Aunt Gloria and cousin Drew, Uncle Charles, and also me. The words were mostly Greek to a little kid like myself, but my father's name was in there (also some other people I knew) and it seemed an important thing about my family. One day, when I was about eight, Mom found me looking at it. She skipped across the room, snatched it away, and said it wasn't for kids. But I could tell by the way she gazed at it that it held some special meaning for her and, of course, that made me want to know about it even more. Unfortunately, she reached up in the closet and put it where I couldn't get at it. Then she went back to working on her loom.

All during my childhood, I never stopped wondering about that binder. Maybe, because I was adopted, I craved information about all the things that happened before my parents took me on. When I got big enough to reach that shelf I'd go in when Mom wasn't around and take it down. Don't get me wrong. I wouldn't read it. That didn't seem honest, after she told me that she didn't want me to. I would just hold it, feel the weight of it. Maybe look at the photos stuffed in the back. Finally, when I was in the ninth grade, I got up the nerve to ask Mom when she thought I'd be old enough to give the whole thing a proper read. She got all thoughtful-mothery like she gets and said when I graduate from college. Dad said good-that-might-give-him-some-incentive-to-finish-the-degree. (:/)

I finished up at NM State this past May and Mom, like always, was true to her word. I've read that binder three times now. And I must say, I learned a lot about my family—and also some things about history I didn't know. Especially how war can mess people up. Now I understand why, every time the subject of what I'd do when I grew up got discussed, Mom always said, "I don't care what you do, as long as it isn't soldiering." Sometimes she'd grip me around the shoulders, look me in the eyes, and make me promise to never take up arms.

I probably shouldn't say much else. You'll read it all inside. Like I said over the phone, with the times we're living through, some people might find it interesting.

Thank you for your time and attention (bcnu),
Arturo Llewellyn-Devers

Letter to Howard Dansiger from Marj Llewellyn

December 21, 1991

Howard Dansiger, Director
Capitol Center for Psychic Wellness
400 North Capitol Street
Washington, D.C. 20004

Dear Howie,
I told you when I left the clinic that I would contact you when I was ready. I didn't think it would take ten months, but when do life's timetables work out as we predict? I realize now that several lines of inner struggle came to a head last winter, the unraveling of one instigating the unraveling of another, until I have come to a place of calm and peace, ready to move forward.

Gary Devers, whom I spoke to you about on a couple of occasions, had a great deal to do with all of this. But I wouldn't say that he was the cause of things, or even a catalyst for the changes I have gone through. More properly, he and I were fortunate enough to find a place where, together, we untangled the overgrown vines of our lives. It was a time of strange synchronicities: events I've come to regard as the hand of Spirit reaching into my life, offering wholeness (admittedly, in this instance, along paths I had never dreamt of traveling).

Gary came to the clinic as a client. You may remember the conflict engendered by my feelings toward him; you counseled me—quite properly, of course—to have his file transferred to one of our colleagues. In some ways (in some only) I wish I had had the clarity to do that. I did not, however, and he and I became involved in ways that at first provoked considerable anguish. But as the days and weeks wore on, an inevitability asserted itself that I came to feel comfortable with. It is likely I will never resolve all the ethical nuances I then confronted.

I know this is hard to understand. It no doubt confuses matters further to say that time has convinced me that in some sense Gary was a veteran, not only of Vietnam, but other wars as well. More importantly, I have come to question whether he ever should have been considered a client. He came as one bearing a message. I would be hard-pressed to name any respect in which he is any more traumatized than the rest of us.

What follows started as an attempt to bring you up-to-date, to try to explain, and to understand myself. Somewhere along the line it became an open song of the heart and perhaps the most honest thing I have ever done. It took me farther afield than I had planned, but it all seemed necessary.

Sincerely yours,
Marj Llewellyn

HEAVEN HELP US ALL

A Report Prepared for the
Center for Pychic Wellness

by

Marjorie Llewellyn, Pys. D.

Voices

INVOCATION

I dreamed I saw the bombers,
Flying shotgun in the sky,
Turning into butterflies above our nation.
Joni Mitchell, "Woodstock"

Weapons are unblessed among tools,
The sober-minded detest them,
They resort to violence only when inescapable,
For their highest value is peace.
Even in victory they do not rejoice,
For martial victory means the slaughter of
    one's fellow human beings,
They go into battle as if attending the funerary rites,
Standing at the emperor's right hand side.
Lao Tzu, Tao te ching

Heaven help the roses when the bombs begin to fall.
Ron Miller, "Heaven Help Us All"

She well knows that by once enlisting under other banners than her own, were they even the banners of foreign independence, she would involve herself beyond the power of extrication, in all the wars of interest and intrigue, of individual avarice, envy, and ambition, which assume the colors and usurp the standard of freedom. The fundamental maxims of her policy would insensibly change from *liberty* to *force* . . . . She might become the dictatress of the world. She would be no longer be the ruler of her own spirit.
John Quincy Adams, U.S. Secretary of State, 1818

Wartime is only the other side of peacetime,
But if you ever seen how wars are won,
You'd know what it's like to wish that peace
   would come . . .
      Michael Brewer and Tom Shipley,
      "Seems Like a Long Time"

Prelude

SUMMER, 1990

WE THOUGHT PEACE might come last summer. It's true, the mayor of our beloved burg—*the capital of the free world*—was up on cocaine charges (it was an ugly trial, with tainted contracts, call girls, an indignant wife, and creditable accusations of a *racist* prosecution). And Lord knows, I'm still not over those women who worked the *stroll*—we had a psychopath on the loose, and city police without a decent lead. But for all our local concerns, somehow manageable for being close at hand, we were crazily hopeful about world events. The seed planted in the Gdansk shipyards ten years earlier had finally borne its startling fruit; we looked on amazedly, month by month, as one crude dictatorship after another toppled to the awakened purpose of manifold peoples longing for sweet *freedom*. Who can forget the sense of elation, with Bush and Gorby talking disarmament like old camarades (or the joyous crowds who, stone by stone, ripped apart the Berlin Wall, forever parting an Iron Curtain)? I know it stretches credulity, but the Cold War bogeyman who had shadowed our entire lives—atomic blast nightmares, "duck and cover," proxy wars near and far—seemed, in one wrenching turn of history, well and finally laid to rest. And then last winter—as if these marvels were not enough!—Mandela was released. Could it be, I wondered, that the world's last re-actionary holdouts had finally kenned that you cannot catego-rize people by the melanin content of their skin? I joined the avenue's cheering throngs when, on a sparkling June day, the graying freedom fighter visited at the White House.

After drenching the capital in its soggy torpor, July burst into wracking storms that strewed our city's streets with lush limbs of maple and oak. In the cooler calm that followed those tempests, Cheryl and I motored out to Wolf Trap to see Jackson Browne. I confess it was a nostalgic indulgence; but it was also rites of summer—and a renewed dialogue with the voice we knew so well from high school years . . .

> *Oh people look around you, the signs are everywhere,*
> *You've left it for somebody other than you to be the one to care . . .*

It had been years since I was surrounded by ladies with hair loose and long, men with sideburns and deep eyes. Then, sweet summer air, blankets on the lawn, the expectant mood of the crowd, —and the poet himself, all brought me to remembrance. *What I'm trying to say is* out among the further rings of the burbs, on a grassy slope arced by greenish sky, I managed to forget the city's troubles and believe that my fondest youthful dreams— peace in the world, racial harmony, and a mellow contentment in one another—were finally coming true.

The benign buzz of that magic evening lingered over the crest of our dazedly bright midsummer. The following weekend the National Gallery's airy spaces, and Brancusi's primal stone silences, made a perfect dreamscape for my serenity—and Jorge a grand companion, with his fine artistic sense and unflagging curiosity. If there was an awkward moment, when we stood before two lovers entwined in marbled bliss (our bosum friend-ship had resisted all temptation to become something more), we wordlessly separated until shared enthusiasm over a polished egg labeled *Newborn* brought us back together again.

Later that week, after the worst of the rush had passed, I motored again to the Virginia burbs to check on my mother. I found her stepping around the patio behind her townhouse, contentedly admiring the scarlet monardas she had planted the previous spring. *Hummingbirds come in the mornings*, she told me, and I pictured her sipping tea and watching them feed. That image rendered me supremely grateful for her garden, and also for the gardening club, about which she shared some inconsequential details. They were a comforting thread to the life we knew when my father yet lived: a house and yard, dark soil, a tool shed, and growing things.

As for the Center for Psychic Wellness, our traumatized veterans seemed genuinely uplifted by the hopeful international developments, if signaled by nothing more than an occasional brightness in the eyes, a cleaner energy in the voice.

But alas! our summer idyll was about to end. As Sarah Tilly would say, Grandmother Spider was weaving a radical shift in the patterns of our lives . . .

& & &

HUSSEIN'S ARMIES invaded Kuwait on August 2nd. I caught a snippet on the late news, sandwiched between items on the mayor's trial, which went to jury that day, and the search for the prostitute killer. Despite the distress war talk is bound to engender in one so familiar with war's ravages, there was yet something of *Arabian Nights* in the royal brother's last, fatal stand (that airy seaside palace, drenched in sun and blue). The weekend was filled with the usual errands, and an exhibit of Yoruban weavings I had been looking forward to, so it wasn't until I settled in with Sunday's *Post* that I realized how serious things were. There were condemnations from all quarters, anxiety over trapped Americans, and a president's resolve to protect our "vital interests." I was already thinking about my mother when the phone rang.

"Did you see the president?"

"Just a clip on the news."

"I don't like the sound of it."

"The worst seems to be over, Ma."

"If he goes for Saudi Arabia, they'll fight him." She seemed to be thinking out loud. "Or if they start hurting those hostages . . ."

"I don't think they'll do that," I countered. "I can't imagine Hussein wants to tangle with the United States."

"If they call up Bobby I'll just die. I can't go through this again. Grenada was bad enough, and they hardly had an army. Saddam has a million soldiers. And poison gas!"

"Mom, try not to worry. Bob was active duty then. Besides, no one's rushing to start a war."

"They're already sending an aircraft carrier," she said. "That's how it starts—the aircraft carrier. I learned that from your dad. And what does the president mean? Watch, wait, learn? Watch what? Learn what?"

Our conversation was clearly fueling her anxieties; I didn't respond. After a moment, she resumed.

"Why didn't they get our people out of there? That's what I can't understand. Some people say Kuwait stole Iraq's oil and ought to be a part of Iraq anyway. What's in it for us? Everybody's talking about oil. They can have their danged oil, for all I care. I'm sorry to go on, but this is so hard for me . . ."

"I know."

"Our anniversary would have been next week."

"Ma?"

"What?"

"I'll be out to visit soon. I'm working on a weaving pattern

I want to show you."

"I'm sure I'll be thrilled to see it."

"And listen, you shouldn't focus so much on the news. It's not healthy for you."

"What else do you expect me to do?"

"Work on your knitting. Get out in the garden."

"Basket weaving at the sanitarium, huh? I knit until my eyes fall out. And there's nothing more to do in the garden."

"You could volunteer somewhere."

"You know I don't like to be away from home."

"It might just do you some good."

"Baby, there's no use finding a purpose for an old crone. I only want peace and quiet—and for my kids to be all right."

"Mom, you're still an attractive and youthful woman."

"And you're very sweet. Will you call your brother? I'm sure he'd like to hear from you."

ಶ ಶ ಶ

Over the coming weeks the Gulf situation grew more menacing: Hussein announced the end of the Kuwaiti kingdom. The emir confessed his heart *squeezed with sadness,* a grief I wished to believe spent as much for a lost brother as a lost crown. President Bush sent warriors and armaments to the faraway desert (*Newsweek* photo: the USS Eisenhower floats through the Suez Canal, its deck bristling with armored wasps, sailors crowded around its rails) at a dizzying pace. Hussein banned the exit of foreigners, his own *desert shield* of human flesh and spirit. By Labor Day some kind of stalemate had been achieved. Officials were confident—this should have worried me—that the blockade would bring the dictator to reason as they saw it.

All this saber-rattling made itself felt among my Vietnam veterans, men who had yet to recover from our last grand descent into mass violence. The glimmers I had so recently seen were gone from their eyes, the music from their voices as they grimly grappled with their losses, their fears, and their regrets. Intrusive visions intensified. Nightmares increased. The steady working through of issues—the normal fare of our weekly support group—gave way to anxious debate over the prospect of a new thrust of American military might.

"Say we do go in. Will Congress let the professionals run the show, or will they just turn the whole thing into another political football?"

"How about the public? Are they going to support a long engagement?"

"Yeah, and who's going to give a rat's behind in ten years about the guys what did the heavy lifting?"

I called Bob one evening as my mother had asked. I still picture the tow-headed tyke Cheryl and I made over, marshaling his toy tanks with that attitude of dazed wonder; then, how he would wake screaming after Dad returned from his last tour, refusing all comfort until I came to his room to make him laugh. Gloria seemed weary when she picked up, so I resisted the urge to chat (beyond simple inquiries into her well-being). We could catch up later on little Drew. Still I was glad that she had answered. It was her voice, warm and open, that let me believe that all was well in my brother's world. His fortress of stoicism no more guaranteed me his safety than duty and honor had preserved our father.

"Yo, big Sis."

"How are you?"

"No complaints."

"Have you talked to Mom?"

"Couple a times."

"She's worried about you."

"No need. They only called up a few units."

"I know, but you know how she is."

In the silence that followed, I wondered, *Does he?*

"You know what the grunts said in Nam," he said.

"What's that?"

"It don't mean a thing."

"You don't believe that, do you?"

"Something to say."

"Stop saying it. Will you, please?"

"I'll try."

"How's the job going?"

"Pretty good."

"You still like working with computers?"

"You know I love gadgets."

"Frankly, Bob, I'm a little worried too."

"Sis, Saddam's not crazy enough for a pissing match with the U.S. He's crazy, but he's not that crazy."

"I hope so. How are Gloria and Drew?"

"They're okay. And you?"

"I'm fine."

"Got a boyfriend these days?"

"None of your business."

"I guess that's a no or, —he's married."

"Shush."

"Listen, tell Mom not to worry."

❧ ❧ ❧

THERE WAS LAUGHTER in Bob's voice as we said goodbye. His sly tease about married men was a clairvoyant probe at my weakest point: for how, I wondered, could he have known about Stephen? Cheryl, to whom I cried bitter tears over my academic mentor, who would not leave his family for all the obvious reasons, would never share my confidences. Since returning from my studies in New Mexico I had tried to forget the whole, sad affair.

But more to the point, how describe Jorge and me? That wandering troupe with panpipes and guitars, he affixed by the sounds of his Peruvian homeland, I intrigued by the musicians' brightly woven vests? Or the way he turned, amid the delighted office workers who crowded the sidewalks of Connecticut Avenue, to share his rapture? With his Hispanic courtesy the perfect lubricant we forged, with unstudied naturalness, an alliance against the city's loneliness—a fortress fashioned from movies and art exhibits, hiking by the river, and tales of a civil engineer's work (hearing of tangible structures that undergird this city, which had always seemed a shifting mirage, gave me a certain comfort). We exchanged ideas and friends, recipes, and phrases in Spanish and English. I adored, of course, the work he was doing toward his doctorate—fantastical schemes for metropoli of the future. And when one caught wind of one of the Cuzco Boys' impromptu concerts, we would ring the other and rush, when appointments and classes allowed, toward that soughing of the Andes' distant escarpments cascading through the city's glass and granite canyons!

If he had tried it on, a few months into our acquaintence (after, I should add, we had each imbibed way too much sangria), my gentle rebuff steered things back into the channels of a platonic friendship which I found—and that Jorge himself gave every indication of finding—not merely diverting, but the expression of a true meeting of souls. His invitation to Cheryl and Dan's annual Labor Day cookout was understood: he has always been a great favorite of theirs.

When I arrived at the rowhouse below Adams Morgan where he rented a second-floor apartment, he invited me up to see the drawings that would constitute the final phase of his dissertation work. They were spread across an oaken antique that served as both dining table and work desk. His manner evinced none of the skittishness that normally accompanied a sharing of his creations, imagined cityscapes that partake as much of the spirit of Escher as of his hero, Piranesi (cloverleafs threaded through luxuriant gardens, shining columns, —recondite grottos holding pieces of statuary!). Instead he projected the sober aura of one whose work has finally found its natural resting place.

I approached the table in a silence made complete by the drone of a refrigerator in the next room; Jorge stood outside a pool of light shed by lamps clamped to table edge. I was instantly beguiled by what I found there—an aerial view of a futuristic city and its surroundings —, so finely balanced, without forgoing myriad details, were the renderings that covered large sheets of draftsman's paper carefully scotch-taped together. There was, first, a central plaza bordered by structures both strong and elegant, in its wide and open center a pavilion, labeled BROTHERHOOD, set off by fountains bursting with jets of floating spray. The entire metropolis was embraced by a circular way, this connected to the plaza by spokes that carried electric trams; concentric rings, also with their trams, echoed from center to edge. Each successive band brought a greater admixture of green, until the final sector consisted of canopied forest. It was amid these shady boughs, I knew through many conversations, that the city's residents would dwell, meeting their daily needs along simple footpaths. The only breaks in the forest occurred at village greens, along the banks of watercourses and at meadows, where animals might find habitat (or lovers collect wildflowers of a summer's day).

I was so immersed in his drawings (one of the meadows, to be exact) that I didn't notice Jorge move around the table, silent as a panther, to a place behind me. The soft pressure of his fingertips on my waist, the dampness of his mouth on the nape of my neck, startled me. My insides began to go liquid. In my absorption, I turned to face him only slowly.

I gently pushed him away.

"I thought we weren't going to be like this," I said. My voice was tremulous.

"I haven't always been so sure."

His hands lingered on my waist.

I slipped along the rim of the table; his fingers glided onto my arms, probed to capture my hands. I pulled until I was free and walked to the other side. For a long moment I gazed blankly into Jorge's drawings. When I looked up, he stood in that immutable way of his and asked, in his most simple manner, did I like them?

As we motored to the far suburbs, the strong sun of a dying summer splayed across the windshield, we confined our conversaton to petty details of the week just passed. But in the silences that cleaved our conversation—ranchers and split-levels flowing by—I struggled desperately to process Jorge's sudden amatory demarche. His gesture portended chaos where I preferred to construct a refuge; threatened me with everything of my past from which our friendship had helped to shield me. When we breached the closer burbs into more open vistas—pristine McMansions, standing aloof amid rolling golf courses and uncut pastures—I groped in vain for the spontaneous connectedness that had always comprised our better moments.

When we arrived at Cheryl and Dan's the long driveway was already lined with cars. We walked around back. Dan was at the grill, his and Cheryl's guests seated in a rough circle sheltered by an aging pear tree's broken shade. Julian, Cheryl's toddler, tilted among the adults on unsteady feet. Her one-year-old, Emmy, bounced gently in her mother's lap. I recognized most of the usual crowd. My old friend Beth Delantis and her husband were there, a couple of Dan's friends, Cheryl's mother, Mrs.

McFarland and her brother, Mark. There were also a couple of workmates she had kept up with since beginning her mothering stint. Children played around the woodpile and on the play set.

After greeting Jorge and me, and making what introductions were required, Cheryl informed us that the group had been discussing our mayor's cocaine trial. The jury had hung on the most serious charges, in spite of inescapable evidence that Mayor Barry—become notorious across the country as a symbol of corrupt municipal government—had perjured himself in regard to transactions in the contraband substance. Several African-American jurors, it was reported, were convinced that the entire enterprise was a set-up by a right-wing federal administration to bring down a populist black politician.

"I'm just glad it's over," Mrs. McFarland said. "The trial was tearing the city apart. A lot of blacks felt that it was a judicial lynching, I think they said."

Her remark was met with awkward silence, until after a moment Donna, one of Cheryl's workmates, came out with, "Now we have Saddam to worry about."

"Don't get me started." It was Mark McFarland, Bob's boyhood comrade in countless war games and, like Bob, a veteran of the United States' armed forces.

"Pleeeeease don't," his wife, Susan, entoned—in jest, but only partly so, it seemed.

"I just think we need to kick some serious butt," Mark stated flatly.

Now Beth DeLantis, so inseparable from Cheryl and me in school that the three of us were widely known as the *Mod Squad*, came in. "If calm heads prevail," she offered in the measured cadences of an undersecretary at a major federal agency, "the situation could work itself out through diplomatic channels."

"It's more likely," Mark McFarland countered archly, "that further dilly-dallying will just allow Saddam to keep stalling until the annexation of Kuwait is a fait accompli."

Now Dan's friend Ron, he of thin face, pleasantly balding and of avuncular manner, came in. "My concern," he began with a thoughtful nod toward Mark, "is that things could spiral out of control. Hussein has one of the largest armies in the world. And he's thought to be harboring chemical weapons. I'd hate to have another Vietnam on our hands. Or, God forbid, worse. Not that I'm comfortable letting the guy gobble up any small nation he develops a sudden yen for . . ."

"Perhaps we shouldn't have built up his regime," Beth said now. "Of course, at the time, the United States government chiefly wanted a counterweight to the anti-American revolutionaries in Iran . . ."

"You don't have to worry about another Vietnam, Ron," Mark McFarland interrupted, ignoring Beth completely. "This isn't going to be another stalemate—or some wimpy rescue like Carter tried in Iran. These boy have learned their lesson. It's like Teddy Roosevelt said, the only sin is 'soft hitting.' No bunch of ragheads is going to stand up to what we're bringing on for ten minutes. You can count on that."

In the silence that followed Mark glanced toward Jorge. I feared he was gauging whether my friend, on account of his olive-toned complexion, might be considered a *raghead*. Apparently satisfied he hadn't offended anyone, he closed his peroration and stared into the lawn.

"You have to admit," Beth picked up again, calmly undaunted, "if it weren't for Kuwait's oil reserves, the United States government would be little troubled by the disappeance of some small, desert kingdom . . ."

Cheryl announced that she had to attend to preparations in the kitchen and, having heard enough, I offered to join her. I scooped up Emmy, leaving Jorge listening attentively to the others.

While Cheryl and I put together a salad, with Emmy plopped on the counter toying with shreds of greens and carrot, I unburdened myself about the episode at Jorge's place.

"He is a man, after all."

"I've noticed that," I said. "It's just that we decided, ages ago, that we weren't going to be like that."

"Yes, you did decide that, but . . ."

Yes, *but*. Cheryl—girlhood neighbor and constant companion, lifelong friend—knew me better than I knew myself. Touching on everything from the oft-unappreciated role of simple hormones in all our interactions with the opposite sex, to the differing evolutionary reproductive strategies of men and women, the lingering effects of my busted affair in New Mexico, the untimely loss of my father—even on Doug DeForrest, the golden boy of my youth (wine-fueled revels in the woods, making out in the back of his brother's car; guitars, motorcycles—sweet love letters!); —finishing with an appeal to the inscrutable but imperious dictates of Eros, she masterfully summed up my life as only someone who truly cared—and who took a Classics masters with high honors—could.

To my question as to whether men and women can even be simple friends (I struggling to steady a squirming infant, offering salad spoon as plaything), she averred with dead certainty that solid and satisfying friendship between men and women was indeed possible, as long as both parties had a very clear idea of what was—and what was not—on offer. She is too considerate, and too sweet a friend, to have pointed out that such a characterization could apply to neither Jorge nor myself: he yearning for more than I could give and I, reluctant to lose his companionship, willfully ignoring signals that no woman with even a jot of her gender's storied intuition could for three years have remained oblivious to. But I took her point and, feeling suddenly hopeless over the tangled conundrums of my life, grew silent.

Putting the finishing touches on the salad (croutons and grated pamesan), the picture of steady, domestic contentment, Cheryl wiped her forehead with the back of one wrist and said, "Well, that's that." Looking up, noting my sadness (for I could hide nothing from her), she rounded the counter, beheld me for a moment, and enclosed both little Emily and myself in a slow and snug embrace. Emmy fingered my mouth and cooed.

I rubbed her back, a film of tears over my eyes. "Maybe I just need one of these."

"They're sweet," Cheryl said. "But it's a lot of work."

Emmy babbled as I carried her outside; Cheryl walked in front, the salad bowl propped between her arms. Dan was taking meat off the grill, his guests gathered round. Jorge returned my smile. I wasn't hungry, so when everyone settled to eat hamburgers, drink beer, and discuss the Redskins' prospects, I walked Emmy around the yard. After exploring the woodpile (*woo-pie, woo-pie*) we got down in the grass to pick wildflowers. As I attempted—with little success—to braid them into her gossamer-fine hair, Jorge came over. He sat on the lawn and, with Emmy as a sort of confessor, said that he was sorry.

I told him that he didn't need to apologize.

"I know we made certain decisions," he said. "It just never seems to make sense."

"It's not easy for me, either."

"I always thought that if two people have a lot in common, and enjoy each other's company, why not take it to the next level?"

"I don't think it's quite that pat."

He grew inward.

"I just don't think I can be what you need. Not in that respect." I spoke with calm objectivity.

"You're my best friend."

"We'll stay friends, of course."

We sat in silence a moment, —until I lost my psych, got all emotional. "I don't know how I would have managed these last few years had it not been for you." My eyes had grown moist; I fixed my gaze into the bright sky.

"I've got so much going on right now," he said.

"I'm sure you'll see things more clearly when life is better settled."

"Who knows where I'll end up when I finish my degree?" he mused to no one in particular. He tore a blade of grass and flipped it aside.

I laid a hand on his and told him not to worry.

"Frankly," he said, "I feel a little lost."

Emmy cooed and blithely patted the lawn, her unreflective existence suggesting the absurdity of analyses. I took her up and rose from the ground; Jorge too rose into the sunlight and we wandered back to an open field where deer sometimes come to graze. This made us feel lighter, and I allowed myself to indulge the counterfeit feeling that here was a family of my own.

Jorge and I drove back to town listening to a piano sonata under a deepening sky streaked with vermilion and lemon. Though we chatted in a natural way, our words possessed a force I was not accustomed to. When I praised his drawings, he revealed anxieties about moving from his theoretical studies (his dissertation: *Urban Utopias: Past, Future, Present*) into the practical realm of city planning work. "I'm sure you'll manage," I said. "Look how far you've come already." Though we were clocking past the big, uptown apartment houses on Connecticut Avenue, I didn't mean to assign superiority to their symmetrical bulk as against the colonial Andean town where he was raised. He was silent as we approached his building. We parted on the sidewalk with a promise to talk soon.

& & &

DURING THE WEEK that followed I put in my hours at the clinic but otherwise lay low. One evening I called to check on my mother. She was glued to the tube, weighing the jumble of bellicose and conciliatory gestures emerging from all sides of the Persian Gulf crisis. "They'll end up going in," she said. "I have a sense about these things."

I told her that I would visit the following week.

On Saturday I passed up a dinner party at the home of one of our colleagues; I felt the need to reconnect with something that seemed to be unraveling, a thread bearing knowledge of self and purpose. And as I sat in the deepening dusk, feeling a quiet emptiness, I decided to bury myself in weaving come morning. That has always been my best form of therapy.

But when I awoke Sunday I just sat staring at the loom, —there, near my bedroom window, where it lives. I tried to envision the tapestry I had been trying to start. It was to be an evocation of the halcyon days of my youth, before tragedy both historical and familial rent it all asunder. Before, that is to say, Vietnam. I had purchased the yarns and warped the machine weeks earlier, but I hadn't been able to settle down to the work. Some dark cloud stood between me and what I have always considered my truest métier. With an effort I pictured myself pumping the treadles, carefully interlacing weft and warp. But it was no good. The instrument was unapproachable. I kicked around and made a cup of tea. Sitting at the window that looks down into the park, I found myself thinking about Jorge. We badly needed clarity in our relationship, and I could conjure nothing to say or do.

I felt restless and frustrated.

Glancing at the kitchen clock, I realized I could still make an appearance at the funky little congregation I belong to. I knew I would be welcome, though I no longer attended as regularly as during those years after I broke with Stephen—when, immersed in a city full of people, but with deep inner loneliness, I sought strength to bring to the ocean of brokenness that constitutes my work at the clinic. The pastor, Richard Dorsey, is a renegade from the mainstream churches. The white-haired widower captivated me the morning of my first impromptu visit when, burrowing into a parable to laud unstinting Love he freely, and without a trace of embarrassment, succumbed to copious tears. He remains something of a touchstone, as does much else about the Union.

It was good to see my friends: Dorothy Robinson, the displaced Jamaican with whom I worked on El Salvadoran relief; Bud Rawlings, the kindly elder who devotes his mornings to the soup kitchen for the homeless; and Tom Mertz, the Midwestern seminary dropout with whom I always discuss ultimate realities (*It's not a question of avoiding suffering,* I hear him say, his congenial smile never wavering, *but a question of suffering with meaning, or suffering with no meaning.*) Richard continued a series of reflections on the life of Gandhi, and there were expressions of guarded hopes for a peaceful resolution to the Persian Gulf crisis. The children, happy to be in community, spent the fellowship hour, while their parents chatted over hors d'oeuvres and coffees, exploring recondite corners of the old building. Their laughter in the hallways reminded me that all was not ill in our world.

I left the Union with my private concerns, and my share of the collective uneasiness, ameliorated. The day was as golden clear as any Washington September and, as I wandered the avenue, I decided to lunch, *al fresco,* at Bruno's. My tapestry was on my mind, to be sure, but I couldn't convince myself to go home and take up the shuttle. I told myself it was too splendid an afternoon to spend indoors, but down deep I knew there was more to it than that. My apprenticeship under a Navajo teacher

of consummate power—*finding her in the desert brightness, the res-
olute peace with which she put each weft into place*—was about much
more than weaving proper, and the making of fabric inevitably
became woven (sorry, but the metaphor is unavoidable) into
every aspect of my life. Yes, Sarah Tilly taught me to employ in-
woven thread to confront my deepest dreams and darkest fears,
so when I am having trouble with weaving work, I know the
solution must be sought at the gut level of my existence.

But this luminous afternoon of carefree friends on city out-
ings did little to encourage a soul-ransacking I was not in any
case eager for. Recalling instead that there was a new exhibit at
Textile House (the city's wondrous homage to all things cloth) I
wondered if I might find, if not a resolution to my creative crisis, at least some trace of inspiration there. And as I finished my
coffee, the idea of wandering the Kalorama hills among pun-
gent mums and the last wan roses, of finally making my way up
the Spanish Steps—our own humble replica of the famous Roman landmark—to the street of ambassadorial mansions where
the museum is located, struck me with an inescapable rightness.

Hearing the lion heads gurgling into the fountain, I passed
the glorious weeping cherry at the top of the Steps and emerged
onto that plateau, with the grassy square surrounded by stately
apartment houses, that has always struck me as more British
than American. And as I crested over land that arches with a
sense of earth straining toward sky, then descended toward the
museum, I thought of what would be awaiting me there: a chi-
noiserie umbrella stand; the quiet foyer with an intern at the
desk; a garden through French doors; and the plexiglas kiosk
with a slot for your five-dollar donation.

Having merely glanced at the circular that came a week
earlier, I knew nothing of the show but its title: *Implements of
Holiness: Jewish Textiles from the Prague Collection*. But I felt the
usual anticipation, for these pilgrimages always yielded good

things of growth and spirit (even when the pieces were as troubling as those Huari weavings last year, covered with arcane symbols suggesting toil, oppression—even unspeakable things!) This I credit to the nature of cloth—always humble and true, it cannot lie—and to the spirit of the weaver: integrating, exploring, surrendering; everywhere, and in all ages, the same!

There is an anteroom between the lobby and the hallway that begins the exhibit space proper; the fresh blue of the water cooler speaks to me of purity, female energies, and resuscitation after an encounter with the numinous. I sipped from a paper cone while a sobering introductory placard pulled me away from the street and its mundane concerns. The exhibit, it turned out, featured objects stripped from homes and synagogues by Nazi stormtroopers during World War II. The items they assembled at Prague were intended to document the culture of an *extinct* people. "The Jewish curators recruited to manage the collection," the placard read, "were later transported to death camps. Notes found among the objects when, at the end of the war, the collection was turned over to the Prague Council, registered desperate pleas for human rescue, but also prayers beseeching divine deliverance.

"All of the textiles on display here," the placard continued, "were created as *tashmeshe kiddusha*, or 'implements of holiness.' The fashioning of lovely objects for ritual use," it read, "is a response to the Talmudic injunction to *hiddur mitzvah*, the embellishment of practices that affirm the supplicant's relationship to the ineffable Mystery:

> *Make a beautiful sukkah in His honor,*
> *a beautiful lulav, a beautiful shofar, beautiful tzitzis,*
> *and a beautiful Scroll of the Law,*
> *written with fine ink and a fine reed,*
> *by a skilled penman,*

and wrap it about with beautiful silk . . .

"This adorning of ritual implements," the placard concluded, "was thought by rabbinical scholars to render even the miraculous possible."

The show sounded intriguing, but I was reluctant to move forward. Though I had not worked with Holocaust survivors, the trauma complexes spawned by that ugly blot on history are of the same stuff as those of the combat veterans whose painful inner struggles make up our everyday work at the clinic. (We therapists, after all, must be careful to give ourselves regular breaks from our work.) But still I took an instinctive step toward the first hallway; and as I climbed the low stairs toward the exhibit, it seemed inevitable that I would find myself at Bruno's at loose ends, that the September radiance would beckon me to wander toward the museum and, that instead of a pleasurable escape—weavings of nomadic Turks, their saddle bags, jug-holders, and woolen carpets the largest part of their material culture—I would be summoned back to those places where healing is most elusive!

I stood for a moment in a twilight dictated by the fragility of the textiles, so that my eyes might adjust, before examining the pieces along the first wall. There were hand-stitched Seder towels for ritual ablutions, woven pouches to hold the unleavened bread of the Passover feast, and meticulously embroidered pillows for reclining after the holiday meal. Some of the objects were in splendid condition, like one satin pillow ringed with striking violet flowers, its vine motifs in green silk and gold metallic thread; others were less well preserved. But the spirit of the work transcended the barriers of time and material, and I found myself sharing the space of pure creation these unknown stitchers had occupied years before I was born.

One of the matzah bags, its ground of undyed linen now

yellowed, was embroidered with lush foliage, juicy berries, and a bird in polychrome silk not unlike the golden creature in one of my own tapestries—a work that used to hang behind my desk at the clinic. The piece transfixed me with its attitude of simple observation, and left a residue of staunch quietude (a quietude infused with subtle joy). I couldn't help wonder about its creator, but all I could know of her life, aside from three Hebrew initials woven into the center of the ground, was contained in a placard beside the case. I copied the words in a blank space in my exhibit brochure. "A Jewish girl of this era," it read, "like many of her counterparts across the globe, was at an early age taught to sew by her mother and other female relations. Beginning with simple stitches for mending clothing, she would slowly progress to more elaborate techniques for embroidering home furnishings and bridal trousseaus. As she matured, she would begin to fashion *implements of holiness*. Some, like the matzah bags, Seder towels and pillows in this case, would be used in the home. Others, like the ark curtains in the galleries ahead, would be presented to her synagogue."

Standing before the display case, I recalled how my own mother once taught me to stitch, the beginnings of a lifelong romance with thread. And that is when I saw—now as one I knew!—that happy girl, surrounded by loving relations; a young wife, fondly stitching a pillow for her beloved; or a wise and skilled matron, dedicating an exquisite piece of handiwork to her synagogue. The exhibit had taken a decidedly personal— and distinctly disturbing—turn. Again I hesitated to continue. But the next case pulled me forward: its richly brocaded mantles clothed standing Torah scrolls. Gorgeous crowns of the finest metalwork made them look like little kings and queens.

Stepping over the museum's fine gray carpeting into the first large gallery, I exchanged glances with a young African guard, his high cheekbones hatched with ritual scars. He shyly smiled and moved away. The high-ceilinged space was devoted to *paro-chets*: broad curtains fashioned to cover the *ark*, that tall cabinet where the cherished Torah is kept in synagogue. The textiles were hung vertically along the walls, one next to the other, and beside each was a photograph of the temple from which it had been looted. Some featured lustrous fields of velvet adorned with fringes and tassels, Hebrew characters stitched in gold thread or regal Lions of Judah. Others were sumptuously embroidered with multi-colored silk fruits, or meticulously appliquéd with seed pearls and glass stones. "These textiles once veiled the most sacred zone of the synagogue," the placard at the gallery entrance read, "the Holy of Holies where the ineffable Mystery is thought to dwell." How various the ways in which that veiling was conceived! Standing before a portal motif, I puzzled whether I should kneel in reverence—or simply walk through, questioning how a piece of cloth, so easily brushed aside, could separate us from all we conceive of as sacred!

When I had absorbed all I could of the masterfully executed ark curtains, I went into the hallway that concluded the exhibit. Its walls were hung with narrow bands of quaintly embroidered cloth. These Torah scroll binders, the placard informed me, were used to enwrap that psychic map so historically crucial for this "people of the book." Sewn by a newborn's mother or grandmother from the infant's first swaddling clothes, the scroll binders would have been dedicated to the family's synagogue to celebrate the presence of the child in the community. Scanning over humble stitchings of childhood scenes, my mind swung erratically between pleasing thoughts of babies, —and an ugly intimation of the diseased hatred that likely carried these women and—what was more unthinkable!—their children, away.

I turned aside in sorrow. The rabbis' miracles, claimed to be invoked by the lovely objects on display throughout the museum's galleries, had failed to materialize for these ill-fated people; I walked sadly toward the exit. But just shy of the doorway, at the end of the hallway, I was arrested by one last tapestry—a strikingly modern one. The piece had been woven by Barbara Greenfield, a textile artist, much revered in weaving circles, who had succumbed to cancer the previous year. The tapestry was commissioned by the museum, its placard informed me, as a corollary to the Prague Collection exhibit. As a child, the placard further provided, Greenfield suffered internment at the Buchenwald concentration camp, where she lost her mother. The artist's last major work, the tapestry was completed only months before her death.

It's title: *Parochet (Ark Curtain)*.

It cost me a long moment to adjust to the work, for I was still hung on the pathos at the core of the exhibit and Greenfield's *Parochet* was, as much as any artwork I had ever witnessed, a study in unadulterated wonder. The piece, as large as the ark curtains hung in the main galleries, was breathtakingly extravagant in design. Shimmering linen threads of manifold hues in minutely gradated washes—a specialty for which Greenfield was famous—created a sense of quietly exultant energy. Mauves and greens, cerulean blues, and deep sunset golds flowed across the piece with an effortless ease, coalescing by the dictates of some dreamlike logic into forms that evoked mountains and trees, rivers and coves, —even the vastnesses of plains, oceans and illimitable sky. I had never seen anything so enchanting in my life. Watercolor rendered in cloth, a painting that you could take up and caress in your hands! It was hard to believe its liquid mergings to be the product of the loom, with that instrument's blocky dictates of weft and warp, for they seemed to have arisen organically from the soft and fertile earth. Hanging there across the wall in front of me, inviolate and unassailable, it felt like truth itself.

Beauty incarnate.

I stood before the piece for some moments in a state of awed amazement. Then, as I grew accustomed to its grandeur, I moved about so that I might view Greenfield's workmanship from different angles. Finally I came very close, where I could examine her incredibly fine washes, washes created by juxtaposing, one after the other, linen threads of subtly varied hues along the color spectrum. In their totality, these washes were the product of painstaking and patient effort. Each was, in itself, a locus of sublime beauty.

I stepped back again in an attempt to digest the wealth of impressions my encounter with Greenfield's tapestry had instigated. Remembering the rest of the exhibit, and its theme, I felt perplexed. What might Greenfield have meant to communicate with her piece, I wondered? It had been commissioned for an exhibit which, to be certain, showcased the considerable talents of a host of anonymous Jewish artisans. But the collection also brought its audience face to face with the most appalling episode of organized savagery in modern history. Greenfield, I reasoned, might have woven a tapestry depicting the concentration camps, with their concertina wire and gas chambers, or referenced the squeletic figures of the dead and dying. Instead she pulled out all the stops of her impressive range of artistic tools to evoke a potent sense of quiet rapture. A remark I once read while researching the trauma complexes of Holocaust survivors came to mind. "The best revenge is living well," a millionaire New York businessman who had survived Auschwitz had said. Perhaps Greenfield meant to express something similar with her piece, I reflected, —though without the businessman's chutzpah. For, in unequivocally affirming such breathtaking beauty in the world, did she not witness that in spite of the pain and trauma inflicted upon herself and her people, she had not merely healed her psyche but had achieved the capacity to perceive life in all its richest abundance?

Taking a last, long look at Greenfield's work, I experienced a sudden upwelling of painful emotions. Judging it to be the undercurrent of tragedy carried by the exhibit (in spite of the wondering admiration its pieces, and especially Greenfield's *Parochet*, had evoked in me) I stepped from the gallery with tears in my eyes. Heedless of the worried expression of the guard, to whom I managed a crimped smile, I emerged into daylight and walked abstractedly toward the Spanish Steps. When I arrived there I sat on the edge of its shallow pool. Frothy, green-yellow streams splashed gently onto its surface from the sculpted lion heads.

Sunlight fell through overhanging branches. I took a deep breath, and then another, and listened to the rilling water. I tried to mobilize my thoughts but, allowing my gaze to drop to the bottom of the pool, it was only scattered, disconnected shreds that floated through my mind. My troubled relationship with Jorge, the impending war in the Persian Gulf, Bob's reserve status, my mother's anxieties . . . all the rubbed-raw pieces of my life pressed upon me with an insistence that was painful to bear. Finally, after some indeterminate amount of time, these worried reflections resolved themselves into a grating frustration over my stalled weaving project. It was as though somehow, in that cauldron of creation, I hoped to put something into the balance against all the unalterable griefs of the world—as Barbara Greenfield had so masterfully done with her final tapestry.

I dwelt like this on how successfully Greenfield had painted life's consoling wonders with thread, and how stymied were my own efforts in that regard until, on the surface of the pool, a wavering form of refracted sunlight—an undulating plaque of glinting gold—came into preternatural focus. My ruminations were abruptly arrested by this extraordinary vision, one that incorporated the pool's depth, its surface, and the echoed sky all at once. I gazed upon the mirage, let it slowly empty me, and was deeply calmed. And when the *trompe l'oeil* faded, some minutes later, I lifted my face with a steadier mind. In spite of my training in trauma treatment, I confessed to myself, I still struggled to see past life's most painful experiences or to participate fully in its abundance. I questioned, naturally, whether it made sense to compare my weaving efforts to the masterpiece of a lauded artist at the peak of her powers (it could even be said of Greenfield's *Parochet*—in how she managed, in spite of the traumas she had suffered, to hold faith in fulsome life— that one of the rabbis' promised miracles had indeed occurred). But I there and then resolved to visit my mother, instinctively knowing that, aside from failing in my daughterly duties, I had forsaken an opportunity to recover something (my mother my first mentor in textiles, as in all things female) that might lead me from my dilemmas . . .

CNN WAS ON the television when I came in. After greeting her I asked Mom to show me the garden. "The monardas are getting weedy," she said, brushing them with her hand as one might caress the hair of a child. "And I don't know what to do about that dogwood in the corner. I'm afraid it's dying, poor thing." Orange sunset colored the sky. I could hear the rumble of the expressway a mile off.

"I didn't really cook," she said, "but I made those biscuits you like. I thought we'd have some frozen dinners with them, if that's okay with you."

The biscuits hadn't been on my favorites list for many years, but I didn't say as much. Instead I hugged her around the shoulders and kissed her cheek. That seemed to fluster her.

"I guess that's a yes," she said, and we went indoors.

I helped her set the table and prepare our simple dinner.

Commentators droned Iraq news from the television, intercut with U.S. officials trying too hard to sound in control. Hussein, for his part, prophesied *rivers of blood* should his armies come under attack. When the microwave chimed we carried our plates to the table. I asked if we could turn off the television.

"Aren't you interested?" she asked.

"Of course," I said. "But I'd rather talk. Just us."

"If you say so." She stiffly wandered amid the living room furniture to find the remote; the TV expired with a thumping click.

After she sat down again she spoke. "Have you talked to Bobby?"

"A couple weeks ago. His feeling was that we shouldn't concern ourselves too greatly about this Iraq business."

"What does he know!" she quietly crowed. "They've already started to call up reserves. Listen sweetie, you have to watch what they do, not what they say. They lie, believe me. I've seen it."

Her remarks echoed those of my veterans at the clinic. I strove not to discount their opinions—based on bitter experience, to be sure—or my mother's, but I tried to remain objective. "The administration still expects the economic sanctions to force Hussein to vacate Kuwait," I said.

"That's right. They say Saddam will back down, just like they said Ho Chi Minh would back down. But look at what they're doing. They're sending in planes, and tanks—and soldiers!"

"That's just to protect Saudi Arabia," I ventured.

"Sure, dominoes all over the place. I've seen where that leads! Just watch"—she put another biscuit on my plate—"in a couple of months the Marines will be landing."

"Let's talk about something else," I pleaded, regretting that I had waited so long to visit. I asked her to tell me about her knitting, and we passed the rest of the meal discussing stitching techniques. After washing the dishes we moved to the living room sofa. She asked about the pattern I had brought.

I confessed that I was having trouble with it. "I'm afraid the plan may be flawed," I said. "Or missing something." I took the folded paper, etched with my arcane weaver's markings, out of my purse. I told her that I had decided to do a tapestry about my youth in Arden Forest, a serene subdivision in Washington's suburbs, a place of broad lawns and over-arching shade trees. "You know," I said, "the house and yard. The woods and the creek. That old cherry tree that bloomed so white every spring." Mom stared dispassionately at the floor. "I started to draw and diagram last year," I said, "but I can't seem to get going with it. I suspect it has something to do with everything that happened with Dad."

"You know I don't like to talk about that."

"I know. But there it is."

"I thought you got over those troubles," she said, "—after that therapy you did for your degree. You told me you had come to terms . . ."

It's true I had accepted the untimely loss of my father— my family's bitter sacrifice to Mars—to the extent that I could live constructively, even work as a therapist. "But this is something different," I said to my mother. "I want to move beyond just getting by toward, well"—I knew I was pushing her envelope—"embracing the totality of things. You know, living with every pore of my being wide open . . ."

"You're losing me, Boop." She emitted a weak laugh.

I described Barbara Greenfield's tapestry, how she had managed to convey such a sense of speechless wonder toward life. Mom, to her credit, made an effort to grasp what I was driving at. "It sounds interesting," she said, but then abruptly changed the subject. "How's that Spanish fellow doing?"

"You mean Jorge? He's Peruvian, Mom, —not Spanish."

"Still dating?"

"We don't call it dating."

"Why, no sex?"

"I told you, we're just friends."

"Seems peculiar. No offense."

"Things aren't so pat as they were when you were younger."

"He seems awfully nice."

"He is. But it just doesn't add up."

"Sweetie, if that doesn't add up, what ever will?"

"Maybe nothing, in that area."

"I can't believe that."

"It happens."

"Not to my daughter, it doesn't."

I scooted over and rested my head on her shoulder. Though I thought her reasoning faulty, I appreciated the caring behind it.

"When I met your Dad, it was so automatic, I didn't have to think about anything. I just loved him. And that's the way it stayed. I don't guess you ever felt anything like that."

I toyed with the idea of telling her about Stephen but realized that, no, it had never been anything like that.

"There was that boy Doug you were so fond of. Grew his hair long and run off to someplace. Bet he got into drugs. Do you suppose he ever came back to his senses?"

Tears were forming in my eyes.

"Now there's something *you* don't like to talk about," she said. "Enough of this folderol. Let's turn on the TV and see what's happening."

Part I

AUTUMN

WHEN GARY CAME, at the end of September, I expected nothing more than my standard first encounter with a client. I found him attractive, even in the faded field jacket, but that wasn't so out of the ordinary. It was only later I saw significance in the way he relaxed into a teal-upholstered chair reserved for men who are scared, tense—even angry—with one leg casually crossed over the other.

"What brings you here?" I asked.

"Karma?" he ventured with upturned hands.

I waited. Nothing more came. "Do you want to elaborate on that?"

"No one escapes the wheel."

Again I waited.

"It's right in the *Dhammapada*."

He spoke as if it were all quite evident. This wasn't going to be easy. What's more, I was handicapped by a lack of records; his folder hadn't been on my desk. I excused myself and went out to Alice, complained about the administrative failing, and took an intake form. When I returned, he was staring into the carpet between our chairs.

I asked had he been in Vietnam.

His answer—*Weren't we all?*—was offered like a stone picked from a glittering streambed, as if he assumed our agreement, as reasonable people, on the matter.

About the particulars of his service he was dismissive. "Places and dates aren't important," he said. "Carnage is carnage. Savagery, savagery."

"Do you have any trouble sleeping?"

"I often wonder if I'm awake."

"Disturbing dreams?"

"We live one every day."

I noted his intellectualizing of trauma. And Gary Devers was obviously intelligent. With an accommodating gesture he stood and walked calmly to the bookcase. He scanned the titles with an occasional comment ("Rollo May, together guy," or "Freud, that crazy bastard") and then moved across the room to the wide windows that face Union Station. After remarking on the view, he turned to take in the Capitol.

"Oh my God, here it comes again."

"Flashbacks?"

"It's all a bloody flashback . . ." He indicated the landscape beyond the windows with a sweeping gesture.

"Wait," I said. "Are you speaking metaphorically, because we don't want to confuse symbol with symptomology?"

"Believe me, it's real enough."

I continued with the intake. In good health (seemed robust). Divorced. Lived alone.

His answers were off-hand, his focus more on the scene outside the window. I was asking about his work when the faint palpitation of a helicopter's rotors arose in the distance. It was approaching from beyond the Capitol: probably, I thought, from Bolling Air Base, south of the city along the river. As the craft drew closer, the thwop of its blades more distinct, Gary inched along the windowsill, away from its approach. The padding of the propellers, a tom-tom played with cotton mallets, grew in intensity until a violent snare drilled the air. When the chopper emerged over the dome of the Capitol I noted his discomfort. As it bore down on our building, and passed overhead, he slunk to his chair. Held his breath until it was gone.

"That chopper seemed to bother you."

"All those hot landing zones," he breathed with a small shiver. Regaining, with a long exhalation, his composure, abruptly folding his arms across his chest, he looked straight into my eyes. He must have sensed my unease, because he quickly averted his gaze to the place behind my desk where my tapestry hung. With an absorbing interest he stepped around me to examine the piece more carefully. He stared at it a long while, and his gaze, through the fabric I had woven, pierced to my most hidden places—though scores of men had observed my creation without drawing any sensation beyond a simple pride of workmanship. Suddenly aware of my dress (a simple style with watery forms in greens and blues), my earrings and the way I had done my hair, I wondered if he had catalogued me as minutely as he was examining my weavingwork! He made flattering references to Georgia O'Keefe and Art Dove, vowed surprise that I had woven the piece myself. There followed a discussion of colors and their emotional resonances, the atmosphere of the southwest desert, and the meaning of the yellow bird in the fabric's center. I glanced at my watch and noted that our time was up.

From my journal . . .

October 3, 1990

In the Greek mode: O Vietnam! How can I paint thee, thou dark and powerful god! paint thee with words, with the threads I ply across my loom—or with the tears that have drenched my life, as the lives of so many others? My father (distant seeming world, sun-kissed suburban stronghold, paragon of manly grace!) laid low, gone, gone, gone. Men of my tribe, older brothers, tender beauty of youth: athletes, lovers, downed on fields of fire, grieving still for names on granite wall. Friends, companions, let us lament the grace-given garden we knew, rent asunder by bitter division (acrimony of ill-tuned city; look inward or out, suffer or deny the pain of sacred wounds)! Women, O women! that we could throw our hearts into the fire of this world, bring it back through some ancient alchemy to the healing glow of our birth-right. Sisters, mothers, that they could know our pain, having birthed this world, to see it destroyed in folly and madness!

I picture myself walking, where do I not see him? He is in every city place, in the bright glare of sidewalks, signs with no meaning, bustling traffic, welling crowds. In the soft dusk, reading in my chair, or asleep in the dream-deep night, he comes to me again. How can I forget, though I make peace a thousand times over (with myself for not saving him; with history and all its crude logic; with the nations of the earth, or the rules of the game that claimed him). With him, after all, for not saving himself! I ask myself, is this madness, or merely the shadow of my loneliness? Yet it is not a haunting as you might imagine. His presence has become a loving one, something I carry like a polished stone that glows with warmth. It has taken a silent struggle of many years to feel that strength, a strength I do not wish to relinquish . . .

April 27, 1991

When Gary was here it began to make sense. I could feel that stone of my father glowing warmer when he was with me. It was as if there were a stone in him that glowed with a similar warmth, and the two stones were happy when they were together. I know this sounds strange, but how else describe it? Now he is gone, no news for weeks, Central American mail. So my loom, where Penelope-like I pass my hours (when I am not typing this report, this assemblage of words, thoughts, dreams, yearnings). The crazy hope is that with colors and shapes, with the caressing textures of yarns, I can finally say what has eluded me these many years; sing what must be sung to put an end to a cycle that returns me again and again to the lawns and woods of my family home, each time emerging with more and less pain, more and less understanding. More and less bitterness! If only Gary were here!

May 11, 1991

I would worry more about him except for the conviction that an angel watches over him—a conviction not diminished by an intimation that the supernal presence I envision is nothing more than a projection of my own caring. My days are spent working on this report, looking out my window at the trees that lead into the valley of the park, or sitting at my loom while my heart takes shape in braided colors. I let myself be guided by distant memories of childhood and youth, stories I've heard from men at the clinic, by times I spent with Gary and by so many other promptings, glimmerings, and previsions. At times I hear the voice of Sarah Tilly in my ear, as clearly as if she were standing beside the loom. She reminds me not only to tighten my selvages, or leave more play in the fabric, but also to take myself out of the way, let my body speak with the loom, to sing its sorrows and joys, until these become the sorrows and joys of the loom itself! When my projects become a sticky film, neither sweet nor bitter but threatening rancidity, I shake off absorption with self (however necessary at this time of reassessing and redirecting) and drive out to the burbs, where Cheryl always welcomes help with the children; stop in on my mother; or, more rarely, head to the projects to do some quilting with Mrs. Pinckney.

May 17, 1991

I have received a couple of letters from Jorge. I love the old-fash-
ioned Peruvian stamps, and also the postmark of the Andean
town of his childhood. We are trying to make peace with one
another, and though it is strange for him to be so far away (I
have always associated him with this city) I believe that the distance can only help. If his flight was inspired, as I believe, by a
gallant desire to leave me free to pursue changes he was bound
to resist, I know it will also prove best for him in the long run.
After he comes to terms with his nostalgia for familiar things
of youth, he will be free to go wherever his extraordinary gifts
lead him—whether it be Washington, Paris, Lima, or Mexico City.
Meanwhile I sense a true Jorge when I breathe the expansiveness
of the mountains, feel the cobblestones under my feet, smell the
aromas of mother-cooked food wafting from the huddled houses
in the evening. Occasionally I wander downtown to find the Cuzco Boys, recalling the many times we sought them out during our
lunch hours. I wonder what we were pursuing in that ethereal cry
that seemed to emanate from everywhere or nowhere; to be five
blocks away or around the corner; panpipes floating through city
canyons, scurrying around corners, piercing the overarching sky
to some Andes of the imagination . . .

HIS VISITS TO MY OFFICE. How strange they seem, looking
over my notes. The two of us: one claiming to be a healer, another
who professes to seek healing. But is it ever that simple? Gary
steps from the chairs where the talking cure is conducted, pulls an
umbrella from the stand beside the door, and holds it, like some
song-and-dance man, before him. He glides to the wall where my
mask collection hangsa silent chorus; there's more space there.
He shuffles and tap dances while he sings, struts and gestures

broadly:

> "It was just one of those things,
> just one of those Cold War flings,
> a trip to Hanoi when you've earned your wings,
> just one of those things . . .
>
> "It was just one just one of those fights,
> got to avenge geo-political slights,
> remember to keep the dinks in your sights
>   (umbrella rifle-like),
> just one of those fights . . .
>
> "If we'd thought a bit of the end of it
> when at Tet they threatened Saigon,
> we'd have been aware, that in foreign affairs,
> you can't control what comes down
>   (open, sheltering) . . .
>
> "So goodbye Ho and amen,
> such a shame about Ngo Dinh Diem,
> 'cause it was great fun,
> but it was just one of those things . . ."

He whistles while he tap-dances a while longer. After a deep stage bow, he returns the umbrella to the stand. A feeling like a memory I can't grasp nags at me. He goes to the windows and gazes down at traffic. I remind myself that I am his therapist, he my client, because everything in my body tells me that something different is going on.

"Not a bad performance," I say, tentatively.

He cocks his head, touches his brow in a courteous salute.

"But what was it all about?"

He turns to look at me. "I thought it was obvious." He rubs his jaw. "Maybe I carried the irony too far."

He comes to his chair and sits down. "You know," he says, "I get tired of talking about me all the time. I'd really rather hear about you."

I'm ashamed of myself for blushing, and know that he notices. "That's not what this is about," I say.

"Why not?"

I get up, go to the window, and stand where Gary had stood moments earlier. A flush of anger rises in my face, which I keep trained toward the window, vaguely taking in the city beyond. Clients don't get over on me, I remind myself. A long moment I let myself breathe. Calm, calm. He is surely behind me, somewhere, and I remember Jorge approaching on jaguar feet. I suddenly turn, expecting to find Gary reaching toward my waist, but he is in his chair, staring at my tapestry.

"Gary," I say.

"Yes?"

"This is your fourth visit, if I'm not mistaken."

"You're not."

I return to my chair; he seems to follow my every movement.

"In order to continue to see you—treat you, that is—I need to come up with some definite diagnosis. At your last session you gave me an exhaustive treatise on the history of the Vietnamese people before the French—"

"Very important for a sharp perspective, particularly their perennial struggle against Chinese hegemony—"

"That may be true, but—"

"Otherwise, we'll never comprehend the depth of feeling that motivated the Viet Cong, or their confidence in the eventual—"

"I just don't know what this has to do with—"

"You've got to read your Sun Tzu," he says. "If you don't understand your enemy, you're—"

He sees my frustration, silences himself, and fastens me with eyes eager to drink up every word. This somehow discomfits me more than his interruptions.

"As I was saying, there's the matter of diagnosis. You've given me some, I'm sure, very important history. And the week before, we discussed communist economics . . ."

"That's right," he says innocently.

"Which, I agree, all has some bearing on the war in Vietnam, and perhaps on your response to your wartime experiences. However, we're not here for philosophical discussions, but to bring you back to health—assuming there's some condition we can treat. We have requirements under the Veterans Administration, according to the terms of the clinic's contract. Paperwork to fill out. I'm afraid we can't proceed unless we unearth more concrete material than we've gotten so far."

He shrugs his shoulders.

"Let's start from the beginning. What can we say is your chief complaint?"

"Easy, an overall feeling of insanity."

"That's too vague. What are the . . . symptoms?"

"Just observe, you can't miss them."

"Observe what?"

"Haven't you noticed what's going on in the Persian Gulf? They're setting up a shiny new meat grinding machine for a nice, fresh batch of raw American manhood."

"You're troubled about the Persian Gulf situation?"

"Who wouldn't be, unless he were a war-mongering maniac?"

"Is it causing you anxiety?"

"Of course it is."

He breathes a moment. "Look," he says, "perhaps Hussein needs to be stopped. But I don't like the whole tone of it. This refusal to acknowledge the absurdity of these ersatz nation-states, map lines drawn willy-nilly by colonial overlords decades ago, now enshrined as sacred entities. Why aren't we discussing some kind of equitable access to the world's resources—including those within the boundaries of the good old U, S of A. Or, for that matter, the kinds of regimes we ought to be supporting? I don't know, given man's current level of evolution, maybe states need to act as if they're half blind. You know, so things don't get too complicated to manage . . ."

Inhaling deeply, looks toward the Capitol. "One thing's for certain," he says, "if past is prologue, when they set our military boys loose, you can bet there's going to be some serious overkill."

The remark makes me uncomfortable. "Gary," I say, "we're drifting back into the kind of philosophical discussion that won't help us achieve what we're here for."

"Fine."

"Let's try and stick to your personal situation."

"I thought that's what we were doing."

"Tell me about those hot landing zones."

"I'd rather not."

He gazes at the floor, avoids my eyes.

I don't push the point. "All right," I say, "let's look at your present circumstances. How's your worklife?"

"Signed, Sealed & Delivered—we're yours!" He perks up with feigned gallantry. "Delivering the nation's capital's messages since 1981."

"You're a messenger?"

"I'm mainly in Dispatch these days, but I'll get on a bike when there's a fire to put out. It's good to move around sometimes, get in touch with the streets."

"Do you enjoy it?"

"I don't know. It's become sort of . . . a way of life, I guess you'd say." His eyes scan the bookshelf.

"Surely you have some feeling about it."

"I used to get more of a kick out of it. It's probably one of those end-of-an-era things."

"Are there difficulties on the job?"

"Naturally."

"Would you like to talk about them?"

He abruptly turns toward me. "I wouldn't mind, but do you really want to hear about operators' sloppy handwriting, I-want-it-yesterday requests, and the occasional run-in between cyclist and automobile?"

"How about your workmates? Do you get along with them?"

"They're a great bunch. You'll have to meet them."

"I'm afraid that won't be possible." I look up from my note-pad.

"You don't know what you're missing."

I ignore his remark, bury my eyes once again in my notes.

"On your first visit you said that everything was a flashback. Would you like to elaborate on that?"

"It just seems we never learn."

I wait for him to continue, but he gazes mutely toward the Capitol.

"I'm concerned that by placing things in an abstract context," I say after a moment, "you avoid dealing with your own, very personal pain."

"My pain, somebody else's pain . . ."

I'm suddenly inspired to cut to the heart of things. "Tell me plainly," I say. "What brought you here?"

"You really want to know?"

"Yes."

"Two things."

"All right."

"One, you."

Seeing my skepticism, he says, "Oh yes, I've been wanting to talk to you."

"Talk to me? But you didn't even know—"

"And, two, Pinky."

"Pinky? You mean—"

"Charles Robinson Pinckney."

I didn't expect this. "You know Charles?"

"One of my best friends."

"I knew he worked in the courier business," I say. "But you two work together?"

"Did."

"What do you mean? Has he changed jobs?"

"Not exactly."

"Where is he?"

"Who knows? He just kind of . . . disappeared . . . into thin air! It's really got the Gathering bummed out."

"The Gathering? Have you called the police?"

"I put in the usual reports. They haven't turned up a thing."

"This must be upsetting for you."

"I'm hanging in there, trying to stay on top of the paperwork." He's silent for a moment. "It's been bad enough with Clark . . ."

"Clark?"

"This other friend of mine. Somewhere in Guatemala, I think. God, I've got people disappearing all over the place."

I note the clock out of the corner of my eye. "Our time's up," I say. "We can continue with this next time."

"Sure," he says. He reaches out his hand, grasps mine warmly before leaving.

⅋ ⅋ ⅋

PINKY: real name, Charles Robinson Pinckney. Fleshy but solid. Skin of rich, dark brown. Eyes . . . like liquid agate. That Gary would bring him up, and that remark about coming for me!—a feint, a dodge, a stratagem of the psychically wounded? And where was Pinky?—or *Charles*, as I prefer to call him. I was tempted to keep Gary over, inquire further. But aside from my long-standing practice of ending sessions on time, there were issues of professional integrity in discussing one client with another.

When I started at the clinic, fresh out of training, Charles was no longer the man who had come half-willing, several years earlier, suffering from clinical depression. I always suspected, Howie, that you assigned me that group not through any faith in my untested abilities as a therapist, but because you knew that he would cover my mistakes, that I would learn from him. A member of the group for three years, Charles had emerged as its leader under the system we still use: a therapist co-facilitating with a veteran chosen by his cohort. Aside from leading discussions, he managed the support system that kept the men connected outside the clinic (the phone tree, the basketball league, bowling nights). Theoretically it was my job to supervise the process. In reality, I took on the role of understudy. With all due respect to my professors at New Mexico, Charles was my most important mentor in dealing with the effects of combat stress—

"Hey," I hear him saying, sharing his stories with the group, "the war forced me to look at myself seriously. When I was thrown into that madness, I didn't know what I was doing. I'm going along thinking I can leave my stuff hanging out. You know, as long as I'm a decent guy, I'll be all right. I was just like any fresh meat, when you think about it. My mama raised me a good Christian boy—pretty good, anyway. But I didn't know thing one about spiritual *warriorship.*

"And then I get to Nam. And what do you know, people are trying to kill me. I mean *kill.* You all know what I'm saying. They're not firing blanks, like some boot camp exercise. The bottom line, I'm in their country, trying to tell them what kind of government they're going to have, and they don't like it. No, them Cong don't care about my dumb butt, how I want to get home, have a nice life. Well, maybe some of them care a little. But mostly they want me, and the entire apparatus I'm part of, out of Vietnam—so they won't have to bide any more dudes from someplace else trying to game their lives."

Charles saw a lot of action in Vietnam. But one incident, and its aftermath, forever altered the trajectory of his life—

"We were going through this little hamlet," he begins in his steady tones, "your typical collection of grass-thatched hooches. It was the usual sweep, you know, searching for weapons and VC. My blood Carl and me were in this sort of granary, trying to calm down this elderly couple—I mean, they were, like, shivering with fear—when we heard a firefight break out on the other side of the ville. We ran toward the shooting, naturally, and when we approached this clearing we saw tracers and smoke. The black pajamas came out of nowhere. Me and Carl stopped short. We weren't more than twenty feet away. The VC faced the clearing, back toward us. In a flash the right hand thrusted down and away, the left reached for the pin. I leveled my M-16, but Carl beat me to it. A full burst from the hip. The grenade dropped and the VC went down. I scooped up that live ordance (in a move that would have made Clemente proud) and tossed it into the bush. Hit dirt as it blows . . .

"When I get up," Charles continues after a long moment, rubbing his forehead with his fingertips, "Carl's on his knees beside this dude we dropped. Only thing is, it ain't a dude. It's this girl, blood seeping all out from her clothes. She's not more than sixteen or seventeen years old. Pretty, too. I know what Carl's thinking—the same thing I am. Under other circumstances, she might have been a friend, a sister . . . a girlfriend. I go over and put a hand on his shoulder, tell him it don't mean a thing. But he ain't buying it. He drops on this girl and starts to bawl his eyes out. I didn't know what to do. I couldn't handle it. After standing there a minute, kind of dumbfounded, I just ran for the clearing. Got myself up with the rest of the squad . . ."

What followed this incident parallels stories I've heard from many another veteran at the clinic—

"Carl got strange after that," Charles picks up again, casting a level gaze around the circle of shared pain. "He wouldn't wash the girl's blood off his fatigues, for one thing. He told the lieutenant to screw off when he bugged him about it. The other dudes figured it was some kind of trophy, but I knew better. It was more like a *penance*. And when we weren't out on patrol, he would just sit and stare at his smoke, or go wandering off in the bush somewhere. Something started to change in me, too. Up to that point, I was doing a pretty decent job of keeping my act together. Mainly due to Carl. We'd talk music we digged, Coltrane or Miles, give ourselves a break from the war. We did a little toking, sure, but we stayed away from all that hard-core buzz. Now Carl got uncommicative on me. And he started to smoke them skags. You know, Kool cigarettes laced with heroin. I steered clear of the serioius junk, thank God. But I definitely got to doing more reefer. And I'd pop just about any pill one of the dudes'd put in my hand . . ."

Moving in this unreal world of dangerous chaos and moral ambiguity, seriously traumatized himself, Charles was ill-equipped to help his psychically injured friend—

"The worst was patrol. Carl would volunteer for point every time we humped the bush. He'd scan the forest the usual way, like he was being properly vigilant and everything. But the problem was, it wasn't for real. I, for one, knew he just didn't give a crap. I should have said something to the lieutenant. But you get this attitude over there. You don't trust anybody. Especially the higher-ups. You all know what I mean. It was even worse for us men of color. Meanwhile, every step Carl takes, he's asking for it. Asking to get wasted. Me? I'm praying under my breath. Don't let him trip a wire, lead us into some godforsaken ambush . . .

"Sure enough, one day we come under some serious sniper fire. We were crossing this paddy dike when they opened up from the trees. We jump in the water, try and get a bead, return fire. But Carl doesn't get down. I can still see him glowing in that hot Vietnamese sun. He's got his arms spread wide, M-16 in one hand, and he's hollering at them snipers like they can understand English or something. Come on, he's yelling, take me out, you bunch of motherfuckers! The whole squad is screaming at him to get down, waving our arms like crazy people. Finally I make a break. Just as they hit him. Hard, from both sides. I can still see the way the bullets shredded his fatigues, the way he stumbled, turned by the rounds. He fell and I ran over. The medic crawled up, and Carl clasped my hand. He tries to whisper something, but I couldn't make it out. His grip gave way, all of a sudden, and that was that."

Charles's experiences in Vietnam, especially the killing of the teenaged female soldier and the subsequent, and related, death of his friend Carl, deeply seared his pysche. Many years had intervened by the time Gary Devers first appeared in my office, and Charles had long since recovered—or so we all thought—from the psychological aberrations engendered by his wartime traumas. Yet if Gary was to be believed, something was amiss with my old mentor and friend. Disappeared.

Into thin air, as Gary put it.

With the noise of another war on the horizon, many of our clients were revisiting old traumas. And as certain as I had been of Charles's healing—as much as he had given me faith in the work we do—I feared some connection between his reported disappearance and his tour in Vietnam. I was prepared to discount Gary's story (I didn't yet know how far I should trust him) but my intuition whispered that I could bank on his basic honesty. I almost wished I had kept him over but decided that, given all the issues, I had been right to end our session on time.

W. E. Smith

& & &

AT MY MOTHER'S, early October. The monardas are dying and, as usual, the news is on. There's more talk of the "offensive option" in the Persian Gulf, just as she had predicted. Grainy images of American hostages tear at our scarcely healed Iranian wound. Eagle tethered, democracy on the ropes, and what's to be done? The Israelis issue gas masks; Primakov, the Soviet emissary, is in Baghdad. The stock market is down, and Congress hears testimony of rape and torture in Kuwait.

"Look at this!" Mom gestures through the pass-through. "Amphibious assault drills in Oman, wherever that is . . . somewhere over there. They're fixing to go in, I tell you."

"Things are looking more serious," I concede from the couch. "But the administration still says they're expecting the embargo to force Hussein's armies out of Kuwait."

"Don't believe it for a minute, hon. They're talking like Saddam's rational. Even they realize they got that one wrong. Can't you see? I knew it the minute I saw him posing with those little kids. Remember, the ones he was keeping hostage? He had this big grin on his face, like it was somebody's birthday party or something. Uncle Saddam! I knew then, the man's crazy, even more than our own government. Playing tit-for-tat with people's babies!"

The news drones on while we wait for our microwave dinners to cook. I smell the meatless loaf I've brought over, only vaguely aware of Defense Secretary Cheney slyly deflecting reporters' questions, President Bush addressing the United Nations, and jets bolting off the decks of aircraft carriers. I let my eyes drift around the room, where each horizontal surface is freighted with family photographs. Arrayed across the credenza are my parents' wedding; Bob, Gloria, and little Drew; and my beloved late grandmother in sepia tones. On one of the side tables sits the faded color image, 1964, of smiling family perched on ancient stone wall, the broad Shenandoah Valley stretching away below. On the other that same bright family, 1966, framed by Atlantic spray and crashing breakers. Presiding from the breakfront, among assorted aunts and uncles, my father stands ramrod straight in dress uniform, spangled honors over breast, jaw set and eyes clear. I let my gaze rest there. I'm world-weary, and it's good to look at him, and also to let him look at me that way. After a moment, oblivious to the television, I begin to hear the tones of his voice. It's the same Kentucky accent as my mother—only a little nasal and a little questioning (the questioning just to make you feel comfortable, because the man always knows his mind!).

My mother says she's going to call Bob. "Bobby," she still says. I mute the television, put up my feet, and close my eyes. I listen to one side of a conversation that covers the usual ground: Drew and Gloria, Bob's job and then the Gulf, the Gulf, the Gulf! Bringing a hand to my brow, pressing hard against closed lids, I begin to feel the light-headedness—my *bête noir*—coming on. I lie back, my grasp on things becoming more and more tenuous, until I am surrounded by . . . ghosts. There are those of my father, my mother as she once was and Bob, so far away. And when I glance toward the glowing screen arise these television specters: soldiers, sailors, airmen, and unknown foreigners in dusty places, draped in their thawbs and keffiyehs. I desperately seek myself, some core to hold to, but find only more phantoms. I fear being pulled into a chasm, a full-on vertigo attack . . .

But then I am reminded—by the aroma of mashed potatoes wafting from the kitchen, by the sound of my mother's voice, and by the still lingering gaze of my father—of verdant lawns that stretched unbroken behind houses of brick and wood (fences would have seemed a rudeness), where stalwart hardwoods dropped acorns in autumn and seed-pods in spring. Across the lawns were the woods, and in the woods the creek where we waded as children, as youths conducted revels of fruit wines and grass. Beyond the woods, Andrews Air Base rises like a fortress in my mind, squadron upon squadron of gleaming beasts my father rode skyward to protect our Eden of lawn and forest, of brick and wood. But it's gone now, as my father is gone. Fences have gone up, not only of wire and board, but more insidious ones; they insinuate themselves into the mind, creating so many ghosts . . .

"You want to speak to Bobby, hon?" my mother calls from the kitchen. "Make it quick, cause supper's almost ready."

& & &

TO CHERYL'S. We motor, Jorge and I, to where the city spreads its ectoplasm ever more thinly, until these zones take on the aspect of separate organisms. The metabolism is so unpaced, the soil of civilization barely held by families who sink sparse roots from aluminum-sided houses, service stations, schools, and shopping plazas. I experience such queer feelings here. There is a lonely vacuity that longs for the city's creative hunger, the cauldron of so many drives, urges, and dreams. But there is also a liberation from the city's tatters, incompletions of other kinds, lock-step nightmares. Here are babies, bulging madonnas, burp-spilled bibs, minivans and car seats: the close suburbs breached, we enter a world of peed and soiled pants, dirty hands and smudged mouths. But it is above all a world of wonder and newness (amazement at leaf falling, tadpole launching its amphibious existence, cardinal at the feeder, mother's love, father's strength, siblings, and ever-remembered playmates).

Cheryl holds me to the time of the lawns and the woods. I picture the swimming pool with planked deck where we sunned ourselves through each bright summer like lazy lizard snake-goddesses, wholly believing that our sole purpose was to luxuriate in every possible pleasure. Later came boyfriends and trials of youth, mutual friends and nocturnal revels, Joni Mitchell and James Taylor; but also Vietnam, the stain of a nation under the grip of apartheid, and assorted crises of family. With growing awareness, and solidarity of noble intentions, our college years were spent apart but never out of reach. Later we ventured into careers and serious love affairs, heartbreaks and consolations. Our lives are so intertwined that our menses still sync, as when we lived next door.

Moon-friend.

Last autumn Emmy was beginning to speak in sentences. Julian was coming out of his shyness, more happy to settle in your lap with a picture book. Cheryl recognized my share in her offspring; it was obvious in how she would leave them in my charge, wander off to take care of things that mothers never have time for. She and Dan had been invited sailing with one of his colleagues; Jorge and I were happy to enter for a time that fertile chaos which is the child. As for our relationship, nothing had been settled. We had only spoken a time or two since Labor Day and had scrupulously side-stepped anything serious.

We sat on the kitchen floor making Play-Doh monsters with the children. Their faces alone, shocked and delighted by turns, were more than worth the drive out to the suburbs. On expedition to find colored leaves, Julian poked the earth with a stick—precious find!—while Emmy, as we improvised silly songs, groped at the delicate white butterflies that twittered jerkily above the lawn. Later, with Emmy sleeping nearby, we sat Julian on the living room carpet and together perused his favorite picture book. The story was about a bunny who searches high and low for a home. On each page the bunny encounters a different animal; to each he inquires whether he might belong in a bird's nest, or a beavers' lodge, or a fox's den. Finally, of course, he encounters another bunny, with whom he shares a rabbit hole. As we turned each page, we asked Julian about the events of the story.

"What do you think the fox is going to say?"

"I don't know," he intoned quietly, and with great reverence.

"Do you think he'll live with the bird?"

"I don't know," he said again, this time with rising mystery in his voice.

"What do you think will happen next?"

And now Julian gleefully blurts his "I don't know!" with tremendous gusto, as if naïve ignorance were the most marvelous boon imaginable! Enchanted by his attitude—wide-eyed toward the horizon, palms up, the simple phrase drawn out with dread awe or great enthusiasm—we played our game until we all tired of laughing over how much we didn't know. Julian was suddenly drowsy and wanted to be held; Jorge and I watched dusk gather in the yard while he slept in my arms. Melding into my moon-friend, I cradled her baby, sat on her couch, and looked out a window where swallows veered hunting insects. Their acrobatics recalled the Thunderbirds' air shows at Andrews and I remembered a vision, and how I knew a teacher I loved would die. I could see that Jorge's thoughts had traveled, too, by the wistful expression I had come to associate with Peru. It was the way he looked when we caught up to the Cuzco Boys, gave ourselves over to panpipes that danced wildly through the air like these swallows. I loved him truly then, as always, and almost reached over to take his hand. But I was afraid that he would misinterpret, that it would make matters worse, not better.

& & &

"SURE," GARY SAYS, "Gorby's bound to say force is unacceptable. With all the credit he's rightly been given for perceiving the fatal flaws of the Soviet system, he's still hooked on the powerful drug of international influence. Iraq was a client state, after all. The patron has to protect its client, or the jig is up. The emperor's nakedness is exposed. It's my guess he'll get on board with the democratic powers, or be benignly ignored."

Gary started in on the Gulf situation immediately upon entering, and I have allowed myself to be pulled into another political discussion. I hoped we would talk about Charles, and not just to allay my concerns for an old and dear mentor. Gary's parting reference to a friend's disappearance—with echoes of other comrades lost in fire and blood—promised an opening to the places of his brokenness. But I decide to play it his way a while longer, remaining vigilant for an opportunity to guide him gently to those griefs he cannot yet face straight up. To be honest, I am in no small measure intrigued by the quirky way his mind works.

"You sound almost eager to see our troops committed," I say.

"Of course not. Who wants to enter the jaws of hell again?"

"Yet you question Gorbachev's efforts to work out a peaceful solution."

"I applaud them. But I question the purity of his motives. Who doesn't want peace? Who didn't want peace in '38? But a few tank battalions in Czechoslovakia at the right moment might have spared humanity six years of mayhem and fifty-million dead. The question of pacifism is perennial. After all, sane people don't enjoy violence. Most of us were raised on the ideal of turning the other cheek. But let's face it, when someone is being violated, you expect the police to show up, prepared to use lethal power, if necessary, to rescue them. It's Augustine's classic justification for war. 'Sometimes love requires force to protect the innocent.'"

"Augustine?"

"Author of *City of God. Confessions.* Church father.aint by Catholic reckoning . . ."

"Oh, yes," I say to avoid sounding ignorant, making a mental note of this concession to my vanity. "I'm somewhat familiar . . ."

"Not a household name, to be sure," Gary concedes (another note—his solicitude for my self-regard). "But for a student of the philosophy of statecraft, impossible to ignore."

"You were a philosophy student?"

"International affairs, to be exact. But I was drawn to the more philosophical corners of the field from the beginning. Yes," he continues with a rueful laugh, "I was all fired up to find the golden ideas that would bring us to the promised land of peace and goodness. But don't worry, I soon found out how little market there is for that kind of thing."

"I don't believe we've discussed your studies."

"It didn't seem important. Anyone can study, but what have you done? I never finished the degree, after all. It hardly seems cricket to give myself credit . . ."

He lapses into silence.

"Was college interrupted by the war?"

"Grad school, more precisely. Doctoral program at Georgetown. Because of the war? That's an interesting question. This was during the Carter years . . ."

"So, you were a doctoral student at Georgetown in the . . . late '70s. But you never finished the degree?"

"The dissertation, to be exact."

I suspect self-defeating tendencies, driven by survivors' guilt. "And now you work in the courier business . . ." I hesitate. It would be a mistake to push too hard, but I sense an opportunity to uncover a fundamental insight. "You don't seem to be working up to your potential," I finally say.

He seems uncomfortable, squirms in his chair. "I'd much rather talk about Augustine, if you don't mind . . ."

I start to protest, but before I can pronounce a word he takes up again, his voice grown suddenly warm with enthusiasm. "I was just absolutely intrigued how this Roman rhetorician," he waxes, "spurred by a child's song heard in the depths of existential despair, gives himself over to the church and how, through the ages, his ideas have shaped the way we speak about the state, war, ultimate meanings, so much else . . ."

"Augustine was the focus of your studies?"

"My dissertation actually deals with the Spanish jurists of the Renaissance," he explains more calmly now. "Figures even less familiar than Augustine—outside the realm of political philosophy, at least. Hoary old churchmen like Vives, Valdes, Suares, Sepulveda. It's funny," he adds wistfully, looking toward the window, "just the evocation of their names suggests the arid calm of the Spanish plains, a sun-drenched cloister. But they were all heirs of Augustine and, like him, they each concluded that violence is absolutely intrinsic to human existence."

He notices my resistance to such talk; my therapist's poker face has faltered.

"I know that's not what we like to hear. But there's not a state on earth, even a community, that doesn't depend on force, or the threat thereof, for its very existence. The Spanish jurists, following Augustine, were brave enough to confront that fact head-on."

For what deeds, committed in rage of battle, I wonder, *did Gary seek atonement?* I venture a bold guess. "Do I sense a need to rationalize acts of violence?"

"Listen," he responds tersely, "my Spaniards were committed to a reign of Christian love. But their conclusion, from what they had seen of the world, was that only potential violence in the hands of the good can check the wanton cruelty which would surely be perpetrated, were the wicked given free reign. You have to admit, that logic can be hard to refute. Just look around. Or consider the history of this fair century!"

I don't respond.

"Don't get me wrong," he resumes more casually. "Speaking personally, I'm most drawn to Vives. He argued that force could one day be made obsolete, if leaders would take responsibility to educate the masses in what he called Virtue. But even Vives admitted the need for some ordering force until that happy day should arrive. The crucial problem with the Spaniards, to my mind, is that they couldn't imagine an enforcing power beyond the head of the nation-state. The 'Prince,' in their parlance. In their world, each prince becomes the sole—and unilateral—arbiter (advised, it is hoped, by wise and righteous counselors) of when to go to war to maintain the rule of right. They weren't in a position to envision multi-national institutions."

"Like the U.N.?"

"Exactly. Though, when you consider how ineffectual that debating club has been in deterring mayhem and destruction, you might appreciate the convictions of my learned doctors."

"Are you against the United Nations?"

"No, of course not. I'm convinced, in fact, that we've reached a point where the only sane option is to finally transcend the limits of the jurists' thinking and make the U.N. a workable instrument. The jurists were enamored of the nation-state, beholding it in all the glory of its youth. Today it's a moribund concept—and one that's rapidly becoming obsolete. Let's face it, the world's gotten too small, and weaponry too destructive, for two-hundred private armies and no overarching referee. The U.N. needs real policing powers. Unfortunately, it wasn't constructed to play that role. But enough of this depressing talk. Let's have some fun."

It's a remark I had never heard in the setting of my practice. "Fun? What are you talking . . ."

He is already up and moving to the wall where my masks hang. "I've really grown to love these faces," he says with a satisfied smile. "It's such a fine collection."

"They speak to you?"

"Oh, yes, in many ways. What's your favorite?"

"They're all useful in the therapeutic context," I say clinically.

"What about this one?" He pulls a colorful mandarin from its hook and lifts it to his face. "Ahh," he says in the worst imaginable Chinese accent, "the inscrutable oriental. Smile in your face, then stab you in back!" He makes an imaginary dagger thrust. "Be careful, Joe! Me look friendly, but me make tiger pit down trail!"

He pulls the mask away. "Is that how you play?" He doesn't wait for a response. "Ah, look at this!" He is lifting an Ashanti warrior off the wall, a polished column of carven wood with exploded eyes and gaudily painted mouth. Slipping the mask quickly over his face, he abruptly whirls around. "Boo!"—he yelps as he begins an exuberant fandango, knees pumping, arms gesticulating wildly overhead. "Black man gonna take away your women, Whitey!" he cries. "Gonna take away your very whiteness, til you be nothing but a shadow. Yeah, gonna beat my jungle rhythm til you can't think straight no more. Break up your little plan to enslave the world! Watch out Cracker, watch your back! Me and China gonna team you up. Got Arab and Latino, too. Gonna take your place!"

He stops suddenly, plops into his chair, and lets out his breath.

"Now you."

"We could arrange a role play," I say as calmly as I can. "But first we need to establish some protocols."

"Protocols," he says, "I've seen where that leads—" He gets up and goes back to the wall. Replacing the Ashanti mask, stepping slowly back, he contemplates the selection anew.

"Gary!"

He ignores me; it appears we are moving toward Gestalt. I stand up.

"Oh, yes," he says, "here's the one." He delicately lifts away a classic toy soldier and places it over his face. Stepping mechanically toward the chairs, he swings his arms stiffly at his sides. Nutcracker-style. He stops abruptly before me, looks me dead-on through the dark hollows of the mask's eye-holes. His voice is mask-muffled.

"I can't believe I killed the whole thing."

"Tell me about it, let it out."

"It was the dominoes. We couldn't let the dominoes fall."

"Dominoes?"

"Yes, it was all a super-sized dominoes game."

I see glimmers of tears through the eye-holes. "And what did you do?"

"The manly thing, of course," the voice now deeply martial.

"And what was that?"

He fixes an imaginary bayonet, mimics a fierce thrust.

"Is it manly to kill?"

"I plead the Fifth," he chokes out.

"That's not allowed here."

"I demand to see my lawyer."

"Who's that?"

"I can only divulge his identity if you wear a mask."

Things have gotten out of hand, but I feel we're getting down to cases. I go to the wall, aware of his eyes following me. I look over my collection; two dozen faces stare mutely back. Most are masculine, a concession to the composition of my clientele. I don't wish to be a man today. Not with Gary. An enameled violet goddess, with moon imagery, is my choice. I step toward the wooden soldier and look straight through my eye-holes into his.

"All right," I say sternly, "no more funny business. Who's the lawyer?"

"Charles Robinson Pinckney, Esquire. A.k.a. Pinky. Only he can enter my plea."

"But you told me that Charles was missing."

"You never know, he might just turn up."

"You've heard from him?"

"Not a word."

"If you're going to play games . . ." I take hold of my mask, begin to remove it.

"Wait," he says abruptly.

"What?"

"If you're concerned about Pinky, be at Farragut Square at ten o'clock on Wednesday morning."

"I can't do that."

He goes to the wall and replaces his mask, leaves the office without a word.

& & &

WHAT WAS GARY UP TO? Telling me that Charles Pinckney had disappeared without a trace, police reports and all, and now to come to Farragut Square if I was concerned about him? *If I was concerned.* I knew this was the key, for I had been here with other clients. Gary needed to know that I could be trusted with his deepest secrets and darkest wounds. Was I *concerned* about him and other vets like Charles, or was I just doing a job—a cog in a heartless bureaucracy? It was possible that he saw me (others had!) as a shill for the VA, instructed to certify him fit so those who sent him off to war could abjure responsibility for his fate. I knew we were at a crucial juncture. The development of a fruitful therapeutic alliance hinged upon its proper negotiation.

Gary couldn't know how truly genuine was my concern about Charles's disappearance. I was vitally interested in his well-being, for reasons both personal and professional. But how could I cede to a wild goose chase, and one so freighted with intrigue? Farragut Square—a city park. Had Charles exiled himself to the streets, tormented by the return of harrowing visions? I dug through my old files, desperate to find firmer ground. I found my vets group folder from the summer of 1980, and as I perused my notes, I pictured Charles sitting among the circle, heard the hearty tones of his voice:

"When I got back stateside it was bizarre." He glances quiiz-zically around the circle at his mates. "What I mean is, too nor-mal. Cars are driving down the street, stopping at lights. People walking on the sidewalks. Nobody's taking cover, doing reconnaissance! Know what I mean? I'm in the back of this taxi from National, and we're slowly cruising through Georgetown. It's a beautiful afternoon, smack-dab middle in the Summer of Love. Sweet, funky music pouring out from all them M Street record shops. Everybody on the street looks blissed out, but I've got this urge to roll down the window and yell, GET THE HELL DOWN YOU'RE GOING TO DIE! Meantime, another part of me is saying I'm crazy. You know, keep my mouth shut, it don't mean a thing . . .

"I took my G.I. Bill, found a place to stay, and signed up for classes. The only problem was, I couldn't concentrate. No, I couldn't shake that feeling that everything was heading south, and in a hurry. To make matters worse, I was having trouble with my girlfriend, Cynthia. She was happy when I got back. I knew she'd been faithful and waited. She was like that. Honest as the day is long. I should have been happy myself. And in some, deep-down way, I probably was. But the crazy thing is, I started to avoid her. Quit returning her calls. I was ignoring the one person in this world who might have helped me get back to some kind of normal! Can you imagine? I knew it was tearing her up. It was killing me, too. But I couldn't help myself. Every time I saw her, or any woman, I'd see that Cong girl, face down in that dark Vietnamese muck. The way I saw it, I had blood on my hands. When Carl bought the farm, you see, he left me to carry the whole thing by my lonesome. After all, if I had been the quicker draw, it would have been me that wasted the girl. I kept asking myself why I didn't do something when he started to go off the rails. Take some responsibility. And I couldn't help wondering, why couldn't I make a faster break on that damned paddy dike?"

Shaken to his foundations by the horrors he had both witnessed and participated in; shocked and disoriented by a world of sudden, random loss; poisoned by an indigestible cocktail of guilt, shame, and grief, Charles soon found himself deep in the woods of post-traumatic stress disorder—

"I'd be walking down a hallway at the college and it would come over me," he calmly recounts, "—panic. I'd freeze. Back into a corner, shivering like some frightened animal. Once I stood there for over two hours. People passing by be looking all worried. A couple of the less generous dudes might even have a cruel laugh at my expense. The only thing that made it any better—the only thing that helped me forget—was dope. Weed or pills. When that wasn't enough firepower anymore, I brought in the heavy artillery. Smack. As you might imagine, before very long I was flunking out . . ."

Escaping the unbearable feelings associated with his combat tour through narcotics ultimately proved no better a solution for Charles than it has been for myriad other vets. After his G.I. Bill was cut for failure to attend classes, he turned to dealing to support his habit. I shuddered to think that he had taken up his old ways, that he once again patrolled the city's darkest corners, seeking to sell or buy a solace which could only bring more pain and ruin! As much as I was inclined to put such a possibility out of mind, Gary's remarks had rendered me decidedly worried.

But of more immediate professional concern: how get to the bottom of Gary's case? Though I hadn't come up with a definite diagnosis, I felt certain there was something to be addressed. At times I suspected standard depression and anxiety, pre-dating or unconnected to the war. Then I would find myself entertaining the possibility of a grief so deep he couldn't get near it. It was all complicated by the fact that I had begun to find his playful digressions entertaining, to look forward to his visits. I fantasized about running my hands through his chestnut hair, or touching his face. And then I told myself that my clinical attitude was sound—even as I considered accepting his invitations! By following the thread of his intrigues to its end, I rationalized, I might unravel the sticky skein of his life and troubles; help him out of his labyrinth as Ariadne had helped Theseus, and yet avoid her fate!

I worked diligently with my other clients, gauged their progress and wrote in their files. But behind each question, nod, or stroke of my pen were thoughts of Gary and Charles, an image of Farragut Square's leafy precincts in mind's eye, and the promise of a reunion freighted with infinite significance. Knowing that I was losing perspective, I made an appointment with you, Howie, for the following Monday. Then, with new resolution, I determined to spend Sunday at my loom, where I hoped to find a surer sense of myself.

& & &

SUNDAY MORNING. I had a light breakfast and sat at my loom. How can I convey the seductive force that armature of wood and wire exerts upon me: a living skeleton, to which I add the flesh of cotton and wool? How many times have I sat before it open-armed, it mirroring my openness, a well of mystery stretching to infinity! It lives, mute androgynous loving god, mute androgynous terrifying god, and invites me to enter where nothing is settled. For even were I to execute the most meticulously planned piece (a traditional Navajo pattern, handed down over generations, that Sarah Tilly taught me so painstakingly) I would emerge from the process something new. Holding the yarns, my senses heightened, I am every woman who has ever woven, stretching back even to the earliest human settlements. I am part of a seamless web that honors sheep at pasture, cotton growing in fields, rain and sun and soil, ranchers and farmers, shearers and pickers, spinners and dyers.

But today—again—I find frustration. The loom offers no point of entry. It is not merely mute, but without life, nothing more than wood and wire. My pattern in hand, I recall epiphanies we have shared, the yarns lain across the warps waiting to be tied.

It is the piece I had spoken to my mother about, through which I have planned to address my childhood and youth. There are to be lawns and woods, a creek and sky and sun and, as its central element, the big cherry that bloomed so white every June. *I still taste the pulpy fruit my mother baked into pies, or that we ate by the handful, straddling the lateral branch, as thick as the trunk itself, that thrust from the yard's edge where the tree grew.*

I toy with the yarns, idly move the treadles once or twice, and allow my eyes to rest on the purple-red I have chosen for the cherries. I take the skein in hand, feel the yarn's texture, and strain toward a space of creative vigor. Still the familiar shadow holds me back. Seeing the futility of pressing the matter, I close my eyes and let my mind go blank. I knead the cherry yarn between thumb and finger, feel its wooliness, so prosaic and real. And when I open my eyes I am again conscious of its color. But now I see blood, not cherry—the dark, sticky blood of poorly healed wounds. I make an effort to dismiss the thought, but I cannot refuse the blood-ness of the yarn. The cherries now become blood, blood-drenched the world I had wished to recreate on my loom. Sun of blood, sky of blood, blood rain falling on lawns and woods, soaking everything in scarlet! I lay down the yarn and get up from the bench.

I walk toward the kitchen but feel the vertigo coming. Staggering unsteadily to the easy chair, the room shifting around me, I sink heavily down. Confused images of my childhood world come floating through my mind, bright or blood-trickled. Then I hear the children laughing. This is the thread, I am certain, to which I must cling if I am not to lose my hold. Following it, the memories come flooding in upon me.

Sixth grade at Tanglevine Elementary School.

What a year that was for all of us! Coming away from childhood proper, I found myself fixed in a group of friends that coalesced as organically as the blooming of the cherry each spring.

With a crazily kinetic energy we noticed for the first time that we were social animals and created our own tribe, with its own rules and values. We noticed for the first time also that we were sexual animals; yet untainted by failure and disappointment, we began to understand *longing*.

There was Deirdre, a favorite of Mrs. Marshall's for her diligence, of the boys for her precociously developed breasts; dreamy Lynda, loyal and a little sad; redheaded Jim, easy-going and harmlessly mischievous; Charlene, exotic with her Tennessee accent; Dougie, my own, already visionary; Spencer, incorrigible flirt; Tommy, delightfully wicked; and of course Cheryl, moon-friend, clear as water. Surrounded by these intimates, school hardly seemed an interruption of our parties and gatherings, but rather another venue where we worked at projects, passed notes and glances, and got to know one another as I have hardly known anyone since.

Presiding over it all was ancient Mrs. Marshall, with her white-streaked charcoal hair, her pointed glasses, and a dogged determination to develop our minds (but also our spirits, for I remember plays and music, art and poetry!).

Incongruous crone or our Sophia, goddess of wisdom?

In the second half of the year the student teacher, Mr. Dawson, arrived. Now we—the girls, at least—had our god and hero: Hercules or Theseus. Muscled, tall, and vaguely martial with his ROTC flat-top, he was also idealistic and patient. We flirted with him unabashedly, I more than any (with Dad away in Vietnam, I naturally craved the attentions of an older male). Discovering a sudden concern that my clothes appear mature, my voice calmly modulated, I began to distance myself from the boys' fooleries.

The old polaroid on my bureau, now fading, tells it all: a field trip to Gettysburg on a spring day. Our coach ride into the rolling Pennsylvania countryside was marked by the usual shenanigans (teasing and flirting, boys with pea-shooters, "Ninety-nine Bottles of Beer on the Wall"); after dispersing, pell mell, from the visitors center, we blithely wandered grassy battlefields in the sun, yet too innocent to grieve for the miseries of those blood-soaked hills. Later we picnicked on the fertile greensward. Before boarding the bus to return to modern America we gathered at a granite pedestal topped by a squat obelisk. We are crowded around its base, old Mrs. Marshall in back. The boys in their sports coats look poised or goofy; Mr. Dawson is hemmed in by us girls. I stand beside him, one arm draped over his shoulder. Claiming him. It is my last clear memory of him before the year ended. We kids went on to summer vacation, Mr. Dawson to pilot jets in Vietnam, discharging civic duty before settling into the teaching career for which he was so obviously suited.

But then that summer, my father just back from his second Indochina tour, we went to the air show on base. I remember my happiness when the day began, still basking in the glow of showering him with confetti—I in my new dress, Bobby in his toy flight suit—buoyed by family friends, colored streamers, and my mother's serene contentment. The MP directed us to parking reserved for officers, a privilege that seemed natural to me (my father clearly superior to other men) but that appeared to strike Dad as if some mistake had been made. He was relaxed and smiling, though, as we skirted the monstrous hangars, his arm draped casually over my mother's shoulders. She stretched one arm around his waist, while with her opposite hand she smoothed Bobby's hair. I walked behind. As we came into the open the runways, stretching on like Nevada salt flats, reflected their hard, acid glare into our faces.

Bobby was getting jumpy. The military hardware that so fascinated him was now in view. Spread across the airfield, it appeared an insect army of fighters and choppers, stout bombers roped off from the crowds, and big-bellied cargo planes, their lowered ramps inviting a look inside. Bobby ran on, unheeding of my mother's admonitions; I came up and took her hand. My father said, "He's sure crazy about that stuff," and I rushed after him. It was good that Mom and Dad relax together, and I wanted to be helpful. I also remembered former air shows, rushing up the ramps of the C-130s, or swinging from the canvas straps that lined the gunships' walls. But when Bobby sighted down the barrels of an ugly black machine gun I felt a sickness inside. I took him by the arm and pulled him away from that game.

I was waiting for the Thunderbirds, for though I didn't share Bobby's fascination with weaponry, I had always found the maneuvers of the Air Force's flying drill team alluring beyond measure (and that summer, when I pictured Mr. Dawson in one of the cockpits, it was almost impossibly exciting). I knew that he would come dead-leveling out of the south, before ramping radically into the sky, as if pulled from the heavens. He and his wingmates would briskly veer into cloverleafs, or coalesce in impossibly tight constellations; finally, after tilting together in balletic movements, they would hurtle straight into the massive blue, as though they would never return. Just before being lost to sight they would drop helplessly, as into an endless chasm, then blithely recover into new formations.

Everyone ate hotdogs, but I confined myself to lemonade. I felt quivery inside, the glare or puberty or the crowds, my mother said, but my father said, "She's just excited about the Thunderbirds. You know how she gets."

We went to the runway to secure a good watching-place.

They started the usual way, which nonetheless provoked in me the most exquisite thrill. A shimmering wave of heat and speed emerged from the distant south, growing closer and larger until the glistening cockpits came roaring past; defying earth's sodden pull with breathtaking nonchalance, the airships pierced straight into the open sky. When they separated to the four quarters to weave ephemeral webs of gleaming glare in plumes of cloud, a rapt mesmerization supplanted my queasiness. Now there was only jets and sky, with the vaguest sense of the glowing runway, my family standing nearby, and the crowds that surrounded us. And then suddenly, without warning, a single brave aviator pointed his craft heavenward. He climbed and climbed, as if determined to break free forever of earth-boundedness. The Phantom's billowing contrail masked his ascent, and I held my breath. And here is where I must have blacked out because, though the jet continued its climb, I was no longer there but in some other place. And the pilot wasn't a Thunderbird, but Mr. Dawson; and his plane wasn't coming back; I knew with awful certainty that his plane. wasn't. coming. back.

When I regained consciousness I was laid out on the runway. My mother cradled my head. My father, Ray-bans masking his eyes, bent over me and spoke softly. "Come on, Boop, wake up now." I opened my eyes a slit but, seeing the crowd gathered round, groaned with embarrassment and closed them again. My father gently laughed, patted my hand, and helped me to sit up. I let myself be hugged, sheltered, and protected; and when I broke in stifled sobs he held me closer. But I couldn't voice the reason behind my tears. Nor would I explain it all that autumn, when we learned that Mr. Dawson had been struck from the sky in Vietnam.

That was my first fainting spell.

O HOWIE! Here it becomes difficult. I promised you I would explain, but how explain what comes next? You will recall my proposing that I meet Gary Devers at Farragut Square, as he had requested during his session. You reminded me, as you should have, that contact with clients outside of therapy is *verboten*, except in the most extraordinary circumstances. You further pointed out (I have the notes of our consult before me) that given my attraction to Gary, and his flirtations, such a situation could only invite disaster. I'm sure you came away from our meeting convinced that I would disregard his offer. I signaled only agreement with your analysis, and we moved on to other issues, other clients. As for me, I left your office as I always had, convinced that our system of checks and balances was solid; that, with you, I had found the perfect working relationship.

But that evening I was prey to other influences, voices that spoke only sometimes in words. More often it was an ebbing and surging, electricity running through the spine, or water and space at once. I couldn't concentrate logically. Memories of childhood and youth—the yards and woods, Cheryl and Doug, my vision of Mr. Dawson's phantom flight—mingled with thoughts of Gary's promised encounter at Farragut Square, until the prospect of that meeting crowded out all else.

Herb tea and yoga did little to settle my mind.

I called Cheryl, but she was putting down the children and said that she would call back. While I waited I stared into the darkened trees outside the window. There was only the meeting in the morning; the only question, would I be there; and not to be felt like *running*. How absurd, I thought, when it should have been so easy. There was a simple answer at hand: put another client's bad idea out of my mind! But despite my hard-won skills in staying independent of clients' distress, I couldn't disregard Gary's disturbing news of Charles—news all the more unsettling for its vagueness. Even more maddening, Gary's tantalizing suggestions were inextricably mixed up with a pull toward Gary himself, a pull with a life of its own.

I went to the closet for my briefcase and pulled from it the folder in which I was still carrying the old vets group records. To suppose that Charles's life had been derailed by resurgent symptoms of PTSD called into question our very capacity to heal wounded psyches. Even more troubling, considering the titanic struggle he once waged to break free of such dependencies, was my tentative hypothesis that he had fallen back into the slough of narcotics addiction . . .

"Sometimes I'd go round to see my mother," Charles is saying, his fellow vets gathered round. "She would give me a good once-over and say I wasn't looking too well." He laughs congenially. "Have any of you guys ever seen a junkie who *did* look well? Usually I'd come up with some bull, you know, about how hard I was studying. Often as not my sister, Jackie, would be there, too. She wouldn't say anything. But I suspected she was on to my game. We've always been tight . . ."

Charles Pinckney was extremely fortunate to have family who were devoted to his well-being. They played an integral role in his ultimate healing—

"Sometimes Mama would send Jackie over with food. I guess she thought I needed some home-cooked meals. So, as fate would have it, one evening she came in while I was working this deal. The customer and me were about to sample some, if you can picture it. Let me tell you, this dude was in bad shape, know what I mean? I was bad, but this dude was *gone*. His body was like a skeleton. And when you looked into those eyes of his, there wasn't nothing but the faintest glimmer . . .

"Anyway, Jackie comes breezing in, all happy like she does, and she's holding this big casserole dish in front of her. Me and this dude are sitting on the sofa, fastening our ties, a nice pile of cash on the coffee table. Jackie stood there kind of dumbfounded for a minute, but it didn't take her long to figure out what was going on. The girl ain't dumb, right? I was about to feed her some bull, but she looks at me like—don't even try. And that look of hers, well, it stopped me in my tracks. And you know what, it wasn't her anger, or even the pity, as bad as they both were. No, the worst part was that I could see that I was breaking my poor little sister's heart. Before the war, you see, it was me always saying how crazy the neighborhood dope fiends were, ruining their chances with a hypodermic syringe! The pushers who helped them wreck their lives burned me up even worse. I made Jackie promise me, like ten times over, never, ever to get mixed up with that crowd.

"Well, she set that lovely casserole down, and left without word one. And me and that dude, yeah, we went ahead and did our thing. But that episode marked the end of my dealing career. When all was said and done, I couldn't get past that look in my sister's eyes. It haunted me when I'd lay down to go to sleep . . . when I was doing junk . . . when a customer showed up at the door . . ."

As countless others have learned, escaping the manifold clutches of the opiate lifestyle was no simple matter—

"First I tried cold turkey," Charles proclaims, mock-heroic. "I figured I was tough enough to break it. I'd gotten through Vietnam, hadn't I? Well," he adds with sardonic laughter in his voice, "in about two days I was back on the stuff. Only now, since I'd quit dealing, my funds were running dry—and I still had this relentless, and expensive, habit to support. So, like many a junkie, I turned to petty pilfering. The only problem, aside from the obvious ethical issue, is that I wasn't any good at it! Before long I'd about stopped eating because, you know, every cent I got my hands on went to dope. Within a few months, I was looking about as rough as that dude was at my place when Jackie came by.

"Then, one day—bless the girl's heart—she shows up again. Walks right in. I'm on the sofa, shivering in this dirty old blanket. Naturally, she got pretty shook up seeing her brother like that. She said I looked like death itself. She's standing there over me, tears in her eyes, and swears she's not going to leave until I agree to come back to Mama's place with her.

"Well, I got pretty emotional, too. My sister standing there weeping like that, it suddenly dawned on me, like I'd been living in this fog or something, that there were people in this world who care about me. Who hurt when I hurt, suffer when I suffer! The truth is, I had a bit of a breakdown myself. She came over and put her arms around me, like I was her baby or something, while I cried my heart out. I knew it would do me good to go home," I told her, "but I couldn't bear to have Mama see me in the shape I was in. So listen." Charles pulls forward on his chair now, rests his forearms on his knees. "There's this old movie I saw on television before I went to Nam. It's called *Man with the Golden Arm*. Frank Sinatra plays the lead character, this jazz drummer, and he's got a vicious heroin habit. At first Sinatra makes an attempt to shake the addiction on his own, but he had about as much luck with that as I did." Charles chuckles deeply; the others smile and nod. "So, finally, Frank recruits his girlfriend—that's Kim Novak—to tie him to his bed. Once Novak has Frank tied up good and proper, of course, he instructs her not to cut him loose, no matter how desperately he begs for smack. For some reason, I never forgot that movie. Who knows, maybe I somehow knew I'd be needing it one day. Anyway, I decided to get Jackie to help me try that same experiment. It worked for old blue eyes, I figured, so why not me? She tied me up real good, and she stayed super solid—I mean, that girl's a brick—until I stopped screaming for dope. Fed me with a spoon. She told my mother I wasn't feeling well—you know, a flu—and that she was staying over to nurse me. That's what she told Mama, anyway. I must say, that girl thinks of everything."

"But I've got to tell you," he continues with a sort of rueful mirth in his voice, "that movie didn't do justice. I mean, soaked in sweat. Cramps, convulsions. Messing myself, upchucking. Deep, down-in-the-bone pain. Finally Jackie just stripped off my clothes, so cleaning up wouldn't be such a hassle. Covered me with bedsheets. After about a week, she bent over me, said my eyes were starting to look more clear. The fact is, I was too worn out to be anxious anymore. Too beat to put up a struggle. After I was calm a couple more days she untied me. Beauty and the beast! I'm happy to say that ended my thing with dope. But I still had a major stretch before I could live with my full self again. Once you quit numbing your psyche with self-medication, you know, there's nothing left but to face down the pain.

"Eat the bitter."

When Cheryl returned my call, I was thoroughly tangled in my thoughts. As he had noted to his comrades, it had cost Charles years of bitter struggle to overcome the internal chaos unleashed by the barbarities he had particiapted in in Vietnam. Yet by the time I met him, he had accomplished what each of us at the clinic considered a textbook case of healing from post-traumatic stress disorder. One sensed that he shared his stories with the group not from some need for catharthis, or to make sense of a shattered psyche but to model, for the others, a healthy openness about the painful difficulties he had successfully overcome. There was a vigorous clarity at the core of his personality that bespoke fulsome pyschic health. And yet he had now—if Gary was to be believed—up and disappeared, slunk away from responsibilities without a word to friends or workmates. This was a troubling development, by any account.

Cheryl heard me out like she always does, though a tad impatient, it seemed, with my penchant for examining every angle of any fraught situation. And I was handicapped by the need to stick to generalities, as sharing details would have compromised the personal information of clients. When I concluded, she simply said that she knew that I would sort it all out properly. I suspected these to be the words of a tired mom with too many scraped knees to mend, wanting to find bed and rest. But at bottom, she was right. There was no answer for my quandary outside of myself. Signing off, I decided to sleep on the matter and simply follow my instincts in the morning . . .

The train pulled up at Farragut North a few minutes before ten. Yes, I was unable to follow your counsel, Howie, though it made sense from every rational angle. My deepest gut told me that destiny lay in the direction of Gary's proposal, and I have never managed to ignore my intuition when it speaks as strongly as it did that morning. Please don't misunderstand. Disregarding your advice wasn't easy. I didn't make up my mind to debark until the car's doors opened; I was fully prepared, in fact, to continue on to the clinic. But the passengers pouring onto the platform seemed a river that must carry me to future, whatever that might be.

The mists had burned away; a soft autumn light bathed Farragut Square. I crossed over K Street into that block of lawns and trees, at the city's core, and stepped onto one of its interlacing sidewalks. In its midst stood the bronze admiral atop his rough stone pedestal, periscope in hand, peering past the White House and on toward distant Mobile Bay. The rush hour had quieted and traffic was sparse; a moment of peace had opened in the city. I walked toward the mammoth statue, glancing around for Gary or Charles. Other than a few office workers lingering over newspapers and carry-out coffees, the only sign of life was a clutch of young men gathered near the base of the colossus. For some reason they were arranging garlands of flowers. Some were wild; others, like the big, red canna lilies they placed in bunches against the monument's plinth, bore a suspicious resemblance to those of the city's public gardens.

I grew absorbed in their operations, which they undertook with great care. Two of them wore the stretch pants of the city's couriers, and I couldn't help wonder if they were connected with Gary's invitation. Before I could muse further over the matter, however, the men rose from their task and, directing their attention up Connecticut Avenue, appeared to comment on something in the distance. I turned and looked toward Dupont Circle myself. At first I was blinded by morning sunlight shearing the towering glass cliffs that border the avenue. But when my eyes adjusted, I saw what had captured the wreath-layers' attention. A phalanx of bicycles, two blocks deep, filled the avenue's shaded southbound lanes.

The riders bore down on the Square in a stately, hushed manner, festive and sad at once. Streamers of black crepe floated from their machines. As the procession approached, I noticed the automobiles, including three black limousines, that followed with headlights on. My wreathlayers rushed to mount bicycles that leaned nearby; they joined the procession as it began a slow circuit of the Square on surrounding streets. Outriders dismounted to hold traffic at intersections. Midway through the cyclists' second revolution, near the front of the procession, his fatigue jacket a dead giveaway, I spotted Gary. He rode gracefully and dignified, body erect and eyes forward.

I rose filled with misgivings. This appeared to be a funeral cortege—though one such as I had never seen—and I feared the worst with regard to Charles. I was so upset that I was oblivious to the approach of the man with the notepad.

"Excuse me, Miss," he began. "I'm with *The Capital Trend*. I hate to do this, but do you mind if I ask a couple of questions?"

"Questions?"

"Just a couple," he said squeamishly. "I hate to disturb you."

"About?" I said absently, not taking my eyes off the scruffy bicyclists. They laid their machines at the verges of the park and moved toward the monument, filtering incongruously through the dapper mourners who emerged from the limos and other automobiles.

"Were you . . . were you . . ." the reporter stammered. I turned to the man. Short, with a shock of stiff, flaxen hair encroaching onto his forehead, he wore out-of-fashion eyeglasses and an ill-fitting shirt. He squinted at me with a pained expression.

"Did you know the deceased?" he finally got out.

"I didn't know anything about it!" I blurted.

I forced my way through the crowd, searching for Gary. I found him at the base of Farragut's statue, where he conferred with three of his companions. I recognized one of them as one of the wreathlayers I had watched earlier.

"I say we do it the way he wanted it," one of the young men said.

"You don't think it'll freak people out?" said the wreathlayer.

"Who cares? It's none of their goddam business, as far as I'm concerned."

"What do you think, Gary?" asked the other one.

"Listen," Gary said, "Tomás was his best friend. He knew him better than the rest of us. What's more, he spoke to him at the hospital. I'm leaning toward doing it like he says."

"What about the parents, the other mourners?"

"I agree," Gary said, "it's problematic from a lot of angles. But there's something about a man's last wishes . . ."

Now noticing me, Gary acknowledged my presence with a hike of his head. He excused himself to his friends and came over.

"So this is it?" I said. "Why didn't you just tell me that Charles had died?" I was shaking. "Instead of all this mystery . . ."

Gary was taken aback. "No, no, no," he said, "Pinky isn't dead. Not as far as I know, anyway." I must have looked faint.

"Come here."

Before I could protest Gary had wrapped his arms around me. After a moment, the scent of his fatigue jacket's vintage cotton remembered me to myself. I pulled away, with assurances that I was fine, and took a deep breath. "Then who is all this for? And . . . where's Charles?"

"That's a lot to explain right now," Gary said. "I thoroughly expected Pinky to be here. The fact that he isn't definitely gives me pause. He was quite fond of Darick. Both of them princes among men, of course."

"Excuse me." It was the reporter again. "I hope I wasn't too abrupt over there," he squinted. "I'm just trying to do my job."

"Who is this?" Gary asked.

"Sorry," the reporter said, holding out his hand. "David Greenhue, *Capital Trend*. I hate to do this. I feel like such a vulture. But the editors want a piece, what can I say? I'll try not to be too intrusive."

"We'd appreciate that."

Gary's friends approached, one of them—the wreathlayer—holding a sheaf of bound papers. Nearby, mourners piled flowers at the base of the monument. Others built a tipi of sticks that looked to be the preparation for a fire. The cyclists began to sing something I didn't recognize, more a chant than a hymn, voiced in some exotic tongue. Well-dressed relatives wept quietly on the periphery.

"Here it is," said the wreathlayer. "I still say it seems awfully personal, if you ask me."

"That's the whole point," the one called Tomás said. "He wanted it personal, don't you get it? Why do you think we're going to burn it after we read it, ride all over the city scattering the ashes? It's about her, every bit of it."

Gary took the booklet from the wreathlayer and began to leaf through it. "Man," he said, "he had it bad. Listen to this."

> In this world, where is holiness?
> In the liquid fire of your eyes,
> your lustral twisting braids,
> your secret mouth of plunging kisses?
> the touch of your hand,
> soft and happy on my neck, my face?
>
> Where is my path?
> Does it run through you, my love,

or in some other direction?
Does it incorporate your sex,
your tongue, your breasts?
Will your weight bear upon me always,
bring me something new yet ancient,
unexpected, though not forgotten?

Pressing on, I leave doubt by the way,
holiness is surely one with union,
Strength is peace, and you are strength to me,
Waters recede, waters flow,
your waters engulf me,
I lose all presence in a world of phenomena,
Happiness is not a given, but
if you can break yourself open,
. . . light can come in.

"I don't know," the wreathlayer said, "with the parents here
and everything. It's pretty raw, don't you think?"

"What about this one?" Gary said. "This isn't too bad."

Dawn is breaking, and
I am not with you;
the world goes on,
the day will come,
traffic fills the avenue,
with its whine, its moan;
Peace in all these things,
yet I still grasping,
for something eternal:
your love, with its endless roses,
the path we share,
with its open horizons;
the solace we lust for,

which will only be found,
when I am in your arms.

"A few touches of poetry there," Gary said. "Here, I like the way this one ends . . ."

> Blooming cherries,
> a dance, the moon's
> new meniscus, smiling;
> waters of the river, surging,
> singing, the touch
> of you always, spring.
>
> Be with me, greet my
> smile, like that moon,
> let it grow; cherries
> blooming, a dance,
> the waters of the river,
> a touch of you . . .

Gary broke off and resumed flipping through the booklet. "Hey," he said, "here the kid starts on a note of irony—so necessary for a proper view of love. If he could just have kept up his psych . . ."

> I have noted your faults,
> with due regard
> in pen and ink,
>
> attempting to cover
> my rear end,
> and other important places,
>
> but you leave me
> no choice
> in the matter:

your eyes, your smile,
your strange,
quiet intelligence,

your rock n' roll soul,
your Debussian fantasies,
your pleasant ways,

your love, your truth,
your running, your standing,
your flight and returning,

I love you,
til I am love
for you,

I want you,
til I am want
for you,

I need you,
til I am need
for you—

"Ouch," the wreathlayer interjected. Gary continued.

I am the river,
surging brown
and turgid,

speak to me,
and my waters
sing,

dance for me,
and my heart
knows strength,

> live with me,
> and my soul
> will fly!

"You know," the reporter said, "I agree. There is a touch of irony in the beginning. But all told, I'd say the guy was a hopeless romantic."

"No argument here," Gary said.

"Can I see that?" the one named Tomás said. He took hold of the booklet and folded back a page. "At the hospital Darick asked me to make sure we read this one. What do you think?"

"Let's see," Gary began to read.

> Since you don't wish to care,
> how I am, or where,
>
> Since you don't want to know,
> how I feel, or if it show,
>
> Since you don't take my hand, or
> mark yours with a golden band,
>
> Since you don't believe in me,
> but choose to ponder who you'll be,
>
> Since you don't live for us,
> but wonder still if you can trust,
>
> Since you don't grieve for time,
> (wasted all if you're not mine)
>
> Since you don't stop to see,
> just how precious life could be,
>
> Since you don't take what's meant,
> but insist on your own bent,
>
> Since you don't live for truth,

we'll both repent lost days of youth,

Since you don't come to me,
but like to say you must be free,

Since the sky still seems blue—
guess I'll keep on loving you . . .

"I don't know," Gary said, "I hate to see him go out on a note of bitterness."

"You really think it's bitter?" the reporter asked.

Gary looked at him wryly.

"I mean, I see what you're getting at. But it does end sweetly."

"I say we scrap the reading."

"What about a man's last wishes, like you said?" Tomás protested.

"That's all well and good," Gary replied calmly, "but sometimes a man's not thinking straight. At such times his friends have to keep him from making a damned fool of himself."

"So we just burn the stuff without reading it?" Tomás asked; but before Gary could mobilize a response, a sudden hush fell over the crowd. Everyone's attention was riveted to the top of the monument, where a coffee-skinned young woman, her loosely braided hair in alternating strands of brown and dyed blond, braced herself on Farragut's outstretched arm. There were tears in her eyes.

"I hate to disrupt the ceremonies," she called out from her lofty perch, "but I just had to set the record straight."

"This isn't the time, Tanya," someone yelled from the crowd. A couple of others booed. Gary turned. "Give it a break," he barked. "Let the lady speak."

Tanya brandished a sheaf of papers identical to the one Gary had been reading from.

"I see this stuff's been making the rounds," she said, "and I

just can't let a bunch of untruth be spread all over the city. I know
a lot of you are blaming me, but I didn't make him dart in front
of that bus on Mass Avenue. How can I be responsible for everything he does? Poor Darick. I was fond of him. We were good
friends. He helped me learn the ropes when I got started with
Signed and Sealed. But he should have understood where I was
coming from. I told him at least a gazillion times I couldn't get
into anything heavy right now. I'm still trying to figure out what
to do with my own life, for crying out loud. That's why I took
up riding to begin with, to get a break from my studies. A little
freedom to find myself. But Darick, he wanted to nail me down.
We could have been close, but he was so insecure. He wanted this
big lifetime commitment. I just wasn't ready for that. He would
get withdrawn. Silent, jealous. I couldn't even sit in this park, have
lunch with one of you guys, without getting an earful. You don't
know what I've been going through. It's true, I did tell him we
needed some time apart. It was the only healthy thing to do. You
can blame this horrible accident on me if that makes you feel any
better. There's nothing I can do about it. I miss him, too. I just
wish he'd been mature enough to take better care of himself."

Tanya draped herself onto the admiral's arm and gave herself over to weeping out her grief. Just then some cops arrived,
pushed their way through the crowd and ordered the fire extinguished. While couriers threw Darick's poetry into the flames,
Tomás did his best to buy time with the officers.

"Damned sad," Gary said. The girl named Tanya had disappeared from atop the monument. A stately older lady in a dark
overcoat, whom I took to be Darick's mother, wept loudly. The
couriers collected their bicycles.

"Where's everyone going?" the reporter asked.

"We're scattering the ashes," Gary said, "per Darick's instruc-
tions. Along the river, up at Dupont Circle, around his alma ma-
ter." He turned to me. "Wanna come? We might be able to get you

on the crossbar."

"I can't." I felt shaken by the whole experience. "What about Charles?" I asked.

"I'll let you know if I hear anything."

Gary walked away. I remained to watch him and the other cyclists form into squadrons and pour down K Street toward Georgetown. After they had disappeared from view I hailed a cab. Shooting a backward glance, as we pulled away from the curb, my attention was arrested by a familiar-seeming form crossing in front of Farragut's monument. It was a man of solid bulk in full camouflage. For a split second he caught my eye, but I lost sight of him as the taxi turned. By the time the cabbie maneuvered his vehicle back to the Square the man was gone.

Vanished.

& & &

GARY'S APARTMENT. Once a week I stop by to collect the mail and water the plants. I walk through the park to that quiet neighborhood, overlooking the zoo, where he rents the top floor of an old rowhouse. There's a skylight, and it's pleasant to pot around with the watering can, listen to his records, or to sit at his desk and peruse his papers. Lest you think me unconscionably nosy, let me assure you that he offered me the use of his writings in putting this report together. We had so little time; he sensed, I imagine, that they would help me get to know him better while he is gone.

He says that his writing habit began with his dissertation; and there is plenty here of the Spanish jurists, who still exercise a certain hold over him, Augustine, just war theories, and notes on Sun Tzu and Clausewitz. But there are also verses copied from the *Tao te ching*, probings of his life and experiences, philosophical flights, efforts at haiku, memories and observations, confessions and resolutions . . .

December 28, 1988

I strive to be the man at the center, and there are times when I dare say I've come dangerously close. When I broke with the Foreign Service, still in the infancy of my career, I was without a conscious agenda. I only knew that I wanted out of that Foggy Bottom of deceit, substitutions and lies, dressed as honor, truth and decency. What then could be more natural than my affinity with the messengers? They seemed so free in the afternoon sun, wheeling along an avenue, or banking through an intersection—feet pushing, thighs, haunches, breast and shoulders lifting and plunging—their bodies aligned with City in a way that seemed to escape the rest of us.

The rest of us with our suits, our briefcases—our agendas.

The sobriety I have begun to learn from Pinky wasn't yet part of my psychic equipment. It was only animal impulse, a corralled mustang, anxious and claustrophobic, wanting to run. When I stumbled into Signed, Sealed & Delivered, needing to keep my nut paid, I wagered that to ride with the couriers might loose my tethers to disenchantment, chagrin and malaise.

The wheel has many spokes, Lao Tzu says, but it's the hub that makes it useful. I remember the day I met Pinky. I played down my degrees, figuring it would only hurt my chances. But he kept probing, wanting more on the Spanish jurists, just war theory, or my reading of Camus and Marcuse and Ortega y Gasset. We were back at his desk, where the spiral stairway goes up to the pool table, the pinball machines, and the chess board. Behind him, on the wall, were bamboo peasant hats from Vietnam, photos of King and Gandhi, assorted paraphernalia of the United States armed forces and a big metal sign that read DEMILITARIZED ZONE. I failed to notice the Vietnam-era flight suit hung from the ceiling, slowly twirling in the void—or the electric-paneled

Shiva that pulsated in meditative ecstasy on an adjacent wall.

He seemed to be sizing me up, and I couldn't help wonder what he was thinking about the man across the desk: scion of the Master Race, with my precious degrees, the legacy of domination. My *whiteness*. There was an impulse to bolt and run, the same equine nerves that sent me fleeing State. But something in his brown-green eyes, or the way he sat so comfortably in his chair, hooked me with the same force I experienced when later I was to stand before the flickering electric idol and feel it's ineffable energy.

"This isn't a regular courier company," he said. "You might want to try someplace else." His eyes bore into me, but with obvious compassion. I could see that he wasn't being unfriendly, or trying to get rid of me. But what did he mean, not regular? Signed, Sealed & Delivered was listed in the directory with all the other courier outfits. I chose them because I liked the name, and the slogan—We're Yours!

"I guess I've had enough of being regular," I said.

Pinky laughed, heartily, and I relaxed a little. He offered me a cup of coffee, and we spent another hour talking the philosophy of statecraft. "How'd you find us?" he asked as I rose to go.

"Yellow Pages. I liked the name."

"Really, you dig Stevie?"

"Of course. He was the first show I ever saw, at the old coliseum. My mother took my brother and me to see him."

"You must have one righteous mother."

"She couldn't stand the nagging anymore."

"When was this?"

"Say, around '67."

"No kidding? I'm sure I would have been there myself, but I was otherwise occupied. See, we had this little proxy war thing going on . . ." He gestured to the paraphernalia on the wall behind him as, rising, he made to walk me to the door. "You might work out all right. You got a bike?"

"Sure."

"Be here at seven. We'll see how it goes."

He held his fist toward me, smiling on my bewilderment at a salutation that was new to me. I rapped it lightly with the face of my knuckles, and when I ventured back into the city it was with a feeling that I had started something more real than what I had left behind.

After that it was simply a matter of getting into the *zeitgeist* of the thing: spandex, pedal straps, safety reflectors, helmet. Add in conversations with other riders on derailleurs, brakes and tires, the mystery of the machine itself; and then, little by little (but all the more inevitably) becoming aware of the Gathering, with its convergences among guys like Tomás, Rick and Ven, or others as they came along. But Pinky was always in the center, as irrefutable as that Olmec head at the National Gallery last year; that same gravity, and the gaze that never wavers.

March 18, 1989

Quitting State took me away from international affairs, but my defection from the United States Foreign Service brought me closer to what is most real. That is to say, my career as a bicycle messenger freed me, once I got used to the routines (pager mooring me umbilically to the dispatcher, the treachery of certain motorists at rush hour) to plunge more fully after that thing I groped toward when I started my philosophical studies, what I now think of as being at *the center*.

I was beleaguered in those years with Cortázar, drawn ineluctably into the precipitant gyre of *Hopscotch* (sometimes struggling with the elliptical Spanish, just as often availing myself of Rabassa's masterful translation). Like all shamanic mystery men the great Argentine, in his magical novel, lays out a world of surpassing reality, even if we cannot help but suspect it all to be smoke and mirrors. Against a backdrop of post-war Paris, moving among the dour French natives and a loose circle of bohemian outsiders, Horacio Oliveira stands in relief, but a relief not overly stark, for Oliveira cannot escape connection to everything around him! Seeking communion, while recoiling from the misery, the inanity, and the sheer inconveniences of life; wanting love, but unable to admit in La Maga a different kind of intelligence; Cortázar's hero searches for his "kibbutz of desire" through a haze of alcohol, sex, art and ideas. I was fascinated, obsessed even, with what I now recognize as the protagonist's self-absorbed comfort-seeking (how much of myself I saw there!) but also with his passion for that open flow between self and world, a flow my Protestant ancestors strove so hard to staunch. O White Man's Burden, how thoroughly I feel it! How bitterly I taste it! But with such familiarity!

Wheels. The wheels of my bike, day after day, making the rounds, rolling over avenues and bridges, skirting parks or the river, piercing buildings' shadows, ever spinning and whirring. My feet circle constant revolutions while my heart pumps inarticulate, knowing infinitesimally more with each rotation of the pedals. I note the wheels of passing cars through goggled eyes as I navigate the great wheel of this city, with Dupont Circle at its hub, avenues spoking out per L'Enfant's plan. Sun and moon revolve an arc of days that begin quiet and dark, build to a maddening crescendo of traffic and noise, then fade with evening into dusky peace and dead night.

Morning ritual. A wheel of couriers gathers in the open space of Signed, Sealed & Delivered. In the middle, earthbound, Pinky speaks for us all. He expresses gratitude for another morning, beseeches for safety on the roads, and enjoins us towards mutual cooperation and service. "Higher Ground" pumps through the stereo (*world, keep on turning!*) while we check one another's machines—a buddy system borrowed from Pinky's stint in 'Nam (brakes, tires, derailleurs, seat fastenings). Everyone helmeted and mounted, a drill of interlaced circles and high fives, Pinky raises the big bay door and we disperse into the city with our first commissions of the day.

Women. Another hub—or a centrifugal force, pulling me into ever-widening circles? Nurturance and pleasure, mother and lover (such is the mind, with its contradictions of language). My own mother: I see her holding imaginary court in her uptown apartment. She surrounds herself with illustrious ancestors in frock coats and billowing dresses; they are diplomats and, before them, missionaries to the South Pacific. What can she think of her drop-out son, about whom she chooses to say, when speaking to friends and acquaintances, that he is "finishing his doctorate?" It is the same pride with which she faces what she chooses to see as my father's fecklessness. Wounded, but constitutionally incapable of descending into chaos . . .

August 3, 1989

At Signed & Sealed a couple of years, I had settled into a different kind of life. I had begun to believe that I could shed the Burden, the need to be a Player. Supporting it all was my relationship with the asphalt, joy in the movement of the body, and the conditioning my daily cycling worked. There was also a steady indoctrination into the ways of the Gathering: morning ritual, evening bells, and hanging in the upstairs lounge, over chess or billiards, outside the glass-enclosed space where Pinky directed each day's web of connections. I could even say that we approached magical heights, with poetry readings and winey parties, breakfasts at Donna's Bakery, and trips outside the city for woodland rites.

Flirting with women was an occupational nicety; they welcomed the advent of us windblown outriders from beyond the confining walls of their offices. Andrea happened to be in the lobby of the foundation where she worked. The receptionist had disappeared somewhere; otherwise we would have never met. We got into a serious talk about her foundation's work on aid issues I had worked at State, and her farewell contained a hint of invitation. The next day I made a deal with another rider to take a delivery to her office, and she agreed to meet at the corner café; she would bring her lunch to the park when our schedules conflated during that spring. I never thought she would take me up on my standing offer, delivered half in jest, but one evening she brought herself to me and we became lovers.

She was attractive, intelligent and good-natured, a minor stubborn streak being her only foible. But perhaps that is what allowed her to achieve a better grounding than I. The fact is, she had come to a *modus vivendi* that eludes me still. The work of her foundation, evaluating health projects in the Third World, was missing the quest for overarching paradigms that has fueled my life. But in its solid, steady way, it was visionary, and it afforded her many quiet epiphanies. Her family had been a disappointment—not only the usual dysfunctions but, as Cortázar writes of La Maga's past, *blows in the corners*—yet she had managed to come through it all with an unwavering idealism. Her work was an ongoing refutation of both her father's brutality and her mother's haplessness. I was in awe of her orderly domestic arrangements, her solid friendships, and the settled nature of her personality. She had found a place from which she could operate, and if she showed any restlessness, it was only to deepen the commitments that had brought her to her métier.

The pregnancy was an accident; for I was in no way ready for the tasks of fatherhood. We found a place together, nonetheless, and tried to make a go of it. And for a while I lived in the zone of Andrea's unshakability, overwhelmed with protective love every time I held little Lila in my arms. But before a year was out, the sense of confinement crept in. It wasn't merely the responsibilities of parenthood, as daunting as they were. Even more, it was a growing suspicion that, as much as I admired Andrea, we would never truly understand one another. I spent my days on the streets, seeking that elusive *center* I had left State to find, while she worked contentedly at her office. The florid ideals that had fueled our lunchtime discussions were replaced by the logistics of child care and shopping runs. This was all natural, of course; and how could Andrea have been expected to know that the man who courted her in a park full of springtime, and bedded her in a funky studio, was a man who would never stop running until he found that thing that had fallen out from under his life somewhere around Vietnam?

When she finally tired of my discontent and departed with Lila, I missed them more than I might have imagined. Allowing the riding to absorb everything of my life I had so far withheld, I came to identify more and more with the organism of the city. The rubber of my tires on its streets pressed impossibly close. If I could only merge with its convergence of earth and sky and history and living people, I might spin out of the gyre a new-made man. Something workable, free of the past. And with time I began, little by little, to gain a new sobriety. I rode quietly, intent on nothing, as I went from office to office to deliver the oxygen of the city's metabolism, with each push of the pedals entering more into the organism of my own being . . .

November 27, 1989

Ah, poetry! It's how we riders incorporate the city more fully into our communion. Our Friday Gatherings witness the distillation of a week's worth of sensations, amblings, smiles, shrugs . . . astronomical events. I remember my first one—a haiku. It came to me suddenly, fully formed, while coasting along the river very early:

a shorebird skimming

> *the river at dawn, one thing*
> *it says to me—be!*

I rode all week with the taste of those words on my tongue, the universe filling me from the inside out. And it was good also to hear my fellows' lines: poems not only about the city but about love and politics and grace and fallen man,. Or the myriad comico-tragedies of the day-to-day:

> *Donna's Bakery,*
> *warm and steamy I find you,*
> *leaving my wheels outside,*
> *I taste your hot cinnamon buns,*
> *and think of Glenda . . .*

November 29, 1989

It was about this time—the time of my first poem—that I returned to my studies, spending my nights with the Spanish jurists, Aristotle, Augustine, Sun Tzu and Lao Tzu. After evening bells I would talk with Pinky. He was always interested in what I was reading. But one idea especially intrigued him, and he brought me again and again to the subject of my stillborn dissertation: Vittoria's conception, which he shared with most of his contemporaries, of war as the perennial state of mankind. I picture him pacing around his desk.

"I can see what they're saying. The state, society, international boundaries, it all comes down to Man against Man. Somebody pushing somebody else around. The problem is, it runs against everything I was taught to believe. My mama raised me a good Christian boy, know what I mean?"

"And the jurists considered themselves good Christians as well," I said. "Most of them were in holy orders, after all. But they were struggling with a conundrum. Their master had taught non-violence. But history, as well as everyday life, convinced them that unless good men—I say that in quotes—were willing to use violence against bad men, bad men would dominate. If that were to be allowed to happen, of course, everything would go completely to the dogs."

"What's a good man, anyway, but a bad man's teacher?"

"Lao-Tzu."

"Right." He paced some more. "But there's something else. I mean, once you've seen it, been in it. It's all well and good, on paper, all these ideas. But watching a brother's guts get blown out. The misery, the grief . . ."

"Vietnam."

"Blessed—Nam. Good God."

May 12, 1990

Vietnam! Dredging you up like an alien poison, a stinking, murky sludge, from deep within the gut. America's misery, can it never be expelled? The retching impulse comes but isn't consummated. The toxin remains to infect one generation, another, how many? Napalm. Mylai. Tet. Free-fire zones. Carpet bombing. Agent Orange. Cut and run. Vietnamization. Cambodia. Nixon. Kissinger. Gook. Dink. LBJ. Thieu. Khe Sahn. Kent State. Each syllable like a spitting and spitting but cannot spit it out. I fear that we have lost the gods who can transform darkness into future. We have failed to bring them the harvest of our hubris in weeping and repentance. And we have failed one another: without honesty, without shame, without humility.

Without apology . . .

"This whole Vietnam thing is so heavy," Pinky says across the billiard table in the upstairs lounge. "It has this special status. Know what I mean? You could say it strikes right at the core of what America means. Look at World War II. Horrendous stuff went down in some of those theaters of operation. Targeting of civilians worse than Nam . . . a lot worse. Think about Dresden,

Tokyo or, for that matter, Hiroshima and Nagasaki. It was nothing but plain, wanton slaughter. And we're supposed to see those guys as heroes, the greatest generation. World War II as our finest moment! How does that happen?"

"Maybe it's because we won that one."

He interrupts the shot he was about to make, slowly raises his gaze.

"You've got a point," he says gamely, sighting down his cue. "Nothing justifies a war like winning it. You know what they say, *vae victis* and all that. And think about it, the communists didn't get in our faces like them fascists did. The Japanese jumped us at Pearl Harbor and, along with Nazi Germany, seemed hell bent on taking down the world in quick-time. I mean, who could argue with stopping Hitler? Is anybody going to stand up for genocide? But Marxist-Leninism, it was looked at more benignly when I was younger. I'm sure you remember. A lot of the hipper folks, the sixties generation, thought it was a great idea. Mao was a hero. So were Che and Castro. Everybody was carrying around the *Little Red Book*. The lack of freedoms under those dictatorships didn't seem to bother people too much. Maybe they weren't aware of what was happening, on the ground, in some of those countries."

He sinks the thirteen ball, steps back and surveys the table. "As for me," he says, "I'd rather take my chances in a free society. If I do right by my fellow man, I figure the Tao's bound to take care of me. That's how I look at it, anyway."

His face grows grave, and as he turns toward the vintage flight suit that dangles over the open space below, he grips his cue stick tightly with both hands. "But listen," he goes on, planting the end of the stick solidly on the floor, "freedom's not something we can do for other people. It's been a rock-hard struggle here, and we're still working at it. Think about it. Every time Uncle Sam gets mixed up in some overseas adventure, even if there's some good intention involved, it's always tainted with selfish interests. Look at Afghanistan, Angola, Central America. Heck, I don't need to tell you. It's like the Buddha said, you start with both pure and impure intentions, you're going to get both pure and impure results. You know," he says, turning again toward the table, considering his options, "the more I read about it, the more I wonder if Marxism wasn't the best some of these societies could have done at the time. I mean, they had to get themselves all the way from feudalism to the modern world. The populations of those countries weren't ready for democracy. And you've got to admit, they've made some pretty impressive improvements in their standard of living. Sure, a lot of it was at the expense of personal freedoms. But how much personal freedom did a Russian serf have, anyway? A Chinese peasant? Fortunately," he adds with his characteristic optimism, "that era's coming to an end. You can see that yearning for freedom in all those places. It can't be denied forever.

"The way I see it," he says after sending the ten ball banking unsuccessfully out of the corner, "Vietnam rubbed the wound of our own divisions—that eternal struggle between group feeling and every-man-for-himself. We can't seem to get it together on that. Like I said, I'm not into some dictatorship of the proletariat, a violent clique ramming their version of the Promised Land down everybody's throat. But I don't mind a little fellow feeling, know what I mean? I've got to believe that we can square that circle. Keep all the freedoms, but still practice some kind of caring for each other."

October 4, 1990

I came to understand that, with Signed, Sealed & Delivered, Pinky made an attempt to build, on a modest scale, a community that reflected his ideals. Everyone is treated with respect, and standing policy is that no one in the company, including Pinky himself, can earn more than twice the lowest paid employee. Morning ritual is mandatory, but other aspects of the operation we consider more *the Gathering* (evening bells, Friday Gathering, woodland retreats) are voluntary. Pinky doesn't ride people. He allows everybody plenty of rein in getting their work done. And the business has thrived. But Pinky set up the basic structures, and he's always been there, subtly adding his judgment, keeping things on course. If a rider isn't working out, has an attitude problem, or is a proven slacker, he'll quietly take him aside and let him know that he has to do better. If things don't improve, he'll cut him loose.

Now Pinky is gone. Fortunately, the systems he put into place have so far proved durable enough to withstand his absence. There is bewilderment and tension, but everyone is striving to provide, as much as they can, the cohesive force for which we have allowed ourselves to rely on Pinky for too long. They come to Dispatch with their sense of loss. They know the Pinkman and I are tight. They bring their half-baked speculations, and seek mine, but I don't have much to offer. And I am not at liberty to share my most intriguing thoughts on the matter . . .

October 17, 1990

To have disappeared so suddenly, and without a trace! I search my memory for some clue, step back from my bewilderment, labor to conceive this thing's meaning. To put the idea of a sudden, violent end out of mind, I imagine benign explanations. One thing I'm sure of: if Pinky disappeared of his own volition, it wasn't done casually, nor as a manifestation of a helter-skelter personality. In the nine years I've known the man, I've learned that even the most casual-seeming decisions arise from a well of constant reflection.

I start with a classic—*cherchez la femme*. I ponder his relationship with the woman I know only as Cynthia, an image seen through frosted glass. High school sweethearts, they shared summer nights and motorcycle rides before the war. She waited for him, but the psychically wounded man who returned from Vietnam could find no space for her in his life, and she was constrained to go her own way. Pinky eventually rebuilt himself and started Signed & Sealed, placed himself at the center of the wheel of the Gathering, the wheel of the city and, I'd dare say, even more comprehensive wheels. After starting a nursing career, Cynthia married a comer in non-profit circles with whom she built a suburban refuge of seeming security and success. When, one day she looked up Pinky, she was the picture of upward mobility, with fine clothes, a nice rock and the smooth skin of spa treatments. They lunched together; old fires were rekindled. After that Cynthia started to come by the shop. I'd see the Benz pull to the curb through the Dispatch window. Stepping out, she would take in the homey familiarity of low-down Washington with a gentle-eyed compassion. But there was also a recoiling, as if she feared not only the immediate menaces of the city, but that these bruised and battered streets might pull her back again into their drab and tattered life.

From the perspective of the Dispatch window, her svelte figure and gracious poise reminded me of a certain soul singer I had a crush on as a kid. Pinky never spoke about where they went when he joined her in the big sedan. But sometimes, when he and I got down to one of our investigations about life, he would refer to his *weakness*. "I know this situation's gotta change," he'd say, "I just don't know how."

Cynthia had two sons in middle school.

I turn over the possibility that something has happened with their *thing*. Maybe the husband found out—a murderous rage. Or is this Pinky's way of ending it? Maybe Cynthia cut it off, and he had to get away. That's it! He didn't feel he could tell the crew what was going on.

But why didn't he talk to me?

THE CAB STOPPED at a break in the chain-link fence. A worn sign confirmed that I had come to the right place: Crawford Terrace, the city housing project where, if she hadn't moved or passed on, Charles Pinckney's mother lived. My fleeting glimpse of his camouflaged form crossing Farragut Square had awakened in me an irrepressible determination to get to the bottom of his disappearance. The uniform was troubling enough. Even more, the way our eyes met—that he saw me, but didn't bother to stop or even gesture—made me fear that something was seriously wrong with my old friend and mentor.

I recalled that Charles had lived with his mother after his return from Vietnam, and his devotion to her. Perhaps, I thought, she could shed some light on his puzzling behavior. I had Alice dig through the clinic's records. She had come up with the Crawford Terrace address.

I paid the cabbie and watched him drive away. The flat gray sky threatened more of the on and off drizzle we had had for a week. A starving locust with yellowed leaves interlaced itself in the scraggly fence that bounded the housing project; scattered tufts of grass prodded through a broken asphalt courtyard surrounded by water-stained brick walls from which blank windows surveyed the desolation. An archway bisected the further wall and appeared to lead to an inner courtyard surrounded by more apartments. Passing traffic was infrequent. I'm not sure what I had expected to find, but it all now seemed impossibly bleak—and distinctly menacing. What was I thinking? I was alone in a neighborhood with a reputation as one of the city's roughest. I lingered at the entranceway, rethinking my decision. I wasn't even sure that Mrs. Pinckney would be here. The number listed in the clinic's records was no longer working, and there had been nothing with directory assistance. I decided to return some other time, and with company. I would walk along the main street. Sooner or later, a cab had to pass.

When I turned to go, we nearly collided. He stepped back, lifted his palms to me.

"Whoa." He pretended not to notice my startled gasp. "Can I help you find something?"

"No, thanks," I said, "I was just leaving."

He was a young man, slightly built, sporting a knit cap with broad stripes in green, orange, and yellow. He moved aside so that I could pass. "Sure I can't help?" he said. "You look lost."

"I was looking for Mrs. Pinckney. Charles's mother?"

"Mrs. P?" he said.

"You know her?"

"Everybody knows Mrs. P. She's like the Red Cross, Salvation Army, and psychiatrist office all in one stop."

"So I'm in the right place?"

"Number 27-B. Right through that arch there, and then to the left."

He looked toward the buildings. My eyes followed his gaze. Penetrating the arch would put me out of sight of the street.

"Would you like me to show you?"

He didn't seem big enough to offer much protection, but he was courteous, and his eyes were kind. "Would you mind?"

He preceded me through the gate.

"You a friend of hers?" He turned his head slightly.

"Charles," I said.

"You mean Pinky?"

"Yes."

"Pinky's the man."

We cleared the arch. The door of Mrs. Pinckney's unit was marked by a quilted wreath with a homiletic message on a wooden slat. My escort turned to face me. "This be it."

"Thank you." I held out my hand. "I'm Marjorie."

"Ralph." He knocked on the door.

The door opened. An elderly woman, her graying skin stretched tautly over sturdy bones, sized us up.

"Mrs. P," Ralph said, "this is a friend of Charles. She's looking for you."

"A friend of Charles?" She looked into my eyes. "Baby, if you're a friend of Charles, come on in. Thank you, Ralph."

"Anytime." Ralph nodded and left.

"Are you really a friend of Charles?" Mrs. Pinckney asked as I stepped into her home. "Sometimes they just say that, when they're from social services and such."

"I'm from the veterans clinic. I worked with Charles's vets group a few years back."

"There's no trouble, is there?"

There was a distinct note of worry in her voice.

"Not that I know of."

"Here, take a seat." She gestured toward a couch. It was only when I looked in its direction that I noticed a girl and a boy playing on the floor beyond it. Mrs. Pinckney walked stiffly toward the kitchen. "Can I get you some coffee, or a cup of tea? We might as well get comfortable, if we're going to talk."

I asked for tea.

She turned and addressed the children. "Babies, why don't you two play in my room for a while."

They stared at me. "This is a friend of Charles. Her name's—"

"I'm Marjorie," I said. "Marjorie Llewellyn."

The boy waved his hand vaguely across the air; the girl smiled, and they began to collect their toys. I looked around the living room. It was full of color and texture, a striking contrast to the housing project's stark exterior. My eyes were drawn first to the homemade quilts, stitched pillow covers, and hand-sewn draperies. Then I noticed, on a sideboard, the family photos. A teenaged Charles stands beside a motorcycle with a pretty girl on his arm, then alone in a private's uniform. I was absorbed in my observations when Mrs. Pinckney emerged from the kitchen with two steaming cups. She set mine on the coffee table and lowered herself into a stuffed chair catty-cornered from me.

I expressed admiration for the quilts and asked if she had done them herself.

"These two I did." She indicated one draped over the couch and another hanging on the opposite wall. "That one by the kitchen was handed down from my mother."

They were of extraordinary workmanship. I complimented her again.

"Thank you," she said. "Do you sew?"

I told her about my weaving work, and how I had learned to crochet from my mother when I was a girl.

"Making things from thread is good for a person, don't you think?" she said. "But tell me about Charles. That's the reason you came, isn't it?"

Her casual tone belied the lingering concern in her eyes.

"You seem worried about him," I said gently.

"A mother always worries about her children, some kind of way. It don't matter how big they get. Do you have any?"

I told her that I didn't.

She looked off for a moment. "He did have that trouble after he came back from his soldiering," she said. "But I guess you know all about that. 'Course that's been a long time now. It looks like they're fixing to start another one. Don't they ever learn?"

"Have you seen him lately?"

She stared at her hands, as if examining her nails. "Not too lately. What about you?"

"Actually, I did see him. Or think I did, briefly. I was in a cab, downtown. But before we could turn around, he had disappeared."

"Disappeared?"

"Do you know where he is?"

She fidgeted with the fabric of her dress, pricking it up in little tufts. "Well, he hasn't stayed in touch like he generally does."

"When's the last time you saw him?"

She looked up suddenly. "Not since summer."

She seemed to have surprised herself with the news she herself had imparted, and we lapsed into silence. When she resumed, she avoided my eyes. "He generally sends me a check every month, same amount every time. But a couple months ago he sent me a big old amount. There was also a note saying he had to take care of some things and not to worry. I figured he was just busy with his company. I know he's got a lot of people depending on him. But I haven't heard from him since."

She turned a perplexed expression to me.

"I see."

She averted her gaze. "A few weeks ago the police came around looking for him. Can you imagine? They must have got him mixed up with some of these hoodlums 'round here. I didn't tell 'em anything."

There was a knock at the door.

"Come in."

A skinny girl with tightly bound pigtails peeked through. "Mama told me to ask could she borrow ten dollars. She said it's just til the end of the month." The girl was out of breath; she nervously shifted her weight from one foot to the other.

"Come on in," Mrs. Pinckney said. "I'll see what I can do. This is Miss Marjorie. She's a friend of Charles."

The girl nodded timidly.

"Have a seat for a minute," Mrs. Pinckney said to the girl. "I'll be right back."

The girl sat on the couch with still shallow breath; Mrs. Pinckney got up and walked back through the apartment. The girl and I exchanged smiles. When Mrs. Pinckney returned, the girl rose and walked to the door. Mrs. Pinckney met her there, holding out a bill. "You doing all right these days?" she asked. "These boys aren't giving you too much trouble, are they?"

"Not really."

"Come back sometime when I'm not busy. We'll work on our stitching. Would you like that?"

"Mm-hm."

"You be well, okay?"

The girl nodded and backed out the door. "Sorry about that," Mrs. Pinckney said as she walked back to her chair. "Somebody around here's always needing something. If it weren't for that check from Charles, I'd have to say no." She sat down again with a weary sigh. "He chastises me for giving it away, you know. He says I ought to spend it on myself." She shook her head in disbelief. "Then he gets to telling me I ought to move! Get out of that hood, he says. All I do is worry about you." She let out an exasperated sigh. "Doesn't he know I'd be lonesome, away from everybody I know? Sooner or later, he's just going have to accept that I want to stay right where I am."

She gazed around the living room, until her eyes rested on the sideboard with the family photographs. "I'm proud of him for moving up, Lord knows. He only had that one bad patch, after he came back from the war. Anybody could understand that. I can't bear to think what he went through over there. It breaks my heart too bad. And him always such a sweet boy. But I'll bet you didn't come all the way over here to hear about this. Isn't it just like a mother to go on about her children?"

I said that I was always happy to talk about Charles.

She stirred her tea for a moment and grew reflective. "For a while there," she said, "I thought he might just get the whole ball of wax. He got back from the war in one piece, at least he seemed all right. And he had that nice girl waiting for him. Cynthia, that was her name. He was even getting the GI Bill. But life don't always work out like we plan. Sometimes God works it in ways we can't fathom, no matter how hard we try. Sometimes don't want to fathom, I suppose. And my son, well, he just couldn't move along there for a while." Her voice dropped to a whisper. "He got involved in hard drugs. But don't you tell him I told you that. He thinks I don't know."

After peering down the hallway to where the children had disappeared, she resumed in her normal voice. "He lived in that room back there a couple of years." She stretched an arm toward the hallway. "Just moped around all day, all moody-like. Depression, they said it was. I'd wake up in the middle of the night, and hear him weeping his eyes out. I'd go in there and take a hold of him, try and help him through whatever kind of storm he was in. I'd ask him what was wrong. But he wouldn't tell me. I guess he couldn't see clear to what was messing with him. Sometimes he'd cry out men's names. Rick! Carl! I figured they were some of the ones that didn't make it back.

"This war's such a horrible business." She shook her head dolefully. "They ought to let us mothers run the show. There'd be a lot less sorrow in this world. We wouldn't be sending our boys around the world to shoot each other up, I can tell you that!"

She leaned over the table and looked into my cup. "How's your tea? Need warming up?"

I told her that I was fine.

"I got to say," she went on, settling back a little, "one lucky thing I did was find you folks. It wasn't easy getting him to come in, that's for sure. I waited in that sitting lounge while he had his first therapy. It was almost like his first day at school. Then, little by little, he started to come out of that bad place he was in. It was like he was crawling through some kind of cave, trying to find the light at the end. I guess a year went by. I don't know what you people did, but one day he goes out and finds himself a job, working as a messenger. That was before he started his own outfit. A week later he comes in here and hands me his pay. And he says, Mama, I'm sorry I worried you so bad. I'm better now.

Well, I didn't sleep that night for thanking the Lord. Down on my knees, praising His mercy. I was so grateful to know my son was sleeping peaceful in the next room, instead of wasting himself away in sorrow . . ."

There was another knock at the door. It was a boy this time. "Mrs. P, my grandma's having sky attic again. She said can you give her a mes-sage?"

"Tell her I'll be over presently. And here's a quarter. If you find Ralph, ask him to come and see me."

The boy stepped over, took the quarter, and ran off.

"I've gone on too much," Mrs. Pinckney said. "I still don't know why you came. I suppose you're looking for Charles."

"I'm not looking for him, exactly. It's just that no one seems to know where he is."

"Have you tried the courier company?"

"Yes—or rather his friend, Gary Devers—tells me they haven't seen him."

"Oh yes, Gary. What about his apartment?"

"They've looked there, too."

She stared into the carpet a long moment, then raised her eyes. "That sounds some troublesome." She looked away, lost in reflection. "As a doctor, you don't suppose he's . . ."

I put my hand on hers. "I'm sure he's fine."

She began to pull herself up from her chair. "I can tell you one thing. Whatever he's up to, I'm sure it's okay. He's not one of these ne're do wells, ruining our community with drugs and shoot-em-ups."

She put on a brave face, but there was again that edge of worry in her voice. I promised to let her know if I heard anything.

A knock at the door. It was Ralph. Mrs. Pinckney asked him to see that I get a cab. "Come and see me sometime," she said. "We'll do some sewing."

I said I would. We clasped hands warmly, and I left with Ralph.

As the cab ferried me toward the clinic building, I considered my parting assurance about Charles's soundness of mind ("I'm sure he's fine") and questioned whether I had merely been offering empty, if soothing, words to a worried mother. I had immediately liked Mrs. Pinckney—she possessed the same grounded honesty and warmth as her son—and I felt a guilty twinge at the mere possibility that I had been insincere with her. The fact is, I had not, consciously at least, drawn any definite conclusions about Charles's unusual behavior. I thought through the events of the previous weeks, winnowing the wheat from the chaff, and concluded that all we really had was the simple fact of his disappearance—along with my brief sighting of the man (at least I was convinced that the figure crossing in front of Farragut's statue, fitted out in full cammo, was Charles) after the courier's memorial service. Both of these factors were troublesome, certainly, but still I struggled to believe that Charles's healing had somehow come undone. Striving to settle on some solid ground, I found myself reflecting on his final session with the vets group, a meeting marked by poignant reminiscences and more than a few tears. I remembered the words he had spoken, a sort of valediction to the group: words to which I have ofen referred when I find myself groping for a way forward with a client's treatment . . .

"You've got to look it in the eye and deal with it," he said in his brotherly way, his warm gaze taking in friends he was preparing to leave. "That's going to be rough," he went on, "but it's the only way. And you've got to give yourself permission to grieve. The people here helped me with that. When all is said and done, you've got to accept that there are certain things in life you just can't control. Number one? The past. It's hard on the ego, no question, but you have to take whatever happened and feel whatever you feel. The losses, the regrets. The mistakes! You've even got to suck up the big one. Shame. Finally, after you've gotten through all of that, you've got to forgive yourself, and anybody else you think might have messed you up along the way. It's not easy to face these kinds of depths, I know. We could be annihilated if we let go of those old mental habits. Things like judgment, self-punishment, grudge-holding. That's what you think, anyway! The therapy process helps. This vets group. It's a blessing to have people to listen and understand. People who want you to be well. Of course, nobody's going to totally get what goes on inside. For me, that's where some kind of higher—or bigger, or better—power comes in. I don't care if you call it Jesus, Buddha, Allah, the Tao, or Captain Kangaroo. I just need something bigger than me to get me through this mess. Plain and simple. And one last thing. We've got to stick together. If we can't do that, there's definitely no way forward . . ."

Hearing the steady tones of Charles's voice in my mind, I felt more settled as the cab pulled up to the curb at the clinic building, at peace with my comforting assurances to his mother. There was no way to be certain, but until we knew more I would operate on the premise that wherever he was, and whatever he was up to, Charles Pinckney continued to enjoy abundant psychic health.

& & &

I'M TRYING TO RECREATE the way things were last autumn, Howie, but you know what a slippery thing memory is. Kierkegaard may have said that we live life forward, and understand it backward, but he failed to add that we can't help but see the past through present eyes. I picture myself last October, the time of my visit to Mrs. Pinckney, and must remind myself of everything I now know that I did not know then: I refer to my times with Gary, the winter warfare in the Persian Gulf, and what later went down with Charles. It has all fermented in these months of waiting for Gary's return, building this report, and weaving the tapestry that gave me so much trouble last year. I am whelmed with a flood of feeling and, placed viscerally back in time, possessed of the need to bring all of these things to bear, so that I might finally be free of them . . .

It became clear, as autumn deepened, that there would be no pristine solution to the Persian Gulf crisis. My mother was more certain than ever that Bob would be called up, and I had begun to share her concerns. Along with these underlying worries, and my day-to-day obligations at the clinic, I was dealing also with Jorge's restiveness and Charles's disappearance. And though he hadn't been at the clinic for two weeks, indeed seemed to have abandoned his therapy altogether, there were insistent thoughts of Gary Devers. I felt more and more surrounded by a host of unresolved dilemmas. They would all be washed away with the watershed of the war.

But I get ahead of myself . . .

I am near Dupont Circle, where I have lunched at the book-store café. I see that the Cuzco Boys have set up in the park.

It is the kind of autumn day we count on every year. There are burnished sun, still lush grass, and leaves of every shade of orange and yellow. Behind it all is the heightened expectancy of frost and winter snows. I don't cross into the Circle but am content to listen from a distance. Pigeons wheel and shuttle over the park's sturdy hardwoods; a group of anti-war protesters, silently abetted by these flighted symbols of peace, chants stridently on its far edge.

As always, there is a sense of kismet in having come across the Cuzco Boys; I recall how Jorge and I sought them out, so avidly—though we don't meet for lunch as we once did. Their music throbs through the air. The park is full of people, the ta-bles around its periphery occupied by gentlemen intent on serious chess play. The angular signs of the protesters work against the fountain's smooth marble, its adamantine waves, and against its silver jet, which refracts the afternoon sun in sparkling sheets.

It was in this moment of outward movement and inner calm (of raucous contention and quiet rapture) that Gary appeared. The cycle came banking around the Circle among others that ply the city's streets, its rider not especially elegant in form, though not without his lanky grace. He subtly moved his head in my direction and my breath deepened; shifting his gaze forward, he deftly maneuvered the cycle through the Circle's shifting traffic. After another two passes round, he moved toward the curb and approached me.

"What's up?" he said casually, planting one foot on the pavement.

I squinted into a sun that hung low over the fountain in the southern sky. "You've missed two appointments."

"Sorry."

"Are you on a delivery? I thought you worked in Dispatch."

"I'm just making a few customer calls," he said. "Stuff Charles normally takes care of."

"No word of him?"

"No, but I feel something in the air." He surveyed the activity in the Circle. "It's almost like he's here . . . somewhere."

We stood and listened to the Cuzco Boys' panpipes and guitars.

He turned to me suddenly. "Listen," he said, "it's a beautiful day. Why don't we go for a ride?" He invitingly patted the crossbar of his cycle. There was a brusque wavering in my solar plexus, and the city began to suck away like an undertow. With my eyes resting on the dull green of Gary's fatigue jacket, I flashed to the boy I had loved in my youth. The queasy throbbings of vertigo threatened. Gary was dangerous, but my only safety . . . the thread I must hold to . . .

The crossbar's steel was hard against my thighs. I tightly gripped the handle bars. Leaning back abruptly when the machine lurched forward, I breathed in Gary's woody scent; he bent toward me until my head lay against his shoulder. We spun out of Dupont Circle, over Rock Creek, and then coasted past Georgetown's shops toward the river. When we crossed Key Bridge, university crew teams crawled over the watercourse's placid skin. On the Virginia side Gary turned decisively, accelerating onto the freeway shoulder toward Arlington Cemetery. Digging hard at the pedals, his chest surged against my back in rhythmic waves, so close I felt the stream of his breath against my neck. After Iwo Jima we ramped past the cemetery's neoclassical gate and wheeled again over the Potomac. The layer cake of the Kennedy Center gleamed before us in the sun; Lincoln's temple rose on the verge. Speeding along past the Wall and the Reflecting Pool, skirting government agencies and office buildings, we made our way toward the clinic . . .

The thought of the clinic broke the spell, and I was again aware of my surroundings. The Cuzco Boys' wildly plaintive "El Condor Pasa" played on and on; protesters chanted loud and emphatic. The burnt autumn sun etched the entire scene (the fountain jetting clean and pure, office workers milling about, musicians and chess players and protesters all floating in a rain of colored leaves) onto my soul. I looked at my watch and saw that I was running late. Turning, I stepped uncertainly toward the subway entrance.

✦ ✦ ✦

MY MOTHER'S. The monardas lean sadly in the waning light. I am expecting her to be anxious. Hussein shows no sign of relaxing his grip on Kuwait, and the U.S. administration is equally intransigent. Bob has missed the first round of reserve call-ups, but there are rumors of adding more troops. I feel it at the clinic. It's in the eyes (the nervous gestures) and a quality in the skin (oily and toxic).

"They're going to do it again," one of them says. "Send a fresh boatload of poor bastards some god-forsaken shithole to get messed up . . ."

Gary has missed another appointment; I wonder what he would say about the latest news. At his last visit we had discussed the administration's strategy. The president had cautioned that the economic embargo would require a substantial interval before it might achieve the desired effect.

"That sounds like an admonition to patience," Gary said. "But did you notice what came next? He said that they were reviewing *all the options*. That's code. You have to realize how things work in these scenarios. They don't say what they actually mean. Mark my words, within weeks we'll see Powell head to the Gulf for a consult with Shwartzy. They'll discuss executing what they call the 'offensive option'—without a shred of irony, I should add. But don't expect them to come out with that before the elections. Their poll numbers are down, and with a budget battle going on in Congress, they're not about to rock the boat with any frightening announcements."

"Let's hope you're wrong."

"I'd love to be," he said. "Escalation would be a questionable move. Once they commit a larger force, a climbdown will be next to unthinkable."

My mother turned on the television as soon as we came in from the garden. Just as Gary had predicted, the secretary of state had visited General Schwartzkopf in Saudi Arabia earlier that week. The details of their talks weren't announced, but the press was on to the scent. Word on the street was that the administration was planning to send more American soldiers to the Persian Gulf. As a reporter interviewed Secretary of Defense Cheney, Mom's eyes were riveted to the tube. Her face was set and her hands, which had been chopping a red pepper, were frozen in place.

"We're not yet at a point where we want to stop adding forces," Cheney said.

"But is it true," the newswoman pressed, "that you're considering adding as many as one hundred thousand soldiers?"

"It's conceivable we'll end up with that big an increase."

Mom's face went white. "Conceivable! What a bunch of malarkey. Why doesn't he just come right out and say it? Pretty soon they're going to have the whole kit and caboodle over there!"

Clenching her teeth, she chopped at the pepper in emphatic, determined strokes. I silently cleaned the chicken breasts I had brought, for no words were needed. I shared her anguished helplessness, recalling the many evenings we had cooked in another kitchen, with a television in another living room, Bobby playing in the yard, and my father a world away and in constant danger.

"And your brother's without a clue," my mother croaked out. "He thinks it's like the soldier dolls he used to play with. He was too little to get what was going on. Of course I tried to shield him. All he knew was that his daddy was a soldier, and that's what he wanted to be."

"He was in Grenada," I said.

"That's the problem. He thinks Grenada was a war. That was a turkey shoot. He hasn't seen the dead and the maimed, week after week, month after month, year . . . and the ones . . ."

I put an arm around her. Where was Dad? Tears seeped from her eyes as she finished chopping the pepper and then turned and dumped the pieces into a bowl on the opposite counter. We ate dinner with the usual ghosts present. My mother had agreed to turn off the television: grateful, I think, for a hiatus from the disturbing rush of events.

My father: two men. The slyly good-natured trickster who teased and called me Boop, tossed a baseball with Bob and complimented Mom on her figure; and the moody, silent specter who, after his last tour, dwelt in the den studying books that did little to cheer him: grim titles like *War Crimes and the American Conscience*; *The Wasted Nations: Report of the International Commission of Enquiry into United States Crimes in Indochina*; *The Pentagon Papers*; and *The Winter Soldier Investigation: An Inquiry into American War Crimes*. And always on his side table, frozen forever on the *New York Times'* front page, Kim Phuc Phan Thi, mouth agape and scorched arms side-dangled, runs naked down the village road, fleeing American napalm that has savaged her tender child's body! How disturbing it had been, and how little I understood! I ran with my friends and pursued our hippy dreams; or slipped away with Dougie, who saved me with his touches, the sweet cherry wine we downed by the creek and with his peace-talk and brotherhood. Afterward I would return home to find my father alone and unkempt, a glass of scotch in hand, the half-empty bottle nearby. That home had always been a shelter, even when he was away; a shelter we preserved in tenderness, knowing he would return one day with life and joy.

But his last tour brought a clinging vesture of death; Vietnam had insinuated itself into his life with an unholy vengeance. Two times he escaped to come back to us whole. Then, at the air show on base, I saw Mr. Dawson ascend away forever but said nothing. And when talk came of Dad doing one last tour, there was that same horrible feeling in the pit of my stomach, and again the vertigo.

But again I remained silent.

"Why so glum?" he asked at the airfield. I said that I would miss him and, lowering my head, let the tears come. He hugged me and said, "Come on Boop, everything's going to be all right. Doesn't your Daddy always come back to you?" But I couldn't answer because, suddenly seeing Mr. Dawson merging into the blue above the air show, I began to grow dizzy. My mother came over and said I would be all right, I was just hormonal and hadn't had breakfast. Bobby saluted sternly, which made Dad laugh, and I was glad to see him happy for a time.

He didn't disappear as Mr. Dawson had. Perhaps that would have been easier, something clean and final. Something other than the entropic giving up of life force which no longer believed in its right to exist! How I tortured myself after he was gone! I told myself that I could have better helped had I not been out sowing my wild oats. And those peace signs sewn into my jeans jacket, did they rub salt into the wound we couldn't see, but from which he suffered so? I even felt guilty for Doug, my one lifeline to clear skies during those times—until he ran off, anyway. Not even Cheryl understood completely. She was, of course, struggling with her own predicaments . . .

Mom and I sat on the couch talking. Our quiet dinner seemed to have settled her mood.

"How's your weaving coming?" she asked.

"Not so great, I'm afraid."

She fussed with a throw pillow. "Are you still having trouble with that tapestry you wanted to start? That thing about the old house?"

"I tried again last week," I said, "but I only got as far as the border. I think it's all this war business. Things are so unsettled. It brings back so many difficult memories . . ."

She laid aside the pillow. "Why can't you just let those times be?"

"We have a concept in trauma therapy," I replied. "It says you can't be truly whole until you consciously incorporate everything you've experienced into your life story, both the good and the bad."

"Maybe some things aren't worth incorporating." She looked toward the television set with a hint of sorrow in her expression. After a moment her face quickened into a purposeful mask, and she turned again to me.

"Instead of dwelling on the past, why not focus on the here and now? Something practical—like getting married, for example. Having a family?" She gently elbowed me, acknowledging that this was an old story between us.

"I'm not dwelling on the past, Mom. And as for getting married, that would depend on meeting the right person."

"You're still not sold on that Spanish fellow? Didn't you say he was finishing his doctorate? You could do worse . . ."

I didn't bother to repeat my Gloria Steinem quote: *Women spend too much time trying to find the right person, and not enough time trying to be the right person.* I had been wielding it since college and, obviously, it had yet to sink in. I was at a loss to change the tenor of our conversation.

"There's a lot to be said for security," she went on, "a little stability . . ."

"Stability comes from doing what you're supposed to be doing," I said bravely. "Knowing your heart, and working from there. Wherever that leads you."

"I'm just being your mother."

It was hard to argue with that. We made tea and watched a couple of sit-coms. I left with a promise to call Bob and return at my earliest opportunity.

& & &

WITH THE DEEPENING of autumn emerged a novel facet of Jorge's nature. Normally predictably present, he was excitably furtive, a quivering that echoed the fluttering of the starlings that flocked in the broad poplars outside my living room windows. He would leave messages saying he had to see me, then fail to return my calls. One late evening he called to announce breathlessly that he was on his way over, but never showed up.

What had become of my dependable friend?

Since our chance meeting on a city street, three years earlier—drawn by the Cuzco Boys' joyous strains—I allowed myself to imagine that Jorge appreciated our friendship in the same platonic vein as I; he could focus on his demanding academic work, I told myself, knowing there was someone to whom he could come, as Joni Mitchell once put it, for comfort and conversation. I should have known, and perhaps in my deepest self I did, that such an arrangement was bound to prove unstable; that as personable, able and, I should add, good looking a man as Jorge could not be expected to forever play the role of attendant to a woman in a sentimental recovery that seemed to find no terminus: his erotic demarche, on Labor Day, left no further doubt in the matter. How convenient it would have been had he sparked in me a fire greater than the comforting warmth of true friendship! But such matters are out of the hands of we mere mortals, and as much as I appreciated, respected and, yes, adored him, I was unable to conceive of Jorge as a lover. He was a real brick, and we shared our fondest ideals; but I doubted he could ever touch my deepest wounds. And if not that, what is a lover for?

I spoke to Cheryl on the phone.

"The main thing is to be clear about what you want."

"That's easier said than done."

"Yes, but it's possible, if you try."

"All I really want is understanding," I said. "Some way for us both to get on the same page, whatever that is. Ideally, I'd like to find a way to stay friends, but sidestep the whole romance thing."

"Given where Jorge seems to be, that doesn't sound like it's going to be easy."

"Still, I want to try."

"It's a tangled web you weavers weave . . ."

Tangled indeed. Things were pushing toward a break, and influences beyond Jorge's restiveness—Charles's disappearance,

Bob's situation, my stalled weaving work—were all playing a role. Nor was the presence of Gary Devers in my life without its effect. I hadn't seen him since the courier's memorial service, but my fantasies persisted. I told myself it was crazy. He was a client, forbidden fruit. I truly believed that I would never see him again.

But I couldn't forget him.

I decided to tell Jorge about my feelings for Gary. I knew it could prove painful for him, but I thought it might help clarify our situation.

Perhaps I was looking for a confessor.

We were at that café on the avenue with the plate glass windows all around, sitting against the afternoon sun. It was a Saturday, and the sidewalks were busy with people.

"So, you wanted to talk."

He sounded oddly formal, distant in a way I had never seen before. There was about him a sad world-weariness

"I'd just like things to be clear between us," I said.

"Yes, I know. So would I. I feel like we've been playing a game of, how do you say, cat and mouse. I'm sorry if I made you feel uncomfortable. You know, that day at my place. I can't help my feelings. I've been struggling with that lately. Hanging around together all the time. I guess it's no use trying to hide it anymore. I've felt this way for quite a while, actually. I don't know if I can do this anymore."

"I'll never forget, and will always be grateful for, the times we've spent together." I wanted to cry.

"Of course. Me, too. I'll be wrapping up my degree soon. I guess I'll be leaving Washington before long."

"I'll miss you. I know you're going to have a brilliant future. And you'd better stay in touch." My eyes were moist, but I tried to put a brave face on things.

"And me you. What about your future?"

There seemed little point, now, in bringing up Gary. "Looking

after of my mom. The clinic. Cleaning up some unfinished business . . ."

He smiled wanly, nodded thoughtfully, and slowly rose from
the table.

"You'll keep me informed of your plans, won't you?"

& & &

WHEN I WALKED into the clinic's reception area, Alice called
me over. "Mr. Devers was here first thing. He left this for you."

The manila envelope was tied with a string. I went into my
office and opened it with hands like butterfly wings. The poem
was written down a yellow sheet of paper with the words *Dispatch
Request* embossed over a blue line at the top:

> spinning wheels do not disclose
> our thoughts or those of city closed
> upon itself in breathing rhyme;
> a missing friend, life's game
> sublime, tragi-comic, without end:
> spiraling deeper, vorticed plunge,
> to the core the mind returns,
> drawn by grace and beauty, heart,
> to the lady's eyes undreamed,
> belief in precious things redeemed (waiting
> in suspension keen) breaking through
> to something clean and pure (your allure);
> down I go but whence, your
> thoughts for a pence, tribal meeting,
> Friday eve'—Signed & Sealed—believe!
> your presence will most welcome
> be. come.

Under the sheet containing these words was a newspaper clipping. Print along the top edge identified the publication: *The Underground Stream*. I include the article in its entirety:

CARILLON PIRATED FOR FANFARE

Arlington National Cemetery's normally peaceful carillon concert was disrupted Sunday when an unidentified assailant forced carilloneur Joseph McElvry to include Aaron Copeland's *Fanfare for the Common Man* in his program.

McElvry was well into a selection of American standards, with dusk rapidly falling across the leafy grove adjacent to the Iwo Jima Memorial, when an intruder entered the carilloneur's booth, twenty-five meters up a metal stairway, and thrust a hard object into the small of his back.

The assailant warned McElvry not to turn around, assured him he that wouldn't be hurt, and suggested that he finish "Camptown Races." At the close of the piece, the assailant asked McElvry if he knew Copeland's *Fanfare*. When McElvry responded that the piece wasn't part of his repertoire, the assailant said, "It is now, unless you know 'Heaven Help Us All.'"

"I had no idea what he was talking about," carilloneur McElvry told the *Stream*, "so I decided to do my best with the *Fanfare*. Fortunately, it's a piece with relatively simple lines. Thank God he didn't demand the *Passacaglia and Fugue*."

Reaching past McElvry to commandeer the microphone used for program announcements, the assailant introduced the piece, adding,

"This one's for the guys with the little white wafers."

"It was pretty scary," McElvry later told the *Stream*, "definitely a whole new level of stage fright."

The Netherlands Carillon was donated to the United States by the Dutch Republic in 1952, a token of gratitude for America's role in defeating Nazi Germany, whose armies occupied the Netherlands during World War II. The weekly concerts on the 49-bell carillon, a stark, modernesque tower of black steel, are normally a time of quiet contemplation at one of America's most sacred national spaces.

At the end of the *Fanfare*, the assailant again addressed McElvry. "I hated to have to do this, Brother," he said, according to McElvry's account. "I started to turn around," McElvry told the *Stream*, "but he told me, real stern-like, not to look back."

McElvry recalls that the next thing he knew, the assailant's arm was around him. "I was ready to fight for my life," McElvry said, "but he just clasped me snuggly and said that I had pulled off a good performance under the circumstances. I didn't turn around until I heard his footsteps at the bottom of the tower."

Military Police are without leads in the incident. A green banana was found at the base of the carillon's stairwell. Investigators are focusing on a disturbed veteran as the most likely suspect.

There was a handwritten note at the bottom of the clipping. "This has Pinky written all over it. See you Friday. Gary."

I read the poem more closely. *A missing friend.* Easy, Charles Pinckney. *A lady's eyes?* Mine I imagined, with both delight and no small distress. T*ribal meeting, signed & sealed.* An obvious reference to the courier company—and an invitation. The address was on the outside of the envelope.

Re-reading the news clipping, carefully considering the assailant's words and actions, I couldn't help but question the investigators' focus on a "disturbed" veteran (that hoary cliché!). Though the assailant's actions were arguably anti-social—and conceivably evidence of a disordered psyche—they were conducted with a calm, even courteous, deliberation. Nor could I credit Gary's suggestion that Charles was involved. That final, apologetic embrace, I was willing concede, evinced a warmth I have come to associate with Charles (and one I could only wish to see more of in the general population!). But that seemed scant reason to suppose that my steady, wise friend would scare the wits out of a defenseless carilloneur, all the while exposing himself to criminal prosecutions!

What was Gary up to? I was sure he understood my attraction toward him—as well as the ethical dilemmas in which it was entwined. Taking the darkest view, he had already once exploited my concern about Charles to entice me to Farragut Square the day of the courier Darick's memorial service. Now, here was another gambit I found difficult to ignore. It involved the same vague references to Charles, but this time with implications of felony investigations! Gary's prescience both fascinated and scared me. In it I saw shades of the Coyote trickster of Sarah Tilly's Navajo folk tales, always striking at your weakest points. I wanted Gary, but hated him for bringing my desire to bear where I would be forced to make painful choices. I loved him already and also wanted to run as fast as possible to the nearest exit. I resented his maneuvers, but was inexpressibly grateful for them.

The cab pulled up to Signed, Sealed & Delivered around eight. A steady stream of out-bound commuters had careened up 7th Street towards their weekends, but this side street of trash-blown sidewalks and broken streetlights was dark and quiet. The cabbie wrote in his manifest and checked in at home, the meter clicking quietly, while I sat in the shadows of his back seat and contemplated whether I really wanted to go in.

This time I hadn't consulted you, Howie, but how could I? After the memorial service, it was clear that our system of checks and balances was hopelessly broken. I hadn't even thought to call Cheryl, as I sat through the wee hours sipping tea by the window that looks into the park, alone in a world of thoughts and impressions I despaired of explaining to anyone. After considering everything *ad infinitum*, fighting sleep, I reluctantly admitted that something was pulling me toward this situation that went beyond logic, reason, and even the ethics of my profession. Either the hand of Spirit was reaching into my life, or I was hopelessly lost.

To ask the cabbie to take me home felt like falling into a void, a pristine void of ethical rectitude; to enter Gary's world, life with its attendant messiness. I paid the fare with trembling hand and stepped out. Signed, Sealed & Delivered's headquarters sat back in an alley, an irregular two-story structure from the upper windows of which a hard yellow light spilled onto an asphalt pad in front of two bay doors. I was approaching a door to one side when I was startled by a scuffing sound on the pavement. When I turned, two young men were bringing up bicycles short. They quickly leaned away from their machines and dismounted. As they removed their helmets, one of them spoke to me. "Haven't I seen you?" he asked, coming closer. Dark hair cascaded in ringlets over his temples. I recognized him, too, but I couldn't place him.

"Darick's memorial service—" he said suddenly. "That was it.

Weren't you there?"

I acknowledged that I had been at Farragut Square that day, and now remembered him as one of the guys who had spoken with Gary about Darick's poems.

"Bummer about Darick," the other one said, a slim young man with long dreads tied behind his head. "We still haven't gotten over it, and all over a love-thing. Were you and him close?"

"I'm afraid I didn't know him," I said. "I'm a friend of Gary's." Then I added, feeling a little compromised, "and Charles."

"Charles? I guess you know he's missing."

"Yes, I know."

"Have you ever been to a Gathering?"

"No."

"Tonight'll be a little different than usual," the one with the ringlets said. "Incidentally, I'm Ben."

I introduced myself.

"This is Henry."

We shook hands.

"Different, how?" I asked.

"Normally things are pretty open-ended," Henry said, "combination rave, shamanic ritual, poetry slam, encounter session . . ."

"Socratic dialogue, public forum, drumming circle," Ben concluded. "But tonight will be more structured," he went on, "what with Charles missing. Gary suggested we put our heads together, see what we can come up with."

"Gary's in charge?"

"Not officially," Ben said. "But we see him as the number two guy, since he's Head Dispatch."

"He and Pinky," Henry added, "they're like this." He entwined the middle and index fingers of his right hand.

"I hope I'm not late."

"You can't be late to a Gathering," Henry said. "Whenever you get here, you just kind of meld in."

Ben opened the door and waited for me to enter. He and Henry followed. I stopped to allow my eyes to adjust to the cool green light that bathed the narrow entryway. An open door on one side led to a shadowy space that, with its stout wooden counters and bicycle frames hung from the ceiling, appeared to be a workshop. A door on our right carried a sign at eye level that read DEMILITARIZED ZONE. Ben opened the door and we stepped into a large open space. It was illuminated by a moody reddish light that pulsated to an exotic music, with droning instruments and piercing strings, that played over a sound system.

I came into the room and took in my surroundings. The space was the size of a tennis court, more or less. A spiral stairway, near the back, led to a loft that partially overhung the main room. Looking up, I noted the metal girders that supported the roof. Hanging from one of these, a stuffed flight suit, with a visored helmet of the kind my father wore in Vietnam, twisted in the void. Psychedelic paintings and prints of Dutch masters bedecked the walls, along with other bric-a-brac I could not identify.

Along the verges of the room were stuffed, folding and bean bag chairs, and three worn sofas occupied by a couple dozen young men and women. Other celebrants stood in small groups in the middle of the room and chatted among themselves. Against one wall a table was loaded with wine bottles and other refreshments. From the back and above I heard the occasional clack of billiard balls, or the mechanical laboring of a soda machine giving birth.

Henry offered food and drink. I walked with him and Ben to the refreshment table, where I allowed Ben to pour me a glass of wine.

"So, what do you do?" he asked. His voice was liltingly friendly.

"I'm a therapist," I said. "I work at a clinic for combat veterans."

"Groovy," he said. He was munching on a cracker. I found his use of slang from before his time oddly charming.

"What about you?" I asked. "I'll bet you're a courier."

"For now," he said.

"Ben's actually a songwriter," Henry put in. "Word is, he's going BIG-TIME one of these days."

"That's the plan," Ben said. He smiled at Henry as he swallowed the last of his cracker. He reached toward a small refrigerator that stood beside the table.

"Do you work with guys who were in Vietnam?" Henry asked.

"Most of my clients are Vietnam veterans," I said. "But I've got a couple who were in Korea, and even one from the Second World War. Post-traumatic stress can be very persistent."

"Pinky was over there—Vietnam—wasn't he?" Ben asked.

"Right on," Henry said.

"And Gary," I added.

"Gary, really?" Ben said. "I never knew that."

"News to me," Henry said.

I had unwittingly divulged information that Gary apparently preferred to keep to himself, and I immediately regretted it. It was a painful reminder of the perils of stepping outside the prescribed therapeutic boundaries. "Tell me about you," I said to Henry, hoping to gloss over my disclosure

"You know," he said, "working the courier thing, taking some courses. Pinky's always telling me how I got to improve myself, make sure I don't end up in the ghett-toe. I'm thinking about getting into computer graphics. Who knows? I've still got time. For the here and now, I don't mind hanging with this crowd." He indicated the assembled company with a broad gesture.

Ben nodded approvingly while he munched another cracker. He handed Henry a beer and turned to me. "Henry's being modest," he said. "This man is a tremendous artist. You should see his acrylic cityscapes."

"Come on," Henry said with a modest laugh. "I can't handle being pumped by you Ivy League dudes."

I looked to Ben.

"Columbia," Henry said. "Don't let the homey look fool you. He's down with the whole academia thing."

"I'd like to see your work sometime," I said to Henry.

"I'd love that," he said. "Maybe I should let Gary know you're here."

I had assumed that Gary hadn't arrived. "All right," I said.

Henry went to the spiral stairway, climbed it, and disappeared into the loft. He soon reappeared at the head of the stairs, followed by Gary.

"You and Gary been friends long?" Ben asked. We were watching Gary and Henry descend the spiral.

"Not long."

"Great guy," Ben said.

Reaching the floor, Henry and Gary approached us.

"Sorry," Gary said. "I hope you haven't been waiting too long."

"That's all right, Ben and Henry have been taking good care of me."

"I'll bet." He cast a sly glance at his workmates. "We're going to get this thing going pretty soon. What do you think, gents?"

"Sounds good," Ben said.

"Cool with me," Henry added.

"Ben, will you bring down the music?"

"Sure."

Ben strode off and climbed the stairway. Gary turned to me. "I'm glad you could make it." I smiled noncommittally. The music tapered off.

"Well," Gary said, "I guess we ought to get started." He turned from me and addressed the assembled company. "What do you all think about getting this thing going? The floor will be open as usual, but we're going to devote this evening strictly to the

Pinkman. While I'm up here, let me introduce Marjorie Llewellyn. She's a friend of Pinky's." He gestured toward me. I held up my wine glass and, wondering how I would fit in, noted Ben bounding down the stairway.

"Who wants to get us started?" Gary asked.

"I've got something." A young man with reddish hair pulled into a ponytail stepped forward from the sofa he had been sitting on with a few others. He removed a folded paper from the pocket of his lumberjack shirt and carefully uncreased it. "Rob," Gary whispered to me, "film student." Rob stood ramrod straight and began to read:

> A band of riders moving on,
> amid the city's dancing churn,
> as autumn falls a leader's gone—
> we carry on through sorrow's burn.
>
> Disparate souls and strangers once,
> we learned to turn together, think,
> that in our spinning, whirring dance,
> we found our way here—in the Pink.
>
> Buoyed up by diverse means,
> morning ritual, evening bells,
> still inside the wailing keen,
> an unabated aching tells.
>
> Whether city's casual harm,
> or yet some more mysterious fate,
> let us raise a loud alarm—
> find the Pink without delay!

Rob bowed, acknowledging the ripple of approval that went through the room. A Middle Eastern man then slowly pulled his lanky frame up from a bean bag chair. Stepping toward the center of the room, he brushed dark bangs from his eyes.

"Ali," Gary whispered. "Iranian refugee, working on his doctorate in economics."

After waving a general greeting, Ali turned to Rob. "Rob," he said, "I liked your poem. Really good." Then, again brushing the bangs from his forehead, he addressed the Gathering. "When I first came to the United States," he began, "I didn't know anybody. My family was refugees, scattered all over the place. Germany, California, London. I came to Washington because I got into American University. Why not, I figured. Capital of the free world, right? I have to admit, I was a little nervous. The hostage crisis hadn't been over too long, and there all that Great Satan propaganda back in my home country. Anyhow, I needed a little extra money, and I saw this ad for Signed, Sealed & Delivered. I can still remember the day I came in for my interview." Ali gestured toward the back of the room, where the wall above a desk was covered with disparate paraphernalia, much of it military in nature. "I've got to tell you," he went on, "when I saw Pinky's army stuff on that wall, I thought, oh boy, this could be trouble!"

He smilingly nodded in acknowledgement of the compassionate vocalizations that ran through the room. He shuffled his feet across the floor for a moment before he picked up again. "Anyway, Pinky must have noticed me looking at it—at his army stuff, that is—because he said that everybody's got to have a country. Good enough, I thought. But I didn't know where this thing was heading, right? The fact is, I was thinking about bolting for the door . . ."

A frisson of laughter rippled through the Gathering. Ali shyly wiped his bangs from his eyes while it subsided. "No, I didn't say a thing," he took up again, scanning the room for the eyes of his friends. "I wasn't going to touch that one. Then, while I stood there like a deer in the headlights, Pinky said that it was normal for a person to love his country, at least in some kind of way. He didn't sound angry or anything, but I still didn't know what the man was getting at. You want to know the truth, I was still glancing at that exit. But then Pinky stood up and said that he wasn't talking about patriotism. He said that the *Tao te ching* says that patriotism's born when the country's in chaos. "Now I'm thinking," Ali went on, "what the heck is the *Tao te ching?*" Again there was laughter, more exuberant this time. "Anyway," he resumed when the room was quiet, "Pinky said that the United States hadn't always done the right thing, but it was the only country he had. These are my people, he said. And I guess I finally got up my nerve, because I told him that I could understand how he felt. He looked me in the eyes, you know how he does, and he said I probably loved my country, too. I was still kind of nervous about the whole thing, but I told him that I did love Iran, even if a bunch of kooks were in charge at the moment. Then, with a little laugh, Pinky sat me down and started asking about Iranian food and music, about Sufism, Persian history . . . all that stuff. We talked about my country for at least half an hour. It made me feel so much more at home. You all know how the Pinkman is . . ."

Ali looked around the room, smiled, and was met with smiles in return. "After that he gave me the usual routine," Ali resumed. "You know, how this isn't a normal courier company? I come from a country run by Ayatollahs, I told him. You think I'm worried about normal?" There were knowing looks and more laughter among the Gathering. "That made Pinky laugh. He came around the desk and put his arm around my shoulders, like he was my favorite uncle or something, and said he thought I'd work out all right. And as you all know, I've been here ever since. I would die for that man. I mean it. He's the best. Whatever I can do. If there's a problem. If the Pinkman's in any kind of trouble. If he needs money, my family's got some. Gary, let me know."

Ali moved to his seat amid a little eruption of applause. A thick-set man with close-cropped hair stood and moved deliberately into the center of the room.

"Roger," Gary whispered to me. "Homeboy from Pinky's old hood."

"Like Ali said," Roger began, "Pinky's a prince. A king! Whatever needs to be done, let's do it. We need to make a supreme effort. Put our heads together. A couple of months ago everything was happy. We're doing our work. I'm going home every night to take care of my wife and baby. A good life. Then Pinky disappears, just like that! How can that happen? That ain't like the Pinkman. You all know what kind of things go down around here. I hate to mention it, but this ain't exactly the safest neighborhood in town." He ground his hands together, filled with unexpressed emotion. "We need to figure this thing out." He wandered uncertainly back to his seat.

Gary stepped forward.

"Listen everybody. Let me caution you about getting too gloomy. We don't have any evidence to suggest that Pinky's in trouble. Or that he's come to harm. I put in the police report the week he disappeared, and they haven't turned up anything."

"They never do," Roger bellowed, "until it's too late. Besides, if it wasn't something bad, how can you explain it?"

"I'm not saying I can explain it," Gary said. "At least not right now. I'm just saying that it isn't constructive to jump to conclusions. We ought to keep our minds open until we have more concrete information."

At that moment a short, stockily built man, Indian in appearance, came forward. "I agree with Gary," he said. "As a journalist, I can tell you, you never know where a story might take you."

Gary stepped back to me. "Subesh, part-time stringer for a couple of the news services."

"So, dude, what are you saying we should do?" Ben asked.

"As an investigator," Subesh replied, "I'd start with whatever leads I could find, follow them wherever they take me. With a missing person, I'd start by interviewing people that know him.

I'd see if anybody knows anything, even the smallest scrap. I'd especially want to talk with anyone who saw him before he disappeared. Did he say where he was going? Did he get there? Did he say or do anything unusual? Then I'd want to look at his things. Appointment books are very useful, for example. I'd also want to check his apartment."

"The police have done that," Gary said. "He hasn't been there for weeks."

"What about his desk?" Subesh pondered. "There may have been something going on with the business. Something we didn't know about."

"Impossible," Gary said. "You know the standing policy, open books. He wouldn't keep anything from us."

"Phone records?"

"Been done, nothing but the usual."

"So what leads have we got?" Subesh said, a little deflated. "We should rack our brains. Who was the last to see him?"

Everyone looked at one another. Finally Gary spoke.

"That could have been me, come to think of it," he said. "It was a Wednesday evening, if I recall. We had finished up the last runs, and I came down from Dispatch. Pinky was sitting at his desk. I asked if he was interested in going out for a beer or some chow, but he said that he had some loose ends to tie up."

"Almost like he knew he would be going somewhere," Subesh said.

"You could say that," Gary agreed. "And now that you mention it, there's something else."

"What's that?"

"Pinky normally does his bookkeeping on Fridays," Gary said. "He's trained me in all these procedures, so I can take over when he's on vacation, or out for any other reason. Well, last week, when I started to get used to the idea that he was gone—and that we still had a business to run—I got out the ledger book, figuring

I would catch us up. And you know, everything was done up to the day he disappeared. Like Subesh said, it was like he knew that he would be going away."

"What about his mother?" Henry hollered from the back of the room. "She's out in Anacostia someplace. Did anybody contact her?"

"I believe the police have spoken with her," Gary said.

"So did I," I volunteered. "I went to see her last week." Everyone turned toward me with keen expectation in their eyes. "I'm afraid she hasn't heard from him either," I added, noting disappointment in their faces. "But she said that he recently sent her a large check, with a note saying he would be out of touch for a while."

"Ah-ha!" Subesh said. "It sounds like his departure was definitely premeditated."

There was an audible sigh of relief among the Gathering.

"It's all so strange," Ben said to no one in particular. "Where the hell could he have gone?"

After a moment Roger spoke. "I'm still concerned about some of these homeboys. The bad actors and drug dealers. I've seen him face these dudes down over at Crawford Terrace. You know how those boys work. They might have him marked."

"Dude, what are you saying?" Ben asked.

"Maybe he's laying low for a while, that's all."

"I can't see the man backing away from a fight," the one I recognized from the memorial service as Tomás put in.

"Sun Tzu says it's better to defend than attack," Rob said.

"I don't know," Roger said. "I think we better get up some kind of posse."

"Wait a minute," Gary said. "Let's try and keep our heads. Pinky's whereabouts are anybody's guess. Rog, I can understand your concerns, but my gut tells me he's not in that kind of trouble. Have some faith in the Pinkman. He knows how to take care of himself."

"I hope you're right."

"Gary," Subesh said, "I still think it would be useful to have a look through that desk. What do you think?"

"If it will satisfy that irrepressible curiosity of yours, feel free. It certainly can't do any harm."

Subesh moved toward the desk at the back of the room. Several others joined him. The rest of the Gathering formed into small groups and talked together. I asked Gary if I could speak with him; he led me to the spiral stairway and gestured to precede him. At its apex we emerged into a lounge with pool table, vintage soda machine, café tables and chairs, sofa, a couple of pinball machines, and a chess set on a game table. He directed me to one of the café tables.

"Will this do? It's our hang-out space."

"It's fine."

"What did you want to talk about?"

"Your delivery."

"Oh."

"The article, more specifically."

"Uh-huh?"

"You said it had Charles written all over it. What did you mean by that?"

Gary thought for a moment. "The first thing that struck me was the request for 'Heaven Help Us All'."

"Yes, I couldn't place that."

"It's a Stevie Wonder track, circa 1970. I'm not sure about the album—"

"Oh yes—" I said, suddenly recalling Wonder's song, a poignant plea for a more humane world. "But what's that got to do with Charles?"

"Charles is rather fond of Stevie," Gary said. "—more than fond, actually. You could say that it's a minor cult. It's not as important as, say, the *Tao te ching*, but it's up there. I especially refer to that period when Wonder spent a few years in the studio with some of the first synthesizers. Do you remember *Innervisions, Talking Book*?"

I remembered the albums well. In fact, I told Gary, I had worn out their grooves during my high school and college years. And now, Gary having mentioned Stevie Wonder, I recalled Charles's occasional references to Wonder's songs during our vet group sessions. (Feeling stronger now on my therapist game, I didn't mention this confidential material to Gary.)

"This was shortly after Pinky got back from Nam," he took up again. "It seems he had some real epiphanies with those Stevie albums. He says Wonder's music was like a balm. That it helped him to heal his mind. He was going through a lot of painful stuff back then. But then, I guess you know all about that . . ."

I didn't respond.

"Not that Pinky—or I—would discount the Little Stevie period," Gary hastened to add, his face brightening into a smile. "In fact, we have this whole thing for that old Motown music. One of us might say something like, 'She met her match,' or 'Mistra Know-It-All,' and it will bring in this whole train of associations. We used to trade off Wonder's lyrics when we rode our cycles together."

"So your theory about Charles and this carillon thing comes down to one song by Stevie Wonder?"

"Well, no, there's also something else. Remember the bit about the grave markers?"

"One for the little, white . . . wafers, I think he said."

"Exactly. I believe it was a couple of years back. We had finished evening bells—this little ritual we do after work—and Pinky and I decided to take a ride. Neither of us were doing deliveries anymore, and we enjoyed getting out now and then, especially at the end of the day. Did you ever notice how, in that magic hour, you can almost melt into the city? Feel it breathe? Do you know what I mean?"

I told him that I did.

"We had gone through the park and crossed Memorial Bridge," Gary went on. "We were coasting near the river, toward the airport, and this gorgeous yellow light just clung to everything. It was like transparent butterscotch. Well, I happened to look toward Arlington Cemetary, and I saw those endless rows of nondescript white markers arrayed across the hillsides. And the way they quivered in that beautiful light, against the rich green of the lawns, they looked almost alive. It was like they might propel themselves right into space! I stopped my bike and pointed it out to Pinky, and he said that he loved those wafers. Yep, *wafers* is what he called them. Go over there, he said, and you'll see all these big, beautiful gravestones, with all this sculpture and filigree, and they take up all kinds of real estate. And if you get up close and read the inscriptions, he went on, you'll note that it's always some higher-up. But that wasn't his crowd, he told me. All the enlisted wafers, he said, they're marching down the slopes like they don't know where they're going. But they're together, he said, and they're more or less in line. That's what he said, *more or less in line*, like the Grateful Dead song. Then he remarked on how, over time, the marble gets worn down on all those little wafers, until you can hardly read the names. After a while, he said, the inscriptions wear down so much you can't read them at all."

"So you think it was Charles who accosted this carilloneur?"

"That's what I'm saying."

"I don't know if Stevie Wonder and wafers is enough to draw that kind of conclusion."

"I do."

"Don't you think it's a little off-the-wall for Charles?"

"If he were here he'd probably say that true straightness seems crooked."

I must have looked puzzled.

"*Tao te ching*, Chapter Forty-Five," he explained.

"Look," I said, "if you're convinced it was him, why didn't you say something downstairs, during the discussion?"

"To tell you the truth," he replied, "I'm not sure they would know how to handle it. In case you didn't notice, these guys tend to get a little, well, excited. And would I really be doing Pinky any favors? Whatever he's up to, it looks like he wants to keep it under wraps. I have to respect that."

"But why call a meeting to discuss the situation, if you don't want to find him?"

"It's not that *I* don't want to find him. In fact, he may want *me* to find him. He knows I wouldn't have missed the clues. But that doesn't mean he wants it broadcast all over town. The kids have been getting restless. They needed an opportunity to blow off some steam. I don't care if they knock themselves out to locate Pinky. If they can pull it off, more power to them."

"Incidentally," I said, shifting my glance, in order to afford him some space, away from Gary's eyes, "Ben and Henry were surprised to hear that you'd been in Vietnam."

"I suppose that's something I just don't like to talk about."

"Why have you stopped coming to your appointments?"

"Do you miss me?"

If he could see that I was flustered, it didn't stop him.

"How did you like my poem?"

"You know there are certain ethical codes. Prohibitions against therapists fraternizing with clients outside of sessions."

"Yes, I do."

"I take them seriously," I said, feeling more than a little hypocritical.

"So do I. Let's go downstairs."

As we wound down the spiral stairway I heard music. Ben and Rob were strumming guitars. Tanya—the girl who had climbed

Farragut's statue at Darick's memorial service—sang with them, and Roger played a hand drum. They were laying down "Stoned Soul Picnic" and it sounded good:

There will be lots of time and wine,
Red, yellow honey, sassafras and moonshine . . .

Everyone lounged comfortably on the stuffed furniture and cushions. Gary offered me a glass of wine, and Laura Nyro's song brought me back to a very sweet place of my youth. I wanted to join them all in their nostalgic dream, but my allusion upstairs to the ethics of my profession was nagging at me. I used the phone on Charles's desk and waited in the green-glowing anteroom until my cab arrived.

ON THE VETERANS DAY holiday I went to my mother's. I had turned down an invitation for both of us to Cheryl and Dan's house. Cheryl's gesture was no less thoughtful for being repeated every year, a nod to the many occasions, in those very different times of Arden Forest, when our families would caravan to the base to take part in solemn festivities. She and I would wear our best dresses and look as serious as our parents, but it was always the get-together that followed, in their rec room or ours, that we most looked forward to. Our fathers would drink and swap stories, our mothers relax and catch up, and we and our siblings play hide and seek or, as we grew older, engage in more labyrinthine games by the creek. I had tried to convince my mother to accept the invitation; I missed Cheryl and also thought it would do Mom good to get out. But her reluctance to leave home was growing stronger with each passing day, and she refused to be persuaded. We sat before the television nibbling from artfully arranged snack trays, scanning the sloping lawns where my father's remains lie. If our gathering was a bit forlorn, it was some consolation to know that Cheryl and her family were no doubt engaging in the same ritual. Later it would be helpful to call Bob and to hear the voices of Gloria and little Drew.

The clinic was closed, but the pager I carried in case of emergencies was only the least of threads that connected me to my work. Most of my clients would be marking the holiday either at private gatherings or at ceremonies downtown. I worried about those who would spend the day alone; though I understood that, given the complexity of the human psyche, this could mean great steadiness as easily as it could portend danger. I half expected to catch a familiar face in the passing images of crowds gathered near the Wall, but those I could make out were only nameless strangers. Nonetheless I knew something of their grief and pain. When the cameras panned over the cemetery to reveal a sea of simple white markers, I remembered Gary's tale of Charles Pinckney's "wafers" and wondered where on earth he might be. My father is buried under one of the stately monuments he had referred to, and I pondered sadly that I hadn't visited his gravesite for some time. In the years after his death my mother and I went regularly, but the custom left us cold. It was the way he left us, Mom would say; for me, his lingering presence made it hard to believe that he was gone. We seldom mentioned it and, even now, as we watched sweeping panoramas of rolling green land fertile with so much suffering, she kept a stony silence, while I inwardly vowed to tend his gravesite at my first opportunity.

After the wreathlaying at the Tomb of the Unknown Soldier the phone rang. Bob had pre-empted our call. We were all on speaker phones, with little Drew piping in, and I suspected Bob planned things this way so that my mother could not buttonhole him and fret over the latest military news. It had been announced that the administration had decided to put the *offensive option* in place, with troop levels in the Persian Gulf raised by one hundred thousand or even more.

"Ya'll doing all right?" Bob asked, sounding more like my father than ever.

"I guess," my mother returned with her weary drawl, signaling not only the weight of the day's solemn ceremonies, but also her displeasure with the recent troop deployments.

"Bugle player did real good," Bob said.

"I've got a flag," Drew chirped.

"That's nice, honey" Mom said.

"You should see her marching around the living room," Gloria put in.

"Sis, you there?" It was Bob.

"Hi."

"How's that boyfriend of yours?"

The usual tease. "What boyfriend?"

"Word gets around, you know."

"Not to me, it hasn't."

"Aunt Marjorie?" Drew said.

"Yes Sweetie."

"Is my granddad in that place?"

"Not really. It's more like his memory. I'll take you there sometime. Would you like that?"

"Yeah.

"We'll take some pretty flowers. How about that?"

"Okay."

"What are you all doing today?"

"A parade!" Drew announced.

"Right in the living room," Gloria said, laughing.

"We'll probably go to the VFW," Bob said. "They're having the usual shindig this afternoon."

"What on earth do they think they're doing?" my mother suddenly piped up, an unmistakable note of dismay in her voice.

"Probably roast a pig," Bob replied, attempting to deflect my mother's fretting. "Pass out door prizes, the normal stuff."

"That's not what I'm talking about."

"Baby and me need to get ready," Gloria said, knowing when to make an exit. "Say goodbye to Grandma and Aunt Marjorie."

"Bye."

As their voices faded into another room, Mom resumed.

"What are they talking about, a hundred thousand? Two hundred thousand! They're going in, I tell you! Why on earth did you have to go into the soldiering business?"

"No one is predicting a war," Bob replied flatly. "Hussein will probably back down."

"Never happen."

"Even so, that doesn't mean they'll call up more reserves."

"Keep dreaming."

Bob exhaled loudly. "Relax, Ma, please. Even if they do call us, we'll probably just end up replacing rear echelon forces."

"Maybe you won't."

Her relentlessness was wearing him down; I could hear it in his voice. "What's the difference, anyway?" he said resignedly. "Whatever happens, I signed up, and I'll do my duty. Isn't that what Dad would have wanted?"

"I'm not so sure," my mother said.

A silent truce.

"Hey, you two," I said, "none of us can say what Dad would want if he were here." I put an arm around my mother. "Bob, Mom's just worried about you."

"Of course I am," she said. "He's my baby, isn't he?" Her voice was suddenly shaky. She groped for a paper napkin, wiped her eyes and blew her nose. "Bobby," she said, "there are things about your father you never knew. You were so young."

"He went to Indochina because he couldn't watch guys with less rank fly combat missions while he was safe at his desk in Washington. I know that."

"That's true," my mother conceded, stifling her tears.

"Bob," I said, "I'm sure Mom's not questioning your judgment. Are you coming home for Thanksgiving?"

"This year's Gloria's bunch."

"Honey," my mother said.

"Yeah?"

"Don't think I'm not proud of you."

"I know."

"And I'm not saying I don't want you to follow in your Dad's footsteps."

"I know."

"He was the most decent, honorable man I ever knew. But even decent, honorable people can't do the right thing when they don't have all the information. You know," she continued with a loud sniffle, "sometimes the people that are supposed to be giving us information, they're not. They're deliberately making one thing seem like another."

"Mom," Bob pleaded, "don't worry. Everything's going to be all right. I'm not going to let anything happen to me."

"I want to believe that."

"We'll be out for Christmas."

We signed off, and Mom and I fixed an early supper. Afterward we sat on the couch knitting and listening to my parents' old LPs, Tony Bennett and Doris Day. I drove back to the city after dark. When I passed the cemetery the crowds had gone; all was quiet rolling lawns filled with fathomless shadows. That night I was awakened by fragments of inchoate dream. I got out of bed and wrote a peculiar entry in my journal:

November 12, 1990

What does the city mean?

If it were a glyph, how would you read it?

Does it continually renew itself, as I suspect, to fill a void—some dark and horrible abyss, before which we tremble with fear—to fill it with noise and activity? The paradox is that the city still retains the properties of a vacuum, pulling us always into its vortex, never relinquishing its grip, even when it appears to be sleeping . . .

It is quiet now. The city feigns sleep.

The only sounds are the hum of the building's airhandlers, and the more distant drone of a streetcleaner along the avenue.

I am awake, though it is three in the morning, and I have a nine o'clock appointment. I've been sitting in this bowl chair since one, when I awoke feeling an odd sense of pregnancy, of something impending and—a remarkable clarity! Gazing up the block on the blinking signals, I sense the city transforming itself within me, like some ancient infant waiting to be born (yes, and I a latter-day madonna, prepared for some immaculate conception, to deliver what I can only suppose, for reasons I cannot explain, is the were-jaguar child from the Olmec exhibit last year; that one on the lap of the jade figure which, the placard said, was worshipped as Mother of God by villagers who unearthed her in the last century)! I find myself enthralled by the sensation that I—yes I—may carry within me some vital seed, a torrent of meaning to pour into the void! How else might I rescue my brood (aren't we all mothers of all, especially those of us who have never borne children?) from its appallingly voracious craw?

I realize that these musings are overwrought, perhaps even megalomaniacal. But what real harm is there? I am sipping nothing stronger than herb tea. Cheryl would attribute it, I know, to my "frustrated nurturing tendencies." She says that I need a real child to worry about. Soon it will be time for a shower and coffee. These strange musings will scatter in the sun like so many sparrows.

Or will they?

I AWOKE before the alarm after a few hours sleep. Daylight was still forming, and traffic wasn't yet heavy on the avenue. I made a cup of coffee and sat at the kitchen table. There was a residue of the day before, with its Veterans Day remembrances, the telephone conversation with Bob's family, and driving past the darkened cemetery afterward. I showered and dressed, walked up the avenue to the station, and boarded the train. There was still an hour before I was due at the clinic, but I felt something—something out there in the world—calling to me. Then, as the train pulled away from Dupont station, I was seized by an overwhelming urge to disembark at Farragut.

I stepped off the escalator to a saxophonist honking Amazing Grace, and pigeons broke in a flurry over the Square. I walked to the curb and stood for a long moment looking into the park. The courier's memorial service—and my fleeting glimpse of Charles from the back of the cab—came suddenly and vividly to mind. I turned, saw the newsstand there, and walked in. In response to my inquiries about the *Underground Stream*, the guy behind the counter gestured to one of the racks. Feeling the subversive journal's newsprint in my hands provoked the same calm I feel when I sit before my loom holding skeins of yarn.

I paid and left.

I found a coffee shop on the block, ordered a cup and toast, and perused the paper. The front page carried headlines on the city's decrepit waste treatment facility, corrupt contracts for municipal housing services, and the woeful state of the city's youth detention home (the juvenile services director was quoted as saying he wouldn't kennel his dog there). There was also an article on anti-war protests in Lafayette Park, with a photograph showing demonstrators hoisting NO BLOOD FOR OIL signs. And then I saw it, in the bottom right corner of the page, a small box announcing, "*Underground Stream* Exclusive: Contretemps at Veterans Day Ceremonies Hushed Up – p. 12." I turned quickly to the article, sensing a resolution to the tensions of my restless night. At the top of the page was a color photograph of a towering pole under the headline: "New Maine Explosion Rocks Ceremonies." The subtitle read, "Military Authorities Squelch News."

Solemn Veterans Day observances were punctuated yesterday by an explosion at the Maine Mast Memorial on the grounds of Arlington National Cemetery. The Memorial is not far from the Ceremonial Amphitheatre, where Defense Secretary Cheney was delivering the customary speech glorifying armed violence following the annual wreathlaying at the Tomb of the Unknown Soldier. The ornate Greco-Roman amphitheatre was full to overflowing when the distinctive sound of an explosion crackled through the air, likened by witnesses to a backfiring automobile. Military Police soon cordoned the area around the mast, and officers sent the curious few who wandered over from the amphitheatre back to the ceremonies.

The explosion caused no visible damage to the mast, a relic of the American battleship whose sinking in Havana harbor served as a convenient pretext to kick off the Spanish-American War. The campaign launched the United States forthrightly on a career of imperialism under the prodding of jingoists like newspaperman William Randolph Hearst, whose tabloids brought readers to a fever-pitch of war hysteria with lurid, if not factual, accounts of the situation on the Caribbean island.

There was no interruption to the Veterans Day program, though Defense Secretary Cheney, on careful observation of a video recording of his speech, can be seen to start as he pronounces the words: "To every veteran, this nation owes a debt we cannot possibly discharge, but will always acknowledge."

A spokesperson for the 3rd Infantry Regiment, which is responsible for the cemetery, declined to comment. Our *Underground Stream* reporter, who arrived shortly after the explosion, was told by Major Russ Blankenship, of the 3rd Regiment's Military Police, that a mechanical malfunction caused the blast. MPs scrambled furiously to collect dozens of brightly colored objects that littered the area within the police cordon.

Homeless veteran Dennis Evans was one of few eyewitnesses to the explosion. "We were just standing here watching the ceremonies," Mr. Evans told the *Stream*, referring to himself and two other veterans with whom he shares a nearby encampment. "We couldn't really hear what Cheney was saying ("Bunch of bullshit," one of his companions interjected), "but we felt we had to be here, anyway. John here was in the middle of saying how beautiful the autumn leaves were when it went off, right behind us. About scared shit out of Tiny. All these things suddenly came flying out the crow's nest, just like submunitions from a cluster bomb. We hit the ground, naturally, expecting the popcorn to do its thing. Nothing happened right off, but we stayed down a few minutes anyway, waiting for 'em to blow."

("Figured it was some terrorist asshole," the one named John put in.)

"Then, when John and I finally get up," Mr. Evans continued, "Tiny's over there checking out the popcorn. We yelled like banshees to get him out of there, but he's got one of them—one of the submunis—in his hand. And what does the goof do? He just looks at us and laughs. That's how Tiny is, unfortunately. So we ripped over there, to get him away from all that unexploded, but by then he's already pried the thing open. And you know what? There's nothing inside but a piece of paper. As for the submuni, it's just a regular plastic egg, like the kind they use for Easter egg hunts."

("Or Silly Putty," John added.)

"About that time," Evans went on, "the MPs showed up. Major running the show. He asked what happened, and we told him. Then Tiny showed him one of the eggs. The major read the paper that was inside, got all red in the face, and ordered the MPs to cordon the area. A few gawkers were straggling over from the amphitheatre, but they turned them back. Then the major made a call with his walkie-talkie, and pretty soon a van pulls up with the munitions experts. Well, they haul out their gear and check out every single one of those eggs. I've got to hand it to them, they were damned thorough. But, no surprise, they determined that there was nothing but what we showed them—a bunch of plastic eggs with papers inside. Still, they went up in the crow's nest and took some evidence. I got to say, the major looked pretty disgusted. After that, the van pulled off, and the MPs collected up the egg shells."

"Except," Mr. Evan's companion John added, "the ones they didn't know about. Show 'em, Tiny."

The man called Tiny then produced three plastic eggs from the pockets of his coat. Each contained a folded paper upon which the following quotations, and accompanying ascriptions, had been carefully assembled using fragments culled from newsprint:

> When Tao resides in the world,
> Stalwart steeds haul dung to farmers' fields;
> When the world succumbs to chaos,
> War horses are pastured on the commons.
> —*Tao te ching*, Lao Tzu

> Heaven help the boy who won't reach
> twenty-one;
> Heaven help the man who gave that boy
> a gun.
> —"Heaven Help Us All," Ron Miller, as
> sung by Stevie Wonder

> "You supply the pictures, I'll supply the war."
> —William Randolph Hearst to Frederick
> Remington, Cuba, 1898

"I'll tell you one thing," John, who declined to supply his last name, commented, "whoever pulled this thing off knew their munitions. I mean, look at that crow's nest. It's hardly dam-

aged! The eggs even stayed intact. They used just enough blast to get the job done, without overkill."

"They ought to talk to our brass," Mr. Evans added, a fitting commentary on an episode that bears remarkable resemblance to an incident at the Netherlands Carillon on October 23rd, particularly in its reference to Stevie Wonder's popular hit of 1970. The *Stream* has been unable to reach Mr. Wonder for comment. But we are investigating a possible link between the incidents, and will keep readers updated.

A link between the incidents? I stuffed the *Stream* in my purse and went out to the sidewalk. There was half an hour before I was due at the clinic. I waited for the light to stop traffic—strange incantatory power—and crossed into Farragut Square. Standing in the middle of the shady park, I remembered again the memorial service, Darick's lovelorn laments, and my fleeting glimpse of Charles. I tried to summon them all back: to know where Charles was, and to decipher whether he might be behind this explosion at the Maine Mast memorial. I was certain that Gary would believe him responsible, just as he believed that he had accosted that carilloneur. And descending into the subway, and as the train sped along, I was certain that Gary held the key not only to this mystery, but to others considerably more private. I put it out of mind as I crossed the lobby and let the elevator carry me to the fifth floor. But throughout the day, meeting my clients, it was he I heard in their voices, saw in their faces, and each of them gazed at my tapestry with sympathetically piercing eyes.

TIMES WERE MORE unsettled than ever. The increase in troop levels, delayed as Gary had predicted until after the elections, brought an upswell to what had been a tepid anti-war movement. Now there were larger and more vociferous protests on the evening news. Daniel Ellsberg, author of *The Pentagon Papers*, led one of those demonstrations. His name was emblazoned on my memory, as it was on the cover of the book that lived on my father's reading table that terrible autumn that preluded his death.

As I watched the aging advocate address the seething protesters, a swirl of manacled memories strove to break free from their cages. There was my youthful love affair with Dougie, our sympathies with the anti-war movement, and late night conversations with Daddy when I would return from running with our crowd. I couldn't help but picture my father as he was then: curious about my generation's drift away from militarism and war, but never signaling agreement or disagreement, only the weariness of one who could not come free of commitments to which he had given a lifetime.

The day after Veterans Day the administration extended the reserve call-up from three to six months. The announcement only affected units already engaged, but along with the increased troop levels, and the now forthright talk of the *offensive option*, it made more tangible my mother's concerns that Bob would be summoned: she spoke of nothing else. What's more, she quit attending the gardening club and put down her knitting. I feared she spent long hours, when not watching CNN in frustration, brooding in silence, as she had done after my father's death.

As for Jorge, we hadn't spoken since our conversation two weeks earlier. The silence hurt, but I allowed it to happen. It seemed a discomfort that must be endured in the interest of greater authenticity between us.

Fortunately Cheryl stayed constant, with her daily routines of nurturance and steady logic. We frequently spoke by phone. Her only response to developments in the news was the reflection that, as a mother, she couldn't imagine sending Julian or Emmy off to war. And I was anchored in those days, I now realize, by something unexpected: my clients. They were going through changes, to be sure, beyond even the harrowing transformations our therapy always engenders. These temporal crises, spurred by the ever louder drumbeats of war, reflected the entire panoply of response to psychic pain—abraxis, catharsis, resistance. Yet their pain, and the courage they brought to engaging it, is what remained constant, they willingly bearing a burden the rest of us prefer to pretend is not our concern. I listened now with new urgency to their tales of Vietnam: tales of the dark sinews of war where it is real. Then it was not patriotic speeches and high ideals, but the shedding of blood, the tearing of flesh, and the maiming of innocents and of innocence. In the presence of these men, the non-stop media buzz pervading our fair city evaporated into a stage play put on by inmates at an insane asylum. Then my clients' world of suffering, the concrete human tragedies that result when men take up arms, became my only truth.

Consider Ron Dixon:

As part of a medical detachment, it was Ron's job to scour wasted battlefields for fallen comrades. This mere youth of eighteen spent the rest of his time in Vietnam in a gloomy morgue at the rear, pent up with mangled corpses. Occasionally his unit came upon a living man: Ron is still tortured by the memory of one soldier, alive but with nothing but bloody stumps for arms, who pleaded frantically to be put out of his misery. "I couldn't stand the screams anymore," Ron says through an almost catatonic gaze, "so I took a pillow and pushed it against his face until he stopped breathing." Hordes of dead—uncontrollable visions!— now give Ron no peace. With outstretched arms and hollow eyes they greedily implore him to join them. They pursue him along city sidewalks, and crowd into the beat-up pickup that passes for

Ron's home. Ron steals his food and he is still, for all intents and purposes (such is the power of the mind!) in Vietnam for weeks on end . . .

And there was Jason Howard:

From observation posts on the Vietnamese mainland, Jason relayed coordinates to shipboard sailors so they might direct their death-dealing cannon against the land of Vietnam. Suffering suicidal ideation and uncontrollable tremors, Ron spends insomniac nights driving far from the city, roaming Piedmont hills in search of an elusive peace. "It's so green and quiet up there," he tells the group. But the foothills of the Alleghenies inevitably become Quang Tri Province, and Jason gapes once again upon the charred bodies of civilian artillery victims—part of his handiwork—stacked like ghastly logs on the roadside outside of Dong Ha . . .

There was Danny Sabatone:

A decorated soldier who led special units into enemy territory, Danny was referred to the clinic after trying to strangle his wife. Danny keeps down a job as a warehouse supervisor, but he spends his off-time inebriated and involved in chronic altercations. He suffers frequent nightmares of combat, from which he awakes screaming, "Call in the med vac!" While in Vietnam he both witnessed and participated in atrocities. He once led his unit's fire on a Vietcong village from which all combatants had fled, killing two dozen women, children, and elderly. They were listed on the after-action report, Danny confides sardonically, as Vietcong soldiers . . .

And think of Vernon Allen:

At the famous battle of Hamburger Hill, while moving up to emplace artillery, the teenaged Vernon witnessed a fellow infantryman have his legs blown off. What bothered Vernon most about the episode was the fact that the hill, which was eventually taken with a large number of American casualties, was immediately abandoned for no apparent reason. It was all so useless, he says; and he has carried that sense of futility throughout his life. In a recurring dream, Vernon is scheduled to leave Vietnam. But something always happens. The airport is blown up, or his unit ambushed before he can get out of the bush . . .

There was also Jonathan Straiman:

Jonathan fatally shot a pubescent boy, though a fully-armed Vietcong soldier, who had approached the brushline where Jonathan's squad lay in hiding. "He didn't fall no more than three feet away," Jonathan relates tearfully. "But there wasn't no way I could help him, what without putting my whole squad in danger." Jonathan was forced to endure the child's pleading eyes while, over the course of an eternal hour, his yet-fledged life ebbed slowly away. When the action was over, Jonathan removed a small red flag from the boy's clothing; he later carried the relic back to the States, guarded in a bamboo box which he never opens. Jonathan now suffers frequent nightmares, as well as daylight interjections of the boy. Debilitating headaches, with bouts of nausea and vomiting, forced him to quit his telephone lineman job year before last. Last autumn he was having increasing trouble with a son who had just entered adolescence . . .

Thomas Melton:

Thomas's squad was caught in an ambush on a battered hillside. Most of the men were able to take cover, but one badly wounded soldier, Randy by name, was stranded in the open. The words of the lieutenant who led the unit, as Randy lay screaming for help, are forever emblazoned on Thomas's memory: "Don't go near him," the lieutenant ordered, "he's bait." Thomas's sense of being "bait" in Vietnam was confirmed by the loss of his best friend in the unit when, a month later, an enemy mortar round hit their camp's ammo depot while the two privates relaxed over coffee. Thomas now lives an isolated existence in a "hooch" he has constructed in the basement of his parents' home. Its walls are fashioned from newspaper clippings on Vietnam, along with subsequent American military actions . . .

And there was Rick Dennis:

Rick endured the weeks-long battering of North Vietnamese artillery at the famous siege of Khe Sahn. One day his machine gun emplacement was overrun by waves of communist soldiers. Rick remained at his post until the enemy was upon him, enabling the rest of his squad to retreat behind the base's perimeter. And such was his terror, when he finally fell back to American lines, that he kept sprinting on toward the mess hall. "There was a blue chair in the corner of the mess," he tells his fellows, "that was my place of safety. Call it superstition, but for some reason, I always believed I'd be safe in that chair." Unfortunately, on reaching the mess hall Rick discovered, with shock bordering on horror, that the entire makeshift building had been demolished by an artillery round. He hasn't felt safe since. Episodes of double vision, in which customers at the electronics store where he works become hoards of attacking communist soldiers, regularly send him to the stockroom to clear his mind . . .

I write that these men, with their harrowing accounts of war gave me, amid the endless noise of the *commentariat,* safe in their newsrooms and television studios, something unassailably real to hold to. And that is true. Just the same, I was not oblivious to the danger we therapists continually run, that our psychic resources may not suffice to cope with our clients' traumas—traumas which must, if we are to be of any help, become our own. Yes, that week after Veterans Day, I was aware of operating very near the line as I welcomed—craved, even—a deeper empathy with the men who came to see me.

I took reasonable precautions to keep myself afloat. I attended our weekly support sessions and shared my struggles with our colleagues. They shared their not dissimilar difficulties.

I spoke, at one of those gatherings, of Charles Pinckney, and saw my concern for him echoed among others who had known him during his time at the clinic. Yet still I was left, after the session, with a hollow aching in his regard. His disappearance, in ways I could not fathom, struck to the heart of all the loose ends of my unsettled life.

I didn't mention Gary at our support group. He hadn't been at the clinic for a month. He had been on my mind, to be sure, but my feelings toward him were not those of a therapist for her client. It was those feelings that prevented me from calling to inquire why he wasn't coming in, a gesture that would have been pro forma with any of my other charges.

& & &

I FINALLY DECIDED to review Gary's file, if for no other reason than to bring closure to the matter. I had never received his service records, in spite of my appeals to Alice. I admit that I hadn't followed up thoroughly. (As you know, Howie, paperwork has never been my forte.)

I asked Alice why she hadn't provided me the records I'd requested weeks earlier. She looked at me sheepishly.

"I can't get hold of them," she said.

"What do you mean? Did you contact the VA?"

"Yes."

"What did they say?"

"They don't have them."

"Don't have them? What about the referral letter? We're always supposed to get a referral letter."

"Well," she said, her eyes downcast, "he didn't have it when he first came, so I told him he could just bring it later."

Before I could scold her, she lifted her face to me. "The thing is, I sort of knew him. He used to come in here with deliveries. Since he worked for Mr. Pinckney, I figured he was all right."

"Really?"

"You know how he is," she said conspiratorially. "He'd look at me with those big brown eyes. Then he'd say how disorganized he was, and that he just forgot it. I kept on reminding him . . ."

Oh, the big brown eyes, I wanted to say; but I suspected my rising anger was of the jealous, not the administrative, variety. I took a deep breath and spoke surprisingly calmly. "What about the Army, did you contact them? Maybe the VA lost the record."

"Yes," she said painfully, "I tried everything. Army, Navy, Air Force, Marines, National Guard. I even contacted the Coast Guard. Nobody can find any service records on him."

"Can you check again?"

"I've already checked twice."

I confined myself to a this-is-not-the-way-things-are-done, but as I walked to my office, my mind swam in confusion. And then it hit me, it was suddenly so clear! This wasn't the standard bureaucratic snafu. It was all too strange—and of a piece. His peculiar demeanor. His evasiveness regarding details of his combat service. His flirtations. And now, no service records! Or referral letter. Who was Gary Devers—if Gary Devers was in fact his name. And what was his game? Was he working some con to bilk the government? And what about those big brown eyes? Is that how he operated with every receptionist in town? I cringed at the thought that I had been stupid enough to fall for his shtick. His gushing over my tapestry. My developing a "thing" for him. But then I remembered—he was Charles's friend. Or was that part of the scam? Yet the couriers at Signed, Sealed & Delivered treated him with a great deal of respect. It was all too much to fathom.

I desperately needed clarity.

Again, but with little deliberation this time, I found myself cabbing up 11th Street through Friday evening traffic. I told myself (and really believed it) that this would be the last time. The location was easy to remember, off the main drag and then down a few blocks to the funny-shaped building set into an alleyway behind the old printing plant. It was not without trepidation that I buzzed at the door. I didn't know what I would say when I saw Gary, but I was determined not to leave without some answers. As it happened it was Ben, the nice young man who had greeted me on my first visit, who opened the door.

"Hey!" he said with a sense of recognition. "Good to see you again. Come on in."

He stepped back into the foyer and held the door for me. His casual warmth took a notch out of my resolve to remain indignant until I could have things out with Gary.

"Glad you came back," he said. I stepped inside. "Marjorie, isn't it?"

His mellow eyes shone softly. "Yes, that's right." I began to take off my coat and he reached out to help. A gentleman, I thought, and more of my anger leaked away.

"How are things with you?" I asked. "It's Ben, right?"

"That's right. Everything's okay, I suppose. As okay as it could be, considering what's going on with the Pinkman. You haven't heard anything, have you?" He hung my coat on the rack to one side of the foyer.

I almost mentioned the business at the Maine Mast Memorial but, remembering Gary's remarks about Charles's privacy, found myself falling in line with his protocols of silence. "Not really," I said.

"And this war scare," Ben went on. "All this chest-thumping is mighty disturbing."

I agreed, and we moved to the door that gives onto the open space they call the Demilitarized Zone. He opened it, and I paused there to let my eyes adjust to the reddish light. A murmur of multiple conversations filtered through a bed of quietly jazzy music. I began to pick out groups of people talking, sipping drinks, and munching snacks. My eyes sought out Gary, but I couldn't distinguish him in the crowd.

"Looking for Gary?" Ben asked.

I regretted that it was so obvious. "I'd just like to speak with him at some point."

"He's probably finishing up Dispatch paperwork. Should I run upstairs and get him?"

"Oh no, it can wait," I said, certain nonetheless that my tone betrayed my impatience. Ben led me into the room; and its bohemian ambience, with the whimsically disparate paraphernalia that lined its walls, further undermined the sense of purpose that had accompanied me in the cab up 11th Street. I was looking over the assembled crowd when Henry approached obliquely and, removing a beret he wore, performed a comical bow and flourish. I was happy to see him.

"To what do we owe the honor?" he asked.

"The honor's mine, I'm sure," I said lightly.

"I think Gary's upstairs. Want me to get him?"

I visibly blushed. Apparently I was now considered *Gary's girl* among couriers all over town. To deflect attention from Gary and me, I said, "No thanks, I came more about Charles."

"The Pinkman?"

"Yes."

"Have you heard something?" There was eager excitement in his voice, and I regretted having raised his hopes.

"No, I'm afraid not," I said. I again kept the Maine Mast episode close to my chest. "I hoped I might learn something from you guys."

"We're still completely in the dark," he said. "But I'm glad you came out. We can put our heads together."

Ben's eyes darted to the stairway at the back of the room and I followed his gaze. Gary's unmistakable form, tall and lanky in his vintage fatigue, spiraled toward the floor. I tensed up. There was a flush at seeing him again, not completely explained by my anger, and the realization that though it would serve him right, I could not confront him in front of the assembled Gathering. I would have to make nice until we could be alone together. I disguised my frequent glances in his direction as he talked with a group near the base of the stairway and then moved from cluster to cluster, greeting and chatting. Eventually he stood to one side, raised his voice, and asked for everyone's attention. It was only then, as he surveyed the breadth of the room, that his eyes found me.

"I want to thank you all for being here and say welcome, whether you're Signed, Sealed, from other outfits, friends"— he looked at me and smiled—"or friends of friends." He lowered his head, thoughtful for a moment, and then raised his gaze again. "Listen," he said, "I know everyone's bummed about the Pinkman. I am, too. I'm doing everything I can to figure out what's happened. The police still haven't turned up anything, and I say that's a good thing. At least they haven't turned up anything bad. I have a feeling we're going to get a breakthrough on this before long. Don't ask me why, call it a hunch. Meanwhile, we're keeping the company going, and we're all here together. They're also good things. I'm sure you people have some thoughts you'd like to express about all of this, and perhaps some other stuff as well."

"No blood for oil!" someone shouted.

"Make love not war!"

"Bread, not guns!"

Gary acknowledged the remarks with a nod. "Like they said. But for now, let me suggest a drumming circle. I think it would do us all some good. Let off some steam, get the mind-body tuned up a little."

"Sounds good," someone said, and everyone began to stir. A chattering contingent left the room through the foyer; when they returned, moments later, they bore an odd assortment of percussion instruments: congas and frame drums, maracas and shakers, tambourines, chestnut rattles and hand cymbals. The rest of us pulled all manner of chair into the center of the room. Ben positioned a crate in the middle of our circle and placed a candle upon it.

Gary looked in my direction and waved as I took a place between Henry and Ben. When the instruments were passed around, they secured me a djembe, the hour-glass-shaped African instrument. With laudable patience they taught me how to properly strike it.

There was a period of experimentation, of twitterings and scrapings and lowings, that finally settled without apparent cue into a pregnant silence. A young man with solid shoulders and steady gaze began to beat out a mournful rhythm on a stout, ovoid drum. The shaking of a chestnut rattle came like rising wind before a storm; it was pierced by the thunder and lightening of tambourine strikes, deft counter-rhythms from frame drums, and the rolling mutterings of a tabla.

With eyes closed I let tension escape from body, mind, and heart. Sensing Ben and Henry close by, I heard their drummings: Henry firm and steady, Ben in delicate filigree against the beat. I even sensed their breathing, and by extension that of the entire circle, which more and more inhaled as one organism. When I felt myself joining that common respiration, I began to tap the djembe near the rim. With my other hand I added syncopated strikes in keeping with the solemn tempo.

The drumming went on and on and on: dissolved in languid, rhythmic waves, my consciousness of time and place grows increasingly fluid. Awash in this hypnogogic state of half-dream, I see the vivid sand painting on the hogan floor. A Navajo shaman shakes his rattle over the returned veteran; he is chanting healing sounds. His song wells from within, gaining force until memory blends with inform noises from around the circle. There are low moans, mumbled slogans, clickings and pops. I ride that wave, allow memory to mix with present, until at last the image fades . . .

I pull my consciousness back into the present moment and

look around. The man who had started the beat hasn't wavered. His gaze is steady, his attention locked on his drum. Others look vaguely into the midst of the Gathering as I now do, their expressions intent but peaceful. A man who looks like Marvin Gaye after he grew his beard emits bird-like calls toward the ceiling. I recognize faces from the last Gathering, couriers from Darick's memorial service and Tanya, who climbed atop Farragut's memorial to defend herself against unkind gossip. They were all one now, intently drumming with an effortless focus.

The aleatory symphony built to an unplanned climax, and the lead drummer indicated a decrescendo with downturned palms. The soundweave gradually ebbed until we were again near the quiet of the beginning. The leader struck the big oval drum three times in close succession before, raising his eyes to the group, he wordlessly signaled a final stoke.

"Yeah!" one of the couriers, rocking his head back and forth, emphatically exhaled.

"Take that at the White House," the man of the bird calls squawked.

"Make drums, not war!"—this from Rob, the film student who had read his poem at the earlier Gathering.

Others commented in like manner, or just nodded appreciatively.

Gary addressed himself to the man who had begun the beat. "Ty, what say we try something a little more up-tempo?"

Ty nodded, looked to the side, and marked an intricate pattern of three low beats, a strike on the higher part of the drum, a trill, and a final stroke at the deeper center of the skin. Hearing the interstices that called to be filled (and those silences that begged to be left alone) I joined in. Others joined as well, and before long a note of joy began to emerge. We were moving from the perplexed, grieving dirge of the first round to an untrammeled expression of life force, with prominent hand cymbals and tambourines, cries in several languages, and raucous parrots in place of the dire keenings of before.

I let myself be carried along in the exuberant mood, occasionally glancing at Ben or Henry to see the risen blood in their faces. I enjoyed the extemporaneous comments of the bird-man ("Yes mama, oh yes, mama") and stole furtive glances toward Gary. I felt not anger now but a blind neutrality, happy to be among others in such an elemental undertaking.

This round eventually wound toward a close, with a gradual dropping away of voices until only Ty remained, playing as steadily as ever. Finally he too allowed his drum to fade, until it merged into the silence that followed.

Everyone gazed downward, absorbing the new energies that had been called forth. Slowly people looked into the circle and met one another's eyes. Then Gary spoke. "Okay, what's on your minds? Let's hear it."

"Like you said," Roger offered, "Pinkman."

"Yeah," others called out.

"All this war business," the man of the bird calls put in. He sprawled against his chair in exasperation.

"Anything else?" Gary asked. He waited a moment. "Okay, let's start with Pinky."

"It's like something has been torn out of us," said Ali, the Persian who had spoken so emotionally of Charles at the earlier Gathering.

"Yeah, it's like the Gathering is spinning into a widening spiral, with no center to hold." This from Ben.

An awkward silence followed Ben's remark. Finally Rob spoke. "Gary," he said, taking in the rest with his eyes, "no one's saying you're not doing a decent job of keeping the outfit going."

"I know," Gary said. "It's been hard for me, too."

"Still no information?" the bird-man asked.

"No," Gary replied. Then he addressed himself to Subesh, the part-time news stringer. "Subesh, you were going to get on this. Anything?"

"I'm afraid not. I've looked at every conceivable angle. You were right about the company records. Nothing unusual there. There were no strange phone calls, either. I've also been in touch with my sources at the police department, and they haven't had any more luck than me. As incredible as it seems, the man has literally vanished."

Henry turned to me. "Marj, you visited Pinky's mother. Have you talked to her lately?"

"I'm afraid not."

Roger loudly cleared his throat. "I spoke to her." Everyone turned to him in eager anticipation. "I know you wanted us to stay cool," he said to Gary, "but I just had to go over there and check things out. Talk to some brothers. See wassup, you know."

"What did you find out?"

He turned up empty palms. "Nada. It was nice seeing Mrs. P, though."

Silence.

"Look," Gary said, "I think we've got to assume that Pinky's all right, and that he'll turn up in due time."

There was a flourish of tablas.

"You might be right," Roger said. "But I'm going to keep my eyes open. Somebody messes with the Pinkman, they're going to get their chops busted."

Ty executed a low roll on the big drum.

"Fine," Gary said. "Other business?"

"Offensive option," the bird-man cried out ominously.

"Desert Shield," Rob added.

"Hostages." Tanya.

"Chemical weapons." Ali.

"Israel." Ben.

"Darkness within darkness . . ." Ty in low, steady voice.

Gary stared thoughtfully into the circle a moment. When he spoke, it was as if thinking out loud. "Hmm, I guess this would be the first real war for most of you. You were too young for Vietnam. Grenada and Panama don't really count . . ."

"Did you hear El Presidente last week?" one of the men said. "He said this wasn't going to be another Vietnam."

"Nothing's going to be another Vietnam," Gary said. "That doesn't mean it's not going to be crappy. Who knows, God forbid, it could be even worse. And let's say the U.S. does manage to pull off this much-advertised antiseptic war—for the American side, that is—with overwhelming air superiority and, consequently, few causualties for the home team. Is that a good thing? I worry about any nation, no matter how just their cause, feeling they can commit war without penalty. It could make the decision to go in just a bit too easy."

"War is completely insane," Tanya piped up. "All this weaponry. What's wrong with people? I mean, who sits around thinking, 'Why don't we see if we can come up with some clever new device for maiming our fellow human beings?'"

"The profit motive," Rob said.

"Capitalism stinks," a guy with aniline hair put in.

"But communism is collapsing under its own weight," Gary returned suddenly. "And the Reds have shown themselves plenty handy at producing the tools of death, without your famous profit motive."

"It's all about oil," someone said.

"Saddam's crazy," Ali put in. "He started a war with my own country. Millions of boys died over there."

"Yeah, but he was our buddy then," a young, blond-haired woman said. "He was supposed to help us stem the tide of Islamic revolution!"

"Why can't we just mind our own business?" Tanya asked plaintively.

"Exactly," Rob said. "We can't get rid of every dictator on earth. Besides, who says we have the right to make the world over in *our* image?"

"If you want to give the administration the benefit of the doubt," Gary remarked in judicious tones, "you could say they're merely upholding standards of international law. The inviolability of national borders, for example. The U.N. charter expressly obliges members to prevent this kind of wanton aggression."

"Yeah," Ben said, "but it seems we observe the U.N. Charter pretty selectively. That is, only when it suits our own interests."

"No argument there," Gary agreed.

"Did you hear what Secretary of State Baker said last week?" Subesh asked. "He basically admitted that this whole thing is about our economy . . . about having access to that Middle Eastern oil."

"At one level," Gary replied, "the showdown in the Gulf may indeed be a naked struggle for resources. But I'm not sure that invalidates it. After all, people need resources to live. And aside from being vital to our economic well-being, petroleum is a strategic commodity, necessary for the fielding of armies and navies. Whoever controls those vast oil fields has the world on a pretty short leash. Preferably that person, or persons, won't be psychopaths . . ."

"Gary," Rob asked, sounding perplexed, "are you saying that you're in favor of a war?"

"Heavens no." Gary seemed taken aback. "What sane person is for war? Especially one who . . . has personally experienced its ravages?"

"Dude!" Roger erupted, "I didn't know you were in the service."

Gary's eyes shot to mine. He seemed alarmed, and unable to hide it. Now the fat's in the fire, I thought. He gazed soulfully at his hands. "I'd rather not talk about that right now."

Gary's friends, taking his remark as a testament to remembered pain, fell into a respectful silence. The bird-man broke the mood with a drum flourish, followed by a few of his unearthly calls.

"Why don't we get the lights on," Gary announced from where he sat. Drums were put away, chairs moved back to the perimeter of the room, and people clustered into groups to chat, drink, and snack. Several guitars were produced. While these were being tuned I made my way to where Gary still rested in his chair, appearing unable to move. He seemed to know that his cover had been blown.

"I need to talk to you," I said.

"Why not?"

"Is there someplace more private?"

He rose and placed his chair against the wall. "How about upstairs?"

He allowed me to precede him up the sprial stairway. When we achieved the darkened riders lounge I stepped aside so that he could direct me further. He threaded his way through the scattered café tables towards where a big sofa occupied the opposite wall. Before we reached it, he pulled a chair away from one of the tables and offered me a seat.

He sat opposite.

"Shoot," he said. (Flashback to him in my office, wearing the toy soldier mask.)

"Gary," I said.

"Uh-huh?"

"You've been lying to me."

"Mm-hm." He raised a hand to his face and began to massage his forehead and eyes.

"You were never in Vietnam."

He slowly rocked his head from side to side.

"You were never in the service at all."

He nodded his assent.

My voice was stern. "Why?"

He ran his hands through his chestnut hair, then rested his face in them.

"Cat got your tongue?"

He emitted a crimped, pained sound.

"I don't get it. What's in it for you?"

He turned up his palms.

"Are you scamming the government?"

"No."

"Then—why?"

"I couldn't think of any other way to get to you."

This surprised me. "You didn't even know me," I said.

"I felt that somebody had to tell you what was going on with the Pinkman."

"That's fine. But why not just drop a note at the clinic? Why all this elaborate . . ."

He shook his head in exasperation. "There was so much going on. It wasn't just Pinky. There was Darick. Clark . . ."

"Clark?" I asked, but then remembered Gary's friend, the one who had gone missing in Central America.

"All this war business . . ." Gary added.

We were silent.

He began again, unsteadily. "Pinky used to talk about his years at the clinic. He always told me what a great therapist you were. And—"

"And what?" I used my hardest voice, determined not to fall prey to his flatteries a second time.

"This is a little embarrassing, but Pinky used to say that you and I . . . well, that we would make a great couple."

I emitted a pshaw! but he soldiered on.

"He said it was like I was the male version of you, and you were the female version of me. I know that may seem odd, but that's what he said."

Fighting the urge to soften, I made no remark. Gary, for his part, seemed to despair of further explanation. "In the last analysis, I guess I was just following my gut," he finally got out. He lowered his eyes, and his shoulders slumped.

"I'm concerned about you," I said after a moment, "that you would carry this thing so far. That bit with the helicopter, for instance. *All those hot landing zones*, I believe you said. There are men who are really suffering, who desperately need the kinds of services the clinic provides. And you, you were just wasting our time."

"I may not suffer like those men," he began uncertainly, "but . . ."

Now he faltered.

"But what?"

"Maybe I've read too much, heard too many stories. Seen too many damned movies! But when I hear those infernal blades slicing the air, I can't help hear the agonized cries of the wounded. I remember those awful times all over again, and how hard it's been for the vets to come home. I grieve for all the people who lost a son, a brother, for the people of Vietnam. Even for the earth, that was so horribly desecrated!" He looked as though he couldn't go on, but then he rallied. "I think about the Pinkman. Such a beautiful guy, and everything he went through—"

His head fell onto his arms, and at first he was still. Then I noticed the slow heaving of his shoulders. I was embarrassed, though it wasn't because he was weeping (I've seen enough of men's tears to fill the seven seas) but because I wondered if this wasn't just another clever act. But as I watched helplessly, my better angels guided me. I felt convinced that Gary's convoluted demarche towards me, however unskillful, was not in bad faith. I skirted the table and took him around the shoulders. After helping him to the sofa, I urged him to lie down and relax. I sat beside him. Voices downstairs sang an old song about a well on a hill, and how you can't kill for Jesus.

Gary covered his face with his hands while I stroked his brow and hair. Stretching myself alongside him, I burrowed an arm beneath the folds of his worn field jacket. He calmed while I rubbed his shoulders and kissed his forehead. Finally I lifted away, looked into his eyes, and asked how he felt.

"Better."

"Good."

"I'm sorry I lied to you. It was pretty stupid, when I think about it."

"Don't worry about it. I know what it's like to suffer for others."

"Yeah, all those guys you work with . . ."

I wanted to tell him how much deeper it ran than even that, but something held me back. I lay my head on his chest, and he stroked my hair.

"Now it's all happening again," he took up after a moment, his tone grown philosophical, "turning up like a bad penny! And these younger folks, it's so sad to watch them deal with it for the first time. To see all their natural inclinations toward harmony and decency undercut by a world of brute, animal force! They're straining toward a utopian future—that's what they're doing— and I'm crazy enough to agree that, as human beings, it's the only course that makes any sense."

"Otherwise it is all pretty pointless, isn't it?"

"And then," he remarked with ironic laughter, "I find myself sounding like Mr. Defender of the Status Quo. Of course I trusted in the same ready solutions when I was their age. Communism, pacifism. But I've come to believe that the road to Utopia, oh, it's just a little more complicated than those arm-chair fantasies would have us believe."

"I think that's reasonable."

"Thanks for covering my back," he said, "but I'm not so

sure myself." He scratched mine lightly, and we were quiet for a moment.

"I sometimes question," he said reflectively, "whether the world has made me wiser, or just harder."

Overcome by a sudden urge, I pulled myself over him, held his face and kissed him deeply and long while he murmured unintelligible things. Later, warm with our loving, we fell asleep. When he shifted under me I awoke and looked into his eyes. We lay and listened. There were low voices downstairs.

"Shall we go down?" I asked.

"We may as well see what's up."

We got up and straightened our clothes. The clock on the wall said ten til two. I brushed out my hair and followed Gary to the head of the stairway and down. The big room was nearly empty. Henry, Ben, Tanya and Tomás (the young man who, at the memorial service, had pleaded the case for Darick's poetry)lounged around a crate graced by a couple of greenish wine bottles. When we were half-way down the spiral they looked up.

"Howdy," Ben said.

"What's up?"

"Everyone else left. We didn't want to bother you guys."

"I appreciate it. What are you up to so late?"

"Just shootin' the breeze," Ben said.

"Trying to make sense of things," Tomás added.

"You know," Henry said, "save-the-world stuff."

"With all this war hysteria," Tanya came in, "we feel we ought to do something. But we don't know where to begin."

"It's not easy," Gary said, "that's for sure."

"And now that Pinky's gone," Tanya went on, "everything feels so different. The way he would stand here at morning bells, there was always something that seemed to make sense. Something solid, somewhere. Now, I don't know . . ."

"We'll figure something out," Henry put in.

"What he said," Gary added sleepily. "But for now, I've got to get this lady home. Let me make a call, see if I can get a cab." He started toward the desk at the back of the room.

"I was about to leave," Tomás said, "I can give you a lift."

We said goodnight and went to Tomás's car. Insisting that Gary and I sit in the back, like honeymooners, he chauffeured us across town to my building. When we arrived Gary got out with me, spoke briefly with Tomás, and walked me to the door.

"Do you want to come up?" I held the collar of his field jacket. His hands bracketed my waist.

"I'd better not." He looked deep into my eyes.

I was disappointed. "Early morning?"

"No." He saw my hurt. "It's just that, it's been so beautiful, I don't want to blow it."

"Funny man." I kissed him, snuggled into his neck, and pressed him close. He held me tightly. I told him that I had seen the Maine Mast article in the *Underground Stream*.

"Pinky for sure."

"Let's talk about that."

"As my lady wishes."

I made my way through the foyer to the elevator; as its doors lumbered shut, Gary pressed his face against the lobby window to make me laugh. While I sat on the bed, removing my stockings, I thought over the evening.

I was madly in love, that much was clear. But now that I was alone, I felt a sticky residue of the suspicions I had harbored only hours before. After all, how could I really be sure that Gary was on the up and up? Had I accepted his explanations, driven by my own emotional—and lets face it, hormonal—needs, too readily? Hadn't he already been caught in one outlandish lie? And even were his protestations as right as rain, when I reflected on how we met, I was beset by a nagging voice—one that shouted to the skies that our love was *illicit*. He was only recently a client, wasn't he? Considering all the facts, I was inclined to dismiss the matter as a technicality. At the same time, I couldn't help but question my objectivity.

My eyes lit on my loom in the corner. There were those same few inches of border; loose, multi-colored skeins dangled over the frame. This was all that so far existed of my envisioned tapestry. I had given up on the project weeks earlier but hadn't had the heart to unravel the weave. Now I resolved to leave it. I still couldn't conceive how I would proceed, but there was a new sense of possibilities . . .

I slept late on Saturday and took care of errands, and on Sunday I cocooned and rested. I wanted to speak to Gary but didn't have his number. I could have tried looking him up, but I was hoping that he would make the next move. Never mind that my own phone was unlisted, and that I had neglected to give him my number at our hurried parting.

On Monday I broke down and looked him up in the clinic's records. But when I dialed the number that evening, it turned out to be a pizza delivery service. That fox! I wondered why he wasn't contacting me. Maybe I had gotten in too deep, too fast. Lingering suspicions raised their ugly head. I realized that I still did not completely trust him.

ON TUESDAY, in spite of my erotic preoccupations, I made an effort to focus on my work. I saw Jonathan Straiman, the client who had killed the boy soldier in Vietnam. His headaches had reached an unbearable level, and he was experiencing more frequent interjections. During our harrowing session, the black pajama – clad youth, standing starkly in my office, brutally taunted him. The boy bitterly hissed that Jonathan didn't deserve to live, further chiding that one day Jonathan's own son would die, terrified and uncomforted, while others looked mercilessly on. Later in the day Vernon Jordan experienced an important breakthrough. He had dreamed again of leaving Vietnam, and this time the plane actually taxied onto the runway and began its take-off. Vernon felt incredible relief, and great portents of joy at the thought of seeing home. But before the craft could leave the ground, the pilot announced that his instruments were malfunctioning and that the take-off must be suspended. Vernon was disappointed, but understood that he was inching slowly closer to leaving Vietnam behind.

When I returned home that evening there was a note from Gary. It silenced all of my doubts:

"Lady of Mercy! Bright-eyed Goddess! Athene, sprung from the mind of God! Now I know it's true, this is a benevolent universe! Your eyes. Your laughter. Don't get me started. I'll never be able to concentrate on the humble life I must carry on without you! Dear heart, blessed one, is it all a dream? Did you love me? Can it last? I'm afraid to know. I must know. When can I see you? Call me, or come by the shop any evening after six. We'll paint the town red! Don't wait one second longer than necessary!" He included two phone numbers and, under a nicely rendered drawing of a flower, signed his name with a flourish.

Thursday would be Thanksgiving; I had made plans to spend the day with my mother. If I were to see Gary it would have to be either the next day or wait until the weekend—and as far as I was concerned, waiting was not an option. I decided to forego a call and show up at Signed, Sealed & Delivered in person. "I'm yours!" The next morning I put extra care into my clothes and hair: sexy but not slutty. I was aware that my clients would be distracted, but what can a girl do? On my way through the front office Alice detained me.

"Ms. Llewellyn," she said sheepishly, "I double-checked those records you asked me about. You know, for Mr. Devers. I still can't turn up anything."

"Alice," I said with a blissful smile, "why don't we just forget the whole thing."

She looked perplexed, though relieved. "Sure," she said. "Thanks, Ms. Llewellyn."

"Don't mention it."

"Ms. Llewellyn?"

"Yes?"

"You look awful nice today."

My clients were buoyed throughout the day, whether by my high spirits, or my short, clingy dress, it was hard to know. I got a cab up 11th Street after work. One of the big bay doors was open, but I went in through the small door to the anteroom. There was activity in the maintenance shop as I passed. Several couriers lingered around the Demilitarized Zone in their riding gear; others made their way up or down the spiral stairway. The daily routine was winding down. Someone closed the bay door. Roger greeted me and went upstairs to find Gary.

A moment later I watched him wind down the spiral stairs, and then walk toward me with deliberate steps. But when he came near he pulled up short and stood apart. Was it self-consciousness before his workmates? I wondered. Or was he rethinking the protestations of his note? But feeling him drink me in with wasted eyes, I knew he shared my exhilaration. I wanted to cast myself upon him, smother him with tenderness, but now it was I who was inhibited by our audience! Finally he walked over and held me for a minute, a minute become an infinity in which everything of my life to that point was washed away . . .

"We've got a piece of Gathering business to take care of before I can go," Gary said. "But who knows, you might enjoy it." He pulled back and looked into my eyes. "Do you mind?"

"No, I'm game. What is it?"

"Oh, just a little ritual we do in the evenings. A sort of vespers for the non-theological."

Couriers congregating in the DMZ pulled chairs into the center of the room. Someone turned out the lights. The sun had set, and a soft twilight filtered through the windows of the bay doors. Ben, striking a match, lit a bundle of sage. He blew on it, coaxing it into a glowing orange pink, and then stepped around the interior of the circle and offered its smoke to each of us. I was familiar with this cleansing ritual from my time among the Navajos. With both hands I wafted the drifting wraith toward me and over my head, bathing myself in it, savoring its sweetness.

After Ben finished his circuit he placed the tightly wrapped leaves in a ceramic dish near the candle and seated himself on a cushion. Without any apparent cue, everyone fell into silent meditation. I glanced around the circle. Each courier sat calmly with lowered face, eyes closed, hands folded on lap or resting on knees and thighs. I too closed my eyes and breathed. We sat in silence for several minutes. Then I recognized the voice of Ty, who had led the drummings at the last Gathering. "I thank Earth Mother for another day of your inconceivable bounty," he intoned flatly. Soon another voice came in, one I couldn't place. "I thank Sky Father for light and illumination." Then, from beside me, Gary spoke. "I thank the Great Mystery for all the unfathomable beauty of this universe."

He reached over and squeezed my hand.

The circle was quiet again for a while, and then Tanya softly spoke.

"May all beings be well," she said.

"May they be peaceful and at ease," another added, spinning out the Buddhist prayer . . .

"May they be happy."

"May they be filled with loving kindness."

We were silent again. Then Henry's voice—

"May Pinky be well."

"May he be peaceful and at ease," Ben added.

"May he be happy."

"May he be filled with loving kindness."

The evocation of Pinky breached a sort of sadness, and Gary again took my hand. Someone in the circle struck a bell three times. When the sound had faded everyone opened their eyes. Gary said, "See you all tomorrow," and the circle dispersed.

He and I rose.

"Pinky," he said merely.

"Yeah." I smoothed my dress, and Gary looked me over.

"God, you're beautiful."

I thanked him. He brushed down his fatigue jacket and combed his straying hair back with one hand. "I guess I should have dressed. I wasn't really expecting you today."

I assured him that he looked fine, but he seemed not to hear me. "I'll be right back," he said and bounded off toward the stairway. When he returned he wore a tweedy sportcoat, and he had neatly combed his hair.

"I keep this around for customer calls," he explained. "What say we blow this joint?"

We went out front, where couriers were mounting cycles and climbing into cars. Gary asked Tomás to give us a lift to Dupont Circle. Minutes later he dropped us in front of the Café Luna, and we squeezed into the same side of a booth. We held hands while we sipped wine. I was terribly happy to be close to Gary, but underneath was the reality of Pinky's disappearance and the threat of war, and the wine became the mournful red fruitfulness of my cherries which had become blood. Gary, sensing my mood, wrapped an arm around me.

"Let's not be down," he said.

"Do you really think Charles is behind these things at the cemetery?"

"I'm practically certain."

"What I'm concerned about," I started hesitantly, "although it seems incredible . . ."

"A relapse?"

"I know it's unlikely, from everything I thought I knew about healing. I've never seen a vet come as clean as Charles."

"Pinky's solid as a rock. There's obviously a method . . ."

"There seems to be," I agreed. "But you know," I added after a moment, "I haven't had a chance to tell you this, but I saw him at Darick's memorial service."

"You saw Pinky?"

"I'm pretty certain I did, after you all rode off. And here's something to ponder—he was in full camouflage."

"Full cammo!"

"What's more, our eyes met, but he made no sign of recognition. Nothing. By the time the cabbie could turn around, he'd fled the scene."

"Wow, that is something to think about."

"I can't help wonder where he's living. It seems so unlike him to let his mother worry. Or to leave Signed, Sealed & Delivered in the lurch the way he has."

Gary struggled to respond. "I hear what you're saying," he finally got out. "But I've lived at close quarters with the man for going on ten years now. There have been other times when I didn't get what he was doing. Things with the company, the Gathering. But eventually, in good time, it's always made sense."

"If I could just talk to him," I said, "know that he's okay."

Gary held me closer. "Listen, we'll figure something out. But for this evening, let's let it be about us. Nothing's going to change overnight. I know the Pinkman would approve."

I acquiesced in his reasoning and we ordered dinner. Afterward he took me to a flamenco show in a restaurant crowded into a big townhouse off the avenue. It was a perfect choice, kitschy enough to pierce the somberness of the times, yet devoid neither of art nor pathos. We walked on the avenue toward midnight and got a cab to his place.

Going to his apartment that first time: through the park, up the hill, and along the ridgeline of Rock Creek's valley. There's a brown rowhouse on the end with a covered porch; up three flights. The first thing that struck me about that studio nestled into the roofline were books spilling out of shelves that lined the walls. Then there was the Persian carpet, an electric keyboard in one corner, and a desk in front of a double window across from the kitchenette. Straight ahead was a raised alcove. Here was the bed, a nightstand, and a slanting skylight above.

I walked to the desk—I've always been drawn to windows— and sat down to evaluate the view. You could see, over the darkened park and zoo, on the opposite ridge of the valley, the lights of Connecticut Avenue: it was a perfect watchtower from which a combat-seared veteran might conduct an unending surveillance. Papers and books lay scattered about. A pewter Buddha sat beside the telephone.

I felt Gary's hands on my shoulders. I eased the rolling chair back and stood to face him. He took my face in his hands . . .

We didn't sleep until dawn came glowing over the skylight across which I remember rapt glimpses of a half-moon arcing through the night. It was Thanksgiving day, and we didn't begin to stir until ten. While I drowsed in bed Gary, with feigned solemnity, played Bach preludes on his electric keyboard. He kissed my hands and made eggs and toast and coffee. Afterwards we walked the holiday-quiet streets of his neighborhood.

"I'm due at my mother's at three," I said as we held one another against the cold. "I hate to go."

"I hate for you to leave, too. But I suppose mothers do need to be attended to."

"What about you?" I asked. "You were so cagey in your so-called sessions, I hardly know anything about you. Do you have any family around here?"

"Just my Mom."

"Are you going to see her today?"

"Natch."

"And your father . . . is he still living?"

"Oh yeah. That old koot's got so much life force it'll probably take a couple tank divisions to bring him down."

"Where does he live?"

"California," he said abruptly, and then fell silent. We walked on quietly until he asked about my father; I told him only that he had died when I was young. I also told him about Bob and learned about Gary's brother, Jim, who lived in Canada. He had gone there in 1969 to avoid the draft, Gary said.

"It caused quite the family rupture," he went on. "My father still hasn't gotten over it."

"What a shame," I said.

We walked in silence again, heard our steps crunch in the dry leaves that everywhere drifted from the big oaks and maples that abound in that old city neighborhood. A crow cawed loudly nearby and Gary, as if cued by its volubility, began again to speak about his brother, about a letter that, in those topsy-turvy days of Vietnam, he had posted to home from college. Jim had gotten involved in the anti-war movement, Gary told me, and had applied for conscientious objector status. He wrote their father that he couldn't go to Vietnam and insisted that he would flee to Canada if they turned down his request. Not long afterward Jim shared their father's reply with his younger brother.

"The old man rehearsed how we come from a long line of military men," Gary recounted, "going back to the hoary old Civil War. The wrong side, I should add. He tried to convince Jim that it was some kind of family duty to take up arms for God, country, and honor." His father, Gary explained, had done his stint in the army after completing an engineering degree. "Fortunately," he went on, "he was inactive by the time Korea started, and he avoided combat. But he still holds the family's martial traditions in great esteem. Basically, the old fart gets on his high horse and tells Jim that he can stop considering himself a Devers if he evades military service. Well," he continued with a little laugh, "Jim thanked him for the advice, but said that he had made his decision and was going to stick with it. That was after adding, before closing, a few choice words about what he thought of my father's value system . . ."

"I suppose your brother didn't get the c.o.," I said.

"No," Gary replied. "We'd both come up in the august Congregational Church—a raft of my maternal ancestors were even missionaries in the South Pacific. But Jim, when he reached the age of reason, began to question the whole theological structure they'd force-fed us in Sunday school. By the time he graduated high school, he'd come to reject any belief in the supernatural as rank superstition. 'Mumbo-jumbo,' he liked to call it." Gary smiled at the memory. "The fact is," he said, "Jim was interested in reforming the way we live in the here and now, based on the kind of rational thinking of which, I've got to say, my dear brother is a passed master. He wasn't expecting so much as a shred of help from some invisible Benevolence.

"The problem with that attitude," Gary continued as we stepped over a curb, "is that it's nearly impossible to get a c.o. based on a personal dislike for violence, or a particular war, or because you think that war is inherently unreasonable. In their endless love of red tape and bureaucracy, the government only respects pacifism if you're part of an *organization* of pacifists. Only group-think is considered valid, if you know what I mean, and Jim had no religion to back him up. Bottom line, they rejected his application, and he headed for the border."

"And he's been there ever since? In Canada?"

"Yep."

"And your father and him?"

"Still not speaking."

"After all these years?"

"Sad, isn't it?"

"What about the amnesty, under President Carter?" I asked. "Couldn't he have come back?"

"Sure," Gary said, "but by then he was settled in. He had married a Canadian gal—my sister-in-law, Diana—and sired a couple of kids. He seems happy enough. They come down from time-to-time, and I go up there to visit every couple of years."

We had made a circuit of the neighborhood and now walked a road that skirted the ridge of Rock Creek's valley back towards Gary's place. We fell in with the simple peace of the earth: with the stone retaining wall along the sidewalk, overhanging branches clinging to their last desiccated leaves, withered mums along yards' edges, and a chill breeze that blew down from the north. When we reached Gary's apartment I called a cab. We hugged hard on the sidewalk and the cabbie took me home, a short drive across the park and up the avenue.

“” “” “”

I SHOWERED, CHANGED, and drove out to my mother's. On the way I listened to PBS news on the radio. I had not followed the Persian Gulf situation for several days and, knowing that she would want to discuss every nuance, wanted to be forearmed. When I had last spoken to her, the previous week, the defense secretary had authorized as many as seventy-five thousand additional reserves for a potential call-up.

The lead story was the president's Thanksgiving Day visit with American troops in Saudi Arabia. He and the secretary of state had spent two weeks globetrotting and lining up support; the following week they planned to lobby the United Nations for a resolution on military force. The always foxy Hussein added a quarter million troops of his own and slyly offered to release, if the peace held for ninety days, his American hostages. World leaders met to declare an end to the Cold War, just in time for a hot one, and Jimmy Carter assailed the escalation of American forces in the Persian Gulf. Daniel Ellsburg conducted campus teach-ins across the country, and Congress scheduled hearings on the legality of the president's actions. Most ominously for my family, the day before, fifteen-thousand reservists of the seventy-five-thousand authorized were called into service.

When I arrived at my mother's, I approached the front door with apprehension. She met me in the hallway and, after she embraced me wearily, I followed her toward the kitchen. Her slumped shoulders and languid gait signaled that she was apprised of the bleak news from the Persian Gulf.

As we passed by the living room I was immediately aware of something out of kilter. There was a lacklusterness about the housekeeping that wasn't like my mother. Stray piles of newspapers lay on the floor, unopened junkmail filled an easy chair, and soiled dishes festered on the coffee table. Making her home a place of comfort and beauty had always been the guiding principle of my mother's existence. The darkness didn't help. Without asking permission I opened the curtains across the sliding glass doors that lead out back. The garden looked weedy and neglected under the gray sky.

The TV was on as usual, but to my surprise it wasn't a news channel, but re-runs of the *Carol Burnett Show*.

I remarked on the programming.

"I had the news on but it made me sick," she said. "All this hoop-la about the president visiting the troops—like he's doing our boys some big favor. You can bet he'll be out of harm's way when the shells start flying!"

She had roasted a chicken and prepared all the customary fixings. Over dinner I had proof positive that, as I suspected, she had been carefully following events.

"We're going in," she said, "no question about it. There's the same feeling as back in sixty-four. Congress is going to rubber stamp the president, just like they did Johnson. You watch."

"Have you talked to Bob?"

"He's cocky as ever. Still thinks he's invulnerable. But let me tell you something, sweetie. Call it mother's intuition. I don't want to scare you, but he's going to be right in the thick of it. I know it plain as day."

The gravity of our supper conversation was only partly relieved by Burnett's crazy antics. When darkness fell I missed Gary and wondered if his family holiday had been any more cheerful than mine.

Driving back to the city I was unable to dismiss my mother's auguries. Her anxieties about Bob's situation were beginning to infiltrate my own psyche, and I didn't feel prepared to face another week at the clinic. I could only hope that Gary and I would be there for one another, as we had been the night before. He didn't answer my call when I arrived at home. I left an extremely fond message and then, exhausted by the previous night's lack of sleep, fell into bed.

I dreamt that night of my father, a nocturnal presence I had believed banished years earlier. I add, with great relief, that it was not the specter of those years just after his death, when in my tortured sleep I again smelled the sick-sweet cooking gas when I came home from school, again saw myself crashing through the living room, knowing with dread certainty that something was terribly, ineradicably wrong! No, now he came to me differently, comforting and playful, as he had been before Vietnam:

"Looks like you got yourself a boyfriend."

Rendered dumbstruck by his presence, I could not respond.

"Seems like a nice fella."

"I think he is," I said shakily.

"That Dougie wasn't a bad kid, either," he said, "just green, that's all. He didn't know what he had in you. Otherwise he'd a never run off."

"That was a long time ago."

"Let bygones be bygones, huh?"

"Yeah, I guess so."

"It looks like there's another war on."

"I'm afraid there may be."

"No, not *may* be. Haven't you been paying attention to your mother?"

He began to recede into a deepening darkness.

"What about Bobby?" I shouted out across our growing distance.

"Bobby? Don't worry about Bobby."

He was almost gone. Then his voice was very close.

"Just take care of Mom. And yourself."

"What's wrong with Mom?"

No answer. I turned. He wasn't there, so I ran toward where I had last seen him. I was suddenly engulfed by the blackness of the darkened wood behind the old house. Before I had gone three steps I was entangled in briars. The more I tried to extricate myself, the sharper the pricks. When I tried to call out for him, sounds of speech would not come from my mouth, only stifled groans.

I awoke in a sweat.

I tried to get up, but I quickly grew dizzy and had to lie down again. I lay there, gazing at the ceiling's blandness, until once again I drifted into dream. There was a beating drum, and the Navajo healer was there. My attention was riveted on the returned veteran, surrounded by his family; that veteran was my father. Bob was there also, and my mother; and the brightly intricate sand painting in the midst of which sat my father was a pattern Sarah Tilly once taught me to weave in woolen blankets. Sarah too was there, chanting her stories of White Shell Woman, psalming how she forever and for all of time knit together a life of strength and meaning with her loom. Coming into half-wakefulness, I feared that my teacher was aware of my neglected instrument, only a few feet from my bed, and would disavow me. But she sweetly stroked my hair and told me that everything would be all right.

I dropped into a deep and dreamless sleep.

& & &

I WOKE around seven and called Gary, wanting to share both the stresses and comforts of my night visions. He had already been out for a morning walk and coffee.

"He's hit again."

"Who?"

"Pinky. I picked up the *Stream* on the street."

"What happened?"

"I won't go into detail. I'm due at the shop. Maybe you can pick up a copy somewhere."

"How was your holiday?"

"The usual cranberry sauce, tales of family greatness past, and the slightly sad call to my brother."

"I miss you."

"I miss you, too. When do you finish work?"

"At six."

"I'll pick you up in front of your building."

"Baby," I said, "the thought of you waiting for me at work is thrilling. But with your history at the clinic, it's probably not a good idea for us to be seen together."

"Hm, I hadn't thought of that. Look, I'll stay in the cab and wait for you around the corner." He sensed my hesitation. "Don't

181

worry. There won't be any problems."

Without waiting for a reply he said goodbye and signed off.

On the way in to the clinic I picked up a copy of the *Underground Stream*. It informed me that on Thanksgiving Eve, while Gary and I got to know one another so much better under a moon-filled skylight, someone was again busy at the cemetery. A photograph taken at dawn showed the sun striking row upon row of Charles's "wafers," each one bearing a simple sign that said merely *Remember*. Again there was a story about the clean-up detail, the stonewalling of the *Stream's* reporter, and bystanding homeless veterans, one of whom remarked, "It was awesome."

After work I went down to the street. I walked around the corner away from Union Station and scanned the cars in the curb lane, looking for Gary. Halfway down the block was a red and black cab waiting for the light with the rest of the traffic. I peered into its back seat. There sat a heavily bearded man, a wide-brimmed fedora pulled over his eyes, sporting dark sunglasses. I made to walk on but the Hasidim beckoned me with emphatic gestures. It was only then that I noticed the familiar field jacket! I stepped to the curb, Gary pushed open the door and, just as the light went to green, I hopped in. Struggling to keep straight faces, we didn't turn toward one another until we were several blocks from the clinic. He pulled off his shades, the beard and the hat, and we embraced.

"Nice disguise," I said, laughing. "But where are we going?"

"There are some people I'd like to talk to."

The cab was doubling back past the Capitol.

"Friends of yours?"

"No, but I have a hunch they can shed some light on Pinky's situation."

"Really?"

"I started to put it together this morning, after I saw the latest *Stream*. How could I have been so blind? It's all so obvious!"

"Obvious?"

"Listen," he said, "how does the *Stream* manage to scoop all these cemetery stories? First, they just happen to be at the carillon concert. That's not exactly a hot ticket, if you know what I mean. Then they're at the wreath-laying when the Maine Mast blew. Admittedly, that's not an unusual beat for them to cover. But now this. The clean-up was finished in half an hour. That's according to the *Stream's* own reporting. So tell me, what are they doing with reporters hanging around the cemetery at dawn on Thanksgiving day?"

"Do you think they're involved with these events?"

He rubbed his jaw. "That's possible, I suppose. But more likely, they're being tipped off."

Shops and restaurants flowed by, and liberated bureaucrats, draped in the first heavier garments of fall, hurried along the sidewalks of Capitol Hill's commercial district. We continued on away from the Capitol, past decreasingly gentrified blocks.

"So, you still haven't told me where we're going."

The cab, turning, made its way up a side street.

In lieu of an answer Gary gestured ahead. The cabbie was pulling up at a rowhouse scantily clad in peeling white paint. Gary paid the driver and we got out. Light shone through second floor windows; we climbed the porch and rang the buzzer. Stenciled across a bay window on the ground floor were the words: "The Underground Stream: All the News, Fit or Not."

A light came on in the foyer, and we watched a man wearing a Grateful Dead tee-shirt, his graying hair hanging to his shoulders, trudge down a staircase. When he reached the door he looked through the leaded-glass window in its top panel and studied us for a moment. He opened the door and asked what he could do for us.

"We want to talk to you about these cemetery stories," Gary said.

"Do you have some information for us?"

"We might."

The man invited us in and then, turning, led us up the stairway to the second floor. We passed through an archway to a large room the bay window of which, part of the same architectural structure as that on the ground floor, faced the street. Several desks sat amid a chaos of paper in scattered piles on furniture and floor. A man with a short afro sat at one of them. When we entered, he turned a questioning look in our direction. The man who had let us in addressed him.

"Mo," he said, "these folks say they have something on the cemetery stories."

"Might have," Gary corrected.

The man called Mo carefully sized us up. He came around from behind his desk and held out his hand. "Mo Bolton," he said. "I see you've met Frank."

"Oh, I'm sorry," Frank said, "how rude of me." He shook our hands. "I've been staring at copy too long. Totally forgot my manners."

We introduced ourselves and they offered us seats. Mo moved back behind his desk while Frank slid awkwardly onto an adjacent desktop.

Mo leaned back in his chair. "Shoot," he said.

"Well," Gary began hesitantly, "we've been following these stories over in the cemetery . . ."

"Okay, and . . ."

Gary seemed uncertain how to proceed and, looking toward the ceiling, seemed to stall for a moment. "To be frank," he finally got out, "it just seems incredibly coincidental that you guys are getting all these scoops."

Mo looked over at his colleague. "Let's just say we've been fortunate enough to be in the right place at the right time. Wouldn't you agree, Frank?"

"Great stories," Frank put in.

Another hesitation, but when Gary spoke again, there was a newly insistent quality in his voice. "That may be," he said, "but I've got to believe that you guys are being tipped off."

Unruffled, Mo toyed with some pens and pencils that lay on his desk. "Now, that's not necessarily the case," he said. "I mean, things aren't always what they seem. Ain't that right, Frank?"

"Righter than rain." Frank twisted around and began to mark up some papers. "Take me and Mo, for instance," he said abstractedly.

"Who'd want us?" Mo leaned back in his chair and gently laughed.

"Who would ever believe that an Alabama Cracker and a Motor City ex-Panther," Frank went on, licking a finger to separate two pages, "would end up partners in the crime of news?"

"Speak for yourself," Mo said. "I happen to believe that the fourth estate's a noble calling."

"Sure it is," Frank said, "on those rare occasions when we actually live up to our ideals."

"Come on now," Mo said, "you're going too hard on us. The main thing is, we keep trying." He turned back to Gary. "But listen," he said, "what's your interest in all this? Didn't you say you had some information?"

"I said I *might* have some information," Gary replied. "But first, I'd like to know how you guys are getting the word on all this stuff."

"That's a sticky question," Mo said. "We're talking about the integrity of our sources. Their privacy."

"Serious issues of journalistic ethics," Frank put in.

"I realize that," Gary said. "But you've got to understand, we're talking about somebody's safety here. He's a friend of ours, and a veteran. This isn't just idle curiosity."

Mo leaned forward with keen interest; Frank also turned to

face us. "A vet?" Mo said. "Tell us more."

"I don't know," Gary said. "We've got privacy issues on our end, too."

Mo settled back. "So you've got your privacy issues, and we've got ours. That's a fine pickle."

"If you could just let me know how we might contact this person . . ."

"Listen," Frank said, "we may not always live up to our principles. But like Mo said, we do like to give it our best shot."

Gary sat staring into their faces.

"I'm sorry we can't be more helpful," Mo said. "But we can't divulge our sources. If you should change your mind, I mean, if there's anything you decide you'd like to share with us—"

"We'd be careful to protect your privacy," Frank added.

"It's not *my* privacy I'm worried about." Gary thought for a moment. "I'll let you know." He looked over at me and nodded, and we began to get up.

Mo also rose from behind his desk and came around to see us off. He escorted us to the head of the stairs. "If you change your minds," he said, "give me a call." He proffered a business card to Gary. Gary put it in his wallet, extracted one of his own, and handed it to Mo.

We descended the stairs, left the building, and walked toward Pennsylvania Avenue. "One thing's certain," Gary said, "they're definitely being tipped off."

Once at the avenue we stood, huddled against the cold, to wait for an empty cab. We were about to start walking toward the busier blocks closer to the Capitol when a taxi pulled to the curb to disembark its passengers. Two men got out of the back. A third swung the front door open but remained inside talking to the driver. I couldn't help notice the appearance of the two men who had gotten out. They were unshaven, unkempt, and not especially clean. One of them spoke to the man in the front seat. "I'm telling you, John," he asserted, "this is the place."

"I don't know," the one called John said. "Something about it doesn't look right."

"But this is it," the other one insisted. "13th Street. I remember it clear as day."

"It's the trees," said the one who hadn't yet spoken, a large, fleshy man with the innocent eyes of a child. "Their leaves are all gone."

"Yeah, that's it," the one who had first spoken said. "Like Tiny said, it's just the trees make it look different."

"What does Tiny know?" John said as he climbed out of the cab. "But what can I do with you guys? If you say this is the place, I'm willing to give it a try. I got no particular place to go, do you?"

He peered at his companions; they gazed dumbly back.

"What about you, Tiny. Got any big appointments? How about you, Denny? An important business trip to London. Paris, perhaps?"

They jostled one another boisterously, and then the one called Denny said, "Follow me. It's down here."

The men walked in the direction of the *Stream's* offices.

Gary held the door of the cab while I got in. The driver turned toward us.

"Where to?"

"Give us a minute." Gary leaned into me. "Did you hear that?"

"What?"

"The guys who just got out?"

"What about them? They looked homeless. It's odd they could afford a cab."

"Did you notice the names?"

"John, I think. Denny. Why?"

"Doesn't that ring a bell? What about the other one—Tiny?"

It was coming back to me. "The article on the Maine Mast incident . . ."

"Tiny, that's hard to mistake. And wasn't there a Dennis?"

Gary asked the cabbie to drive toward the *Stream's* building. When we arrived there, Frank was ushering the three men from the cab through the front door. Gary asked the driver to pull to the curb and wait. He recovered his disguise from the pocket of his field jacket, donned the moustache and beard, and handed me the Fedora. I pulled it over my face and we shrunk into the seat, enveloped in the cab's warmly humid darkness, its cheap air freshener, and strains of vintage jazz coming from the cabbie's radio.

After a few minutes the *Stream's* upstairs lights went out; a moment later the front door opened. The men from the cab, along with Frank and Mo, stepped onto the porch. Gary and I sunk more deeply into the taxi's back seat. The homeless men began to walk toward the avenue, while Frank and Mo disappeared into an alleyway behind the building. After the headlights of their cars came sweeping across the windows of the cab, Gary asked our driver to get underway. When we approached the scruffy trio, they hailed our cab. The cabbie made to pass them, but Gary asked him to stop. He rolled down the window.

"You guys wanna share?"

"Maybe," the one called Denny said. "Where're you headed?"

"Where are *you* headed?"

"Arlington."

"That's right on our way!" Gary said with feigned surprise. "It's awful cold out there, and cabs can be pretty hard to come by on a Friday evening."

"He's right about that," the one called Tiny said.

"It's mighty nice of you to offer," said Denny, nonplussed at this unexpected act of kindness.

"Let's go, for chrissake" the one called John clamored. "It's not getting any warmer out here." Gary and I moved to the front seat, and the three men piled into the back.

After a moment John leaned forward. "Hey," he said, "weren't you the same driver brought us over?"

The cabbie looked sidewise at Gary, and Gary stretched a twenty dollar bill across my lap; the driver folded the note discreetly in his hand. "Still in the neighborhood," he said, "had to stop for gas. You guys going back to the same place?"

"Near," Denny said. "We'll show you."

We ran into a back-up on the 14th Street Bridge to Virginia, and while we waited in traffic, the men in the back deliberated.

"He gave us enough for two cabs," Denny said. "Now that we're sharing a ride, that leaves us fifteen dollars clear."

"What do you suggest we do with our grand fortune?" John said. "Buy a swanky condo? Take a deluxe vacation to Hawaii?"

"Fifteen dollars is fifteen dollars," Denny said.

"Shouldn't we give him back the extra?" Tiny asked.

"Of course not," Denny said. "He allotted a certain amount of money to get a job done. What's it to him if, through intelligent efficiencies, we get the job done cheaper than anticipated?"

"I don't know," John said, "Tiny has a point. There are some definite ethical issues involved here."

"I say the money's ours," Denny said. "Look at defense contractors. You ever see any of them give excess profits back to the government?"

We finally got across the river into Arlington. The driver exited the freeway just past the Pentagon, and at a nondescript place along the road the men asked him to pull over. Gary told them the fare was taken care of, and they got out amid an animated discussion of the additional windfall. Gary and I moved to the back.

"All right," the cabbie said, peering straight ahead, "where to now?"

"Listen—" Gary pulled off the moustache and beard. "I know this seems odd . . ."

"Hey," the driver said cooly, "it's not my job to know what folks are up to. I just take them where they want to go. I don't care if you're CIA, DIA, FBI, NSA, or just plain sneaky. Actually, I'd rather not know. As long as I get my cash, I'm cool. So, where to?"

Gary gave him Signed, Sealed & Delivered's address, and we got underway. "This is amazing," Gary whispered to me, "what luck!"

"When the spirit is eager and willing—"

"The gods join in. I see you've read your Aeschylus."

"Those guys are obviously the *Stream's* sources."

"Obviously."

"But why didn't you say something?" I asked.

"What was I going to say? Hey, we've been stalking you guys, and now we want to pry into your business?"

"I suppose you're right. But we don't know anything more about Charles than when we started."

"Yeah, that's true. But we know where these guys hang. We'll figure something out."

When we arrived at Signed, Sealed & Delivered, the Gathering was in full swing. A poetry slam was going down, and a young woman with straw-blond hair tucked under a painter's cap, whom I recognized from the last Gathering, had the floor. Roger, another man wearing a dashiki, and Tanya sat behind her coolly jamming on various drums. The blonde spoke rhythmically and emphatically, with grace and power, anger and beauty . . .

> . . . say they're protecting the status quo,
> call it international law; we know
> the trip, make sure that oil flows!
> the western world on a feeding frenzy,
> got us in its grip (a dance
> with death, and we don't care)

too worried about what we're gonna wear,
exploitation, homeless, genocide,
legacy of America's pride,
poverty, hunger it's obscene—
(stay tuned to your television screen)
mind control everywhere, lies,
big business, get your shares,
sexism, porno, mis-ogy-ny,
you won't see the president on his knee,
begging forgiveness for his sins,
(all the same if your side wins)
in his house of white he sits,
I wonder if he gives a shit?
about your sister, daughter, son,
all forgotten when the battle's won
or lost, what's the cost—to humanity,
when so-called leaders refuse to see,
the effects on you and me,
it must be fun (a world to run)
manipulate the masses,
rig the news, don't get the blues,
go down heroes in history,
(sowing untold misery)
with bombs and exploitation,
fill the bill for any nation,
resistance is the only hope,
don't be counting on the pope,
or Congress, Amnesty, it's a joke—
sold to industry, can't you see?
all we've got is you and me,
and taking it to the streets!

Smiling, amid raucous cheers, the blonde raised a fist in the

air. Roger stepped forward, and she handed him the microphone.
He paced before the audience for a moment, drummers vamping
behind him, before beginning his rap:

> Born to mean streets, sixty-five,
> lucky now to be alive,
> crack-free, hoping for a future
> better than a bullet wound suture,
> looking at the world with eyes
> focused on the prize, of happiness,
> a woman and child—my pride,
> making my way, on the glide,
> thanks to Pinky's intervention,
> missed a life of federal detention,
> now look around, ain't something wrong?
> (you know I hate to ruin the song)
> but everywhere I hear the noise
> of warfare weapons played like toys,
> by little boys who ought to know better
> than to put this whole wide
> world in a tether,
> fresh meat sent to desert sands
> to keep an oil empire in our hands,
> I tell you dude it makes me weep,
> the company that my nation keeps,
> or thinking bout my brothers offed
> in their prime by a Kalashnikov,
> tell the truth, I don't mind saying
> by dark of night I'm sure nuf praying,
> frankly for some better weather
> (having trouble keeping it together)
> a low-down dirty stroke of luck, just
> when I thought I'd had enough,

> and what is worse is where we're going,
> with no leader showing, the way,
> the dude who brought my life around,
> taken off for unknown ground . . .

As Roger walked away from the drummers their playing intensified to a fever pitch. A chant erupted that was soon joined by everyone in the room.

"NO WAR! NO WAR! NO WAR! NO WAR!"

The chant went on for several minutes. When it finally subsided, Ben came to the center of the Gathering with his guitar in hand. He pulled up a stool, sat down, and began to pick out a melody I easily recognized. The room grew hushed as he voiced the youthful Bob Dylan's visionary plaint of a white dove who longs to sleep in the sand; of the yearnings of a disenfranchised humanity for an end to injustice and violence. The Gathering was silent, mesmerized by Ben's lovely voice and intricate guitar work. I looked over at Gary but he was beyond my reach; I took his hand. Some of the couriers began to sing along. The energy in the room had shifted from frenetic tension to something approaching peace. When Ben finished, everyone just breathed for a moment, until the blonde stepped to the center of the room with microphone in hand.

"Beautiful," she said, wiping away a tear. "All right, the floor's open. Here's your chance to stick it to the man."

Gary extricated his hand from mine and began to rise. "I think I've got something, Sheila." He went to the center and took the microphone amid hoots of encouragement. Setting his gaze into an imagined distance, he began to speak, pausing occasionally to organize his thoughts, to search out a rhyme:

> Mankind always and ever errs
> hence this world of constant cares,
> but shall we ditch the stars and stripes

for just a few ill-thought-out swipes
at dictators who'd have us scrape,
the ground beneath and bend the nape?

You say this hilltop city's dead,
we've made a farce of liberty,
what history calls a patriot's tread
is just the stomp of tyranny;
that greed and grasping motivate
our each and every sallying,
the people numb to contemplate
with bread and circus dallying.

But what if better angels yet
may guide this country's heart of hearts,
from sea to shining sea don't bet
we've lost all our most noble parts;
just look around you, seeing here
a brotherhood of friends most dear,
free to speak and free to choose
each to each and private muse . . .

Youth is ever dashing forth,
as it is and yet should be,
still not far from child's true north,
what's out of joint in life they see;
with piercing pain they're driven on
to rectify the wrongs they feel
(youth our treasure, promise, hope,
the future of our commonweal!)

But if my time is any guide
there's just one thing I'll dare impart,
(hazarding at thirty-eight,
sounding like some dumb old fart):

the world's a stage of struggle still,
mankind yet to find its way
to the peace that's promised well,
by every avatar to date.

And in this murky, mucky place
we strive to find a course that's right,
but much to our complete dismay
it's seldom marked in black and white . . .

Here Gary paused, seeming at a loss. He turned and faced the
drummers; they beat out their steady, rhythmic undercurrent with
renewed energy. Appearing to gain new inspiration, Gary turned
back toward the Gathering and plunged on . . .

Can it be that tyranny
has clasped its hands around the throat,
of this, our land of liberty?
(If that's the case, don't gloat, don't gloat!)
Do war-mongers and twisted souls
monopolize our destiny,
and we in meek submission gaze
upon a wrecked humanity?

I cannot look upon such scenes
without a loss of soul most deep,
yet evidence piles up and up,
a mountain back to home most steep;
But still within me something stirs,
an old belief in something fair,
a pull that's brought us through the years,
the promise of—America?

And at a loss to calculate, the ups
and downs, and summarize,

> it seems the only path that suits
> is through the heart, with open eyes;
> honor every thing that's true,
> cherish every living soul,
> count on love to bring us home,
> each to each and make us whole . . .

Gary hesitated again, as if perplexed, this time, by his own words. He shook his head, handed the microphone to Sheila and, to a smattering of uncertain applause, marked a small bow. One of the drummers played a flourish and the others joined in. Gary came to me.

"I'm not sure what that meant," he said.

Guitars now came out and the Gathering devolved, as it usually seemed to do, into an open jam session. Gary and I were tired and got a cab to my place. We spent much of Saturday in bed resting and loving. Daylight was fading when we went to the living room, sipped tea, and decided to go out for dinner.

We walked down the avenue to my regular Chinese place. While we waited for our dinners Gary and I read about our astrological signs on the placemats. He's a horse: "idealistic and humanitarian," "gifted speaker," but also "needs absolute freedom of maneuver," and "born seducer." I'm a sheep: "changeable free spirit," "warm-hearted," "disorganized and extremely vulnerable," and also, "makes a good artisan."

We strolled on the avenue after dinner. We considered a movie, but none of the celluloid dreams on offer seemed half as rich as our time together, and we wound our way back to my place.

From Gary's papers:
November 14, 1990
Shades of childhood fairy tales. You, marvelous princess, alone in high tower to which I, through mysterious stroke of fortune,

gain entrance. Entrance and entranced, Rapunzel let down your hair! At the loom you showed me your ways, told me the tapestry of your youth. I see the previsioned forms in beginning border strokes, earthen browns and greens, red of cherries, blue of sky, darkness of death. Guiding my hands, you taught me how to thread the weft with arcing loop before pressing down, counting warps and looping back, making the world anew in woolen hue . . .

And then: interrupted life, lost father, lost youth. Desert vastness; Navajo weaver, strong and true; White Shell Woman and healing times. You brought yourself to me like this and then, sitting on your bed, took my old field jacket in hand (paternal relic) and with your needle began to stitch. You hummed old songs while you marked the design—I singing along—adding filigree most fine until it appeared like a star. You offered me the magic coat, blessed with your sign of peace, and laughing fell on me like rain.

Sweet Baby James and Laura Nyro; Neruda and Barrett Browning out loud; candle crystalline bath in the wee hours; sleeping like cats intertwined and furry; in the morning, orange juice and coffee and the *Washington Post* . . .

& & &

SUNDAY MORNING we lounged over the paper. Gary sprawled across the easy chair, partly obscured by newsprint. Wrapped in my kimono, he was a different man than the one I had known only vaguely a week earlier—now that I had covered him with my kisses, poured myself into him and he into me. In the night he spoke of many things: Vietnam and his brother Jim, how his father absconded to California with a younger woman, his own ill-fated attempt at marriage and the child he fathered. Tears came to his eyes when he talked of his daughter, to whom he'd given up custody. She and her mother were in Switzerland, where his ex's job at an international foundation had taken her.

But this morning he was bright as, with wry detachment, he analyzed the newspaper's contents. "Look at this," he said, "*China Presses Crackdown on Dissidents.* They're taking advantage of the democracies' distraction with the Persian Gulf, of course." A little later he laughed over a commentary: "Can you believe that crazy Kissinger, still talking balance of power like some latter-day Metternich!"

We gaily made waffles and eggs together; but after our flurry of preparations we just sat at the table staring into our plates, suddenly aware of what we had almost forgotten while we rested and grew closer—Charles. Our eyes met, and as a kind of grace Gary said, "I hope he's all right." We ate quietly. After coffee he got up from his chair, collected the newspaper into a pile and said, "Let's go out there and see what we can find."

We drove along the river until the Pentagon loomed beside the parkway, and Gary guided me through a series of turns to the stretch of road where the homeless men had de-cabbed Friday evening. We pulled onto the shoulder and got out. The weather was turning; the sun was bright, but a stiff wind blew out of the northwest. The Pentagon lay between us and the river, obscuring, with its stolid bulk, the city's monuments. At a little distance we could see the hillsides of Arlington Cemetery, flecked all over with their white gravestones.

Walking along the road, we scanned the margins for any sign of human habitation. Sunday morning traffic was light. We went over an intersection and down the embankment on the other side, and then moved back along the freeway toward the river. We searched nooks and crannies, all places hidden by brush or otherwise out of sight. Finally, doubling under an overpass, we came upon what we were seeking. Partially hidden by a series of abutments, sheltered by the roadway above, an encampment was signaled by sleeping rolls, duffle bags, a plastic tarpaulin, and the smoldering ashes of a fire.

"This could be it," Gary said.

"Or—any homeless camp."

"Whoever it belongs to," he remarked, poking in the embers with a stick, "it looks like we just missed them."

"What do you want to do?"

"I suppose we could wait around."

He hugged himself against the cold. His light field jacket, barely sufficient in the sun, was woefully inadequate in the frigid shadows of the overpass. My long fall coat was little better; I wrapped my arms around him.

"We could walk around, see if we can find them."

He thought for a moment. "I'd hate for them to feel they were being pursued."

"Oh, we wouldn't want that." Lost in concentration, he missed the irony.

"What say we get this fire going again."

"Are you sure they wouldn't mind?" Now I was in earnest. "I mean, this is their home, for what it's worth."

He agreed that we'd be taking liberties but convinced me that, under the circumstances, they would understand. We collected some brush and rekindled their fire, over which we crouched with arms extended. We stayed this way for some time, occasionally climbing up to the overpass to survey the area, hoping to see them trudging our way; or walking in brisk circles to keep our blood flowing. An hour passed. We glanced at their meager belongings and exchanged weak smiles. It was heartbreaking to see the conditions under which they lived. Yet I was grateful that they had secured this shelter, for all its primitiveness. They had been pushed to the margins, but at least no further than this!

I began to feel we had outstayed our welcome, such as it was. Goldilocks, I remarked, at the home of the three bears.

"I don't suppose any of these beds would be just right," Gary reflected.

"Nor the porridge."

We got up and smothered the fire, climbed the overpass, and scanned the landscape one last time before returning to the car.

I dropped Gary at his place with an agreement to meet that evening. We went to a violin concert at the Phillips Gallery and dined at the Afghan place across from the Hilton. We both needed rest and decided to sleep in our own beds for the night.

We made a plan to return to the homeless encampment the next evening.

I took my car to the clinic on Monday and arrived at Signed, Sealed & Delivered at six-thirty. Couriers were dispersing in cars and on bikes. I found Gary tidying up at Charles's desk in back. On our way through the anteroom he voiced surprise at seeing lights through the workshop door, which stood ajar. "Come on in," he said, "there's someone I want you to meet." He pushed the door open and we went in.

Bent intently over an upside-down bicycle frame was a slender man, his features obscured by a face shield. He grasped something with a pliers in one hand; in the other he wielded an acetylene torch. Gary and I stood clear and watched. The welder's thinning hair was pulled into a ponytail that looped over his visor's strap and fell below the nape of his neck. Working with deft deliberateness, he constantly shifted position to obtain the desired angle on the joint he was repairing. After a couple of minutes he made a few finishing strokes and rose up. It was only then that he noticed us.

"Well, well," he said, lifting the visor, "look who's here. I didn't see you come in."

"I didn't want to disturb you in the middle of the weld," Gary said.

"This thing gave out on Kem this afternoon," the welder said.

"I promised him I'd have it ready by morning."

"You're indefatigable, brother. Have you met Marj?"

"I don't believe I've had the pleasure." He held out his hand.

"Randy's our Vulcan, and also our resident Zen master."

"You're too kind."

I recognized Randy from a couple of the Gatherings. He was older than most of the couriers, mid-forties I guessed, with a penetrating gaze and a welcoming smile. We exchanged greetings.

He turned to Gary. "What's going on, old boy?"

"Other than the usual Dispatch business, mainly puzzling over this Pinky thing."

"Who isn't?"

"What do you make of it?"

"I don't know." Randy drew out his words thoughtfully. "It's certainly strange of him to disappear like this. That is, assuming nothing grave has happened to him."

"I think it's got to do with this Iraq situation," Gary said.

"Really?" Randy's eyes grew deep. "What makes you say that?"

"I don't know, pieces of evidence here and there."

"You must know more than I do," Randy said. "I mean, we have very little to go on. Just the fact that he's gone, really." He thought for a moment before continuing. "Sure, he was in the service, but I don't see what that would have to do with it. He's not in the reserves, is he?"

"No, but there are other things." Gary looked toward the windows that ran, just below the ceiling, along the shop's front wall.

"Other things? Like what?"

"I probably shouldn't talk about it."

Randy directed his gaze to the bicycle he'd been working on. "I see."

"I don't mean to be mystifying."

Randy's eyes met Gary's. "But if you can't talk about it, there's really not much I can say. Know what I mean?"

Gary nodded.

"Anyhow, I better get back to work. If I don't finish this thing, I'll never get out of here. Maribel and I have our book club. But if you decide you want to tell me what's on your mind, let me know. You've got me intrigued."

"Right."

Randy took Gary by the elbow. "And listen," he said, "you can count on my complete confidence, whatever it is."

We left the shop and got into my car. Our progress was good as we headed south against the current of the rush hour, but once in the heart of the city, joining hordes of commuters fleeing into Virginia, we lurched to a crawl. We crept over the 14th Street Bridge slowly enough to see several planes take off and land at National Airport.

Once on the opposite shore, Gary directed me around a series of cloverleafs to the overpass where we had found the homeless encampment. We pulled over and got out. The wind had dropped since the day before and the weather was milder. We stood together on the shoulder.

"What's our plan?" I asked.

"Good question."

"They seemed friendly enough."

"Why don't we just play it by ear?"

I tugged at his sleeve and we climbed down the embankment, strobed by the headlights of passing cars. Once at the bottom we saw smoke emerging through the abutments that shielded the homeless men's camp. Gary straightened himself and took my hand as we wended our way through the concrete pylons. Just before we reached the encampment, he released my hand and moved ahead.

I followed.

They didn't notice our arrival until we emerged into the glow of their fire. The largest one—the one they call Tiny—started violently and reached for something. I reflexively grasped Gary's arm and shrank upon myself, while the other men restrained their companion with strong arms and calming words.

"Easy," the one called John said, "get a grip. It's just a couple of regular folks."

Tiny, panting heavily, dropped the piece of board he had picked up.

"Come on over," Denny said. "He's all right. Tiny just don't like to be surprised, that's all."

John looked toward us. "You're not cops, are you?"

We assured him that we weren't the law.

"Good," he said, "cause if we get run out of one more stinking place, who knows what'll happen to us."

Gary and I approached. I crouched down and apologized to Tiny.

"It's not your fault," he said, his breath still jagged and shallow. "I'm more skittish than most."

I placed a hand on his shoulder and briefly met John's eyes. Then, looking toward Denny, the man the *Stream* called Dennis Evans, I noted that he was intently staring at Gary.

He seemed puzzled. "Hey," he suddenly said, "don't I know you?"

"I don't think we've met." Gary cast a quick, apprehensive glance in my direction.

"But I feel like I've seen you someplace," Denny insisted.

"Yeah," John said, turning now toward me, "you too. I've got that same feeling, like I've met you both somewhere. I just can't get a decent bead on it."

Tiny scratched his beard and looked us over. "Aren't you two with the newspaper?" He looked to John and Denny for their reactions.

"Well, yes," Gary suddenly improvised, "that's correct. We are, in fact, with the paper."

"Yeah," Denny drew out, addressing his companions, "it was the first time we went there, remember? There were a bunch of people in the upstairs room." He turned to us. "We must have seen you then."

"That seems right," John said, "must be it." His gaze shifted between Gary and me. "Do Mo and Frank need something?"

"It's about the guy who's doing all this stuff in the cemetery," Gary eked out slowly, choosing his words with care. "We'd like to get some information on him."

"We already told Frank and Mo everything we know," John said, "—everything we're at liberty to divulge, that is."

Gary seemed at a loss. His eyes flashed me a silent S.O.S.

"We know that," I heard myself putting in. "But people don't always remember everything at first. Telling something a second, third, even a fourth time can really jog the memory."

"Exactly," Gary said, getting his bearings now and not missing a beat. "So if we could just ask you a few questions . . ."

"There ain't that much to tell," Denny said. "But I guess we could go over it all again if you'd like. Let me get ya'll a seat."

He disappeared into the shadows and returned with two large plastic paint cans. He placed them upside-down near the fire and invited us to sit down.

"Shoot," he said.

"For starters," Gary entoned with his best reportorial inflections, "what's the man's name?"

"That's easy," Tiny chuckled.

"Name's Chuck," John put in.

"Last name?" Gary asked.

The men looked at one another. "Never got a last name," Denny said.

"Just call him Chuck," Tiny said flatly.

"What does he look like?" I asked.

"Well built," Denny said. "Not too tall. Black guy."

"Funny eyes," Tiny said, squinting his words out.

"Green and brown," John said, "like . . . like . . ."

"Like agate?" Gary asked.

"Yes, that's it! Exactly!"

It was definitely Charles.

"When's the last time you saw him?" Gary asked.

The men deliberated among themselves for a minute or more. Finally Denny responded. "That would have been about a week ago."

The others nodded.

"Where was he?"

"Right here," John replied and looked toward me. "Right where you're sitting."

"He comes here?" Gary asked.

"Sometimes."

"How often, would you say?"

They exchanged glances among themselves. "It's hard to say," John said. "He sort of comes and goes."

"Comes and goes?" Gary repeated.

"Every now and then he stops in at dinnertime," John went on. "Sometimes he shares our mess, sometimes brings something in."

"He brought a real nice Thanksgiving supper," Denny said.

"With all the fixin's," Tiny gleefully added.

"He might of been here last night," John said. "We were away. Somebody came, anyway. Made a fire."

"Usually he stops in late to chat," Denny said. "It must get lonesome."

"Does he stay overnight?" I asked.

Tiny shook his head as the others voiced a long no.

"Any idea where he's living?" Gary asked.

"Out there." Tiny stretched an arm away into the darkness.

"Out where?"

"There," Tiny repeated, stretching out his arm again.

Gary looked in the direction of his gesture. "Over by the cemetery?"

"No," John said, "not *by* the cemetery. *In* the cemetery."

A chill ran through me.

"But where, exactly?" Gary's voice was a little shaky. "The cemetery's a big place."

"Wait a minute," Denny said to his fellows. "You're giving these folks the wrong impression. It's not like we know the man's coordinates all the time. He never told us flat out that he was living in there. Let's face it, this is nothing but rank speculation."

"An educated assessment, I'd call it." John said.

The men were silent.

"Let's go back to basics," I said. "What can you say you know for absolute certain?"

"Saw his bivouac couple a times," Tiny offered.

"That's right," Denny agreed.

"Could you direct us to it?" Gary asked.

"You don't get it," John said. "He doesn't stay in one place. The guards'd have him in a heartbeat."

The others seconded his remark.

"The way we figure it," Denny said, "he stays on the move. Only makes a camp after dark, somewhere with good cover. Maybe he was LURP, Phoenix. Who knows?"

"We asked him," Tiny put in.

"Asked him what?" I said.

"Where he lives," John replied.

"Remember his answer?" Tiny crowed mirthfully.

"Something crazy," John said, "I remember that much."

"Crazy?" Denny protested. "It was from the Bible. Didn't you learn your verses in Sunday school?"

"Yeah," John said ruefully. "But they ended up with everything else I learned in Sunday school—down the drain in

Vietnam school."

"Say it," Tiny blurted, laughing quietly to himself.

"The bird of the air has its nest," Denny recited. "The fox has its hole. But the son of man has no place to lay his head. I for one remember my Bible verses."

Tiny laughed out loud. The others gazed into the fire.

"He said that?" I asked.

"Nutty, ain't it," John said. He poked in the fire with a stick, stirring the embers into a fiery, fushcia-peach glow.

"Sometimes he asks us to take something over to the paper," Denny said.

"Pays good," Tiny added.

"Messages for the *Underground Stream*?" Gary asked.

"You should know," John said. "That's where you work, isn't it?"

"Of course," Gary replied awkwardly. "I'm just checking the facts . . ."

Denny broke the embarrassed silence that followed. "We were about to have some grub when you folks arrived. It's humble fare, but you're welcome to it, if you'd like to join us."

We thanked him, but declined his offer and took our leave. After climbing the embankment, we made our way to the car through passing headlights more infrequent than when we had arrived. Our mission had been a success. We had proof positive that Charles was alive (the agate eyes) and that he was behind the recent events in the cemetery. But we felt little exaltation as we crossed the river into town. Charles was alive, true enough, but it was doubtful whether he could be said to be well. His current life sounded even more marginal than those of the men under the highway. And that biblical quote—likening himself to Jesus—had he developed a messianic complex? Were my worst fears con-firmed? A serious relapse?

Gary took exception to my worries.

"You've got to realize," he said, "the man's not incapable of irony. You can't read his comments too literally."

"Still, I'm concerned."

"Naturally. The situation is far from ideal." We lapsed into an anxious silence as we coursed up Connecticut Avenue toward my building. I was negotiating the traffic clotted at Dupont Circle, sensing all around us colored electric lights and scurrying pedestrians, when Gary spoke again.

"I don't feel great about lying to those guys."

"Neither do I. But it seemed necessary, given the circumstances. We'll find a way to make it up to them."

"What to do now?" he said. "That's the real question."

We discussed searching the cemetery; but if Charles established his shifting bivouacs after nightfall, as the homeless men averred, the prospect of scouring the place after closing, eluding MPs all the while, was daunting from several angles. There was also Gary's finely tuned respect for Charles's privacy.

"Chasing him down just doesn't seem right," he said. We were pulling into my building's garage.

"Forgetting about him doesn't, either."

"No one said we're going to forget about him."

"I know." I reached over the console and took his hand. We were both a little at sea, trying to process what we had learned at the homeless encampment. We went quietly up to my place, made dinner together, and held one another long and lovingly into the night.

& & &

DURING THE LAST WEEK of November my clients were more restive than ever. With Bush and Baker furiously lobbying the U. N. for military action against Iraq, there was the scent of imminent violence in the air. Jonathan Straiman's child soldier gave him no peace, and his migraines returned with a vengeance. Former morgue worker Ron Dixon's macabre hordes assailed him relentlessly down the city's sidewalks by day, and at night besieged the dilapidated pickup where he slept in ragged fragments. Forward artillery controller Jason Howard's nocturnal ramblings took him ever further afield, until he finally roamed the distant hills of West Virginia. He had failed on two occasions to arrive at work on time and was afraid he would soon lose his job. But despite the horrid visions he encountered there, he was ineluctably drawn to the road . . .

They were all at our Thursday evening vets group, and there was fresh news from the media outlets. The U.N. had passed an American resolution authorizing "all necessary means" to drive Iraqi forces from Kuwait. The atmosphere was electric. Ron Dixon, peering through and beyond us to invoke his phantom legions, signaled the horrific specters with a sudden sweep of his arm: strange, ghastly prophet. Thomas Melton revealed that he had begun to fortify his basement hooch; he now plastered articles on the Persian Gulf crisis among his yellowed clippings on Vietnam, Grenada and Panama attempting, with such brittle shields, to thicken the walls of his isolation against another storm.

Finally Jonathan Straiman, driven to the wall by his somatic symptoms, extracted from his knapsack the bamboo box in which he had for years kept the relic of the boy soldier he had shot and then helplessly watched to die. We looked on spellbound as he lay the box on his lap and, carefully opening it, tenderly removed the tattered red flag. Holding the square of cloth before him, he tearfully blurted out his anguish, pleadingly asking the boy's forgiveness. Most of the men responded with quiet reverence and compassion.

But then Danny spoke. "When it comes right down to it," he said cooly, "it was him or you, wasn't it?"

Danny's comment elicited an embarrassed silence. Looking indignantly around the group, he pressed his point. "Well, I'm right, ain't I? Even if the kid was a runt, he was packing, wasn't he? I mean, if you want to cut it that fine, we're all nothing but a bunch of war criminals. Ain't I right?"

"Speak for yourself," Thomas said.

There was another strained silence.

Danny leaned into into his chair back and took a more conciliatory tone. "Don't get me wrong," he said. "I'm all for letting it out, if that's what floats your boat. It might even do the rest of us some good. Who knows?"

He then rose from his chair, walked over to Jonathan, and opened wide his arms. Jonathan too rose to his feet and the two men embraced. The others joined in with similar gestures, awkward coughs, and not a few tears.

After they were all seated, Danny spoke again.

"All right," he said, "now we got that out of our system, there's something I wanted to show you guys." He glanced around at his cohort and added, "if you don't mind moving on, that is."

No one objected, and I encouraged him to proceed with what he had to share. Reaching around to the back of his jeans, he pulled a sheaf of folded newsprint from his pocket.

"I don't know if any of you guys follow this rag," he said, "but you know me, I like to keep on top of the *subversive* viewpoint." He displayed to the group what I immediately recognized as a copy of the *Underground Stream*. A photograph of the JFK gravesite at Arlington cemetery, cordoned with bright orange police tape, graced the front page.

"They've been running a series lately on some bizarre happenings over at the cemetery," he went on. "Today's may be the weirdest yet. Listen to this."

He removed a pair of glasses from a breast pocket, adjusted them across the bridge of his nose, and began to read:

> Visitors to the JFK gravesite at Arlington Na-
> tional Cemetery were greeted by a police cordon
> this morning after a strike at one of the coun-
> try's most hallowed monuments. According to
> *Stream* sources, the cemetery command closed
> the gravesite after discovering that alterations
> had been made to the memorial overnight. The
> *Stream* was unable to verify details with Fort
> Meyers, and military authorities are not allow-
> ing anyone near the grave.

"I saw that on the news," Vernon interrupted. "They said there was a problem with the gas line for the eternal flame."

Danny looked quizzically over the rims of his glasses. "So that's the malarkey they're feeding the mainstream media, eh? Well, just keep listening." He began to read again:

> According to the *Stream's* exclusive source,
> overnight on November 28 a new inscription
> was added to the stone ellipse which bears
> excerpts from Kennedy's inaugural address, in-
> cluding the famous vow:

> *Let every nation know,*
> *Whether it wishes us well or ill,*
> *That we shall pay any price, bear any burden,*
> *Meet any hardship, support any friend,*
> *Oppose any foe, to assure the survival*
> *And the success of liberty.*

"Us dumbasses really fell for that one, didn't we?" Ron Dixon commented.

"Yeah, for all the good it did anybody," Thomas Melton added wearily.

"But there's more," Danny said, "listen up. He found his place again and resumed, reciting now in stentorian tones:

> **The memorial bears the even more famous**
>   **exhortation:**
> *Ask not what your country can do for you,*
> *Ask what you can do for your country.*
> *My fellow citizens of the world, ask not*
> *What America will do for you, but what together*
> *We can do for the freedom of man.*

"Yeah, right," Rick Dennis put in, "some freedom."

"Hold your laughter," Danny said. "I'm not to the best part yet. Where was I?" Scanning a finger down the page, he placed a hand over his heart and took up now in solemn cadences:

> *With a good conscience our only sure reward,*
> *With history the final judge of our deeds,*
> *Let us go forth to lead the land we love, asking*
>   *His blessing,*
> *And His help, but knowing that here on earth,*
> *God's work must truly be our own.*

"That's the best part?" Thomas said. "It sounds like some kind of damned sermon."

"What do you expect us to do," Ron chimed in, "get down on our knees, for chrissake?"

"You have to admit," Danny said, "that Ted Sorensen—Kennedy's speech writer—was one consummate bullshit artist. But have a little patience, we're just getting to the gist of it. Let's see, here we go . . ."

> **After the memorial's final excerpt, a new quo-**
> **tation had been roughly, though not unartfully,**
> **hewn into the low wall that encircles the hal-**
> **lowed gravesite:**
> *It's like taking a drink:*

*The effect wears off
and you have to take another.*

"Taking a drink?" Jonathan Straiman put in. "What's that got to do with anything?"

"If you can just wait a god-forsaken minute," Danny said. "It's all explained right here."

"Fine."

Danny peered into the newsprint and picked up where he had left off:

> **The *Stream's* research has uncovered that the added quotation is from the autumn of 1963, when Kennedy was discussing introducing American troops into Southeast Asia. "They say it's necessary to restore confidence and maintain morale," Kennedy had said. "But it will be just like Berlin. The troops will march in. The bands will play. The crowds will cheer. And in four days, everyone will have forgotten. Then we will be told that we have to send in more troops. It's like taking a drink. The effect wears off, and you have to take another."**

Danny settled back in his chair and removed his reading glasses. "That Kennedy was a real card. He fucked up the Bay of Pigs, big time. But at least he learned something from that whole fiasco, not like these bozos we've got running the show nowadays . . ."

Our time was nearing its end. Danny passed the newspaper around the circle. The men squinted at a photograph on the article's back pages, clearly taken with a long lens, that documented what appeared to be freshly hewn inscriptions on the polished granite of the late president's memorial.

"Anyway," Danny said, "this commie rag says they think whoever did this is responsible for a couple other of these shenani-gans over at Arlington. If you want my opinion, it's most likely some wise-ass. Or a complete fruitcake. Defacing federal monu-ments is serous fricking business." He paused while Rick Dennis returned to him his copy of the *Stream*, and then added, "not like I give a crap or anything."

❦ ❦ ❦

FRIDAY AFTER WORK I cabbed to Signed, Sealed & Delivered. Gary and I walked down the block to a little Jamaican restaurant, and when we returned to the shop the Gathering was coalescing. There was a lot of disquiet over the latest Gulf news, and copies of the *Underground Stream* passed from hand to hand. A few of the couriers had begun a loose-jointed drumming session, and in one corner someone casually strummed a guitar. Gary and I were standing near the refreshment table chatting with Tanya when Henry approached.

"Gary," he said, "there are some guys outside say they want to speak with you."

"Who are they? What do they want?"

"I don't know," Henry said. "They didn't want to give their names."

"They're probably looking for a job. Do you mind asking them to come in?"

"I did," Henry said, "but they wanted to wait outside. I got to tell you," he added quietly, "they don't look so hot. Kind of like they're homeless."

"How many are there?" Gary asked.

"Three."

Gary and I exchanged a meaningful glance.

"Okay," Gary said. "You say they're out front?"

"Yep."

Gary and I excused ourselves to Tanya and followed Henry towards the anteroom, put on our coats, and went out. There they were—Denny, John, and Tiny—standing in a rough circle chatting with Ben and Tomás. When we approached, they looked with surprise in our direction.

"These gentlemen have a message for you," Ben said. "They say it's from *Chuck*."

Henry's eyes widened.

"We didn't expect it to be you," Denny babbled.

John stepped back and peered up at the building's signboard. "Signed, Sealed & Delivered. What kind of place is this, anyway? Why couldn't we just come to the paper, like usual?"

"The paper?" Ben asked. He looked toward Gary.

"It's a long story." Gary turned to speak to the homeless men. "Listen," he said, "I can explain everything. But wouldn't you like to get out of this cold? We can go up to my office, where we can speak in private."

"We're not used to being inside," John said. "It makes us kind of nervous, frankly. Especially Tiny, here."

"The food and drink's good," Henry coaxed, "and everybody's friendly. Why don't ya'll join us?"

"Don't know," Tiny said. His big, soft eyes swam vaguely in his fleshy face.

"If you don't mind my asking," Ben piped up, addressing our ragged visitors with obvious agitation, "tell us more about this *Chuck*. Is that *Chuck* as in Charles? As in Charles Pinckney?" After a glance toward Gary and me, he redirected his gaze to the homeless men.

"Don't know anything about Charles or Pinckney," Denny said. "Just Chuck is all we know."

Ben stared insistently at Gary, but receiving no response, turned once again to the trio of envoys. "Could I ask what this

Chuck looks like?"

"Well-built, black guy," John said.

"Dons full cammo," Denny supplied.

"Eyes like cammo, too," Tiny whispered. "Green and brown . . ."

Upon hearing this, Tomás ran off toward the shop. Gary called after him but he did not stop. Ben was speechless. He looked to Henry, who was no more prepared to comment.

"What the heck," Denny said to John, "may as well go in a minute. Tiny, I guess you can wait out here if you don't care to join us."

We escorted Denny and John into the building, leaving Tiny near the entrance, hugging himself against the cold. Ben sidled up to Gary as we crossed the anteroom.

"Gary?!" he exclaimed in a forced whisper.

"I'll explain everything," Gary mouthed under his breath. "Just let me talk to these gentlemen first."

When we walked into the DMZ a full-blown drum circle had erupted. The beat was solemn but forceful, and it was accompanied by an insistent chant: "Pink-Man! Pink-Man! Pink-Man! Pink-Man!" Denny and John looked startled and uneasy as Gary directed them toward the refreshment table. While they loaded their plates, casting nervous glances toward the circle, Gary took me aside. "I'm going to take these guys upstairs. Do me a favor, if you don't mind. See if you can't keep a lid on things down here while I hear what they have to say."

I took Ben and Henry each by the arm and directed them toward the circle, soliciting their assistance. They secured me a drum and sat on either side of me. When Gary passed with John and Denny, couriers called to him over the chanting.

"What gives with the Pinkman?"

"Yeah, tell us about *Chuck*!"

Gary turned and the drums quieted. "Listen," he said, "these gentlemen came to talk with me. They're my guests. So I ask, for the moment, that you give us some peace. Then we'll see where we are."

Gary, Denny, and John climbed the stairway and the drumming recommenced. I played in stone silence, trying to offer a calming presence while others made animal calls, shouted anguished slogans of freedom, or hummed unnamable tunes.

We were in the middle of a second round when Gary and the homeless men reappeared on the spiral stairway. Denny and John, standing stock-still, observed our circle in open amazement. As the Gathering became aware of their presence we stilled our drums and looked expectantly in their direction. Gary escorted his guests down the steps and towards the circle. When they reached us Gary stopped, brought the two men around on either side of him, and addressed us.

"Okay," he said, "let me introduce these gentlemen. But before you go and get all excited, I want to say a couple of things. First, as you've already guessed, they bring news of the Pinkman."

Whoops and catcalls erupted from around the circle.

"Let me finish," Gary said. "The other thing I want to say is this. What these guys are about to tell you may be a little shocking. All I ask it that you take an adequate amount time to digest it. Don't rush off and do something impulsive."

"All right, already," Ben said. "Quit lecturing us and let the gentlemen speak, will you?"

A flourish of drums.

"Fine, then," Gary said, "let's get down to it. This is Denny and John." The two men nodded in greeting. "They're going to fill you in on what they know about Pinky. Denny, do you want to start?"

"Sure." Denny stepped forward uncertainly and looked around the circle, seeking out our eyes. "Heck," he said, "we didn't know Chuck had stirred up such a ruckus. We figured he was just out there doing his own thing. You know, like us. Gary told us how he up and disappeared on you. That must have been pretty upsetting."

"Where is he?" someone called out.

"I'm getting to that," Denny said. "But I want you to bear in mind that what I'm about to tell you is merely speculation."

"Not really," John countered.

"John and I have our differences on that."

"Where is he?" came the call again.

"Let the gentlemen finish," Gary said.

John put himself forward a little. "He's in the cemetery," he said bluntly.

A shocked silence, punctuated by gasps and moans, came over the room. Gary, immediately realizing the misunderstanding, spoke to dispel it. "No, no," he said, "you don't get it. Pinky isn't dead." There was a collective exhalation of relief. "Do you want to continue, John?"

"Will do," John said. "Like I said, he's in the cemetery. But like Gary here just told you, not dead. He's living . . . *in* the cemetery. I know that sounds creepy, but it is what it is."

"What cemetery?" someone called out.

"The big one. You know, Arlington. Heroes' last resting place and all that schmaltz."

"Living there?" Tomás asked.

Denny stepped forward. "Listen," he said, "we're not certain he's living in there. We've just seen his bivouac a couple of times."

"With all due respect," John said, "my friend Denny here doesn't know what he's talking about. Where else is the guy going to live? We reconnoiter the area every day, and we never see him anywhere else. And when he comes to share our mess, he always leaves in the same direction—toward there."

"I still say it's speculation."

The two men fell silent. John rolled his eyes and looked away.

"John, Denny," Gary said, "what about the messages?"

"Oh yeah," Denny said. "Chuck gives us these messages, and we take them to the *Underground Stream* newspaper. He pays us real decent for our labors."

"Dig it," Sheila cried out. "The *Stream!*"

"Messages?" Ben erupted. "What do they say?"

"We can't help you with that," John said. "It's like we told Gary, we're sworn to secrecy."

Denny nodded in agreement.

Gary addressed Denny and John. "Guys, remember what I told you upstairs. We're among friends here. I think it's time these people know what's going on."

"Hey," John said, "you can say whatever you want. But we're not about to rat out a brother. Not after he's sworn us to silence."

"All right," Gary said, "but I think these people need to know. I hope you guys understand."

The homeless men shrugged noncommittally, as if washing their hands of the matter, and Gary turned to the Gathering. "You know these stunts that have been going down in the cemetery, at least according to the *Underground Stream . . .*"

"All the news that's not fit to print!" Sheila shouted. She waved a copy in the air, and there was a stir of laughter throughout the room.

"Well," Gary said, "we have reason to believe—"

"Reason to believe?" Ben snorted. "Get it out, for chrissake."

"Pinky's doing them!" Henry guessed.

Gary's nod precipitated an immediate uproar. He asked for quiet. "Pay attention," he said, "because this is super important. Like I said, don't you guys do anything rash, like running over to Arlington to check out the situation."

"Why not?" Sheila said. "This is totally awesome!"

"Why not?" Gary repeated. "For one thing, as best we know, the Pinkman only makes his camps at night. There's super tight security in the cemetery after hours, bound to be even tighter with what's been going down over there lately. You could get busted for trespassing on what is essentially a military base, not a pleasant prospect. Second, Pinky is now wanted on several criminal counts, and he has obviously taken great pains to remain under cover. You could blow that cover if you go poking your nose around where it doesn't belong. And last, but not least, the man probably wishes to be left alone. After all, if he had wanted any of us to join him, he could have simply invited us."

The Gathering turned quiet.

"Try to understand," Gary said. "I'm not saying that Pinky's dissing us. We all know better. There are just times when a man's got to do what he's got to do. And sometimes, he's got to do it by himself."

"But how is he surviving?" Roger remarked from across the circle. "I mean, it's getting pretty cold out there."

"That's true," Gary said. "But remember, the man got through Vietnam. He's sharp and resourceful. You all know that. He's taken care of Signed, Sealed & Delivered all these years. And one other thing, very important to remember. Loose. Lips. Sink. Ships. Got it?"

A few of the couriers nodded.

"Let me hear you!"

There was a general affirmation, and the circle slowly broke up. Some of the couriers came up to talk with Denny and John. I took a plate of food out to Tiny, who again declined an offer to join the Gathering. He and I were still chatting when Gary came out with his friends. We said goodnight to the three men and watched them lope toward the main drag to catch a cab. Gary and I went inside. Another drumming had commenced, this time powerful, triumphant, glorious and happy: the gnawing tensions of three months dispelled by Denny and John's welcome news. The graver points of Charles's situation were overweighted by the simple fact that he was alive, and by awe at the acts of political theater he had engineered at Arlington.

Gary led me to the spiral stairway. Once we were upstairs, I said, "So, the cat's out of the bag with the Gathering."

"There didn't seem to be much choice." He pulled a chair out from a café table for me. "Besides, I've got to believe that *Chuck* wanted them to know. He's too sage to think that he could send envoys out here unnoticed on a Friday evening."

"Well, it makes things less complicated for us, in any case. I mean, we won't have to dissemble any longer about what we know."

"Perhaps."

At my request, he then filled me in on his conversation with Denny and John. They had added little about Charles's situation, though they had seen him earlier that day, when he asked them to act as envoys to Gary.

"But wasn't there supposed to be a message?"

"Ah, yes, the message," Gary said with a wry laugh. "Here it is." He removed a folded paper from the pocket of his shirt and handed it to me. I uncreased it. One inscrutable sentence flowed across the page in a low and fluid longhand: *You're acting like a knight trying to move like a rook trying to move like a bishop.*

I was flummoxed. "What do you make of this?" I asked.

"Cortázar."

"Cortázar?"

"It's from *Hopscotch*, a favorite book of mine. I'd say that *Chuck* is yanking my chain, in a way he knows is sure to get my attention."

"That doesn't sound like Charles."

"I'm not saying he's being hostile. Just look at it as playful banter—but banter with a purpose, if I know the man. And the chess metaphor is apt. It recalls certain knock-down, drag-out struggles conducted under the hardwoods of Dupont Circle."

"Do you think it's some kind of clue?"

"Your guess is as good as mine. I'll have to give it some thought." His distant expression betrayed no sense of what was on his mind. To lighten the mood, I told him that my father had once tried to teach me chess but that I had been a poor student.

Gary smiled and seemed to snap out of his preoccupations. He took the paper from me briskly, returned it to his pocket, and offered me a lesson; we moved to the table where the company's board lived. After he explained the slyly oblique movements of the bishop, the rook's square stalwartness and the knight's gallantly off-centered leaps, I spent an hour trying to sneak past his airtight defense: all to the accompaniment of exuberant drums from below. If any of this was supposed to suggest some enlightenment regarding Charles's situation, neither of us managed to grasp it. To distract ourselves further we played the pinball machines; downstairs, the drumming shifted to guitars and the customary jam session. Finally we sat on the sofa and rested, my head on his shoulder, as the music below abated to excited murmurings of conversation.

We had grown sleepy and decided to go home. As we descended the spiral stairs, we saw several couriers bent intently over something on the floor. When we crossed over to them, they parted to display the object of their concentration. It was a large piece of poster board over which Henry crouched, art marker in hand, expending meticulous care.

"We were so psyched about the Pinky news," Ben said, "we had to do something."

"Man, he inspired us," Tomás enthused.

"You're not going overboard, I trust," Gary said.

Henry spoke between strokes. "We were just shooting the bull," he said, "and Tanya brought up these army recruiting ads they show on TV. You know, how they make the military look all glorious and everything. *Be all you can be*," he went on with deep

TV narrator profundity.

"They make it sound like a perfectly normal way to boost your career," Ali remarked.

"Fun places to go," Roger said.

"Yeah," Ben put in, "one big vacation."

"We got to talking," Sheila said, "about how they never mention killing people—or getting killed and maimed yourself. You know, the cold, raw business of violence."

Henry sketched in a few last strokes before pulling abruptly away from his handiwork. "Anyway," he said, "this is what we came up with . . ."

Gary and I stepped around to where we could properly assess Henry's efforts. In harsh and garish colors a soldier, jut-jawed and eye-bulged, ruthlessly bayoneted a downed adversary. With blood high-geysering from his chest wound, and outlandish gobs of sweat flying from his face, the prostrate victim, his cavernous mouth brutely gaping, cries in vain for mercy. Background images, overlain without particular regard to proportion, relate to the foreground only through a dreamlike logic: burning huts of Vietnam vintage, massed tanks, fleeing refugees, roaring bombers and a mushroom cloud. In the upper left corner a woman in widow's weeds, a folded flag in her arms, mourns over a coffin. The slogan KILL ALL THAT YOU CAN KILL screams from the top of the poster in bright red lettering. On the bottom: JOIN THE WARMONGERS.

"A touch of Dada," Henry said.

"Affecting," Gary commented.

"A thing of beauty," Ben exulted.

"A masterpiece," Ali concluded.

"What do you think, Marj?" Henry asked.

I confessed that I was still trying to digest it all.

"What do you plan to do with it?" Gary asked.

"Oh, we'll find something." Henry surveyed his friends with

his gaze.

"Yes, we'll definitely find something," Ben agreed.

"These walls are pretty crowded already," Gary, gazing around the room, remarked.

"We were thinking of a slightly wider exposure than the shop," Ben said slyly, exchanging a conspiratorial glance with his companions.

"This piece definitely deserves it," Ali seconded.

"Have fun. We're splitting."

& & &

WE DROVE TO GARY'S PLACE where, gazing at a dark rectangle of sky, we lay and listened to Glen Gould's *Goldberg Variations*. Gary effused over J.S. Bach, saying that he practically invented Western music, as we marveled at the intricate sound patterns the old master had woven. In the morning Gary sat at his keyboard and worked through the *Inventions*, stopping at intervals to comment with envy on Gould's prowess.

Afterward he grew animated and paced aimlessly across the little apartment until, with sudden inspiration, he suggested we take a cycle ride. I could see he needed some outlet for his restlessness and so, still waking up after our late night, cautiously assented. We descended to the rowhouse's first floor; in the back of the hallway were several bicycles. Gary deliberated for a moment before pulling one from the collection, sizing me up, and offering it to me. He then took one for himself and we left through a back door. On the patio, he helped me to adjust my seat and handlebars.

The weather was pleasant and traffic light as we coasted out of the alleyway and into the park, skirted the zoo and pedaled along Rock Creek into town. We passed under the arching bridge of the lion statues, which looks so like an ancient Roman aqueduct from below, and continued past Georgetown until we reached the Potomac. Cruising along the riverbank we stopped to examine a statue dedicated to the obscure inventor of the screw propeller; further on the city's workers recreated with soccer and frisbee across the wide and level playing fields that there border the river. On the low bridge across the Tidal Basin we dismounted. After leaning the bikes against the bridge's railing we stood in the sun to take in the monumental views.

"Ah, the heart of the national shrine," Gary commented, "the Shiva *lingam* of the Washington Monument and, right in view, the curvilinear *yoni* of the Jefferson. The phallic and the feminine, the essential human archetypes. And presiding over their eternal duality, we have Lincoln in all his lofty transcendence. And each of them so much larger than life!"

Hearing him talk like that made me want to touch him, and I hugged him closely. We watched gulls play over the water for a while, and then mounted again and cycled along the Mall. When the Capitol's shining dome loomed ahead we veered into its shadows and pulled up before the sprawling Grant memorial. Straddling our machines, we admired its straining teams of bronze horses, Union soldiers struggling with mud-mired cannon carriages, and the brooding general astride his powerful war-steed. "I can't spare this man," Gary mouthed wistfully, peering up at Grant, "he fights!" Noting my befuddlement, he merely said, abstractedly, "Lincoln."

Pedaling on, we slowly circled the Peace Monument's draped figure of Grief mourning on History's shoulder and then, wheeling back, climbed past the Library of Congress. As we coasted toward the offices of the *Underground Stream* we were assailed by sweet aromas from a bakery busy with the wakening denizens of Capitol Hill. At my suggestion we stopped and sampled their wares.

Having regained the cycles, Gary banked onto a side street and I followed. After several blocks he pulled up at an expansive square ringed with autumn-bare trees. Here we laid down the bikes to examine a darkly worn statue of the Great Emancipator, his blessing hand raised over the heads of crouching slaves. After reading a plaque about the freedwoman who spearheaded the campaign to build the memorial, we wandered across the park to examine another bronze image—that of FDR advisor Mary McLeod Bethune, herself the daughter of formerly enslaved people. Standing full in the sun, leaning on a cane given her by Roosevelt himself, the high councilor passes her scroll of wisdom to a boy and girl who stand nearby, their hands outstretched to receive her legacy. We gazed lingeringly on Robert Berk's sculpture, I remarking that it compared favorably to the artist's massive JFK bust in the airy concourse of the Kennedy Center.

Outside a corner market, across from the park, we sipped coffee before mounting the machines again and heading downtown. Though Gary led without apparent plan, he seemed to bear some purpose—as if he were retracing steps I could not fathom. In front of the National Gallery, he arrested our progress at a stone fountain surrounded by signs of the zodiac and proceeded to expound, in the most scholarly fashion, upon Masonic symbolism that he claimed underlies much of the city's public art. He went so far as to quote private letters of the Founders, letters which evinced their desire to bind our nation's fate to the highest celestial influences. According to his colorful exegesis, Demeter, the grain-bearing goddess of the ancient Greeks, was at the heart of our nation's founding ideals.

With me wondering upon our white-whigged Founders' enchantment with ancient mysteries and pagan goddesses, we wheeled past Constitution Avenue's galleries and museums until we skirted the Reflecting Pool. When we reached the Vietnam Wall, we pulled to the curb. Gary's attention seemed torn between the scene directly in front of us (a long queue that disappeared into the shallow depression where the Wall is buried into the earth) and our holy Parthenon, temple to our martyred demigod, rising up ahead.

"Pinky and I used to sit on those steps and talk at the end of our rides," he said after a moment. "I still remember him telling me how he heard King deliver his 'I Have a Dream' speech up there. Can you imagine . . ."

I was registering Gary's words, but my eyes were riveted to the solemn figures before me, filing into the earth as Odysseus had descended into Hades in search of lost loved ones. I reflected painfully that my father's name was not among those carved on the massive granite slab, though he was as much a casualty of Vietnam as those so recognized by the raisers of the memorial. Gary, seeing my moistened eyes, held me closely as I tearfully mouthed inarticulate phrases about my family.

When I had recovered myself we pulled across the avenue and biked up and along the front of the State Department. There we dismounted to look through expansive plate glass at the panoply, hung across its high-ceilinged lobby, of the world's nations' many-colored flags. In the quietude of a precinct little frequented on weekends, Gary recalled tersely how he had worked here for a time, before disenchantment over government policies put an end to his Foreign Service career.

Mildly dazed by thoughts of diplomatic mission and high purpose, I followed Gary dreamily through Foggy Bottom; we briefly rested before a forgotten Civil War general who stands stiffly bronze-silent amid rows of narrow poplars in a quiet and forgotten park. Cycling on, we cornered the baroque wedding cake of the Executive Office Building; across from the White House we pulled up to chat with the man who holds a perennial peace vigil there. Before riding on we perused his signboards, an ongoing witnessing to the horrors of Hiroshima and Nagasaki . . .

The crowded sidewalks of Dupont Circle bustled with Saturday gaiety as we pumped up the hill where the avenue leaves that quarter of the city. At its crest we laid down the machines and rested below a colossal equestrian statue of George McClellan. Gary archly commented on the Union commander's martial bearing and proud stance. "Sure," he said, "he looks bad now—over a hundred years too late. The problem was, the guy couldn't figure out which side he really wanted to win!"

Without further comment we collected the cycles, coasted easily through the mansions of Kalorama (I pointed out the Textile House), and then climbed arduously along Embassy Row to the nation's cathedral—situated, as was the custom in medieval times, on the city's highest ground. After we parked and locked the bikes, Gary led me around to a door near the back. Entering into the dim quietude, we spent some half an hour taking in the cavernous nave before wandering the building's occult far reaches: its hidden chapels and underground passageways. Upon our return to the nave Gary spotted a friend walking through the choir. They warmly greeted one another, and Gary introduced me.

"Donald's a sexton here," Gary said.

I confessed that I didn't know what a sexton was.

"I'm responsible for the church's facilities," Donald said. "Gary and Charles have been handling our courier business for several years now. Let me tell you, they've bailed me out more times than I can count."

I remarked that he worked in a lovely place.

"True," he said, glancing up toward the towering columns of Indiana limestone, the high vaulted ceilings, and the radiant stained glass windows of monumental proportions. "But to be honest, it can get tiresome when you're stuck in here all week. Maybe it's the low light." He gestured to Gary. "Here's the guy I envy, free as the wind."

"I don't know about that," Gary said. "Trapped in Dispatch would be more like it. Especially with Pinky gone."

"Pinky gone? I hadn't heard."

"Not permanently," Gary hastened to reply, calming a worried customer. "It's more like an extended leave of absence."

"What's going on?" Donald asked, a distinct trace of concern in his voice. "Traveling? He's not ill, is he?"

"Oh no," Gary said gamely. "Everything's fine. It's nothing to worry about. He's just taking care of some . . . personal matters."

"I see," Donald said, seeming to sense that his inquiries were unwelcome. "Anyway, I'm glad you two stopped by. But I imagine you'll be wanting to get back to your outing. Incidentally," he said to Gary as we walked toward the exit, "you haven't been in to use the organ. Remember, you're welcome any time after hours. I spoke to the music director about it."

Gary replied that he felt he ought to be in better practice before approaching the cathedral's grand instrument, thanked him, and we said goodbye. After collecting the cycles, we glided easily down a leafy side street back to Connecticut Avenue, crossed the bridge with the lion statues and in minutes again swung through Dupont Circle. From there Gary turned up Massachusetts Avenue to a broad mansion on its south side: "There's one last thing I want to show you." He spoke briefly with the caretaker at a desk in the lobby, with whom he seemed well acquainted. Then he led me around to a garden at the rear of the structure, the centerpiece of which, in Gary's eyes, was a large Buddha resting serenely beside a quiet fountain.

"I love the incongruity of it," he said. "The Buddha presiding over the starchy old Society of the Cincinnati." En route back to the Circle he told me about the Society—descendants of Revolutionary War veterans—and his visits there as a courier. Feeling the exertions of the ride, we lingered over lunch at the bookstore café before pedaling leisurely back to his place.

In the afternoon I recommenced embroidering Gary's field jacket. Doing my best with his rudimentary sewing kit, I started at the peace sign I had sewn into the back panel the previous weekend, adding filigree, and then began what I envisioned would be a garden of flowing vines. The Cincinnati Society's Buddha was to occupy a prominent place. While we listened to Brazilian music on the radio, and the end of an opera, Gary leafed through a mélange of handwritten and typed pages, newspaper clippings, and photocopies.

His friend Clark was on his mind.

He pulled a page out of the pile. "Here it is," he said, "the last letter I got." He spread it before me on the bed.

"He's the one in Guatemala, isn't he?"

"Yes," Gary said, "he went down there to gather material for a book he's writing on U.S. policies in the region."

I put aside Gary's jacket and took up the letter:

Things could start getting dicey here, Clark had written four months earlier. *I've been poking my nose into places that make the forces of disorder uncomfortable. I don't want to end up like Nick Blake[1] if I can help it. I believe I'm safe for the time being, holed up in a village in the interior (one which must, for reasons I'm sure you'll understand, remain nameless). You never know who's reading this (how many nuns have you tortured and raped today, you bunch of assholes?). This Ortiz[2] case could wake folks up. People start to pay attention when our Third World henchmen take to targeting our own women.*

The administration will ballyhoo the upcoming elections as a sign of progress, and perhaps they have a point. But the mainstream press will miss the rest of the story—that the oligarchs still have their tentacles everywhere. They don't need the army anymore now that, thanks to El General, they've got the Patrullas Civiles. Speaking of Montt,[3] I hear our guys are trying

1 Nick Blake, Gary explained to me, was an American journalist killed by Guatemalan paramilitary forces while investigating death squad activity there in 1985.

2 Dianna Ortiz, an American nun of the Ursuline order, was kidnapped, tortured, and raped by Guatemalan paramilitary forces, she claims with CIA involvement, while working with indigenous Guatemalan children in 1989.

3 Efraín Ríos Montt was a Guatemalan dictator and U.S. ally responsible for some of the worst human rights abuses of our time while ruling Guatemala in the early

to keep him out of the presidential race. Even they can see he's a public relations nightmare. We prefer that our dictators, once they've done our dirty work, get out of the way in time for a celebration of "democracy."

Anyhow, some people (including myself) question my sanity for getting involved in all of this. But I don't need to tell you, hombre, our people are partly responsible for this tragic mess. The least I can do is try to spread the word about what it all comes down to. Maybe relieve a little suffering down the line . . .

I don't get much news around here. But from what I'm hearing, this Persian Gulf business doesn't bode well. Especially all this "Vietnam syndrome" talk. Some of these boys are pumping to prove we're not a bunch of sissies. You know where that leads!

I miss home, but I'd hate to leave now that I've finally developed some great sources. I hope everything's good with you. I expect a draft of your magnum opus when I return. No excuses!

Clark

I put down the letter. "It sounds dangerous," I said. Gary walked to his desk and peered out the window.

"It is, to say the least."

"He must feel strongly about what he's doing."

"Oh, he does." Gary came back and sat beside me on the bed. He rested his elbows on his knees, supported his chin on the back of his clasped hands and grew reflective. "We were both so jazzed when we were at Georgetown," he recalled.

"In the foreign service school?"

"Yep." He nodded. "We really thought that Carter's human rights doctrine heralded a new era in American foreign policy. You know, after the self-interested realpolitik of the Nixon-Kissinger years. We actually believed we'd be able to serve our country as diplomats and still hold our heads high."

---

eighties. The Patrullas Civiles were a militia that operated outside the control of the civil authority of the state—all per Gary.

This last reflection occasioned a mirthless little laugh.

"It sounds like that didn't work out."

"No, I'm afraid not. We both ended up at State, in the Latin American section. Naturally we were psyched to be working together. But no sooner had we started our careers than the Reagan gang came in. Then it was back to the old 'enemy of my enemy is my friend,' and 'the end justifies the means.' In brief, before long we were thick as thieves with every two-bit dictator, petty tyrant, and sadistic death squad operator who claimed to be against communism."

He exhaled in exasperation; I gently rubbed his back.

"They started to politicize the Department," he went on with rising passion. "Old hands were fired, people with priceless experience and wisdom, to make room for right-wing ideologues. The environment was intolerable! Clark bailed before me. But I suppose I'm ever the procrastinator."

"You're probably just more deliberative," I remarked.

"I don't know about that. It should have been plain when they fired Ambassador White—for the condign crime of denouncing death squads. And then—oh, get this—they appointed Thomas Enders assistant secretary. Enders was the guy who directed the illegal bombing of Cambodia! The terrible irony is that the Reagan crowd considered the likes of Enders too *dovish*! They ultimately fired him, too, when he had the audacity to suggest a peaceful, negotiated settlement to the Salvadoran situation. That sealed it for me. Unfortunately, I'd already begun to feel like I had something unclean sticking to me."

"I'm sure it's nothing that can't be washed off." I transformed my backrubbing into a decided scrubbing. I hated to see him get so down on himself. Feeling him twist under the pressure of my efforts, I relented. He peered toward his desk and concluded his recollections:

"Clark got involved in journalism, writing pieces on the Central American situation. That's why he's down there now. What's needed, more than anything, is reliable information. And Clark's the guy who can do that."

"What about you?" I asked.

"Me? I hooked up with Signed, Sealed & Delivered, as you know. It may seem a strange career detour, but that crowd is more trustworthy, in my eyes, than the entire State Department put together. And being associated with Pinky, when it comes right down to it, has provided me an education not only in the reality of war, but in a whole new level of personal integrity. As for the more philosophical end of global affairs, that's what these papers and notes are all about." He gestured across the bed, where he had splayed his papers to seek out Clark's letter. "It started as my dissertation on so-called 'just' war theories. Now it's morphed into I don't know what. But I would like to see it amount to something one of these days."

I told him that I had every faith that his work would someday prove beneficial. Then I pulled him down onto the bed and held him, and we rested together. When Gary dozed off I went back to my sewing. Thinking about Bob and my mother, I reminded myself to check on them when I got the chance, wondering all the while what they would think of my new love. Glancing over at him while he slept, I also remembered my promise to Mrs. Pinckney, to let her know if we learned anything about Charles. When Gary awoke, we discussed the matter and decided to visit her the next day.

We eventually roused ourselves, changed, and went to dinner on the avenue. Digging through the *Post's* "Weekend" section over coffee, Gary noted a showing of Michael Cimino's Vietnam drama, *The Deer Hunter*, at one of the city's repertory cinemas. When I told him that I had never been able make it through the Russian roulette scenes, he promised to hold my hand. But it was his eyes that grew moist every time Stanley Myer's haunting guitar theme filled the theater! Both of our faces were soaked with tears, I am not abashed to admit, when Michael Vronsky, finally returned from war, crouched alone in his motel room, exiled from all he loved by his soul-twisting experiences in Vietnam . . .

It was near midnight when the long drama ended and, still seeing De Niro bounding up a mountain crag in the final scene, we made our way back to my place. In the crisp morning of the new day we drove my car down the quiet avenue, nearly deserted on an early Sunday. Sunlight glinting off the bright office squares around Dupont Circle rendered luminous the pigeons that shuttled incessantly, weaving their aerial tapestries among the cornices.

& & &

IT WAS ALMOST NINE-THIRTY when we arrived at Mrs. Pinckney's neighborhood, pulled the car to the curb and got out. The project looked even more desolate than on my first visit, its few trees and bushes now completely denuded of greenery. It was only with marginally less trepidation than on that earlier occasion that I walked with Gary through the broken gate, over shattered glass, and then across the courtyard toward the archway that led to Mrs. Pinckney's home. The blinds were drawn and no one answered when we knocked. While we stood on the stoop deliberating, a neighbor's door opened. The head of an elderly woman emerged.

"Ya'll looking for Mrs. P?"

"Yes, thank you."

"She's gone to church."

"Of course," Gary said, striking his forehead with the heal of his hand.

Mrs. Pinckney's neighbor told us where the church was located, and we walked the four blocks to a brick building with a high façade. Over the entrance, a marquee read WE'RE NOT WAITING FOR HIM; HE'S WAITING FOR US. We proceeded up the steps into a foyer, where we were greeted by the surprised stares of a couple of men and several teenaged boys gathered to one side. They wore nearly identical dark suits, those of the boys mostly ill-fitting. One of the men stepped forward, introduced himself as the pastor, and asked if he could help us. We told him we were looking for Mrs. Pinckney.

"She's here somewhere," he said, a little distractedly. "Either fixing food or practicing with the choir. Anything I can help you with?"

I explained that we'd come to speak with her about a personal matter.

"Is anything wrong?"

"No, it's nothing urgent."

"Service will be starting soon," he said. "I hate to interrupt her, and we're in the middle of a youth group here." He gestured toward his charges.

I apologized for taking up his time and asked if we could stay around and speak to Mrs. Pinckney after the service. "Sure," he said—somewhat doubtfully, I thought. He gave Gary, with his field jacket, a once-over. "Everybody's welcome here." Then he drew me aside and lowered his voice. "You know," he said awkwardly, "this is a, well—pretty much a—a black church."

I assured him that that was fine with us.

"Well, then," he said, "you're welcome in God's house. Go on in and have a seat."

He returned to the boys and they resumed their discussion. Gary and I entered the sanctuary and quietly slid into an empty pew near the back. It was old and battered, as were the others; tattered hymnals rested at sporadic intervals in the racks attached to the back of the pew in front of it. I gazed around the high-ceilinged space. A banner across the front, depicting Jesus in flowing robes, carried the inscription, "I am the light of the world. Whoever followeth me shall not walk in darkness." A low rail marked off the chancel area, and a pulpit stood to one side. On the other side of the chancel an electric piano, a drum set, and a couple of guitars huddled together in front of a stately organ.

A number of older men and women were already scattered in the pews. More came in as we waited; a little later mothers with babies and small children began to arrive. Gary fidgeted. He said that it had been a long time since he'd been in a church. Perhaps it was those New England missionaries in his pedigree, he explained: too much of the patriarchal, punishing, and puritanical God of his forebears.

The boys and men in the foyer suddenly broke into song behind us; shortly afterward they came filing up the aisle. The pastor disappeared through a door at the front of the sanctuary and the others seated themselves. As the space filled, Gary and I noted that people were avoiding our pew. We knew we seemed out of place. But shortly an older man, distinguished not only by his understated brown suit and finely shaped bald head, but also by eyes that bespoke struggles forborne by inner strength, patience, and resolve entered the pew and sat beside me. He introduced himself and welcomed us. I explained that we were friends of Charles and had come to see Mrs. Pinckney.

He was about to respond when a robed choir poured in from the door through which the pastor had left, along with four young men; these latter presently took up the musical instruments. The pastor himself followed directly. Mr. Wood—that was the man's name—stood and faced the front of the sanctuary, and Gary and I followed suit. The musicians began to lay down a rousing vamp, the choir clapped their hands, and the congregation joined in.

The pastor announced the hymn and I reached for the nearest hymnal. I looked toward Mr. Wood, hoping to catch the hymn's number, but he sang along with the rollicking gospel that now filled the church from memory. I noted that most of the congregation did the same, many with great feeling. I searched through the index, finally found the hymn's words on the last verse, and added my voice. Gary, looking dumbly on, sounded sporadic and doubtful syllables, as if trying to decipher a long-dead language.

I spotted Mrs. Pinckney in the choir as we sat down with the rest of the congregation. The pastor, after offering a prayer of thanksgiving, shared a few words about the situation in the Middle East. The choir sang a number with the band, the pastor read a few biblical excerpts, and collection plates were passed awkwardly down the aisles by the dark-suited boys from the youth group.

The pastor, a compactly built young man in a navy blue suit, devoted his sermon to an impassioned plea for personal responsibility. Gesturing toward the banner that hung across the chancel, he exhorted the congregation to embody the highest ideals of Christian life—compassion, service, forgiveness, and tolerance. He conceded that we were living in dark times, with war looming and so much work to be done in our communities, but claimed that these challenges only heightened the need for each of us to cling resolutely to the greatest truths.

He strode energetically down the center aisle as he loudly preached and around the pews, calling out his parishioners and demanding their responses. In return he received shouts of acclamation, hallelujahs, and amens. The band supplied a welling undercurrent, one I noticed only as I grew aware of being pulled into its irresistible energies. Finally the preacher returned to the front of the sanctuary and announced an altar call. Gary and I rose with the others. The congregation began to sway with the ensemble's surging gospel, a soulful concoction underpinned by plunging bass lines and punctuated by ringing chords from the pianist. A few of the older members took up positions behind the chancel rail; Mrs. Pinckney was among them. The pastor raised his voice over the music.

"If you're hurting!" he called out vibrantly, "struggling with things you just can't wrap your mind around! Hey, I know how it gets sometimes! Come down here and accept this wonderful blessing!"

Someone shouted an "Amen!" and another cried "Glory be!" The band members played on, the texture of their hypnotic weave growing denser, tighter. . .

"What's that?" the pastor cried again. He probed down the center aisle, looked to his left and to his right. "You're unsure of your relationship with God? Just remember, He came down here personally to get us out of all these messes we seem to be constantly getting ourselves into!"

"Right on!" someone shouted.

"Praise the Lord," came another voice.

The band pushed the music deeper, broader, stronger . . .

"But wait," the pastor suddenly called, his hand raised to the congregation, his voice resounding throughout the sanctuary. "You say you've been abused? Suffered loss? Well, let me tell you, my sister and brother, you're not alone! Come step into God's heavenly river, His mighty river of peace and blessing!"

"Lord have mercy!" cried a lady at the end of our pew. Gary turned sharply to look upon her, a distinctly worried expression on his face. He appeared to be rendered supremely uncomfortable by this display of untrammeled spiritual longing. I took his hand and squeezed it firmly.

Worshippers had begun to step from the front pew and kneel along the chancel rail in prayer. A few exchanged quiet words with the deacons who stood before them; others bowed their heads to receive a laying on of hands. As these rose, congregants from the second pew stepped up to take their places. The choir now joined in with the band, singing in precisely measured, yet deeply impassioned, tones:

> *We need to hear from you*, they sang,
> *We need a word from you,*
> *If we don't hear from you,*
> *What will we do?*

At the second verse members of the congregation, in a swelling wave, added their voices:

> *Wanting you more each day*, the words rang out,
> *Show us your perfect way,*
> *There is no other way*
> *That we can live . . .*

Led by the choir, the assembled gathering repeated these verses, adding rising harmonies, with new and illuminating touches supplied by the guitarist and organist. All the while the pastor continued to encourage his parishioners, pointing up the gospel's lyric in impassioned outbursts. Now one of the teenaged boys we had seen in the foyer stepped forth from the choir. It struck me, here in the church where he had been raised, that this might have been Charles as a budding man; a glance from Gary suggested that he shared my impression. The boy's voice possessed the clarity of youth, and the authority of youth's innocence, as he declaimed forthrightly above the accompanying chorus:

> *Destruction is now in view*, he cried in his man-child's voice,
> *Seems the world has forgotten about you,*
> *Children are crying, and people are dying,*
> *They're lost without you—so lost without you!*

With the congregation answering, in a call and response pattern, the boy took up again with a sort of fractured passion:

> *You said if we seek, Lord, if we seek your face,*
> *And turn from our wicked, our wicked ways,*
> *You promised to heal our land,*

Father, I know that you can!

As the boy stepped back into line, the organ swelled to fill the sanctuary with its magnificent, throaty power. With bell-like chords chiming from the piano, the choir took up their verses again, pleading for Heaven's help with earthly dilemmas: *show us your perfect way!* As the back pews emptied, the congregation joined in with rising intensity, swaying and rocking, until the sanctuary was soul-shakingly alive with the yearnings of so many for peace, harmony, and the natural wisdom we so easily forget. I looked to Gary; he seemed almost paralyzed by the potency of these exuberant rites; I was half afraid his knees might buckle.

When our pew began to empty, Mr. Wood turned to me in a gesture of invitation. Not wishing to appear ungrateful, I followed him toward the aisle. I held Gary by the hand, and he too came without protest. Ever the diplomat. I directed us to where Mrs. Pinckney stood, and as we approached her, our eyes met in sudden recognition. Gary and I knelt at the rail and bowed our heads. I felt Mrs. Pinckney's warm hands on my shoulders and breathed the comforting, earthy scent of her woolen skirt. Letting myself go completely to the music, and to the spirit of the ritual, I felt deeply at home among these people. Gary too received Mrs. Pinckney's blessing; we rose and returned to our pew.

At the close of the service Mr. Wood shared fond memories of mentoring Charles in Sunday School. "Oh, he had his moments," he said as we lingered in the pew, "like any child. But he was always on the up and up. Anybody could see that." In response to his inquiries about Charles's present situation, we offered only non-committal generalities.

He led us through the door at the front of the sanctuary and down to a basement, where the congregation was gathered at tables and along a buffet. Mrs. Pinckney and a couple of other women stood serving an assortment of dishes both warm and cold. When she saw us approaching, she put down her utensils and came to greet us. After she and Mr. Wood exchanged some pleasantries, her eyes took in Gary and me; she smiled in wordless recognition that we were a couple. She took up my hands.

"I'm still waiting for you to come over and do some quilting."

I pleaded how busy I had been. She turned to Gary.

"And look at you, stranger," she said. "Where have you been keeping yourself? I don't believe I've seen you since last summer—that day you stopped by with Charles. You two were on your bicycles. Gone clear down to Mount Vernon, I believe."

Gary concurred.

I told Mrs. Pinckney that we had news of Charles. "Really?" She turned a wordless plea to Mr. Wood and he stepped away, a vaguely worried expression on his face.

Mrs. Pinckney directed us to an empty corner of the room.

"Is everything all right?"

"We think so," I said. "Remember, I told you I'd let you know if we learned anything about Charles?"

"Yes, I remember."

"Well, he sent Gary a note the other day."

Mrs. Pinckney was obviously relieved; the taut skin of her high-cheek-boned face relaxed a little. "I'm mighty glad to hear that."

Gary and I remained silent. We hadn't thought to plan how we would break the news of Charles's peculiar situation to his mother—or even whether such a revelation would be helpful. Unable to bear the suspense any longer, Mrs. Pinckney finally turned to Gary. "Well, where is he?"

"I'm afraid . . . I can't say."

"Now Gary," she said, "quit teasing me."

"Mrs. P, I wouldn't joke about something like this."

"We know it sounds unusual," I put in.

Still doubting we were serious, Mrs. Pinckney countered with a jest of her own. "If I didn't know my son better, I'd swear he was in trouble with the law. I mean, the way you two are carrying on . . ."

"It's nothing like that," I lied.

"Of course not," she said. "Then what is it?"

"What we've learned," Gary said with slow deliberation, buying time, "is that Charles is involved in some very important veterans work."

"That's no surprise," Mrs. Pinckney replied. "He's been involved with those groups for years. But why can't you tell me where he is?"

Gary now took an unctuous tone. "Mrs. P," he said, "there are so many hurting vets out there." I gazed in astonishment upon my lover's smooth elaborations.

"I suppose I know that as well as anybody."

"The thing is," Gary continued, seeming to gain momentum from his own increasinly fanciful assertions, "they're spread all over the country. So, with the work Pinky's doing, he moves around quite a bit. He doesn't stay in one place more than a day or two. It wouldn't make much sense to give an address. By the time the mail caught up to him, he'd be on to the next town."

"He could at least drop a postcard now and then, couldn't he?" There was obvious hurt in her voice, and Gary was at a loss. But Mrs. Pinckney seemed to sense his discomfort and was too kind to press him further. Her face brightened.

"It seems awful peculiar," she said. "But it probably can't be helped. I'm sure it'll all make sense in due time." She took us each by the arm. "Why don't you two come over here and get some food. We're not going to sort anything out on an empty stomach, that's for sure."

She led us to the buffet, where we loaded our plates with flapjacks and grits, scrapple and bacon, stewed tomatoes, and black-eyed peas and greens. We all chatted pleasantly (Mrs. Pinckney on one side, Mr. Wood on the other) until it was time to go. On the way to the car I said coyly that I couldn't help wondering whether it was wise to get myself involved with a man who was such a facile liar.

"It must be the diplomatic training," he said lightly.

"We'll have to see what we can do about that."

Taking a more earnest tone, he said that it seemed senseless to tell Mrs. Pinckney the raw truth: that her only son was bivouacked in a cemetery, camping outdoors with the heart of winter coming on, and committing acts that could earn him a lengthy stay in the federal prison system. He argued that we should attempt to satisfy our concerns about Pinky without burdening his mother with details that she could do nothing more than worry about. I was, of course, obliged to agree. On the way home we stopped at the newsstand on Farragut Square. We picked up the Sunday papers, Gary a copy of *Le Monde Diplomatique*. We went to my place, loved each other faithfully, and spent the afternoon catching up on the news.

Much had happened since the U.N. resolution on military force only days before. The United States had offered talks with Hussein; the dictator accepted on condition that the question of Israel and Palestine be included in the discussions (Gary: "A deal-breaker if I ever heard one"). Defense Secretary Cheney said in an "off the cuff" interview that it appeared that Iraq possessed the capacity to outlast any sanctions the U.S. and its allies might impose (Gary: "That's it—they're going in"). Thousands attended a peace rally in Boston, and Hussein permitted deliveries of food to Americans trapped in our embassy ("A useless propaganda ploy!"). Meanwhile, the doctrine of "invincible force" was much bruited by the administration ("They obviously haven't read their Sun Tzu").

During the afternoon Cheryl called with an invitation to a holiday party two weeks away; accepting, I told her that I would be bringing Gary along. I demurred about any further details on my new beau, promising to fill her in later.

In the evening, while Gary and I sipped tea in the living room, a call came from Jorge. We hadn't spoken for weeks. I went to the bedroom extension, wondering how I would explain it all to Gary, to whom I had mentioned neither my friend nor our recent difficulties. After brief inquiries into one another's well-being, Jorge said that he was done with his academic work and planned to leave for Peru in a week's time. He added that he didn't know when he would return. Speaking into a hollow void on the line, I congratulated him on finishing his degree and suggested a send-off. He replied formally that, with everything he had to do, he doubted he would have time. I asked him to write and let me know how he was doing, and we signed off. Gary appeared to detect the sadness in my bearing when I returned to the living room. I began to explain about Jorge and me, but he cut me short and assured me that I owed him no explanations. He laid down his paper, helped me crowd into the bowl chair he occupied, and put his arms around me.

Before we went to bed I called my mother. She sounded world-weary, and I was struck by the fact that she made no mention of developments in the news.

The days that followed were less eventful than those of the previous week, and I was able to take my bearings a little. At the clinic I bore down and tried to understand, as best I could, the changes that my clients were going through. I told Gary that I could use a couple of quiet nights, hoping he wouldn't think that it was about Jorge—though I myself knew that that was part of it. He replied that he also needed some personal time, and we didn't see one another for several days.

One morning he called the clinic to alert me to the *Underground Stream*. I picked up a copy during my lunch break. A front-page photo showed, gathered at the Army's downtown recruiting office, a crowd gawking at the poster, now affixed to its storefront window, that Henry had fashioned with his workmates. "General jubilation and rejoicing," Gary said of the couriers' reaction to the publicity.

The men in the vets group seemed also to sense a caesura. They were taking stock, along with the rest of us, of the shocking developments of the last several week: developments whereby a society so lately rejoicing at the outbreak of peace found itself staring bleakly down the gun barrels of another war. They steadied themselves—and leaned on one another for support—as they strained toward a way forward not merely for themselves but for their nation. To my continuing surprise it was Danny, the unrepentant, the irreverent, who held the group together. He flourished a copy of the *Underground Stream*. The paper was folded to display a close-up of Henry's mock recruiting poster.

"Did you guys see the latest?" Danny crooned. A couple of the men visibly winced. "I know whoever did this is probably a jerk. But I got to be honest with you, there's something about it I find refreshing. Maybe because the guy seems to have a great bullshit meter—that's a Hemingway quote, in case you guys don't think I do any serious reading. All this glorious patriotism crap, international law, world-order hoo-ha . . . us guys know better, don't we? It's like Napoleon said, God's on the side with the biggest artillery. The fact is, we're oil gluttons. We're too lazy to walk or ride our bikes, and too impatient to wait for the bus or take the metro. We made an arrangement with the Saudis and all those other petty dictators to keep the Texas tea flowing. The boys in charge are just afraid they won't be able to cop the same deal with Hussein."

The men hesitated to respond.

"Listen," he went on, "I'm not saying that means we shouldn't intervene. If we live in a dog-eat-dog world, maybe you need to be the meanest dog on the block. It's not like Hussein's going to use his oil riches for the benefit of humanity. He'll probably just build a few more palaces. That guy's one of the biggest bastards that ever graced the stage of history."

The others weren't completely satisfied with Danny's reasoning, and the lively discussion that ensued brought them each eventually around to their own deepest struggles. It was a decently productive session, and I returned home feeling that my life might soon settle into a more steady pattern. But when I arrived I found a disturbing message on the answering machine; it was from my mother, and it was brief and to the point. "They've gone and called up Bobby," she said, on the verge of tears, and then abruptly hung up. I returned her call immediately. Bob was to report to a base in Georgia the following Friday; he told Mom that he would come through Washington on the way. She lamented that he wouldn't be home for Christmas. I promised to visit the next day, then called Gary with the news. I said that I wouldn't be at the Gathering but that I would come to him afterwards.

THERE WAS A DUSTING of snow Friday afternoon, and traffic was painfully slow on the way to my mother's. Lost in a sea of crawling automobiles, I listened to the radio and tried to remain calm. There was what, at first blush, sounded like great news. Hussein announced that he would release his American hostages. I felt a surge of hope that war might be averted, until a commentator glibly dismissed the gesture as a cynical attempt to manipulate United States and world opinion. Another pundit, going even further, reminded his listeners that the only tangible barrier to an American invasion had now been removed. When I got off the freeway I stopped at a video rental store. I needed something to distract my mother—and myself. I found an innocuous comedy and drove the few remaining miles to her townhouse.

Her place was dark except for the kitchen light, whose faint glow I detected through the front window when I pulled in. She came down the hallway, hugged me, and led me back to where she had something boiling on the stove. President Bush's gaunt face flickered from the television screen. He said that he welcomed the hostage release and was open to negotiations, but he remained firm in his demand that Iraqi forces evacuate Kuwait.

"That bit about negotiations," Mom said, "it's just for show. I hope you realize that."

I didn't respond. The hostage release (to her mind, just another feint in an ignoble game) had merely tightened the screws of her distress.

"They've already decided to go in," she went on, "even if Saddam leaves Kuwait, —now they've gone and made such a big fuss about it. Before you came, the CIA director was on. He said the sanctions would take nine months to have an effect. Nine months! And now the president says he's losing patience. Well, just add it up! That's how they break the news, without coming right out and saying it. They're going in, sure as day."

I was about to remark that Gary had said much the same over the weekend, but I remembered that I hadn't yet told her about my new love. I decided to wait for a calmer opportunity.

We continued watching news while I helped with dinner. A silver-haired senator appeared on the screen demanding that Congress be consulted before military action be taken. Without warning, Mom strode into the living room. She flicked off the television and, with sudden fury, pitched the remote onto the couch. "I can't take it anymore," she cried pitiably as she returned to the kitchen. I tried to initiate a conversation but her answers were minimal, her mind elsewhere.

Over dinner she flatly recounted the details of Bob's deployment. When we finished she picked up the plates and took them to the sink. After I helped her load the dishwasher we sat on the couch and watched the movie I had brought. The inattention to housekeeping I had noted on my last visit had grown yet worse; I felt constrained, when we paused the video so that she could use the bathroom, to tidy up. She returned to find me stuffing odds and ends into the kitchen trash. She seemed a little embarrassed but made no explanation. I hugged her hard at the door before leaving. She said she would call when she knew more of Bob's plans.

I took the George Washington Parkway into town, knowing that proximity to the deep and fertile gorge of the Potomac would do me good. The roads were clear, but there was a delicate frosting over much of the landscape. Coasting high on the river's palisades, I saw our spreading metropolis through the misty air and thought of my bicycle ride with Gary two weeks earlier. He knew the city so intimately, seemed to regard its monuments and parks as living companions. My love for him grew as I reflected on his enigmatic character. What new mysteries he had brought into my life!

Descending from the heights and with the cemetery at my back crossing Memorial Bridge, I was piercingly aware of my father's grave, of Denny, John, and Tiny, and of Charles, all nearby. Although the heater drove at full blast, I felt a chill, and instinctively made for Gary's place. He wouldn't be back from the Gathering yet, but I didn't want to go home. I feared the dreams that might beset me should I fall asleep alone.

He came in around midnight, answered my drowsy inquiries and, under the snow-dusted skylight, folded himself around me. In the morning we reconnected after a week spent apart. Over breakfast we touched briefly on what had transpired with Jorge. He said helpfully that difficult feelings were normal even at inevitable partings, and we said little else about the matter. What preoccupied him more was Charles, and more especially that peculiar message—the quote from Julio Cortázar's novel—that the homeless men had brought to the Gathering at Signed, Sealed & Delivered.

From Gary's papers—
December 2, 1990:
You're acting like a knight trying to move like a rook trying to move like a bishop. Yes, old man, you make plain what I've always known, that is, that you see right through me! No doubt you pity my attempts to avoid committing myself to one course, my truest self on the line (or really putting myself at the disposal of others, despite the lip service I pay to such fine ideals). I hear you remonstrate with softening words, lauding the efforts I make at the company. Killing me with faint praise. You're too kind to point out what you see as clearly as I—that my entire life has been one long delaying action!

I remember you reading *Hopscotch*. It wasn't long since I'd started working at SS&D. I was still feeling the exhilaration of leaving State, and the even deeper thrill of that great book! I wondered if you too might come under the Cortázaran spell, find yourself roaming the streets of Paris or Buenos Aires, as I did then, in the shoes of Horacio Oliveira. I didn't yet realize that you weren't interested in living through books. For you, books were strictly a means of obtaining information to make concrete, in the present moment, some praxis worthy of our human-ness.

Maybe it was Vietnam made you that way, I don't know. I see you now, as I've seen you so many times. I have come out to the lounge to get a break from the strain of Dispatch (sorting that stream of requests, a city map before mind's eye; plotting the positions of couriers; balancing the peculiarities of clients, the vagaries of traffic, the strengths or weaknesses of riders; dealing with the inevitable crises; hoping the day will end with a sense that, in some small way, we found the Tao). I lean at the rail and look down to where you stand beside your desk, silent and centered. Your arms arc as steadily as a stalking heron; legs are flexed, your feet rooted in the earth. I think of how you taught me to feel the city from the streets up, stood beside me while I learned to negotiate the endless scraps of paper flowing from Dolphine and Lisa. Sensing how hard it was for me to stay fixed in the present, you patiently drew me away from a mediated view of the world that was the inevitable result of my upbringing, my education, and my personality. Later you showed me those exercises you do after the riders have taken to the streets, the morning rush has passed, and initial fires have been extinguished. *Chi Gong* or *Tai Chi* or *Kung Fu*: you've always been vague about terminology, preferring to refer to that series of maneuvers taught you by an elderly Vietnamese as ancient Taoist arts. My own practice is like much else in my life, sporadic and uncommitted. But I've done enough to sense the crazy power in these simple-seeming gestures designed to awaken inner resolve . . .

You're acting like a knight trying to move like a rook trying to move like a bishop.

Knight—service to others, purity of character, courage.

Rook—fortress, defense, under siege.

Bishop—the sacred co-opted by the state.

Of the three I prefer the knight (natch) and feel flattered that you so characterize me. But it is equally true that I have often walled myself off, not heeding Lao Tzu's caution: "the greatest misfortune is to prepare to defend yourself." As for the state co-opting the sacred—a not-too-subtle hint at my stillborn Foreign Service career? Or is it my eternally stalled dissertation on "just" war? Why not, for that matter, maternal ancestors in far flung places, spreading the gospel of prudery and Protestant work ethic under the aegis of the stars and stripes?

You open up a can of worms, my friend, a fine can of worms. No doubt you meant to strike at my indefensible regions—not out of malice, certainly, but to develop my reflexes, to point out my vulnerabilities while there is still time to make corrections. Still, your message was a body blow. In the week since your envoys visited the shop I have felt paralyzed, my failures trailing before me, a sad parade of human frailty. I could list them, if for no other reason than to prove that, like Marj's favorite troubadour, I have not forgotten them. But the most piquant of the lot must be the child I willingly gave up, already six years old now and living in distant climes with her mother. (She now has a new daddy who, unlike yours truly, is comfortable taking responsibility for the lives of others.)

Vietnam you treacherous, you insidious! Why should I have expected life to make sense after Kim Phuc Phan Thi, Christmas bombings, Kent State, or My Lai (as if MAD, fire hoses at Birmingham, and starving farm workers were not enough?)? My own strange path was clearly on a collision course with History—the Christian upbringing, replete with pious ancestors; indoctrination into the cult of America, home of the free and of the brave; and all those schoolbook lessons about a City on a Hill: always kind, always just, always justified! We were the redeemed people, come to the Promised Land. But O how many shadowed, hidden truths!

Then there is my own poor family, with its own silent brokenness. My father, flown to California, carries on as he always has. He nurtures his engineer's values, values that work as far as they go—as far as they go! But does he ever grasp what has happened? To himself, to his marriage; to his sons, to his nation? Holding on, but to what? Seeking peace, but where? Meanwhile my mother holds court in her uptown apartment, her quiet poise masking only to those who don't know her (the charity societies, the DAR) her underlying griefs. Yes, I see the lines in her face where grimaces of pain have traced their histories. I visit and chat over tea, sit at the piano and, singing old songs, knock myself out to bring on a faint smile. It's the best she can do; the best she can do!

Jim, brother, where are you? I've always thought of you as the quintessential American. Direct, optimistic, and sociable. Of course I understand, going to prison would have been worse. But when you passed on Carter's amnesty, admit it, it wasn't only about Diana, or the friends you'd made in Canada. America offended you and, sensitive lout that you are, you cut your ties and didn't look back. Would that my choices were so simple! Sentimental idiot that I am, I don't easily get over my attachments: to the past, to this throbbing city (sometimes heartless, but always full of life!) and even to this crazy nation, traducing its ideals as often as it honors them. In the evenings my mind travels north, over rivers and mountains it soars, questing through forests and swamps like those we roamed as boys. But I never find you . . .

Oh brother, I never find you!

And when it all comes down, I'm left with the fond hope that if I pour enough of what I've seen, done, and felt into these pages, people and places I've known and loved, I'll arrive at some unassailable place: a place where I can stand against all comers, receive them in decency, kindness, and truth. It started with my ill-fated dissertation, it is true, but how far things have spun since those wooden commentaries on "just" war theories! My mind was then as cloistered as the medieval churchmen who first tried to justify violence; who, in telling us that war was the "health of the state," conveniently forgot "resist not evil" and "turn the other cheek!" How many of my intellectual attachments, I now realize, can be explained by a refusal to accept the proposition that there is no justification for much that has gone down in the name of liberty and justice for all?

And now Marj! Mysterious and wonderful, delicate and unbreakable at once. In your own, unassuming way, with what heart you live! *A comfort and a mercy, through and through*—I can't but help quote your valiant troubadour. I recall that first night, and how apt his words: *sister, won't you soothe my fevered brow!*

I picture the loom in the corner of your bedroom. It has witnessed our loving and heard our confidences. Stretched along its warps, in earthy browns and greens, the stalled tapestry groans for your touch to bring completion and fullness (as do I). It sings to your piece at the clinic, deepening the conversation you keep with spirits you came to know desert-bound, progenitors back to Time-before-Time, when White Shell Woman walked the Dreamscape. I see that solitary bird of yours, the one in the clinic tapestry, soaring eternally over ochres and umbers in pale sky-blues.

Peace and freedom. But also an undeniable loneliness.

How I wish I could salve your wounds! But caught in this mystery, I can only wonder and be strong, at every turn finding a father on whose story you touch with teary eyes. Vietnam you treacherous, you insidious! But how I admire the forthright path you've taken, right to the heart of the matter. And how I envy men at the clinic, to bask in you and feel your warmth. More deeply, I hesitate before you, realizing how much I still don't know about your true soul's purpose.

Nothing left but to accept, humbly, my good fortune. And when I worship at your Goddess temple . . . O lady!

❧ ❧ ❧

SATURDAY MORNING GARY pushed back his chair, tossed the newspaper onto his desk, and asked me to drive him across town. He directed me first down into the park and over Rock Creek, and then up onto the avenue and toward Dupont Circle. Once over the lion statue bridge, at the crest where McClellan straddles his monumental steed, we turned. Entering the neighborhood of ambassadorial mansions where Textile House is located, I felt a certain comfort in coming into a zone I think of as hallowed. We motored up and down low hills until the grassy square rose ahead. We parked along its verge, opposite where the museum is situated, and made our way toward one of the stately apartment houses that border its perimeter.

Gary told me about his friend Herbert Mayfield on the drive over. He worked with him at the State Department, before Herbert was purged by the Reagan administration's right-wing ideologues. Some time later, Gary and Charles encountered Herbert at Dupont Circle, where stone tables with inset chess boards ring the shady park. An acquaintance was renewed and the three began to meet regularly for chess and conversation. Charles's cryptic message still weighed on Gary, and he had convinced himself—it was the chess metaphor, perhaps—that Mr. Mayfield might be able to shed some light on Charles's situation.

"Herbert worked in Southeast Asia in the fifties," Gary went on as we approached the building, "and then with Kissinger's gang in the Nixon White House. He did some time in Latin America in the interim. Pinky and I used to spend hours talking politics with him. He's quite informed—and not a bad chess player. You should see he and the Pinkman—who's no slouch himself—go head to head."

Gary picked up a telephone receiver outside the building's door and punched a code into the keypad. There were a half-dozen adults in the park with accompanying children and dogs. The trees were bare, and a blustery wind blew parched leaves along the high, exposed ground. Gary said a few words, a buzzer sounded, and he opened the door. We stepped into a foyer all Louis Napoleon gilt and satin and walked to the elevators. Mr. Mayfield awaited us at the door of his apartment.

He greeted Gary with a crooked smile, drew him close, and as he slowly pumped his hand asked where he had been keeping himself. "And who's this lovely creature?" he added before Gary could respond. He turned to me. "I suppose you're the reason I haven't been seeing my friend lately."

I blushed under his flattery but managed to return the banter. "Not true," I said. "I release him from his manacles at least one afternoon a week. You know, for exercise."

"You're quick," he said while he shook my hand. "I like that." After inviting us in he strode in a low, loping fashion to a sofa laden with books and papers, which he presently began to cart to a dining table already piled high with similar items. "Sorry about the mess," he said. "Charlotta's still in the Bahamas. I can't seem to get motivated to keep things straight with no one here but me."

Gary, who had stepped over to help him clear the sofa, asked when he expected Charlotta to return.

"You never know with her," Herbert said. "She keeps her own counsel on the subject. Never liked Washington, anyway." He turned to me, flushed with exertion. "After four wives," he said wryly, "you get used to the idiosyncrasies . . ."

The sofa clear, Herbert offered Gary and me a seat and a drink. Seeing me glance at my watch, he added, "or a cup of coffee, if you think it's too early to start with the good stuff. I can brew a pot, if I can only figure out where Charlotta put the filters." He got up from his chair and walked stiffly to the kitchen.

"I usually just go out," he explained, opening cabinets at random.

"Don't go to any bother," Gary said. "A glass of water would be fine."

I signaled my agreement with a nod.

"You sure?" Herbert rummaged through the clutter on the kitchen counter. "Those filters have got to be here someplace."

"Listen," Gary said, "I've got a better idea. Why don't we take you to brunch on the avenue? I'll bet we can find a place with some decent liquid refreshment."

Displacing one last pile of junk with a wave of exasperation, Herbert peered through the kitchen pass-through. "All right," he said, "you got yourself a deal. But on one condition, you're my guests. I'm paying."

Gary agreed and we all left the building. The sun shone brightly as we made our way across the square and down a sloping street toward the avenue. Gary related the essential elements of Charles's goings-on, while Herbert directed us to a restaurant he liked, a dimly lit place down a short flight of steps from the sidewalk.

"The décor's not so hot," he said as we entered, "but the food's decent. And the bartender makes a great martini."

We sat at a quiet table from which we could watch, trailing by outdoors, the feet and shins of passing pedestrians. Herbert ordered his martini with an omelet; Gary took a beer and a sandwich; I, tea and a salad. After the waitress left, Herbert placed his elbows on the table and leaned in toward us.

"He's playing with fire, you know" he said decisively. "I mean, Arlington, that's the Holy of Holies."

Gary gestured his assent.

"You get these flag-waver types," Herbert continued, "nothing gets their undies in a bundy like striking at their symbols. Of course, after you get to know them, you find out why. The symbols are all they've got. They don't give a rat's behind for what they stand for."

Gary nodded.

"I just fired off a letter to a few old friends in the Division. I can't sit back and watch the bullshit that passes for reality in this town. Look at the fast and loose way they're playing with the War Powers Act. Congress is going to roll over, just the way they did with the Gulf of Tonkin Resolution. The spineless weenies won't take responsibility for declaring war, but they won't oppose it either. I guess they figure that's the best way to keep their mindless constituents happy. So much for democracy! But I'm getting off the subject. We were talking about Chuck."

"Chuck?" I asked.

"Oh," Herbert said. He smiled as he shot a glance at Gary. "I just call him Chuck when I want to razz him—usually when he has my back against the wall at the chessboard. Let's see what you'll do now, *Chuck*, that kind of thing. The problem is, it never seems to throw him off his stride. . ."

I pointed out that Charles had been referring to himself as Chuck with the homeless men, though I didn't know what significance, if any, to attach to that factoid.

"He's obviously upset about this imbroglio in the Middle East."

"That's an understatement," Gary said.

I remarked that the lingering effects of Charles's experiences in Vietnam could not be discounted. "I see it every day at the clinic," I added.

Herbert looked thoughtfully into his martini. "Yeah," he said, "we thought we were so damned smart, re-ordering the world in our image. The problem is, we bungled it. The communist bogeyman had us on the run. One thing I've learned, you don't make good decisions out of fear. But let me make sure I understand. Are you suggesting that Pinky's having some kind of psychological . . . episode. A relapse, or . . ."

I told him that I would be surprised if Charles were operating from any but the most rational of bases, but that there were aspects of his situation I found troubling. I mentioned his abandoned mother, and the bewilderment his disappearance had created at Signed, Sealed & Delivered.

"And apparently," Gary added, "he's been stalking around town decked out in full cammo."

"Really?" Herbert said. We sat in worried silence until he spoke again. "He must be aware of the risks he's running, don't you think?"

"I would have to assume . . ." Gary said.

The waitress brought our drinks. After sampling his beer, Gary slowly rocked his head in bewilderment. He looked up at Herbert. "He sent me this cryptic message the other day, something from

Cortázar's *Hopscotch*."

"I'm afraid I can't help you there," Herbert said flatly. "I never did get that existential drop-out stuff you and your friends were into." He twirled his swizzle stick in his martini. "I mean, I admit the guy can write . . ."

"I feel like Pinky's playing some sort of game with me," Gary said emphatically. "But I don't know if I'm supposed to make a move, or just sit back and enjoy the joke."

"There's nothing more serious than a game," Herbert said, "and don't you forget it." He drew deeply from his martini. "But I don't see what Chuck hopes to accomplish with this one, unless it's a stretch in the federal prison system. Frankly, it all seems pretty kooky, if you ask me."

"That may be," Gary said. "But what's sanity, after all? United States foreign policy?"

"You know me better than that, my friend," Herbert said, a touch combative now. "I've been battling that nuttiness since the sixties." He turned to me and softened his tone. "I worked in aid programs in Southeast Asia," he confided, "and I could see that we were missing the 'hearts and minds' piece in a big way. A big way. Defense approached social action like a bunch of engineers. McNamara and his numbers! He figured, what the heck, it had worked for the Ford Corporation. Sure it did. But what they didn't calculate is that you can't engineer people into liking you. That requires things like sincerity, decency, and actually caring about them. When it's all just a load of crap, they can sense it. Let's face it, for our so-called best and brightest, the Vietnamese people were just so many little brown pawns on the geo-strategic chessboard. There was no understanding, no feeling. How else could they have foisted Diem off on them, not to mention Ky and Thieu—or bombed their country into the stone age? They were all out in their own, private little La-la-lands. Between you and me, I doubt the current crowd is going to do any better by the people of the Persian Gulf.”

The waitress came with food. Herbert exhaled his frustration, took up his utensils, and gazed upon his omelet as if he didn’t know what to do with it. He cut it up mechanically and, after a sip from his martini, took a couple of aimless bites.

“Look at it, Gare,” he picked up again, “the same mistakes were repeated in Central America. We didn’t learn a thing! Incidentally, how’s that friend of yours down there? Look, I can understand you two quitting. That’s what I should have done, before they gave me the boot. *Rien ne vous tue un homme comme d’être obligé de représenter un pays*—ha ha!” (Gary turned and translated for me: “nothing kills a man like having to represent a country.”)

Herbert addressed his eggs now with greater relish. After eating this way for a minute or two, he resumed. “By the way,” he said to Gary, “you really ought to get back in the game. I mean, what do you expect to accomplish by sitting on the sidelines?”

He went back to his omelet. Gary stared thoughtfully into his beer, either unable or unwilling to respond.

“Listen, I know how it is,” Herbert went on after wiping his mouth with his napkin. “I remember when my idealistic cherry got busted. 1949. The so-called ‘wise men’ running the show. Acheson and that crowd. All the blasted French wanted was their Asian colony back, and we bought into the whole commie scare—agreed to finance their war against the people of Vietnam. These were the same generals who had collaborated with the Nazis!”

“Do you really think that France would have gone red?” Gary asked.

“You don’t get it, my friend.” Herbert’s voice grew tense. “You just don’t get it! It doesn’t matter whether they would have gone red. The point is, the generals said they would, and they had our boys convinced that they were ready to step in. You’ve got to understand the kind of Neanderthals we were dealing with. Think Dreyfus affair. We should have taken them on in France for democracy, rather than get involved in their dirty colonial war in Indochina."

Herbert pushed his plate aside, as if he might so easily dismiss his frustrations over his nation's many blunders. He wiped his mouth again and settled back. Slowly lifting his martini to his lips, he took a long and leisurely sip. This seemed to calm him. "I can't say that I'm happy about this business with Chuck."

"We're worried about him, too," I said.

He set his drink on the table. "I certainly hope he hasn't lost it. You know, he really put me onto something with that Taoism. It's great stuff. Ought to be required reading for all foreign service recruits. We've got to learn how to understand the larger forces at work. In the complicated world we're living in these days, good ol' Yankee pluck and ingenuity just ain't going to cut it."

Unable to interest Gary in another beer, Herbert called for the check. "Those exercises he showed me," he said, "do 'em every morning. Not bad for a geezer, eh?"

Gary said that he envied his consistency.

"You've got to stick with it," Herbert said. "And listen, find some way to get involved again. Really. We can't afford to have good minds like yours sitting out the game."

We climbed the hilly streets toward Herbert's building. On the way he revived the subject of Charles's disappearance, his voice rising choppily over the drone of cars drifting up from the avenue. "If you really want to understand what Chuck's up to," he said, "take a bit of advice from a man who's been trying to checkmate the character for several years now. Expect him to stand his ground. He's not going to react—or be intimidated. It's all Sun Tzu. Better to defend than attack. Or, best of all, to win without a battle. Also, expect the unexpected. Count on him to turn up when you'd least anticipate it."

We came to the high ground and made our way across the grassy square to Herbert's building. He invited us up to take a look at some rare books he had acquired, ancient Taoist texts on attaining immortality. They were fanned across one end of his dining table, a small oasis of clarity amid the clutter. After examining them, Gary with great interest, we prepared to take our leave. Herbert had to attend to some business involving the sale of several helicopters to the Canadian government.

"It's just a few Sikorskis," he explained as we approached the door, "but there's decent money in it. That's one thing I learned from Kissinger," he added with his crooked smile, "cashing in on the connections. Of course, the old fox is way ahead of me in that department."

Herbert held the door while we said our goodbyes. We left the building and walked into the square. I hugged Gary there in the park and then, responding to an irrepressible urge, took his arm and directed him toward Textile House.

We each slipped a five dollar bill into the plastic kiosk and stepped over the heavy ceramic tiles to the French doors that lead to the museum's garden. After examining its Renaissance statuary, we wandered to the stone balustrade at the garden's far end. From the high ground on which the museum is situated you can sight over the city toward the State Department and, beyond that, the river. Our meeting with Herbert had done us both good. I felt the calming influence of a wise elder, both within myself and in the way Gary, placing one arm comfortably around me, pressed me into him.

The Holocaust items had gone; now there was an exhibit of Japanese resist-dye tapestries. Gary seemed as charmed as I by the shimmering linen surfaces and bold designs, most of them from nature, meticulously realized by painting wax onto the fabric in successive dyings. A smaller gallery upstairs contained a collection of ancient shawls from Guatemala; neither of us mentioned Gary's missing friend, Clark, though thoughts of him were woven into every strand of the richly colored garments. We looked over the balcony onto the main galleries below. The Japanese textiles looked strangely different from above, the other museum-goers timeless in their absorption.

We browsed in the gift shop before leaving. Gary bought me a shawl, I a warm scarf for him. We drove back to his place, made dinner for ourselves, and listened to some music. I went home early Sunday morning to catch up with personal chores and prepare for another week at the clinic.

❧ ❧ ❧

MONDAY I HEARD from my mother. Bob would be coming through town on Thursday, and we were to have an early Christmas celebration. She asked if I would be able to pick him up at the airport. I begged off, pleading my client schedule, but assured her that I would be there for dinner.

Tuesday morning Gary called me at the clinic.

"I just spoke to Cynthia," he said breathlessly, without other greeting.

"Cynthia?"

"Pinky's woman."

This was the first I had heard of Charles's ongoing relationship with the lover of his youth. "Really. Tell me more."

"I was up here in Dispatch," he went on, "and when I got up to stretch and looked out the window, —there was the Mercedes, sitting on the opposite curb."

In response to my probings, Gary provided a brief sketch of Charles's lady friend. He said that he used to watch Charles drive off with her to parts unknown, returning only hours later. According to Gary, she resembled a beautiful Motown singer of our youth. He spoke of his friend's infrequent, elliptical, and often pained references to their irregular relationship.

"I wasn't completely sure it was her," he said, "because there was a lot of glare on the window. But when the sun went behind the clouds, there was no question. I went back to work, but I got up now and then to peek out, and she'd just be sitting there, like she was waiting for Pinky to come out. I wasn't sure what to do. I wanted to respect her and Pinky's privacy, but I couldn't bear her thinking that he was intentionally ignoring her."

He asked Randy to cover Dispatch.

"I felt no small misgivings as I walked toward the Benz," he said. "But it seemed the only thing to do."

When Cynthia saw Gary coming toward her she pulled up, as if she would drive away, but he waved to her to stay around. Rolling down the window, she tilted toward him an open expression.

Gary introduced himself, and Cynthia replied that she had heard a great deal about him. He told her that Charles had been away and asked whether she had heard from him. She said she hadn't. Clearly distressed at his unexplained absence, she was desperate for any information Gary might be able to offer.

"It didn't seem like the time—or place—to go into details," Gary told me. "Frankly, I wasn't too sure how to handle it. And I had to get back inside. Randy doesn't know any more about Dispatch than I know how to weld a frame."

He offered to meet Cynthia after work and, after a silent calculation, she agreed. He also suggested that I come along. An old friend of Charles, he said.

We met at a bar near Farragut Square. On the way Gary filled me in on Charles and Cynthia's long but broken history. I was already familiar, from Charles's participation in the vets group, with the story's early chapters.

Her elegant spirit expressed itself in a trim woolen suit of subdued earth tones. "Let's not be uptight about this, okay?" she asked right away. We were seated at a quiet booth in a dimly lit corner. "I mean, you both know the story, right?"

We agreed.

"It's not that I feel okay about it," she said with downcast eyes. "I had to lie just to meet you two. I told Russell I had more Christmas shopping to do." She touched a big department store bag that sat beside her on the booth bench. "Sometimes I wish I'd never gotten into this situation. But it's so complicated. Chuck and I were high school sweethearts . . ."

She started to choke up. I reached over the table and laid my hand on hers. She excused herself, pulled a tissue from her purse, and wiped her eyes. "This whole thing, him disappearing on me, it's like when he came back from Vietnam. There's the same waiting, and him not being there. Not *really* there. Do you know what I mean?"

I assured her that I did.

"You haven't heard a thing?" Gary asked.

"No," she said. "We don't talk that often. I have this meeting in town once a month. That's when I come—after. The last three times, he didn't come out of the shop."

There was silence. She looked down briefly, and then into my eyes. "It started so simple," she said. "I'd heard he was back on his feet, and that he had started his own business. I just wanted to see for myself that he was okay. I never felt right about us. About ending things after the war. But what else could I do? He pushed me away. And I didn't understand anything. We were both so young—"

She closed her eyes tightly, repressing a still-sharp grief. A waitress approached and took our drink orders. After she left, Cynthia took up again.

"We met for lunch. If I had known what was going to happen, I would have never come. That's what I tell myself, anyway. But all the old feelings came back. Things that have never really been there with Russell. He was the Charles I used to know. Except stronger, more solid. A man, not a kid."

"The past can be very powerful," I said.

"We didn't know what we were getting into." She looked off across the restaurant. "It was bigger than both of us. We kept saying we'd cut it off, wait until my boys are grown. Run off . . ." She was unable to explain further. She looked at the wine the waitress had delivered, brought the glass to her lips and tasted it.

Gary fleshed out Charles's situation with great delicacy, I occasionally interjecting a clarifying remark. Cynthia listened intently.

"I remember our last conversation," she said when Gary fell silent. "Charles said there were times when a man had to stand for something. He and I, he said, had gotten ourselves into a place where he didn't know what we stood for. Then he said something strange. He said there were some things he had to do, and that to do them his life had to be as clear as water. That's the way he put it. *Clear as water.* I wasn't sure what he was talking about. It seemed so totally out of the blue. I'm not sure I wanted to know. Maybe he couldn't take the strain anymore." She looked at me. "Marj," she said, "you don't think he—"

She couldn't finish.

"I don't think so," I said.

We walked her to her car. She lightly embraced us both, and we promised to keep her informed.

Part II

WINTER

BOB GREETED ME AT THE DOOR in jeans and a check-
ered flannel shirt. Taller than my father, but with his mouth set
in the same eternal question, he looked trim and relaxed. We
hugged and, as my mother called out a cheerful greeting walked
toward the kitchen. I looked around: the house was well lit, im-
maculately clean, and gorgeously decorated for the season. The
heady aroma of a roasting turkey filled the rooms, with under-
tones of a baking pie. Mom wore a deep red velvet dress and
her best shoes and had her hair done in a nice sweep. One of
my parents' old Christmas albums—Mitch Miller, I think—was
on the stereo. The table was set with the best china, and candles
floating in aromatic oil.

While Mom and I fixed dinner, Bob leaned against the
counter and chatted about his flight, congestion at the airport,
and traffic on the way to my mother's. After we exhausted these
topics, occasioning a lull in our conversation, I asked about
Gloria and Drew.

"They're doing all right," Bob said in his stifled way, a manner that has always struck me as a determined effort to avoid
anything having to do with his emotional world.

"How are they dealing with Daddy going away?"

"Fine," he said matter-of-factly. "Drew cried a little, but she doesn't really know what's going on."

Mom began to remove the turkey from the oven. She asked for our help, and now final meal preparations absorbed all of our attention. As we placed the last dishes on the table, she said, "All right, no more talk about Iraq." She went into the living room, turned down the stereo, and returned to the table. Sitting at its head, she asked Bob to carve the turkey. When our plates were loaded she extended her arms, closed her eyes, and squeezed our hands in a wordless grace.

As we began to eat, Bob inquired about his childhood playmate Mark McFarland, Cheryl's brother. I told him what I knew of Mark's circumstances, and he began to reminisce.

"I guess we had it pretty good," he said, "with the woods out back. Me and Mark used to love to play army out there. We had that rope swing over the creek. Great for special forces training. I wonder if it's still there."

I told him that much of the old woods had been lost to development.

"Let bygones be bygones, I suppose," Bob commented, plowing forthwith into his turkey and stuffing.

My mother didn't comment.

Bob suddenly looked up from his meal. "Remember that pool?" he blurted. "I don't see those much anymore. Above ground, with the wood deck. You and Cheryl used to spend all summer working on your tans out there. Whatever happened to that, Mom?"

"I can't remember," she said. "Marj went away to school—"

Bob went back to his turkey. "After Dad was gone," he speculated, "I guess you couldn't keep up with the maintenance."

"I'm sure Mr. McFarland would have been happy to help," I said.

Mom maintained a stony silence; Bob and I exchanged a

quiet glance.

"I still have those albums you left at home when you went off to college," Bob said after a moment, and I was grateful that he had changed the subject. "Gloria and I listen to them all the time. Drew likes them, too. I hope you don't want them back," he added with a laugh.

I said that he could keep them.

"You're a pretty good sister, I guess."

"As a brother, I'd say you're fair."

My mother smiled, more comfortable with our sibling banter than with painful reminiscences.

Setting down his silverware, Bob slyly trained his eyes on me. "Okay now, Sis," he said, "tell us about that boyfriend of yours."

It was the usual tease, but announced with such certainty, and so like my father, that I hesitated to answer.

"She doesn't call it boyfriend," Mom said. "She says they're just *friends*."

"Really?" Bob leaned back in his chair, focusing that eternal question on me with all my father's steady force.

I was considering how to respond, but it really didn't matter, because the vertigo started. I vaguely remember Bob and my mother getting up, and then hearing my mother's words: "Now we've gotten her upset. It's probably her time of the month. She shouldn't have had that wine." The next I remember I was lying on the couch, with Mom and Bob sitting opposite sipping coffee. They took note when I stirred; Mom came and sat beside me while I collected myself. Afterwards we cut the pie and had dessert.

I interrupted our meandering conversation to volunteer that Bob had been right. "Actually, it so happens that I do have a man in my life these days," I said. "And Mom, I'm not talking about Jorge."

"Well," she said, "I guess I have to wait for Bobby to come home to find out what's going on with my own daughter."

A satisfied smile came across Bob's face. I resisted my mother's entreaties for more information, uncertain how I would finesse how Gary and I had met. "You'll learn about him in due time," was all I said, realizing how far I had projected our relationship into the future.

"I'd say this calls for a toast," Mom said, "—but we'd better not give you any more wine. I expect you'll bring him around some time."

I didn't argue.

It was getting late, so I agreed to stay over and drive Bob to the airport in the morning. After cleaning up the kitchen we all performed our ablutions and settled into our bedrooms. Was it my imagination, or could I hear them breathing through the walls? I wanted to go down the hallway and tuck them in. As I lay in bed, my mother's little townhouse seemed to float above the earth, insulated from a world of fighting and trauma by the love of my family . . .

It started with an intimation of his presence, the sound of heavy chains, and a horrible scraping. I previsioned terror, caught my breath, and reached for something to hold to. Suddenly he was there, grinning in amusement. "Sorry, Princess," he said, "I just wanted to get your attention."

"It wasn't funny," I pouted, though I couldn't help but smile at the kitschiness of the haunted house motif.

"Sometimes life isn't so funny, either," Dad said.

"But after we've had such a nice holiday celebration. . ."

"I didn't mean to upset you, Boop. I just thought you might get a laugh out of it."

He was fading away.

"Daddy," I cried, reaching into the darkness. "Whatever happened to the pool?"

"Forget about the pool!" he called out, as if from across an abyss, and he was gone.

We were up early. I stood in the foyer with my mother while Bob loaded his things into my car. Mom had decided to stay behind.

"Sure you don't want to come to the airport and see him off?" I asked. "I've got plenty of time to bring you back before I'm due at the clinic."

She gazed toward where Bob hoisted his duffle bag into the trunk through the frosty air. "Honey," she said with a low tautness in her voice, "I gave them one man. I'm not about to watch them take another one away."

But when Bob stepped up to the door, she bravely pressed down the shoulders of his uniform, held him to her, and kissed his cheek. I embraced her also and walked with Bob to the car. We looked to wave before we pulled away, our always ritual, but the door was closed, the curtains at the window drawn tight.

On the way to the airport I was able to learn more about Bob's deployment. His reserve unit was attached to a regular Marine tank battalion. It sounded likely they would be part of any ground assault on Iraq. Bob was to be in Georgia for two weeks before flying to Saudi Arabia with the rest of his company. He wasn't sanguine about the possibility of a peaceful settlement. Secretary of State Baker and Iraq Foreign Minister Aziz were engaged in cat and mouse negotiations, each insisting upon conditions which they knew the other could never accept.

"Releasing the hostages was a dumb move, tactically speaking," Bob said. "Now we're completely free to go after him."

I reminded Bob of his confidence, at the outset of the whole mess, that Hussein wasn't crazy enough to court war with the world's sole remaining superpower.

"That's just the thing. Saddam doesn't think he is courting war. He thinks he can peel off our allies with gambits like this hostage release. No, he's not crazy. He's just not as smart as he thinks he is."

I said I wished our leaders were smart enough to find a way to settle things without getting my little brother involved, resting one hand on his shoulder while I drove. He gazed out the window with benign neutrality, as if his personal fate were not important.

After parking at the airport we went in and sat together at the gate until they boarded his flight. When we hugged I didn't want to let him go; but when I saw that he was getting embarrassed I kissed his cheek, told him that I loved him and stepped back to watch him walk, straight as my father, down the ramp.

& & &

I DROVE FROM THE AIRPORT with part of me bulleting through the winter sky on a plane I had watched rise through plate glass windows arced with early light. Freeway traffic was heavy into town, the air fuzzy with a palpitating frozen dampness. There was a hole in my gut I didn't wish to fill with the radio, the passing scenery, or thoughts of the day ahead. Seeing Bob march off to war touched on the most painful traumas of my life, and I knew how excruciating it had to be for my mother. I couldn't conceive how our poor, truncated family could bear another tragedy.

I walked though the lobby of the clinic's building feeling bereft, my only consolation the thought of finding Gary at the Gathering that evening. It seemed my clients sensed my mood: restraining, even, their expressions of distress so as not to trouble me unduly.

The proud bearing of stalwart centurions standing high and stony guard around Union Station's vaulted ceiling little staunched my worries while I dined after work in the terminal's cavernous concourse; flesh and blood soldiers passing through the station shouldering duffle bags only sharpened my distress. It was still early when I finished half-eating a salmon filet I don't remember tasting. so I spent an hour absently browsing in the station's shops before going to Signed, Sealed & Delivered. I didn't feel up to chatting with the couriers while Gary finished paperwork upstairs.

It was near eight when I arrived at the courier company. Randy, the welder, was stepping out of the maintenance shop when I entered the foyer. He turned out the light and pulled the door behind him; we greeted one another as I got out of my coat.

"I don't know if Gary's around," he drew out slowly, reluctant to impart bad news.

"Really? I thought he always comes to the Gathering."

"That's basically true," he said, "but I think he said goodnight a while back." Reading the disappointment in my face, he hastened to add, "But who knows, maybe he came back. Let's take a look."

We went into the DMZ, where people were clustered in small groups making conversation. While Randy went upstairs to look for Gary, Ben and Henry called me over to where they talked with several others.

"We didn't think we'd see you tonight," Henry said, "what with Gary not being here."

I said I hadn't known that he was gone.

"He said he had some things to take care of," Ben said.

"Yeah, very mysterious," Henry added.

I proffered the best smile I could manage when Henry introduced me to some of their friends. Randy returned to say that he hadn't found Gary, but I decided to stay anyway. It seemed unfriendly to refuse and, besides, I had nowhere else to go. Henry fetched me a glass of wine.

The couriers were discussing ideas for another act of street theater. It had been a couple of weeks since the last communication from the cemetery—the addition to the JFK memorial—and a week since the riders graced the windows of the downtown recruiting office with their subversive poster.

"I wonder if he's planning something, even as we speak," Ben enthused.

Roger was there. "I just hope he's all right."

"He's fine," a guy named Hiep, Indochinese in appearance, said. "He took on the Vietcong, didn't he, and lived to tell the tale?"

"Listen," Ben took up again eagerly, "have you guys ever been to Roosevelt Island? It's out in the Potomac River, near Arlington."

"I have," Randy said. "There's a colossal statue of the old Rough Rider pontificating into thin air, and all these stelae, I think you'd call them, situated around a wide open plaza. It's not a bad place for a hike. There's a footpath all the around the circumfrance of the island . . ."

"That's the place!" Ben said. "But what about the inscriptions on those stelae?" He pulled a folded paper from the back pocket of his jeans.

"I don't know," Randy said. "If you're suggesting messing with the memorial, you're talking about a federal felony."

"Yeah," Henry said, "but only if we get caught."

Ben scanned the paper he had pulled from his pocket. "Listen, Randy," he said, "just try and picture it. Alongside the inscription that says, *Alike for the nation and the individual, the one indispensable requisite is character*, wouldn't it be nice to see, *I took the Canal Zone, and let Congress debate; and while the debate goes on, the canal does also?*"

"You'd better seriously think about this," Randy said.

"What about this one?" Ben went on, unheeding of Randy's

cautions: "*It is of incalculable importance that America, Australia, and Siberia should pass out of the hands of their red, black, and yellow aboriginal owners, and become the heritage of the dominant world races?*"

"Roosevelt said that? God, that's ugly," Henry said. "Let me see that thing, Bro." Taking the paper from Ben, he began to peruse it.

"Give it some time," Randy said. "I'm afraid you guys are just copying the P-man."

"Isn't imitation the sincerest form of flattery?"

"I'm just suggesting you come up with something of your own."

"Listen to this," Henry said: "*I don't go so far as to think that the only good Indians are dead Indians, but I believe nine out of ten are, and I shouldn't like to inquire too closely into the case of the tenth!* Man, this guy was president? No wonder the country's so screwed up." He handed the paper back to Ben.

"I can already picture it," Tomás said, looking off dreamily.

"Whatever," Randy said, "I'd just urge you to think about the consequences." He began to walk toward the refreshment table.

"Wait," Ben called out to his back, "just one more: *The pacifist is just as surely a traitor to his country . . . and to humanity . . . as is the most brutal warmonger.* What would you think about that one?"

"The dude had one twisted mind, no question about it," Randy tossed over his shoulder, before moving out of earshot.

Ben stuffed the paper back in his pocket, and he and his friends continued their discussion. Only vaguely listening, I began to wonder what Gary was doing. I excused myself, went to Charles's desk, and used the phone to try his apartment. Receiving no reply, I left a message.

A drum circle was organized, but I climbed to the upstairs lounge and settled on the couch. At ten o'clock Gary still hadn't come; I was on the verge of tears. My mother was right about my time of the month: my emotions were keyed up. What mysterious things might Gary need to take care of, I wondered. I couldn't help picture receptionists all over town whom he had subjected to his considerable charms over the years. Maybe he secretly resented my troubled reaction to Jorge's departure and was acting out. We didn't have a date, but after our meeting with Cynthia we had mentioned seeing one another at week's end. It was all reminiscent of my sad history with Stephen, my academic mentor-cum-lover—never there when I needed him.

I decided to go home.

Despite my weariness I was reluctant to go to bed, for I feared further nocturnal visions of my father. His spectral appearance of the previous night had been so oddly truncated, as if a sequel were in the offing. I made a cup of tea, sat in the bowl chair, and thought over the holiday celebration at my mother's. Neither her immaculate housekeeping, nor the bright Christmas décor, nor her apparent disinterest in the Persian Gulf deceived me. I had seen it all before: the game face of the military wife. I knew that deep inside she seethed with a helpless rage. It was evident, to one who knew her well, in how she closed herself off, door closed and curtains drawn, when Bob and I drove away.

A midnight call to Gary's place was again greeted by the annoyingly svelte voice of his answering machine robot. I told him how I had taken Bob to the airport and asked him to call no matter what the hour. Thinking I might escape unwanted dreams by avoiding the bed, I tried to rest on the couch. There were no dreams, but no sleep either. At five o'clock I got up and made coffee. Another attempt to reach Gary rendered the same result as the earlier ones. How could he repeatedly sleep through the phone, not more than five feet from his bed? I left another message telling him what a horrible night I had had and added woundedly that it would have been nice if he had called. Unable to bear my apartment any longer, I put on warm clothes, went out to the avenue, and made for downtown.

Few people were out and about. A man made deliveries to the coffee shop across from the zoo; another filled newspaper vending machines. I was tempted to walk through the park and across to Gary's place, but got hung on the thought that he was intentionally eluding me. At the worst, it occurred to me—and with a sharp pang of distress—was the prospect that he was not alone! At the very least, after three voicemails in one night, pitifullly pleading for comfort, there was a distinct possibility that he might classify me as "high-maintenance."

A passing car made me wonder where anyone would go so early on a Saturday morning. I didn't know where I was going, either, but the sound of my footsteps on the sidewalk was the only barrier between my life and some abyss I didn't wish to deal with. Clouds bloomed out of the dawning sky beyond the bridge with the lion statues; apartment houses that line the avenue on the opposite rim of the creek's deep valley were stone quiet. Their denizens were all no doubt still sound asleep, as oblivious to what had happened the day before as to what tomorrow would bring. Passing the McClellan statue, then continuing on down the slope into the city's commercial district, I felt more alone than ever. All the traumas of the world, and my little piece of it, were irrelevant to these empty blocks of granite and glass. There wasn't even yet any place open to get out of the cold and have a cup of coffee! The city's pigeons shuttled over the avenue and settled on their window ledges; I stood on the sidewalk and shivered. My outing had brought me no solace, and with a weary resignation I trudged my way back up the hill. When I reached its crest I sat in McClellan's shadow and watched my breath in the cold air. It seemed so wrong, my brother going off to war. Hadn't we learned anything? The pusillanimous general, mutely frozen on his gleaming horse, had no answers. I reflected on how my mother must be struggling, and I began to cry. Passing cars had now become more frequent, but I didn't care. I buried my face in my mittens and allowed myself a full-on pity party.

"Darling—" I was startled by his voice, "what on earth's the matter?"

He stood astride his bicycle, only feet away from me.

"Where have you been?" I sobbed. But before he could answer, I blurted, "and do you always have to wear that stupid field jacket!"

After laying down the bicycle, he proceeded to calmly remove his father's old garment. Exposed to the cold in his flannel shirt, he offered me the faded green cloth in wordless sacrifice. I laughed at myself, went to him, and took the jacket from his hands. I helped him to slide it again over his arms and to button it, fretted about him catching a cold, and kissed his neck and cheeks.

"This thin fabric's not adequate for this weather. You have to layer more."

"I was in a hurry," he said. "When I heard your messages, I was worried about you."

"How'd you know where I was?"

"You said you were out walking. I figured you had to be around here someplace."

I let him hold me. "It was so hard to watch Bobby go."

"I can imagine."

I kissed him again and apologized for my outburst, pleading hormones, and we walked toward my place. "Why didn't you answer my calls?" I asked.

"I was out," he said distractedly.

"All night long? Where were you?"

"Just . . . out."

"Catting around?" I asked quietly. I tried to sound arch and aloof, but inwardly I dreaded his answer.

He hugged me close and kissed my hair. "Nothing like that, dummy."

We walked in silence for a moment.

"I was just doing some riding . . . and thinking."

We were crossing the lion statue bridge. He stopped at the rail and looked down into the valley of the park.

"Was something the matter?"

He thought for a moment before he responded. "That message from Pinky—about the knight, the bishop—it seems to have set off something inside of me."

I said that I could tell he had been troubled by the note.

"I feel it's like a challenge," he said. "To get my act together, I guess you could say. At the company, the Gathering, they all come to me now. They don't say it, but I feel like they expect me to take Pinky's place. And frankly,' " he added quietly, "I don't think I'm up to it." He looked off into the distance and turned upon himself. After watching cars lumber across the bridge's traffic lanes for a moment, he leaned back against the railing and stared at his shoes. "And then," he picked up again after a minute, "when we talked to Herbert Mayfield the other day, —well, it got me questioning some of the decisions I've made. Here we are, descending into the savagery of war again, and what good do all my fine thoughts do, committed to my notebooks for my eyes alone? Maybe I should have stayed at State. I could have had some influence. Worked for peace . . ."

"You followed your heart," I said. "I wouldn't question that."

"I know," he said. "But still—" He was at a loss, and he fell silent as we walked on. But before we reached the end of the bridge, he stopped and again moved to the railing. "There's also something else," he said now, "—something else that's been bothering me." He looked down into the gulf of the valley for a long moment before he went on. "It's about Clark," he said, "about something I said before he left the country."

"Yes?"

"I didn't take it seriously myself when I said it. Clark was about to leave for Guatemala. It was almost a joke. Like some kind of line from a movie." He hesitated, subtly rocking, and grasped the bridge's railing with both hands.

"Well, what was it?" I asked gently, tugging lightly at his sleeve.

He looked off over the crowns of the valley's trees and spoke reluctantly. "I said that if he didn't come back, that I was going to come in after him. I was really just clowning. You know, in a sort of faux-Rambo way. I didn't actually think that he would up and disappear on me . . ."

"And now—"

"That's exactly what's happened."

I held him tightly. "Baby, you've got a lot on your mind."

"I'm sorry I missed your calls. I didn't get in until dawn. I came right away."

I said that he was my hero and kissed him madly right there on the sidewalk. I assured him that everything would be all right and that I would be there for him no matter what came down.

He promised me the same. We stopped on the avenue for breakfast; afterward we went to my place and passed the rest of the morning buried in the warmth of my bed. In the afternoon he went home to catch up on his chores before Cheryl's party, which was scheduled for that evening.

❧ ❧ ❧

I HARDLY RECOGNIZED the man who came down the porch steps of the rowhouse in an elegant overcoat and jaunty cap. When he got into the car and opened the overcoat, I also saw the sports coat and tie, fine worsted slacks and brightly polished loafers.

"You didn't have to dress up." I figured I had rattled him with my outburst about the field jacket.

"I wanted to make a good impression on your friends," he said. "Besides, I wanted you to know that this one-time diplomat can still cut a figure when he has to—in case you should ever need an envoy, for instance. Incidentally," he added, and he shifted to face me, "you're looking pretty swell yourself."

We drove to the burbs across the fleeting vectors of city-flung arteries, past tract houses strung with colored lights and shopping plazas festooned with holiday decorations. Gary said that he had been thinking about the stress we had each been under. He remarked that the courier business would be slow between Christmas and New Year's, and opined that he thought it would do us both good to get away.

"What would you think about finding a cabin in the mountains somewhere?" he asked.

I was thrilled with the idea, I told him, but said that I would have to see if things could be arranged at the clinic.

As we approached Cheryl and Dan's the CBS news report came on the radio. The United States government, citing unacceptable conditions, had cancelled its scheduled talks with the Iraqis: we had ratcheted yet another notch closer to war. The news cast a somber spin on the big wreath, full of holly berries, that hung on Cheryl's front door. Through the bay window we saw the other guests crowded into the living room. We entered without knocking, and after we put up our coats I led Gary to the kitchen to find Cheryl. Little Emmy, more steady on her feet than the last time I had seen her, rushed over to be picked up; while she force-fed me a Christmas cookie Julian looked on in his bewondered way. Gary patted him on the head and called him sport, and the presence of Cheryl and the children made the weight of the times more tolerable. Dan came in and introductions were made all around. He led Gary to the other guests in the living room, while I stayed back to help Cheryl put some trays together.

"So that's him," she said.

"That's him."

I laid cookies in concentric rings while she arranged wedges of cheese in circles of crackers. Julian stood beside me and pulled at the fabric of my skirt.

"You never told me how you two met."

I thought for a moment. "Through work."

"Is he a therapist?"

"No, more a friend of a friend."

We concentrated on the trays for a moment.

"What does he do?" she asked.

Dispatcher at a courier company didn't seem to convey Gary, with his *magnum opus*, his poetry, his Bach and the Gathering. "He does a lot of things. He's very talented." Then, thinking how he had offered me his field jacket that morning, I added, "and very sweet."

"Sounds mysterious," she said as she put the finishing touches on her tray.

We carried the hors d'oeuvres into the living room. Cheryl was beautiful in a black and red holiday dress with sequins, high waist, and fine pleatings. The fire was ablaze, the mantle hung with stockings I had seen since I was a girl. Across its top were other McFarland Christmas heirlooms—the plastic Santa with a sack slung over one shoulder, a top-hatted snowman on skies, a pair of wooden reindeer.

Gary had taken up with a group that included Mark McFarland. As we approached we could hear them talking about the cancelled negotiations.

"I never saw the point in all that chit-chat anyway," Mark was saying. "We may as well go in and get it over with."

"There's a certain logic in what you're saying," Gary said, though I suspected that he was merely being *diplomatic.*

"I guess they want to be able to say that we did everything we could to avoid war," Mark said.

"I'd imagine that's the biggest part of their motivation," Gary remarked. "And who knows, if by some miracle Hussein were to vacate Kuwait . . ."

Cheryl and I set our trays on the coffee table and Cheryl, moving toward Mark, asked for everyone's attention. "There's only one rule tonight," she said, "—no talking politics. Oh, and everyone has to at least try and sing a few carols." She made her announcements with such good humor, immediately commencing to collect empty glasses, that she hardly seemed bossy at all. I marveled at her finesse. After returning from the kitchen she went back to Mark and affectionately squeezed his shoulder. When he told her that Gary had been in the diplomatic corps, she stepped back to take in my lover's height and breadth. "The mystery deepens," she purred, smiling coyly before disappearing to other hostess chores. Gary cast me a quizzical glance, Mark inquired about Bob, and we all discussed his deployment.

Cheryl soon reappeared to suggest that we prepare to serenade the neighbors. While the other guests went for coats and scarves, she led me to the dining room, where it was darkly quiet.

"I've been so scattered," she said, "I didn't even get a chance to ask you about Bob's visit."

I abbreviated my response. Bob's stoicism, my mother's display of normality: these things I hardly needed to describe. Cheryl's was also a military family; she knew the drill. Then I mentioned, almost in passing, that my father had once again begun to haunt my dreams.

She pressed together her lips and nodded. I could see how many things were on her mind, and my family's troubles were now among them. "Let's talk about that later, can we?" Her expression grew thoughtful and she squeezed my hand.

The neighbors were mostly delighted by our revels, and I enjoyed watching Gary hoist Julian onto his shoulders, to carry him from house to house, almost as much as I liked gently rocking Emmy while we sang. The party broke up after midnight, with hugs all around. Gary and I slept well, and in the morning he made us blueberry pancakes.

& & &

THE HOLIDAYS are always difficult for me. It was during this season, against the backdrop of the infamous Christmas bombings of North Vietnam, that my father took his life. For years our family gatherings were dark and mournful. But over time we learned to split our awareness; to celebrate the season, while never ceasing to remember him. Last year was much the same—except now there were new complications, with the coming of another war, Bob in danger, and my old mentor Charles Pinckney's strange doings.

There were few geopolitical developments during the two weeks between Cheryl's party and the Christmas holidays. An effort was underway to reschedule talks, but nothing concrete had emerged. Our government remained adamant in its demand that Iraqi forces vacate Kuwait, while Hussein and his envoy, Tariq Aziz, threatened the now *de rigeur* "rivers of blood" should their armies come under attack.

The men in the vets group were at sixes and sevens. The imminence of war hung over our nation, yet the stalled talks created a lull, something Danny called "phony war."

"Hey, that doesn't mean we're not going to get the whole enchilada," he said at our Thursday evening session. "The same thing happened after Hitler grabbed the Low Countries. First you get the mobilization, and then there's a load of trash talk. It just takes a while to see who's going to make the first move . . ."

I had begun with relaxation exercises, using guided imagery and deep breathing. After we exhausted the Iraq situation, with only minutes remaining, Danny spoke out of the blue.

"Hey, I wonder what's happening with that character at the cemetery. For some reason I can't get him out of my mind. Maybe it's because somebody's doing something, for chrissake."

He looked toward me. I had frequently promoted the healing effects of positive action. My only response was a noncommittal gesture of the eyes.

Danny turned back to the group. "My subversive sources haven't come up with anything new," he said, "but you can bet the authorities haven't dropped the investigation. That thing with the JFK memorial was serious freaking business. This guy has cojones, whoever he is. He strikes, lets things chill for a while, and then he hits again. That's what he's doing now. Security over at Arlington must be tighter than a nun's—well, you know what I mean."

"They got the eternal flame open again," Thomas said.

"Hey, you don't say?" Danny replied, and he lowered his voice. "You know, I've been thinking. Maybe we ought to go over there and take a look, see if we can figure out who's pulling this crap."

The men turned skeptical expressions his way.

"Why are you looking at me like that? This guy's obviously sharp, but I've got some stuff up my sleeve, too, you know. I say we go over there and reconnoiter. Come on, I wouldn't mind talking to this guy, see what kind of crazy bug he's got up his derriere. Then, if he's an asshole, we can bust him."

The men were quiet. I didn't like where things were heading, and I suggested to Danny that he carefully consider his motivations.

"That's easy," he said, "I just want to make contact." He looked around at his comrades. "Maybe you got to be a vet to understand."

I took the group's silence to be an affirmation.

The group broke up with plans for Saturday night basketball. While getting my things together, I looked ahead to the last weekend before Christmas . . .

On Friday, Gary and I went to a party at Signed, Sealed & Delivered. There was a lighted Christmas tree and wreaths, but also a menorah at the refreshment table, Henry's paper mural depicting the ideals of Kwanza, and a Diwali house with a statue of the elephant-headed god, courtesy of Subesh. There was a radiant energy to the drum circle, with heartfelt wishes for universal peace and harmony. After the echo of the last beats died away, a discussion broke out about Charles's situation. The couriers were nonplussed by the silence that had reigned over the cemetery since the episode at the JFK Memorial, and Ben lobbied again for a move against the Theodore Roosevelt monument. The idea was debated, along with other acts of street theater, but no definite plans emerged.

On Saturday Gary and I braved blustery downtown corridors to walk between shops and department stores with a growing load of presents. We spent the evening wrapping, listening to music, and sipping cognac. Sunday morning we stopped by Herbert Mayfield's apartment. We watched him unwrap his gift— Troung Nhu Tang's *Memoirs of a Vietcong*—and accepted his offer of holiday cheer. His home was tidier than on our last visit; he was expecting Charlotta later that day.

From Herbert's place we drove to the projects. Mrs. Pinckney had just returned from church, but she sat us down and loaded us with sweets she had baked for the holidays. She showed us a Christmas card she had received from Charles; it afforded her great comfort. "He says he's involved in vets work, just like you two told me," she said, much to our astonishment. "I still think it's peculiar he's so hard to reach, what with the postmark right here in town. Maybe it's some kind of military mail system."

She was genuinely touched by a shawl I had bought her at Textile House, and before we left she took up one of the throws I had admired on my first visit, folded it carefully, and handed it to me. "Please take this," she said. "I'm sorry it's not store-bought, but it's hard for me to get out shopping." I was reluctant to accept her gift, but she wouldn't be refused. I told her that her handmade piece meant more to me than anything she might have purchased, and she took our hands as we stood by the door. "I'm so glad you came," she said. "You two are about the closest thing to Charles I've got right now."

From the projects we drove to the cemetery. The gifts we bore for Denny, John, and Tiny were mostly practical things, food and thick blankets, but there were also a couple of optional items that Gary couldn't resist (classic comic books, a portable radio).

They were happy to see us. We made a lunch of turkey sandwiches from a roasted bird we brought for their holiday meal and ate them by their blazing campfire. We learned that they had seen Charles the previous week, when he had stopped by their camp one night.

"That real cold one," Denny said, "remember? He said he wanted to warm up a bit. No way he can build a fire where he's bivouacked."

"The MPs would be all over him," John said.

Tiny, who was flipping through one of the comic books, let out a spurt of gay laughter.

"He's got a solid sleeping bag, anyhow," Denny said. "Rated twenty below."

"Yeah," John said, "but they're never as good as the rating."

"Ever the cynic," Denny countered.

"Realistic, I call it."

Gary asked if they had been to the offices of the *Underground Stream*.

There was an awkward silence.

"We probably shouldn't talk about it," Denny finally said.

Tiny laughed again.

"It's not like you're just anybody," Denny added.

We waited expectantly.

"Still," he concluded, "we're in a pre-operation black-out." He poked in the fire with a piece of rusted rebar.

"You'll find out soon enough," John supplied.

Gary didn't press the matter, and we chatted amicably while we finished lunch. Leaving the high-tech gloves and insulated vest we had brought for Charles, we said our goodbyes. Gary was clearly affected that his friend had been in the men's camp so recently. He wanted to scope out the cemetery, presumably in hopes that he might find some trace of him there. Remembering that I hadn't tended my father's grave, as I had resolved to do a month earlier, I agreed, and we parked at the visitors center. We got out of the car and climbed up through the rolling hills. All the while Gary's eyes darted across the landscape, as if he expected to spot Charles at any moment.

At the top of a rise we came across a funeral and stopped still, not wishing to disturb the solemn rites. A caisson bearing a flag-draped coffin stood at rest behind six powerful black horses; the mourners, with their emptied faces, looked on. A military band played hymns from a nearby grove. When their instruments fell silent, the mourners dispersed to a line of cars behind the caisson and the cortege began to move. The ritual hadn't changed since my father's burial rites, and much else was the same: the season, the bare trees, even the clouds of steam that rose from the backs of the draft animals. Without words

I directed Gary down a hill and up another rise toward my father's gravesite. The faint strains of taps drifing through the air were followed by the cracking reports of a twenty-one gun salute.

When we reached the grave I was surprised to find it decorated with a Christmas wreath and flowers, for I was that certain my mother hadn't come. Gary suggested that Bob had visited the site without telling me, but that wouldn't explain the freshness of the blossoms—nor the can of sterno, embedded in ferns, that blew a cool, blue flame into the frigid air. Gary knelt to examine the contrivance more closely and then looked up at me.

"Pinky," we each mouthed, almost in unison. Gary stood up and we surveyed our surroundings. There was nothing out of the ordinary, just death and mourning everywhere . . .

We wandered to the far verges of the cemetery, where Gary separated brush all along the fenceline, probing for traces of Charles's encampments. On our way back to the car we stopped at the JFK memorial. The granite facing after the final quotation was smooth and pristine; the ghostly yellow flame fluttered in the mild wind.

Coming down the slope toward the parking lot we noted a crowd gathered around the visitors center, where the muffled tones of a public address system waffled through the air. We advanced our pace to join the throng. They gazed on high— their expressions running the gamut from bewilderment to outrage, from amusement to reverence—toward a rooftop speaker that projected a steady, mellifluous voice over the landscape. Christmas carols played in the background. The voice was one that Gary and I immediately recognized, just as we recognized the ancient words:

Blessed are those who hunger and thirst for righteousness,

for they will be filled,
Blessed are the peacemakers, for they will be called sons of
God . . .

You have heard it said, eye for eye, and tooth for tooth. But
I tell you, do not resist an evil person. If someone strikes
you on the right cheek, turn to him the other also . . .

You have heard it said, "Do not murder, and anyone who
murders will be subject to judgment." But I tell you that
anyone who is angry with his brother will be subject to judg-
ment. Therefore, if you are offering your gift at the altar
and there remember that your brother has something against
you, leave your gift in front of the altar. First go and be
reconciled to your brother; then come and offer your gift . . .

You have heard that it was said, "Love your neighbor and
hate your enemy." But I tell you: Love your enemy and pray
for those who persecute you, that you may be sons of your
Father in heaven . . .

Blessed are those who hunger and thirst for righteousness,
for they will be filled . . .

"Do you think he's up there somewhere?" I asked Gary.

"No, no way. He probably rigged up a recorder with some kind of continuous tape-loop."

A military truck came pulling up. It presently disgorged about a dozen soldiers; these wedged through the crowd under the barking orders of a major. Three of the men took a ladder from the truck's roof and placed it against the building, and one of them began to climb. Some in the crowd applauded, others booed, as the soldier crept across the roof and disabled the speaker. The major ordered the crowd to disburse.

Gary was visibly inspired after hearing Charles's voice. Nor was I unaffected.

"He was giving them more Christianity than they could handle," he said as we pulled away.

I remarked on the military mindset, how it deplores anything unplanned.

"I suppose they get enough of that on the battlefield," Gary said.

I agreed and we were silent for a while. Then, somewhat reservedly, I asked Gary if he would accompany me to a Christmas Eve service at the Union.

"You know that me and religion don't mix so well."

I told him that the Union wasn't a typical church, and that Richard Dorsey always said that the matter of the sacred was more an open question than a set of answers.

"I know," he replied, "and I can't say I disagree with anything Pinky said over that loudspeaker—though some of it's probably too extreme to put into practice. What really bugs me about Christianity is the vindictive father god, and all that cosmic mumbo jumbo about being saved by the blood of Jesus. Not to mention the group-think . . ."

I assured him that that wasn't how the Union operated.

He declined to respond, but there was a softening in his expression.

I went on to say that I couldn't easily explain my own involvement with the Union; only that I carried, perhaps as a result of childhood imprinting, a radiant vision of an avatar wholly given to unstinting love for all beings. I was drawn to that vision like a moth to a flame. "There are a lot of intelligent people in the congregation," I added as I took his hand.

"Do I have to wear a suit?"

I HAD NO APPOINTMENTS on Christmas Eve but went to the clinic to spend some time at my desk. Gary had rented a cabin in the mountains of West Virginia; a couple of colleagues had agreed to fill in for me, and I wanted to organize my notes for them. Gary was working an abbreviated schedule at Signed, Sealed & Delivered. We were to visit his mother that evening and then attend a candlelight service at the Union. On Christmas Day we would dine with my mother, and on the 26th depart for the mountains.

Mrs. Devers was polite and friendly, if not overly warm; I don't know what I had expected. She was stately in a way I did not find unpleasing, the reflection of a solid core that, for all I could tell, held the universe together. Her apartment, with its high ceilings, spacious rooms, and large windows, was regally though not flamboyantly appointed. With frock-coated ancestors watching from their frames on a sideboard, she served us tea and desserts and gave us each presents. We sang carols, Gary accompanying on the piano, and finally called Gary's brother in Canada. We chatted briefly with his wife and children—Gary's nephew and nieces—and left with an invitation to return for dinner. Mrs. Devers seemed not to dislike me; I decided that I could live with that for the time being.

The Union had organized their Christmas Eve service around presentations about people, near and far, who could use to be kept in our thoughts. Dorothy reported on an effort to set up rural health clinics in Nicaragua; Bud Rawlins briefed us on the soup kitchen he ran out of the church's basement; my friend Tom Mertz described an outreach effort he had spearheaded for the city's isolated elderly. We sang folk songs from around the world and lit candles for "Give Peace a Chance."

After the service I introduced Gary to Richard Dorsey, the pastor, and they quickly lost themselves in Gary's Spanish jurists and just-war theories. Later, when Gary joined Gladys

Turner and me, he listened eagerly to my octogenarian friend's accounts of her anti-war activities in the thirties, and of the career of her late husband, an international economist. Before leaving we spoke with Dorothy about the clinic in Nicaragua; on our drive home I asked Gary if his friend Clark might be near there. "Who knows?" he said, and presently fell into one of his brooding silences.

We arrived at my mother's late on Christmas afternoon. The cold, static air begged to be filled with wind and blizzard. When I removed my coat she remarked on the sweater Gary had given me that morning. Hand-woven in Peru, it was banded with designs that suggested both esoteric knowledge and the simplicity of earthy things.

She wore the same red velvet dress she had worn for Bob's visit and the Christmas decorations were still up, but her housekeeping had lapsed again into slovenliness; I tidied up while she tended to supper preparations. We ate from a roast with vegetables and then sat in the living room sipping coffee. We chatted about the cabin in the mountains, Cheryl's party, and Gary's work at the courier company.

Gary showed great interest in my mother's childhood in Kentucky's rolling farm country: the thoroughbred racing horses, Appalachian folkways, and obscure pioneers who first floated out the Ohio River, contending with Shawnee Indians in their audacious bid to push a fledgling nation's borders westward. She responded to his tactfully insistent queries, but I could see that her mind was elsewhere. When Gary lapsed into momentary silence, his curiosity seeking some new tack, she suddenly stated, out of the blue, that she had gotten a call from Bob. His unit was preparing to embark for Saudi Arabia. We called Ohio to check on Gloria and Drew.

Later that evening, while we watched a holiday special on television, I noted Gary's restlessness. When my mother left the

room I urged him to return to the city and complete his preparations for our trip. I wanted to stay with Mom for the rest of
the holiday and had already packed my bag. He could take my
car and pick me up in the morning, I told him.

From Gary's papers:

The Llewellyn family: perfectly unique, and like many others
I have known. Coming up in Washington during the "American
Century," with signs of Empire everywhere (civil servants and
Pentagon workers, diplomatic families and military brats, the
Washington Post) it is hard, nay, impossible, not to be swept up in
its celebrations of power. Until it is difficult (nay, impossible!)
to distinguish power's uses from its abuses. Until, like the characters in Durrell's *Alexandria Quartet*, we become the city's flora
and fauna, its creatures . . .

Mrs. Llewellyn, hard to describe without resort to paradox.
A soft toughness. She is incalculably feminine, beautiful with
many yearnings, many sorrows, but also a core of strength by
which she survives them all. There is a lushness which echoes
the Kentucky hills where she was nurtured, a surface as yielding
as those grassy pastures! And there is a warmth that I find—
lucky man!—reflected in Marj. But I also detect a pervading
sadness, one she accepts with neither bitterness nor any perverse morbidity, but in the way those hills of her youth accept
the rain that greens them. So unlike my own mother, with her
crisp appearances; yet, in the last analysis, that same stoical
grace! I have only just met her, but I feel that I can say these
things with confidence.

When Marj walked me to the car she said that Mrs. Llewellyn
hadn't been herself lately. She took this to be the reaction of
any mother with a son going off to war, but also symptom-
atic of still-clinging shreds of her husband's untimely death.
Lord knows, the presence of the colonel was palpable in that

place, and not simply in photographs arrayed across the credenza against the living room wall. Straight and alert in dress blues, climbing into the cockpit of an F-14 with a thumbs-up, or clowning with his children at the beach, you can't escape the eyes' steady flame, an inner warmth, and a readiness to sacrifice in every gesture. His absence and presence merged with Bob's, as their images merged in those photographs: Bob as a child, a youth, and then in the uniform of a Marine sergeant. It all ended with me feeling that my simple male-ness rendered me a stand-in for these missing men. Though without a warrior's credentials, I hoped that in some way I was able to allay the spirit of desolation that seemed to hang over that house.

Tomorrow I see Marj again, five days alone together! In those cloven mountains might we cleave one another, create valleys whose riverbanks are spread with fruitful orchards of love and memory! How odd that she asked me to bring along the old field jacket; I've avoided wearing it after her little upset. But that brings me to something else about the colonel. That warrior spirit—I see it in his daughter. No, I could never conceive of Marj wielding a weapon. But his clear-sighted courage is one of his many legacies to the woman I love. The steady, piercing eyes, they are hers, alloyed enough with her mother's fertile softness to make her the object, for me, of the most extravagant fascination! I ache at the mere thought of her. Morning come!

After Gary left, Mom and I cleaned the dishes. Bob was on our minds, but we scrubbed along in silence, not daring to mention our worst fears. "Gary seems like a nice man," she finally said as we put the last of the dishes into the rack. I braced myself for the expected analysis of his career prospects but it did not come. She just folded the dish towel and placed it over the oven's door handle. I asked how she was feeling and said that I was concerned about her spending the rest of the holiday season alone.

"Don't worry about me," she said. "You just go and have yourself a good time."

I didn't mention the growing disorder of her household, nor her oddly distracted moods. She had been taking care of herself since the death of my father, I told myself, perhaps a little too optimistically.

"Frankly," she said, interrupting my thoughts, "I'd just as soon have some time to myself."

Her remark startled me, for she had always loved nothing more than having family around. I hugged her affectionately and we went upstairs to bed.

That night my father made the reappearance I had been both anticipating and dreading. This time I was in the rear seat of a fighter-bomber and Dad was the pilot. Below was the emerald-green countryside of Vietnam. Though we flew at a great altitude, I could see every detail of the landscape, down to the leaves of trees, birds and other animals, even the faces of children who played in the villages.

Dad spoke jauntily. "How we doing back there, Boop? Beautiful day, ain't it, airman?"

I joked with him in return. "Quite beautiful, Sir. Yes, Sir." I spoke with military crispness, and we both laughed.

It filled me with joy to be with him again, surrounded by a preternaturally blue sky, with towering cumuli in the distance. Gorgeous rivers ran down the tropical mountainsides; the clouds cast great moving shadows over the slopes. I distinctly heard bird and monkey calls, the laughter of children, and the quiet conversations of gentle elders rising from the villages below.

"Ready for some fancy maneuvering back there, airman?" my father said, snapping down his visor with decisive force.

"Go for it, Sir," I barked, and cinched my seatbelt tighter.

With a long, swift pull to the joystick the aircraft marked sharply upward. I pushed back into my seat as my father proceeded to execute a display of loops, spins and dives that at first made me laugh but soon provoked a creeping dread. My fingers clawed at the edges of my seat. "Daddy, I finally cried out, "make it stop!"

He must not have heard me, for the craft now spun through a series of maneuvers so violently erratic that I would be hard-pressed to describe them. I cried again for him to end his stunts, but again he did not respond. Fighting the G-forces, I clutched the back of his seat and pulled myself forward, so that I might speak to him. But to my shocked amazement, when I peered around the seat back, I found the pilot seat empty! Only my father's helmet lay there, ominously abandoned. I felt a sense of doom in the pit of my stomach.

The craft, responding to some occult direction, leveled off, and I climbed into the forward seat. I could no longer see the details of the countryside, nor hear its sounds. All below was an undifferentiated gray; colorless too was an enveloping sky which I sensed as an airless, crackling void. The screen on the bomber's instrument panel showed various coordinates and vectors. I couldn't read them but understood with an eerie prescience that we were on a bombing run, and that these queerly moving lines and dots marked our targets. It was also manifestly certain that those targets included the children I had seen in the villages, the animals in the forests, and the gentle and quiet elders. I wanted to abort the mission, but no matter how hard I pulled the joystick, nor in which direction, the craft continued on its course. A sudden voice boomed over the intercom: "Prepare to release load! Prepare to release load!"

My fingers danced desperately across the instrument panel's buttons. Seeking some way to cancel the attack, I was terrified that anything I push might release the bombs instead.

It didn't matter. The assault presently began.

Now, amid the thunderous concussions of an earth-wracking bombardment, I was freshly aware of the ground below. It was engulfed in flame and chaos. Then, suddenly, and without warning, I found myself among the people who faced that armageddon. The scorching heat pierced my skin and the jagged, razored shrapnel. I witnessed my parents, siblings and children maimed and dying, and I ran with others in mindless terror. Finally one mother explosion, more stupendous even than the others, sucked all oxygen from the air. Suffocation. The earth began to sink away. Piercing my despair, my father's voice rang out forcefully. "Mayday! Mayday! Eject! Eject!"

I groped for the eject lever, pulled without thinking, and found myself floating through a calm, blue sky. Presently, hanging from his own chute's wires, my father appeared beside me. He reached over and took my hand.

"How we doing, Boop?"

"I feel horrible." I gasped for breath. "Why did you leave me like that?"

"Sorry, princess. I just needed you to understand. I couldn't think of any other way . . ."

We floated in silence.

"We were supposed to be fighting for peoples' freedoms." He looked away, choking back his emotions. "Somehow it all got horribly bungled up . . ."

My mother was shaking me. I was in a cold sweat. She peered into my eyes.

"I heard you screaming."

I propped myself on one elbow and scraped wet hair from my face. "It was just a bad dream."

She rubbed my arm. "Do you want to talk about it?"

I told her that I would be all right. She held my hand awhile and then returned to bed. In the morning Gary came with the car. Mom wished us a pleasant trip, and we got on our way to West Virginia.

THE CABIN at Lost River was perfect, with walls of sturdy pine and a big stone fireplace. It started to snow the second day. We hiked through the canyon where the cabin was situated and across the ridge to a pasture that overlooks the surrounding valleys. Gary read and worked on his notes; I embroidered his field jacket until I had graced every panel with signs of fertility and peace. We listened to cassette tapes on a boom box and one day went up the ridgeline to conduct a Japanese tea ceremony in a gazebo capped with snow. We made love like maniacs and lounged in front of a blazing fire. I liked to watch him split wood in the cabin's yard; he looked so quintessentially American.

After the snow came a bitter cold that ice-glazed the cabin's windows; when we walked to the park office, the unyielding snowpack returned a dull crunch with every step. There was a payphone outside where I called my mother, but she didn't answer. Probably running errands or napping, Gary said, but still I worried about her.

On New Year's Eve we drove back to town to attend a party at Signed, Sealed & Delivered. I reached my mother from a roadside diner when we stopped for a meal. Her voice was listless, her responses to my questions vague. One would almost have thought that she was drugged. When I told her that she didn't sound well she simply said that she was tired. I made a mental note to check on her the following evening.

We listened to the radio as we approached Washington; the city's bitter weather was in the news. A homeless man had died of exposure, and when we passed the cemetery, Gary fretted over Charles.

"Maybe he's taken shelter somewhere," I said.

"I don't know. I sense that he's out there somewhere—in it. Imagine how cold he must be!"

We arrived at Signed, Sealed & Delivered around ten. There were the usual music and refreshments, but the sense of cheer was cut by thoughts of Charles, alone and likely exposed to deadly weather. Shortly before midnight a general discussion of his situation erupted, and various stratagems for contacting him were recommended. Tomás urged that we go straight to the cemetery. The suggestion created a buzz, but Gary argued against it.

"Listen," he said, "you've got to consider how tight security must be, with everything that's been going down over there. We've been over this before. Didn't you listen to a thing I said? You'll end up getting your butts arrested, and maybe blowing Pinky's cover. He's a big guy. He can take care of himself."

Gary's admonitions met with disappointment and some protest, but with midnight fast approaching we broke off our discussion for a toast. The new year was welcomed with hugs all around, and then someone suggested a drumming. I was looking forward to an exuberant release, but as the Gathering organized itself into a circle, Gary told me, with barely concealed urgency, that he wanted to go. Standing by the door to the anteroom, he addressed his cohorts one last time. "Listen to me," he said, "don't do anything crazy."

Once we were in the car, quite unexpectedly, Gary asked me to drive to the homeless men's encampment. Parking on the shoulder of the freeway and descending the embankment, we found them huddled around their fire. Gary questioned them about Charles, but they hadn't seen him since before Christmas. Gary then had me drive around the cemetery's perimeter while he peered through the cold darkness. It was only with great difficulty that I was able, using his own arguments to the couriers, to dissuade him from getting out to explore the fenceline more closely. Finally, frustrated and dejected, he asked me to drive back to town.

We drove over Memorial Bridge and across the broad avenues near the Mall. The wide sidewalks of the federal district, devoid of commerce and nightlife, were dark and deserted. Across from the art gallery, near the fountain with the signs of the zodiac, we came upon a band of homeless men. They crouched on a grate, huddled in a wispy cloud of vapor that provided the only warmth they could find on this frigid night. Gary got out and spoke to them, and they seemed to recognize him. When he returned to the car he asked me to drive to an all-night convenience store. He purchased food and hot coffee and we returned, where he delivered the supplies to the men. This expedient—what I took to be, at least in part, a vicarious gesture toward Charles—only slightly eased Gary's distraction.

New Year's Day brought no relief from the cold, and TV announcers warned of frostbite from single-digit temperatures and strong winds. There was a story on the homeless man who had died of exposure. The screen showed his lifeless body, wrapped in an old blanket, being carried into an ambulance. Gary paced the floor. I tried to interest him in the Rose Bowl parade but it wasn't any good. Finally, exhausted from anxiety, he napped on the couch. I put my affairs in order for the coming week.

When Gary awoke, darkness had fallen among the trees outside the living room windows. Sleep seemed only to have lent his worry a keener edge, and his agitation was uncontained as we ate a soup I had prepared in the morning. He ate hurriedly, wiped his mouth with a quick stroke of his napkin and said, "Can you give me a lift somewhere?"

In response to my queries as to our destination he responded that he hadn't time to explain and would direct me once we
were on the road.

Assuming that he wanted to check with Denny, Tiny, and
John again, drive around the perimeter of the cemetery, or deliver more supplies to the men on the grates, I assented and
went to the bedroom to dress warmly. Moments later he interrupted my preparations to ask if he could borrow my eyeliner.
I was a little surprised, of course, but he implored me not to
ask questions. When I finished dressing, I found him in the
bathroom blacking his face.

"What are you planning?" I asked.

"I've got to satisfy myself that Pinky's all right . . . and not
turning into the Iceman out there."

"He's got that twenty below sleeping bag."

"Like John said, they're never as good as the rating."

"Wasn't it you who said that Charles knows how to take care
of himself?"

"I say a lot of things."

"But do you really think you can find him? And how will you
avoid the MPs?"

"If I don't at least try, I won't be able to live with myself."

"What about everything you said at the Gathering, about
getting caught, about blowing Pinky's cover?"

"That was for them. You know, they're so exuberant. They
get all hyped up, lose track of what they're doing . . ."

"And you, I suppose, are a paragon of aplomb?"

He smiled, and I was glad that he hadn't lost his sense of
humor. But it was equally plain that there wasn't a chance in the
world of convincing him not to go. He put the finishing touches on his face and handed me the eyeliner; after I forced him
to layer with sweaters we put on our coats. He looked peaceful-
ly martial, with his war-painted face and that field jacket now

completely covered in my delicate threads of many colors.

We parked on the far side of the cemetery; and when Gary opened the door, I reached out to restrain him. I took the eyeliner from my purse and, against his objections, began to darken my own face in the rearview mirror. When he said gallantly that he didn't want me in harm's way, I told him that I was not afraid. He looked me long in the eyes and came to a sudden resolution. "All right, then," he said, "let's get moving with it." I hastily completed my camouflaging.

I had expected that he would satisfy his desire of the previous night to explore the cemetery's outer fenceline. But when we reached the net of galvanized wire, near a thick clump of brush, he clasped his hands together and invited me to step in. He lifted me over and followed behind.

It took two hours to make our way across the frozen ground around the cemetery's perimeter. Having turned up no sign of Charles there, we crisscrossed its interior along lines that Gary carefully calculated at each turn. All the while both of us scanned the rolling landscape for MPs.

It was on a rise not far from where we had seen the funeral cortege that we sensed that something was wrong. We stopped to listen. At first the sounds were so faint that it was difficult to put a meaning to them. Then we began to make out the barking of dogs in the distance. Next came human voices and the rapid clomp of heavy boots on the hard earth. The only avenue away seemed down the slope, toward the cemetery's visitors center.

We ran as quickly as we could on the glazed ground, dodging gravestones, and once slipped horribly. All the while the voices and dogs grew closer; engulfing us from behind, they funneled us into an increasingly narrow path. In this confusion, halfway down the slope we saw, to our great surprise, others fleeing before us. All were rushing toward the fence at the cemetery's edge. As the lot of us crowded past the visitors center I was able to make out the faces of our fellow fugitives. Ben and Sheila and some of the other couriers were there, along with Tiny, John, and one of the publishers of the *Underground Stream*, the one called Mo. And when we reached the fence I noticed, with no small alarm, Danny and the rest of my vets group!

Standing at the fence's base, his hands clasped as Gary had done with me, Danny was hoisting people up and shouting, "Up and over! Up and over!" Now the barking dogs were nearly upon us, and soon uniformed MPs poured around one corner of the visitors center. When their spotlight found us, Danny looked into my face and, with surprise, deciphered my features through the camouflage. His face was also darkened.

The MPs reached us in moments.

Nine of us didn't make it over the fence. There were Gary and I, Frank and Mo from the *Stream*, Danny and Rick from the vets group, Ben, Sheila, and Tiny. We stood exposed in the garish beam of a searchlight, guns trained upon us and German Shepherds barking wildly. As we all reached fearfully toward the customary sky, Danny addressed the MPs.

"Take it easy, fellas," he said coolly, "nothing to get excited about. We're just checking some things out, peaceful as you please."

"Keep your hands up. You're all guilty of trespassing, and we're going to have to take you in."

"Take us in?" Danny said. "Do you have the vaguest idea to whom you're speaking? I was fricking LURP! Do you even know what that means? I was getting my butt shot at for this country when you were still crapping in your diapers!"

The MPs didn't respond. Danny whirled around in exasperation.

"Just keep your hands up." I heard the crisp clicks of multiple safeties being released.

After they searched us for weapons, a military van pulled

up and we were ushered into the back. Gary glared at Ben and Sheila. They returned his stare with expressions that conveyed both embarrassment and vindication. I asked Danny and Rick if they were okay and they nodded yes. "Tiny, how are you?" I asked. He shrugged his shoulders, made a funny noise and laughed quietly to himself.

The van carted us to Fort Myer, adjacent to the cemetery, where we were brought into a drab, windowless room. Shortly an officer entered with one of the MPs. He said that we were under arrest for trespassing in the cemetery after hours and that he would be taking us, one at a time, to another room for questioning. I asked the officer—a Major Russell—if I could speak with him privately.

He led me into the hallway.

I felt silly with my blackened face, and found it difficult to look the major in the eye, as I explained that I was a therapist, Danny and Rick veterans under my care. I asked him to consider that they were sufferers of post-traumatic stress disorder—vaguely implied, even, that we had been conducting a therapeutic ritual in the cemetery.

The major listened politely, and when I finished he said, "Look, this little trespassing charge wouldn't be any big deal, but there's been a series of incidents lately. An assault, for one, and several serious acts of vandalism. We just want to make sure none of these men is connected with anything criminal."

"I can guarantee you they're not involved with anything like that," I said.

"How can you be so sure?"

"I know my clients," I improvised.

"What you're saying is probably true," he said. "But there are still some unanswered questions."

He stared at my camouflaged face.

Perhaps it was the major's sympathetic air, or the stress of our pursuit and capture, but what I did next was not wholly rational. "My father's buried over there," I blurted, then broke down sobbing, right in the hallway.

After a moment's bewilderment Major Russell put an arm around me. He held me in the most paternal fashion and comforted me with soothing words. It was the far-reaching embrace of the "military family," and at that moment I appreciated it. Patting me stiffly on the back, the major assured me that he would take my clients' conditions into consideration (privately thinking, no doubt, that I was a serious flake). When I calmed down he ushered me back to the holding room and summoned Rick, who sat nearest the door.

After Rick left the room, those of us who remained exchanged glances. Everyone tried to speak at once, then we all fell silent. Gary glared at Ben.

"I'm sure you think we totally disregarded your advice," Ben said. "But we didn't. We considered it carefully. We just couldn't deal with the Pinkman freezing out there. We wanted to bring him some supplies. We didn't figure you'd find out."

"You'd best guard your remarks," Mo said from across the room. He pointed to the walls and the ceiling.

"I don't believe we've met," Ben said.

Mo held out his hand. "Mo Bolton, *Underground Stream*."

"The *Stream*! No kidding?" Sheila blurted. "That's awesome!"

"This is my partner, Frank Davis."

"Wait a minute," Danny said, "you guys are with the *Underground Stream*?"

"That's right," Mo said.

"I don't suppose I need to ask what you were doing out there. A little investigating, perhaps?"

"Probably the less said the better." Mo again gestured toward that walls and ceiling.

"Worried about Chuck," Tiny came in.

"Chuck?" Danny asked, "who's that?"

"Had to bring a extra coat. Couldn't find him. Too smart." Tiny laughed.

"Whatever you say, brother." Danny cast a wry look at the rest of us before again addressing Mo and Frank. "Listen," he said, "I think this guy, whoever he is, was some kind of special forces. I mean, the way he calibrated those explosives in the mast—and the stealth! Take it from a guy who knows this stuff."

"You said you were LURP?" Mo asked.

"Yes, sir," Danny said.

"What class?"

"Sixty-seven and eight."

"Me and Frank were 25th infantry. Quang Nai Province. Same years."

"Really, you guys . . . ?"

The door opened and Rick entered. He was followed by the MP, who beckoned Tiny. After they left, Frank pointed toward Mo with his thumb. "You know, this guy saved my life over there."

"Now, Frank," Mo said, "do we have to—"

"It does me good to tell it," Frank said. "Besides, we might be here all night. We may as well shoot the breeze."

"I'd like to hear about it," Gary said.

"Me, too," Ben seconded.

"Can you at least make it quick?" Mo leaned back into his chair and closed his eyes.

Frank rested his elbows on his knees; he collected himself a moment, let out a sigh, and then raised his face to us. "Before I tell this story," he began, "there's something I need all of you to understand. When I arrived in Vietnam, and it causes me great inner pain to say this, I was the most unregenerate bigot you ever saw. The fact is, I was a card-carrying member of the

Ku Klux Klan. I'm not kidding!" he added in response to our skeptical expressions. "I went to meetings with the white hood, burned crosses on people's lawns. The whole, sickening, disgusting business . . ."

He noted our continuing looks of disbelief. "It's a fact!" he affirmed. "You can ask Mo. I was just plain mean. When I arrived in country, I asked my superiors to send me right out to the bush. You know why? I wanted to get down to the important business of killing those little brown gooks as soon as possible!"

Mo smiled benignly at this, his partner's confession. Frank squared himself in his chair and, with a nod toward Mo, resumed. "As it turned out," he said, "I ended up in Mo's unit. They were on a break at base camp when I arrived for duty. Now, Mo wasn't the only African-American in the squad, but for some reason he bothered me more than the others. I guess it was the way he carried himself. There was this quiet dignity about him that really offended that messed-up cracker who used to dwell within me."

I glanced toward Mo; he appeared to be nodding off.

"It wasn't long," Frank went on, "before we had our inevitable dust-up. Mo had unthinkingly parked some of his stuff on my bunk. No big deal, right? But, bastard that I was, I spitefully tossed his gear on the barracks floor. What's worse, I added that I'd appreciate it if he'd keep his *nigger* crap off my bed."

Mo emitted a small laugh. Frank, a tad nervously, responded in kind.

"Mo came toward me real . . . slow," Frank continued, glancing around the room to find our eyes. "And me, well, I started to tense up because—as you can see, Mo's not exactly some ninety-pound weakling. I even thought about going for my M-16. Fortunately, I had enough sense to keep that crazy urge under wraps. Instead I just looked him in the eyes, all squinty-hateful like, bound and determined not to flinch."

We all looked over at Mo. He slowly rocked his head from side to side, rubbed a weary hand across closed eyes. Frank noted our regards, nodded toward Mo himself, and turned our way again.

"Mo came up real close," he said, a little hoarsely now. "Got right up in my face. He didn't raise his voice or anything. No, he just said, cool as a cucumber, to wait until we got out in the bush. 'Wait until we get you in the bush,' he said. 'Then we'll see what that cherry ass of yours is made of.' That was all he said. Then, in that dignified way of his, he walked over to my bunk, steady as can be, and picked his stuff up off the floor."

Mo seemed to have dozed off again. Other than his steady breathing, the room was dead quiet.

"As fate would have it," Frank went on, his voice more clear now, "our unit was soon out humping the bush. As for me, I couldn't get that dust-up with Mo off my mind. All I could think about was what Mo referred to as my *cherry ass*—and what it was made of. I even began to forget my yen to kill gooks. I just wanted to show Mo here—myself too, I suppose—that I wasn't some kind of yellow-bellied coward."

Frank looked toward Mo yet again, but Mo's face remained expressionless. After a thoughtful silence, peering straight ahead, he spoke as if re-living a dream:

"One afternoon, not long after we left camp, we got into some serious action. We were crossing this bog, and there was a forested enclave, oh, a couple hundred feet ahead. I was carrying one of the unit's two M-60s (that's a sixty-caliber machine gun, for those of you who don't know your weaponry—big old thing, and deadly as hell). Anyway, suddenly, and without warning, rounds start to come at us from the tree line, thick as rain. The lieutenant in charge of our squad, God love him, calls a retreat, and we start to pull back. But the Vietcong, smelling blood, advance out of the woods and into the marsh. I'd say there were about a hundred of them. Hot dog, I figured, here's my opportunity to show Mo I'm not the wuss he insinuated I was at base camp! So I get down on my knees in the muck, brace the M-60 best I can, and let loose with everything I've got. That fearsome barrage slowed the Cong down enough to let our guys get out of the bog and back into the jungle. They dig in and start to return fire, and after a bit things are starting to go pretty good. But then I get hit. Pretty badly. Fortunately, by this time our guys have gotten the other M-60 set up, and they're laying a wicked hail of suppressive fire into the enemy. The Vietcong, seeing which way the wind is blowing, withdraw back into the woods on their side of the bog.

"Now, after a few stray shots, everything goes ghastly quiet. There wasn't a sound, except for me calling for the medic, my mommy. All the usual stuff. Then I hear the lieutenant talking to the guys. He's saying that I'm dead meat. 'Leave him alone,' he orders. 'Stay under cover.' The Vietcong are already taking pot shots into the marsh. The lieutenant knows they're watching from the trees, waiting for one of our guys to be stupid enough to come into the open."

Frank took a moment to breathe. Around the little holding room reigned a silence as still as that which must have overtaken the rankly fertile bog where, so many years before, Private Frank Davis found himself rapidly bleeding out—and desperately stranded.

"Well?!" Danny, with characteristic impatience, implored.

Frank swallowed visibly. "The next thing I know," he picks up again with a glance in Danny's direction, "the lieutenant's yelling STOP, and he's calling somebody 'Dumb-Ass.' I crane my head back, best I can, and what do I see? It's Mo, slogging through the marsh with his M-16 slung over one shoulder. Rounds start to pour from the Vietcong like hell-fire incarnate.

But still Mo's coming on, coming toward me, moving in this hypnotic pattern like he can mesmerize the bullets into missing him or something. When he reaches me he clasps one arm around my chest. With his other hand he takes up the M-60, starts to really pour the metal into those trees. What a damned hero! All the while, under all that enemy fire, he's dragging me back through the marsh, inching his way along, step after excruciating step. About that time our air strikes arrived. You should have seen it then. They turned that whole damned forest into a blazing inferno!"

Tears are rolling down Mo's face now. "All that killing," he said, rocking gently back and forth in his chair.

"Sorry, Mo," Frank said, "I didn't mean to upset you."

Mo waved the away comment and wiped his eyes. "S'all right," he said. "Does me good."

"Never want to forget," Frank said solemnly.

Everyone was silent for a couple of minutes, absorbing with difficulty the horrors these two men had lived through in their tender youth. Mo straightened up and began to stare at Gary and me. "You two—" he began, trying to place us. He concentrated, "Ah, yes, I remember . . ."

"That's right!" Frank turned toward us himself. "I didn't notice myself at first. What with the blacking . . ."

Mo again indicated the walls and ceilings. "Why don't we talk about that later?"

Gary nodded. The others, mystified, stared at Gary, then at Mo, and then again at Gary.

Finally Frank spoke again, breaking the stalemate, as it were. "Listen," he said, "if you really want to hear a great story, ask Mo to tell you about his career with the Black Panthers."

"Come on, Frank," Mo pleaded, "can't we leave it alone?"

"These stories deserve to be told," Frank protested. He turned toward the rest of us. "I keep telling him he ought to write his memoir. But he's just too damned modest."

"The Black Panthers!" Sheila enthused. "They were super radical, weren't they?"

"I guess you could say that," Mo replied. "Shooting people, blowing things up, all in the name of some ideology. Something like the United States government, when you think about it."

Frank laughed heartily.

"Actually, there's not much to tell," Mo went on after Frank had quieted. "Once you get to where you're willing to carry a gun for somebody else's freedom, you begin to figure, why not your own? There was just too much irony in the way they indoctrinated us to disparage the Vietnamese. All those racial slurs they tossed around in boot camp. Dinks. Gooks. You're seeing these people of color terrorized by the man and, what do you know, something starts to strike a familiar chord. Selma, Montgomery. Know what I mean?"

"Word," Sheila said.

"Pretty soon you start to wonder who's side you're on. Or ought to be on, anyway," Mo continued. "And to make matters worse," now he hiked his thumb toward his partner with a neutral smile, "you've got guys like Frank, here, pulling their master race act on you."

"I was such a bastard," Frank conceded.

Mo dismissed Frank's comment with a wave of his hand. "In a perverse way, though," he said, "some of those white dudes did me a favor of sorts."

"Really," Ben said. "How's that?"

Mo hesitated to go on, looked around the room. "I don't want to offend anybody," he said cautiously.

No one objected and so Mo, after staring ahead for a moment, began with calm sincerity. "Coming up, you see, in a society diseased by racism," he said, "I was brainwashed to believe that I was inferior to people with lighter skin. I was supposed to be animalistic. Crass. Crude. Unclean."

"The dirty logic of apartheid," Frank put in.

"Exactly," Mo said. "But what I want to say," he went on, "is that Vietnam cured that complex for me. I mean, I witnessed whites over there doing things more animalistic than I could imagine doing in a million years."

"Like what?" Ben asked.

Mo hesitated again.

"Tell him," Frank said.

Mo leaned back. "I don't know that it would do any good. And with ladies present." He glanced at me and Sheila.

"Hey listen," Sheila said, "we can't suppress the ugly truths. That would just give the man a pass to do whatever the hell he feels like."

"I'm a psycho-therapist," I supplied. "I doubt you could shock me. But if you're not comfortable talking about it . . ."

"Go ahead, Mo" Frank said. "People need to know these things. They need to realize there's no such thing as a clean war."

"It was awful," Mo said. Slowly rocking his head, staring at the floor, he retreated into silence.

"Our company was out in the provinces," Frank himself volunteered now, accepting his friend's reluctance to speak. "Mo had been assigned to reconnaissance, and he and his squad mates—a couple of real cowboys—were out cruising in a half-track."

Mo agreed with a nod.

"The area was known to be crawling with Vietcong," Frank continued, "and Mo and his companions were understandably jumpy. They were cruising along slowly, eyes peeled to either side of the road, and when they came around this bend they saw something move in the bush. And what do you know? Without bothering to check things out, Mo's comrades let loose with everything they had."

"Typical," Danny said.

"We went over to investigate," Mo came in now. There was a catch in his throat, and he spoke with obvious difficulty. "It turned out it just was a couple of peasant women. And they were . . . totally wasted. I mean shot to pieces."

Tears welled in his eyes.

"I'll bet they were listed in the body count as Vietcong soldiers," Danny said. "Weren't they?"

"It was worse than that," Frank said.

Silence.

"They raped them," Mo stammered. "I mean, the bodies."

"Gross!" Ben said.

A shiver ran through me.

"Brother, that must have been rough," Danny said.

Mo nodded. He was too choked up to speak.

An MP entered and summoned Sheila. She made a face at him as she got up.

"God, that's gross!" Ben repeated.

"The whole bloody business is gross," Mo got out. "And don't ever let anybody tell you different."

We sat in a heavy silence, until Mo spoke again. "Okay, listen," he said. "Since Frank insisted on telling you how I saved his butt, it's only fitting that I share one more story. How he saved mine."

"Come on, Mo."

"You had your turn, now just be quiet for a damned minute."

Frank, though with obvious reluctance, silenced himself.

Mo looked toward the floor. "I won't go into details," he said, "but I got involved in some pretty serious action with the Panthers. Bottom line, I ended up getting busted. Bank heist. One day Frank shows up at the pen. And the thing is, I hardly recognized him. His hair's down to here, he has beads around his neck, and he's sporting this tie-dye tee-shirt with a peace sign in pink and purple. I mean, he was completely hippied-out!" We all looked at Frank; he smiled sheepishly. Mo laughed quietly at the recollection before he took up again. "Anyway, Frank tells me, sitting there in the visiting booth, that he'd come into some family money, and he wanted to put a high-priced legal team at my disposal. It was an intriguing offer but, as you can imagine, I didn't know what to think of it. What I mean is, I didn't know how I felt about having a cracker like Frank on my case. I told him he didn't owe me a thing because of what happened in that marsh. But we talked a while, and I began to dig that he had really changed. In fact, it appeared he'd gotten himself genuinely radicalized. He'd even started this underground newspaper. He showed me a copy. They were pushing a lot of anti-war stuff, peppered with free verse and thought-pieces on ecology and gender equality. Some of it wasn't half-bad. In short, we ended up having a serious heart-to-heart about the state of the world, racism, and this infuriating country we all live in. Right there in the visiting booth! Later, at trial, he testified about my combat service. Thanks to that, along with the Brooks Brothers legal team he lined up for me, I got off with a pretty light sentence."

"And me, I ended up with an editor second to none," Frank said.

"Far out," Ben crowed.

Mo addressed Gary. "I like the jacket," he said. "That's a 121st Engineers patch, isn't it? Your unit?"

"My father's, actually," Gary said. "I was never in the service."

"You might want to take that off before they take you in there," Danny advised. "No offense, but they're going to take you for some kind of wise-ass with that peacenik crap sewed all over it."

We passed the night, while the major finished his questioning, exchanging further stories all around; as the excitement of the arrest wore off, I considered the implications at the clinic. Most notably, I regretted having divulged my occupation to the major. My arrest could cast the Center for Psychic Wellness in a bad light.

But Howie, you already know where all of this led. Despite the major's good nature, the military bureaucracy was implacably efficient for once; you were contacted about the whole affair before the week was out. I don't blame you for what came next. You had no choice but to put me on leave while an ethics committee was constituted to determine my fate. I promised you this report, having no idea that it would take this long, or extend to such reaches of my life.

I suppose I could end here, having arrived at the incident that occasioned the suspension of my work at the clinic. But it only seems right, since I've gotten this far, to finish what I've started. So with your forbearance, allow me to relate what happened in those weeks leading up to the winter warfare in the Persian Gulf.

⁐ ⁐ ⁐

WE WERE RELEASED from detention near dawn. Major Russell was unable to draw any tangible connections between his suspects and the recent incidents in the cemetery. Sheila and Ben stuck to a story about a dare to wander among the dead at night; Frank and Mo flashed their press credentials; Danny went on about his brothers in arms; and Tiny, with his cryptic references to "Chuck," left the major convinced only that he wasn't operating with a full deck. Gary wore Russell out with constant digressions into United States warfare doctrine, and all the officer garnered from my interview was a sense of commitment to my clients and unresolved grief over my father.

After informing us that the investigation would continue, the major directed us to a subordinate, who arranged for transportation back to the visitors center.

I went in to the clinic with only an hour's sleep. I tried to stay with my clients, but on top of my drowsiness, and anxiety over the disaster at the cemetery, worries about my mother nagged at me; the outlandish events of the previous evening had scuttled my plans to call and check on her. I tried her during my break, but she didn't answer. Nor did she return the voicemail I left for the remainder of the day. That wasn't like her. She seldom went out, and on those rare occasions when she did not pick up the phone, she always returned my calls. As much as I hated to cancel out of the vets group, my intuition was on overdrive. Hearing her dispirited voice during our telephone call on my return from West Virginia, I felt an imperious need to check on her without delay. Paulette DeHaven, to whom I spoke after my last appointment, agreed to cover for me. Telling her to be prepared for some wild stories, I entreated her not to jump to any conclusions and drove out to the suburbs to see what was going on with Mom.

Her car was out front, but she didn't respond to my greeting when I let myself in. The place was dark, and there was a rotten odor in the air. I walked back through the house and found her in the living room. The Christmas tree was dry and brown, remnants of assorted meals still on the table and in the sink. She sat on the floor, facing the credenza where our family photographs are arrayed, clutching an object I readily recognized as my father's old flight cap. I spoke to her but she did not respond; she seemed, in fact, oblivious to my presence. Years of professional experience offered me no map as to how to proceed. I knelt beside her and rubbed her back, trying without success to get her to respond to me, and considered whether she might need to be hospitalized. After several minutes she began to weep and said simply, "I can't stand it anymore." She eventually agreed to come to the couch and lie down. While she rested, I did my best to straighten up the house.

The presence of family, and practical work going on, helped bring her around. She spoke drowsily.

"What day is it?"

I told her. She wasn't sure how long she had been sitting on the floor. When I finished tidying up I went to the kitchen and cooked dinner. I didn't say anything about my inglorious foray into the cemetery, but I recounted the trip to the mountains in some detail. She said that she had had no word from Bob, but I had no way of knowing if, like me, he had tried to call her without success.

I called Gary to tell him that I would be staying the night, then helped Mom get ready for bed and tucked her in. Walking down the hallway to my own room, I almost longed for a vision of my father, something that might guide us; but my dreams were only scattered images and disconnected vignettes. I commuted to the clinic from the suburbs for the rest of the week. Gary called on Thursday. When he asked about my mother, I told him that she was gradually resuming her routines.

"Listen," he said, "I know you've got your Mom to look after. But the Gathering has something planned this weekend that might interest you."

It seemed the couriers were more restless than ever. "They're full of angst about this war coming on," Gary said. "They're waiting for a sign from Pinky, but it just doesn't come."

I remarked that Hussein's envoy had agreed to a resumption of the stalled peace talks.

"Yeah," Gary said, "but don't get your hopes up. All Baker's going to do is present the same tired ultimatums. That'll go over like a lead balloon."

I somehow knew that he was right.

"Randy, God bless him, suggested we get out to the country for one of our woodland retreats."

"But it's so cold," I said.

"True," he agreed. "But things are supposed to warm up some by weekend. Besides, cold will be good for the sweat lodge."

"Sweat lodge?"

He told me about friends of Randy who owned a farm in the Maryland Piedmont. "They're a bunch of old hippies," he said. "They let us use the property, and we've built a lodge out there."

I told him that I had attended sweat lodge ceremonies when I was doing my graduate work in New Mexico; they are a key element in the world of Navajo healing practices that Sarah Tilly introduced me to.

"So you know the drill," he said. "I think it'll be good for all of us. We can clear the channels. Get in touch with ancestral spirits and higher powers."

I thought the idea splendid, I remarked, but said that it would all depend on my mother's condition.

When I came down to the kitchen Saturday morning Mom was up and fixing breakfast, and she had bathed and put up her hair. Though she was quiet, she otherwise seemed fine. I told her that I was considering joining the Gathering in the country, and she assured me that she would be all right. I said that I would return Sunday evening at the latest.

The farm was an hour and a half out of town. A dirt drive, lined with parked cars, dipped beside a weathered barn before climbing to an old farmhouse. A few of the couriers were gathered around a fire when I arrived. I pulled the car off near the others and found Gary in the barn arranging a stack of firewood. We embraced. What appeared to be the Gathering's drums lay along bales of straw that lined the barn's open area.

I asked where everyone was.

He gestured toward the house. "Still asleep," he said, "—most of them, anyway. We had a late one last night. Lots of drumming, jamming and wine."

He asked about my mother. I said that she was better but told him that I would need to keep tabs on her.

"The lodge was getting pretty decrepit," Gary said, "so we thought we'd do some repairs. Some of us will go down to the creek this morning to find saplings. We'll need to soak them in water. They're pretty brittle this time of year. Tomorrow morning we can put the new lodgepoles in place and get the fire started. We'll conduct the sweat in the afternoon, after Star gets here."

Who was Star? I asked.

"He's this itinerant medicine man," Gary said, "from down in the Carolinas."

I asked if I could help to cut saplings: for some reason, I felt an urge to wander in the woods. He said that he felt certain it could be arranged and we went out to the fire. Ty, who always anchored the Gathering's drum circles with his big floor drum was there, as were Sheila, Henry, and Tomás. Randy soon came down from the farmhouse with David, the farm's owner. We all walked over to inspect the framework of the sweat lodge, a skeletal turtle whose bones were dry, brittle, and broken. After some deliberation a detail was formed to collect saplings. The others would stay back to dig the fire pit, cut firewood, and clear brush.

David led Roger, Sheila, and me down the fields and into a wooded area that lay at the bottom of the land. We stepped through piled leaves and broken brush, equipped with axes, machetes, and loppers, until we came to the bank of a creek that ran fresh and cold. After offering a sacrificial wad of tobacco in the hollow of a tree, David instructed us to find willow saplings with straight trunks and no forks. He said that before taking a tree we should speak to it, ask if it wished to be taken, and attempt in some telepathic fashion to feel its response. We spread along the creek and began our work; as the saplings piled up in a clearing, David trimmed them of excess branches. When we had collected fifteen suitable lodgepoles we gathered them up and climbed back to the barn. Everyone was up now, the area between the barn and the lodge filled with activity.

We filled a large trough with water and, after placing the saplings in it, spent the remainder of the day making further preparations for the ceremony. David retrieved an old carpet, cut to the dimensions of the lodge, to be used as flooring; in the barn was a stockpile of blankets that would cover the lodge's skeletal framework. We went through them and discarded some that had grown moldy. I salvaged healthy patches from others that were torn and damaged and stitched them together with sewing implements I borrowed from David's wife. When it was discovered that there weren't enough stones for the fire pit, a group went into the fields to prospect for more. Around noon we stopped for a meal, chatted together, and made ourselves familiar with the farm's dogs.

I called my mother from the house. Her mood was holding steady, but she thought she was coming down with something and felt feverish. Her stress, I theorized, had now manifested itself somatically. I urged her to go to bed early.

The shaman Star arrived late in the day. Solid and barrel-chested, he stood in a relaxed manner, with feet firmly planted on the earth. He sported a fringed coat, dark blond hair pulled into a ponytail, flowing moustaches and curvilinear tattoos across his elongated earlobes. A white man in his forties, he was said, when young, to have divorced himself from civilization to live in the Smoky Mountains as a hunter-gatherer. Afterwards he apprenticed himself to a venerable Cherokee shaman. When his preceptor died at the age of one hundred and four, Star inherited the lore and regalia of his lineage. He now traveled up and down the Appalachians, bringing ancient healing ways to all who requested his services.

After dinner we gathered around the fire to tell stories and ask Star many questions. He gestured into the night sky toward celestial bodies he claimed would bear upon our healing rites. When it grew colder we moved into the house; there, while Star held open shamanic portals with his drumming and chanting, we journeyed to other realms on ethereal steeds. Afterward he sprawled back in an easy chair like a big, tired bear. He had suggested abstinence from alcohol, in order to approach the next day's sweat lodge with clarity, so the Gathering availed itself of non-chemical means of intoxication; a drumming circle was organized. As the evening wore on we each and all, separately or in couples, wandered off to find places to sleep, some in spare bedrooms, others on the living room floor.

In the morning we reclaimed the saplings from their soaking. They were now supple enough to bend into position as lodge poles. Under Star's direction, we removed the more brittle pieces of the lodge's existing frame and lashed fresh saplings into place. As we worked through the frosty January morning, Star touched on various aspects of the lodge of the Great White Mother Bear. The ridge pole formed her spine, he explained. The cross poles were her twenty-eight ribs. The pit in the lodge where the heated stones would be placed was the heart of the bear and the altar, a low earthen mound outside the lodge's entrance, her head. We spent a couple of hours getting the poles in place, we then covered the frame with layer upon layer of blankets. Star cautioned us to leave no gaps where air might escape or light enter.

The stones, each the size of a lunch pale, more or less, were placed in a deep pit, not far from the lodge, over which the men criss-crossed great lengths of stout firewood. David stepped forward to ignite the fuel and soon wild, jagged flames burst into the cold, still air. We lunched nearby while the wood, consuming itself, fell into the pit in brazen embers. Star checked on the stones at intervals. When he judged them sufficiently roasted, he gathered us around the pit. With forthright prayers, he tossed cedar shavings onto the embers and invited us to bathe in the aromatic smoke the sweet wood produced. He then calmly informed us that we would presently enter the womb of the Great White Mother Bear. He said that we should release all feelings of negativity and fear, adding that if anyone did not feel prepared for spiritual cleansing, she should not enter.

We had been instructed to wear bathing suits under our clothing, for there would be little need of garments in the intense heat of the sweat. We each and all stripped down.

Moving toward the lodge, Star enjoined us against stepping between the altar and the lodge entrance, as this would entail treading on the neck of the Bear Mother. He folded back the entrance flap, got on his hands and knees, and began to crawl through.

"Greetings, Grandmother!" he intoned gruffly.

The rest of us followed, each voicing, as Star had done, "Greetings, Grandmother!"; once inside we crowded around the circumference of the cramped lodge. Those most eager for purifying heat moved forward, right to the edge of the shallow depression where the super-heated stones would be placed. Gary was among them. Star then instructed David, now calling him Raven, to bring seven of the twenty-eight scalding stones from the fire pit outside. "Raven" left the lodge and returned bearing one of the blocky, pinkish objects on a pitchfork. He lifted it carefully through the lodge entrance and placed it before Star in the lodge's stone pit.

"Greetings, Grandfather!" Star called out resonantly, and we repeated his words. Raven brought six more stones, each greeted like the first; Star carefully maneuvered each into place with a well-weathered deer antler. Finally Raven crouched through the lodge entrance, carrying a large bucket of water, and secured the flap. The candent glow cast by the white-hot stones was sufficient only to discern the vaguest presence of my nearest neighbors.

The lodge quickly grew uncomfortably warm. Star removed aromatic herb from a leather pouch and tossed it unhurriedly over the stones in small handfuls. In his deeply resonant voice he invoked the Great White Mother Bear, soliciting blessings for us all and for those we loved. His prayers included a special plea for one of his own sons who, like my brother, was part of the American military contingent in the Persian Gulf. Then, without warning, he took up a ladle and in quick succession dished several ladlefuls of water over the scorching stones; each splash burst into a cloud of scalding steam that roiled over our bare flesh. In the anguish of that lacerating heat Star broke into exalted chant, accompanied by wildly energetic pounding on his ceremonial drum. The lodge grew warmer still. Others joined Star's song, one by one, until the lodge of the Great White Mother Bear rocked with raucous sound.

From time to time someone cried out in beseeching. Some prayed for Charles's well-being; others voiced wishes for a peaceful outcome to the Persian Gulf stand-off. With masterful abandon, Star tossed ladleful after ladleful onto the sizzling stones, conjuring the seething steam to burst over us again and again. Sweat seeped from every pore of my body, until I felt helplessly compressed against an oppressive wall of heat. Though I sensed their presence, I was unable to see my companions in the lodge; this initiation, I realized, was one that I would face alone. My mind, in search of refuge, struggled to reorganize itself. Under the most dire compulsion, I inwardly voiced my own, private prayers. I called upon the soul of my father; I beseeched Spirit for protection for my brother, and for a quiet mind for my mother.

Three times more the flap was opened; three times more Raven fetched in the searing stones. Burning different aromatic herbs with each new round, Star took us ever deeper into the world of the Great White Mother Bear. Speaking in hoarsely plangent tones, he told the tale of Uma'al the hunter and of Raven, and how mankind was saved from the bear's righteous craw by a sly trick. With a simple sincerity he urged us to invite Red Wolf Brother—the hunter's ally—to prowl the shadow-places of our lives so that he might sniff out the unhealed places, carry them to Grandmother Bear in offering. When in the third round Star ladled the water with a finely calibrated recklessness—coaxing the heat now to an excruciating intensity—I felt as though I were under the broiler of an oven. With each hissing burst the scalding steam poured over me, until my bathing suit was as drenched as if I had been submerged in water. The discomfort was almost intolerable; only a sense that I was coming near to something essential kept me rooted where I sat. Forcefully diverting my focus from the painful feelings on my exposed skin, I pressed shut my eyes in an effort to simply bear the ordeal.

The glaring red wolf-eyes appeared before me without warning. Stalking closer . . . probing. Just as suddenly other visions crowded against my closed lids: Mr. Dawson climbing away from the air show; my father in his easy chair, lost and uncommunicative; his beloved body, still and lifeless, on the kitchen floor; a flag-draped caisson pulled by powerful black horses. I feared blacking out but the vertigo did not come; instead, refusing to give way to oblivion, I began to feel a sense of exaltation. I chanted freely with Star and the rest of the lodge and now sensed that Eagle Brother soared the heights of my soul. From time to time someone cut through our singing with a naked cry of pain, giving voice to the difficulties we all shared.

"God, it's hot!!" Ben exclaimed.

Finally the flap was opened and Raven fetched the remaining stones. The final round was gentler; after the intensity of the third, almost cozy. When it was over we each crawled out of the lodge and greeted one another in a makeshift receiving line. I approached Gary. The far-seeing clarity in his eyes suggested a successful inner journey. Anxious to get back to my mother, I didn't stay to congregate in the farmhouse with the others.

When I arrived at her townhouse I found her in bed with a fever. Her temperature was over one hundred and one. We discussed going to the emergency room, but she was adamantly against it. Her face glowed with sweat and her thin nightgown clung to her skin around the neckline. I gave her aspirin and sat with her into the night, taking her temperature at intervals. Her erratic thrashing regularly awakened me as I dozed fitfully in an easy chair nearby. At times I sat beside the bed to hold her wrist and feel her pulse. Notwithstanding the cold compresses I applied to her forehead, the fever topped one hundred and two before dawn. When sunlight came streaming through the windows, she seemed to rest more quietly. I too fell into a sound sleep. Her fever was abating when I awoke at ten. She accepted more aspirin, and I went downstairs to find something to eat. She sat up for lunch and in the evening came down for dinner.

& & &

I DROVE TO THE CITY to get ready for the next day's work; and Howie, you know what awaited me at the clinic. The major's inquiries left you with an unsettling picture of me leading our clients on a wild gallivant through the cemetery. What's worse, you had spoken with Paulette. The vets group's account of the episode, replete with references to Gary (whom they recognized from his few appearances at our sessions) included intimations that we were a couple. How could I respond, sitting in your office with the door closed? I didn't want to discuss Gary and me, for I myself questioned whether, in some technical sense, a breach of ethics had been committed. I almost said that it had all been about Charles Pinckney, but that didn't seem to fully explain things, either. The best I could do was to assure you that everything had been done in the best interests of veterans and their families. Our meeting ended with an enforced sabbatical and my promise of a full report. Meanwhile, a peer committee was formed to look into the matter.

I stepped onto the sidewalk holding my folded tapestry in my arms. My work at the clinic had provided the ground reality of my life for several years. Now I had no idea where to go. It was all very painful. Sitting at the Au Bon Pain café in Union Station with a hot chocolate, I wished Gary weren't working. I called from a payphone and tearfully told him what had happened.

"God, baby," he said, "I feel guilty. I should have never let you come."

"Nonsense. I insisted, as you recall."

"Still, I feel terrible." He offered to leave work and come to me. He wanted, he said, to put his arms around me and give me comfort. I told him that I had to check on my mother and assured him that his offer was solace enough. I said that I would drive out to see her and, if all was well, come to him in the evening.

She was knitting when I arrived, the television murmured softly nearby. I couldn't have imagined a more welcome sight. And her temperature was near normal. I finessed why I wasn't needed at the clinic, not wanting to upset her—or myself. She was making some things for little Drew. I settled in, took up yarn and needles, and joined her. We chatted about our women's work, laughed at the absurdities of daytime television, and wondered about Bob. Around noon I made lunch. Later in the day we both napped.

Over dinner I could see that she was better. She was not merely recovering from her fever, but seemed to be coming back into her old self. I almost protested when she turned on CNN; but though she took in the news with the same avidity as always, there was a novel serenity that could not be explained by her weakened physical state alone.

Perhaps, I reflected, prayers in the lodge of the Great White Mother Bear had not been without effect.

After dinner I drove to Gary's. The clear notes of his electric piano wafted down the stairwell as I climbed to the third floor. We touched briefly on my dismissal from the clinic.

"You can always live here," he said.

I told him that I had sufficient resources to keep my apartment for the foreseeable future.

"Still, if you need it . . ."

I commented approvingly on the music I had heard coming up the steps. He said that he had been practicing more and went back to his Bach. I lay on his bed and let the old master's interlaced lines of sound—a multi-dimensional tapestry of the most delicate weave—engulf me. After exhausting his repertoire, Gary put on Glenn Gould. We lay and listened, holding hands and dreaming together.

I stayed with him all that week. My days were occupied with looking in on my mother, or trips to the clinic and apartment for things I needed. On one such errand I ran into Paulette, and we briefly spoke. She was apologetic about ratting me out but pleaded that she felt that she had had no choice. I agreed and assured her that I bore her no ill will. I added that things were not as they seemed, and promised her that everything would be explained in due time. She lifted my spirits with an account of the vets group. The men were greatly buoyed by their trip to the cemetery, in spite of its inglorious finale, and they had recounted their adventures with positive energy. It even seems that Danny, after speaking with Tiny, was inspired to do something concrete for other vets; he convinced the group to organize an effort to support the homeless.

Gary grew more intense that week; I could see that something was eating at him. Every evening he played his Bach in great earnest. He knew it calmed me; but he clearly sought solace for himself as well—and guidance, as if within the intricacies of the great master's lines lay some definitive statement as to what is most real. Betweentimes he grew introspective and distant, listening to me and conversing, but not altogether there. Before bed we watched the late news. The United States and Iraq had scheduled talks again, but there was little hope that war could be averted. Night after night the screen showed American troops and armaments moving into their positions, while commentators coldly discussed scud missiles and poisonous gas. Who could promise me that the armor of Bobby's tank would protect him from such horrors?

From Gary's papers:
January 14, 1990

So here it is: war again. And it has caught me, I'm afraid, with my pants down. I hadn't been expecting this. I thought I had more time with my *magnum opus*, time to suss out man's heart, to find some core of rationality at the bottom of this bloody beast. I'm more a child of the Enlightenment than I had thought, convinced that man must have his reasons; and more a child of the Church than I've been willing to admit: convinced those reasons must be just ones and kind. Perhaps, more than anything, I am a child of the City on a Hill, believing like a sacrament that America must be a Light to all Nations. Even if I can say, with others, that Hussein should be stopped, still I hurt my head looking for reason, justice, kindness, and light in this gory business. It always comes down to a bloodletting ritual from the depths of our shadow self.

The Gathering, what a blessing! The retreat didn't remove my difficulties, but it brought me face to face with the well-springs of my being. Sweat lodge visions, marvelous and frightening! Frock-coated ancestors, missionaries and military men; and was that really Sherman I saw, gruffly intoning, "War is hell?" And even Lincoln: "Military glory—that attractive rainbow, that rises in showers of blood—that serpent's eye, that cleanses to destroy!"

I find myself dwelling on Pinky and Clark, my own personal disappeareds, and not a word from either of them. Brothers, as real as mine by blood, and I cannot find them! I see no way forward without knowing their fate; for in them I see sunny sanity, reason, justice, kindness, and light (like Jim of my blood). That reminds me, I'll have to call him. And somewhere, beyond all this, I see Marjorie and me, happy as clams. But mountains to climb before we get there!

And which way now?

& & &

WHEN GARY AND I arrived at the Friday Gathering a lively discussion was in progress. Sheila stood in the middle of the room, holding aloft a recent edition of the *Underground Stream*. A color photo showed the crowd at Arlington's visitors center listening to Charles's Christmas messages.

"This is the way to do it," she said. "We've got to take it straight to the people!"

"Take what?" someone hollered out. "What are you talking

about?"

"You know," Sheila said, "our whole thing. Poetry, drumming, morning bells, evening vespers. I'm sure Pinky would approve."

"I can get together a P.A. system," Ben called out from the back of the room.

"We'll need some signs," Sheila said. "Henry, can you work on that?"

Henry agreed.

"But Sheila," Subesh put in, "where can we do this thing? The cemetery's out of the question, don't you think? I mean, after what happened the other night . . ."

"The cemetery wasn't what I had in mind," Sheila said. "No, I was thinking of something more vital, more—living. Hey, why not Dupont Circle? Let's take it to the breathing, beating heart of the city!"

Her suggestion met with enthusiasm; Rob volunteered to document the experience on film. Amid hoots and catcalls, the drums came out. Then, in the crazy way of the Gathering, things condensed into a vortex of communal energy. Ben and Tomás played a couple of tunes on guitars while others sang and drummed until, without missing a beat, Sheila stood forth and began to rap:

> Stare down the barrel, what do you see?
> man on a rampage, making his-story,
> what's in the barrel, glossy and black?
> can't get that petro-monkey off our back,
> mothers and brothers, prepare for weeping,
> all these years that we've been sleeping,
> arrangements were made by the highers up,
> now we'll drain their bitter cup,
> warfare, violence, endless strife,

> what kind of excuse is this for life?
> sisters, brothers, can't you recall,
> the Garden, our birthright, before the fall . . .

Sheila continued in this vein for some time; I marveled at her stamina. I turned to Gary from time to time but, remote and inward, he seemed not to share my reactions. When Sheila finished, and Ben took the mic to offer another song, Gary tugged at my hand and hiked his head. He wanted to leave. We stood in the anteroom and put on our coats.

"It's too much for me," he said.

I didn't know how to respond.

"They're so young," he went on, "so exuberant. They think they can convince *them* to change their ways with mere heart and good will."

We drove to his place. The Geneva talks between Secretary of State Baker and Foreign Minister Aziz were scheduled for the next day, a last prophylactic against the conception of a monstrous child. Gary depreciated the negotiations, but I could tell by his quietly expectant demeanor, when we awoke in the morning, that he hoped for some egress from the bind in which our nation, along with millions of voiceless Iraqis, found itself.

In the afternoon we listened with suspended breath to a press conference on the radio. The talks, as everyone now knows, were a brief and pointless failure; the president reiterated his determination to drive Iraqi forces from Kuwait with military violence. Gary sat at his desk and stared broodingly out the window. I reminded him that we had plans to attend a concert at the cathedral that evening. His friend Donald had sent tickets to Signed, Sealed & Delivered for the Bach Society's performance of the master's *B Minor Mass*. Gary had gushed over what he said many considered Bach's greatest achievement, but now he showed scant interest. With some little prodding I convinced him to walk with me into the park. The air was moist and electric, and insistent flurries whisked among the bare trees beside the creek. It was dark when we returned. We had a simple dinner of soup and sandwiches and knocked about, at odds with ourselves, deeply in love but somehow profoundly lonely. We cuddled and listened to old records but it wasn't any good. I finally coaxed him to play his keyboard for me, but he quickly lost interest. I sensed that he felt the diminutive plastic instrument insufficient to express the depth of his feelings. There was still more than an hour before the concert; but the apartment had become oppressive, so we bundled up and got into my car.

The flurries had developed into a light snow. We parked on one of the streets behind the cathedral and walked to a side entrance. We had doubted that we could gain admittance so early, but to our surprise the heavy oaken door opened to our pull. The strains of instruments and voices wafted out into the cold and, as we stepped into the transept, we saw the small orchestra seated across the front of the church. Behind them on risers was a chorus of more than a hundred men and women; the cathedral was otherwise deserted. We stood watching for a moment. When the conductor, a stooped man with thick, wide-rimmed glasses and a reddish mop of unruly hair, stopped the orchestra to explain some point of interpretation to the chorus, a nicely dressed older man got up from the front row and came toward us.

"If you folks are here for the concert," he said, "I'm afraid we're not letting people in just yet. Doors open in twenty minutes."

Gary mentioned his friend Donald and showed the man our tickets.

The man pulled back a little, took in Gary, and then recognized him. "Oh, yes," he said, "of course. That's different.

Maybe you'd enjoy watching the rehearsal. Why don't you two have a seat?"

We sat in one of the frontmost rows. I felt steadied by the snippets of music, somber, seeking, or glorious; by the high reaches of the cathedral's vaulted ceilings; but more than anything by those choristers: arrayed in rows of black and white, they stood with poise and purpose, as if the gravest human tragedies might be amended within the confines of the scores they held before them! Gary followed the rehearsal with interest. He put an arm around my shoulders, seemed to relax, and occasionally whispered a comment.

After fifteen minutes the conductor adjourned the session and the musicians and singers filed out through the back of the church. Presently a murmuring crowd began to filter into the chairs around us, filling rows that occupied the cathedral's stupendous nave almost to the front doors. Gary and I perused our programs, but he soon grew restless, his eyes darting around the building's interior. He took up my hand, dropped it again, and shifted in his chair.

When the audience had settled in, covering the cathedral's worn slate floors from front to back and side to side, the instrumentalists filed again onto the makeshift stage, the choristers onto the risers behind them. After they were in place, the conductor, raising one hand to quiet the round of applause that had burst forth, stepped up to the podium. He shared a few remarks with the audience, greeting and welcoming us, before turning pensively around to the orchestra. A deafening hush fell over the cathedral when he raised his baton to signal the somber strains of the *Mass*'s first movement.

An oboe, alone and forlorn, voices the plaintive theme. Accompanied by a violin, it is underpinned by a sad and stately bass. More instruments join in, lending complexity to the fabric of sound, until the chorus, in alternating sections, begins to sing. I don't need the program notes to follow the translation from the Latin, for the first movement's text consists of only two words: *Kyrie Eleison* (Lord have mercy). The movement builds upon the theme introduced by the oboe, with counter-melodies weaving throughout, while different sections of the chorus repeat, in overlapping voices, the ancient words: *Kyrie Eleison, Kyrie Eleison, Kyrie Eleison.* Lord have mercy, Lord have mercy, Lord have mercy! The dread and somber basses now announce, with greater and greater authority, their dirge for the inner christ we kill daily with our enmities, hatreds, and violence; the chorus, a hundred and more strong, layers their voices with ever more density, building finally to an excruciating power: *Kyrie Eleison! Kyrie Eleison! Kyrie Eleison!*

I felt Gary fidgeting and looked over. Tears ran down his face. He began to rock like a stalled horse, claustrophobic and anxious; then, with no more warning then a tap on my thigh, he slipped out of our row and bolted toward the exit at the rear of the nave. Audience members craned their heads to gawk as he rushed down the aisle. After a moment of bewilderment I got up myself. Clearing our row just in time to see his back disappear through the arched-stone doorway, I hurried to the exit myself. When I emerged from the cathedral he was striding across the wide front lawn through snow showers that had grown heavier than when we had arrived. I ran toward the avenue after him; by the time I reached it he was on the opposite sidewalk, trying to hail a cab. I made my way to him through the snow and traffic and took him by the arm.

He peered doggedly up the avenue.

"It's so clear now," he murmured distractedly. "It's right in the first verse of the *Tao te ching*. Darkness upon darkness, the open door to bewilderment!"

I didn't bother to question the meaning of his prophetic utterance. I'm sure it all made sense within the framework of

Gary's complicated inner world. Nor did I need to ask what he was doing—and knew equally well that it would be pointless to attempt to talk him out of it. Before long an empty cab pulled up, and Gary asked him to take us to the Virginia side of the river. We disembarked on a high ridge at the verges of the cemetery, where the bronzed heroes of Iwo Jima raise their forever flag over the capital. The city's snow-blurred lights spread glazed and glittering across the river.

"You should wait here," he said.

"You think so?"

He looked over the city's breadth, then toward the cemetery, and briefly into my eyes. Without a word, he turned and hurried down and across the slope that lay before us. I watched him for a moment, unsure what to do. But when he was almost lost to me in the snow and dark, I realized that I had no choice but to follow and went running down the hill after him. I dared not call out, for it might draw attention. He skirted the shadowy mass of the Netherlands Carillon, where Charles had briefly held a stunned carilloneur captive, and straddled a low stone wall into the cemetery proper. After struggling over the wall myself, I wove without direction through the monuments and grave markers, straining vainly through the snow for a glimpse of my lover. Just as I was despairing of finding him, I heard an impassioned voice ring through the night. "Pinky!" he called. "Damn it, where the hell are you!"

I ran in the direction of Gary's voice; he continued to hail Charles at intervals. I found him walking along an open area beyond the Tomb of the Unknown Soldier.

"Darling, with all the noise you're making, the MPs are sure to come after us again."

He stared at me, breathless, and seemed to remember himself. While he made an effort to regain his wind, I took his hand and looked around. Heavy, dense flakes floated down;

the whole place was hushed with the cushioned quiet of snow. But then came the raucous barkings of dogs in the distance. "What will I tell the major this time?" I thought, and Gary and I looked toward one another. He began to speak but immediately broke off, suddenly attentive to another sound: the rotors of a helicopter, somewhere up there, moving closer! When moments later the chopper's cone of heavenward light swept over the frosted headstones, Gary seemed paralyzed—speechless and frozen. The barking of the dogs grew nearer. I tried to mobilize myself, come up with some plan to lead us away, but felt impossibly hemmed in.

At that moment a familiar, if distorted, voice rang from the edge of the cemetery.

"Homeboy!"

We looked in the direction of the voice. At first there was nothing but darkness. Then a pool of light appeared along the cemetery's fenceline. The voice came again, scratchy and buzzy.

"Homeboy! Get out of there!"

We ran in the direction of the spot of light and, at the chain-link fence, found a flashlight hooked in its mesh. Beside it hung a walkie-talkie. A jagged hole gaped where the fence had been cut. The voice again squawked through the walkie-talkie's tinny speaker. "Listen," Charles said, "just do what I say and we'll get you out of there. First, turn that flashlight off. But take it with you. You might need it." Gary unhitched the walkie-talkie and the flashlight from the fence and turned off the light. We looked around for Charles. "Don't try to find me," the walkie-talkie voice said, "I'm well hidden. Now, get through that fence on the double and start moving to your right."

We crouched through the hole in the fence and followed Charles's directions. He led us through a gully and a stand of trees until we emerged along a road. It seemed that we were near the area where the homeless men lived. With the helicopter droning overhead Charles directed us to an underpass. "Wait right there," he said, "you're out of sight. Just chill until they move on."

After a moment, Charles addressed Gary.

"They sure got you with that chopper, Bro," he said, laughing now. "They must know you or something."

I was relieved to hear Gary laugh in turn. "Where the hell have you been?" he said.

"Here and there," Charles replied. Then he said hello to me. "I'm glad you guys finally got together," he went on. "I always said you two would make a nice couple."

"You really said that? I figured that was just one of Gary's lines."

"I wouldn't put it past him. But that one was for real."

"Listen," Gary said, "are you all right?"

"I sound all right, don't I?"

"Sure, but how long are you going to keep this up? It's getting old, isn't it? Not to mention— . . . cold?"

"A lot of things are getting old, my friend. Bombing raids, mutilated children . . ."

"Did you hear today's news?" I asked.

"Yeah," Charles said. "The only thing left is Congress. And we know what they'll do. I hate to say it, but it's all over but the killing and the crying."

We were quiet for a moment.

"You really got the kids fired up," Gary said. "They're ready to take the city by storm."

"I'm glad they're getting off their butts," Charles replied. "Showing some spunk."

"What are your plans?" Gary asked. "You're not going to stay in there forever, I suppose?"

"Not if I can help it. I'm just doing what I think needs to be done. What about you? How's everything?"

"Not bad, I guess."

"Listen," Charles then said, his voice suddenly grave. "How's that buddy of yours, Clark? You heard from him lately?"

Gary revealed that he hadn't heard from Clark in months.

"You remember what you told him when he went down there."

"I haven't forgotten." Gary cast a slow glance my way.

"Time might be coming," Charles said. "You can't let a brother down."

"I know." No one spoke for a moment. "Look, Dude," Gary finally said, "thanks for getting us out of there. I'm glad we got to talk. Come back soon, will you. We miss you around the shop."

"Yeah, I miss you guys, too. But I knew you'd be able to keep things going."

"These are screwed up times, aren't they?"

"Sure enough are," Charles said. "I think you two are in the clear now. Just move along that road til you get to a stoplight. There's a diner down that way where you can call a cab."

"All right," Gary said. "But do come back soon. We got to keep the Gathering going."

"We'll see. You never know what kind of changes might be coming."

"Hey, Chuck," Gary said.

"What?"

"Got one for you."

"Hit me."

"*I had a dream . . . So did you—*"

"You kidding?" Charles said, "that's a cinch. *Life was warm. Love was true—*"

I easily remembered Stevie Wonder's famous old chestnut: "*Two kids who followed all the rules,*" I offered . . .

There was a pregnant pause before Charles's voice broke

through again. "Yeah, yester *fools*." His hearty laughter was suddenly truncated. "I got to get out of here," he clipped out. "Somebody's coming. Later." The walkie-talkie emitted a harsh cloud of static, and Gary set it on the ground. We hurried along the road and slipped inconspicuously into the diner.

FINDING CHARLES, and Charles's inquiries into Clark, seemed to resolve something for Gary. He now spent his free hours brushing up on his Spanish grammar, listening to conversation tapes, and studying detailed maps of Guatemala's highlands. He combed through Clark's letters and old newspaper clippings, and he returned from the library one evening freighted with books on Central America.

Hearing Charles's voice had also been good for me. There was no question that he was still the open, kind, and clear-sighted man I had come to admire years before. I began to adjust to my newfound unemployment. Evenings were spent with Gary, afternoons occupied with visits to my mother. Mornings I sat at my desk wrestling with how I would approach this report. Often I would turn and stare at my loom, sometimes rise to handle the yarns hung from the warps or run my fingers along its frame.

On January 12 Congress passed a resolution granting the president authorization to drive Iraqi armies from Kuwait. The city held its breath and waited for the next shoe to drop. Gary and I drew inward together, sheltering one another from the coming storm.

The bombings began overnight on the 17th; the city was abuzz with the news. Television screens flashed jets taking off from aircraft carriers, explosions in the night skies over Baghdad, tracer fire and anti-aircraft missiles. American ground forces waited at their staging areas in Saudi Arabia; my heart clenched with every thought of Bob being thrown into that mayhem. The television networks bookended their coverage with fancy graphics and flourishes of martial music, as if they meant to suggest—abetted by the breathless excitement of their commentators—the festive aura of a Super Bowl. To wit, one American commander swaggered about more troops coming in to join the *party*.

"They won't be showing the guts of the whole thing—no pun intended," Gary said one evening during a commercial break. "The Pentagon learned that lesson in Vietnam. They aren't about to let the press mess things up by showing the public what war is really like. Everything's got to be cleared through military channels, and reporters won't get anywhere near the action. Ergo this inspiring display of technological prowess. Sanitized war. What's missing is the carnage down below. With no air defenses, those Iraqis are sitting ducks. You can bet those poor boys—unwilling conscripts, most of them—are being slaughtered in droves. Plenty of civilians, too. The administration likes to tout their smart weapons, but most of those bombs are good old dummies, dropped from forty-thousand feet. Even with the best aiming imaginable, once the winds start to play on those things, it's anybody's guess what, or who, they'll hit."

We soon sickened of the television coverage and took to garnering our news from the *Underground Stream*. I took a copy to my mother one day and she seemed to profit from it. In spite of her worries about Bob, she was holding up well. I convinced her to volunteer with a ladies auxiliary offering support to families with soldiers in the Gulf, and it did her good. When she was at home we spent a good deal of time knitting together; little Drew was amply supplied with leggings and sweaters that winter her father was away at war.

The bombings continued with unabated fury over the following weeks—more explosives were dropped on Iraq than all those loosed during four years of World War Two, according to the *Stream's* backgrounding. Our commanders crowed about a "turkey shoot." Gary and I attended peace vigils: one at the Union, another at the Cathedral, and one in Lafayette Park. We occasionally went by Dupont Circle to see the couriers mount their ongoing poetry slam. We carried them coffees and hot chocolates and stood with crowds who applauded their efforts to express an unease that most of the city's denizens, buttoned up in their suits and houses, hadn't the time or energy to voice.

The week before Valentine's Day Denny and his friends showed up at the Gathering. Gary and I were summoned to the anteroom.

"Glad you guys are here," Gary said. "What's up? Want to join us?"

"Thanks," Denny said, "that's mighty kind of you. But first, there's something we think you need to know about." With a glance at Ben and Sheila, who stood looking on, he sidled up to Gary. "It's pretty, well, confidential."

Gary led Denny and his friends into the maintenance shop. "So," he said, "tell me what's on your minds."

"To be blunt," John said, "we're concerned about Chuck."

"Why would that be?"

"It's this message he gave us for the *Underground Stream*," Denny said. He held out a piece of paper.

"When was this?"

"Yesterday," John said. "You know we hate to rat out a brother, but we're worried he's taking this thing too far. I mean, what with this war on. Those Pentagon security boys are on a hair-pin trigger, if you know what I mean."

Gary took the paper and read it. It said something to the following effect:

*It's time to take it to the top. This one's for the big
brass in the E-ring. I'm sick and tired of them
hiding behind their press black-out. South Entrance.
Midafternoon. Valentine's Day, the day of Love.*

"Worried about Chuck," Tiny lamented.

"I can understand." Gary thought for a moment before adding, with careful deliberation, "but I'd wager that the man knows exactly what he's doing."

He handed the paper back to Denny.

"Are you sure," John asked, "cause we sure as hell ain't."

Gary paused in thought again, and then he said, "Yes, I'm sure."

We persuaded Denny and John to come into the DMZ for food and drink. The ever-shy Tiny remained in the maintenance shop, where I brought him a plate and kept him company. After the three men left I took Gary aside and asked him what it all meant.

"I'm not completely sure," he said, "but it's something about the Pentagon. The hallways inside are built in concentric circles they call rings. The E-ring, the innermost one, is where all the top brass have their offices. It sounds like he wants to try and get to them somehow."

"But how could he possibly get past security?"

"Who knows?"

"I'm thinking about what John said," I went on. "They're going to be very jumpy over there. Do you think Charles understands what he's getting himself into?"

"We questioned the man's judgment once before," Gary said. "But when we investigated, we found the same, solid Pinky we've always known."

I conceded his point. But still I was nervous, and when Valentine's Day came around Gary agreed to humor me. I picked him up at Signed, Sealed & Delivered and we drove to the Pentagon. If anything bad were to go down, I told him, I would rather be on the scene than to hear about it afterward.

We parked along a quiet road that runs beside the cemetery. The Pentagon's South Entrance, a gap in the tall fence that surrounds the complex, with a no-nonsense guard shack to one side, was within view. We sat in the car with the heater running, listening to the radio and waiting, until we were roused by the startled blare of multiple car horns from behind us. One of the cemetery's caissons, pulled by six majestic black horses, came clopping steadily down the road. We jumped out of the car and ran to meet it. The caisson carted a flag-draped casket; Charles stood at its reins. A banner on its gunwales carried a quotation, *Don't cheer boys, those poor devils are dying*, with the added ascription, *Captain John Philips, Battle of Santiago, 1898*. Stop signs, presumably purloined from nearby intersections, were affixed at each of the vehicle's four corners. Little by little the caisson gathered speed until, in one sudden jolt, it hurtled at breakneck pace straight toward the South Entrance! I can still hear the furious drumming of the horses' hooves pounding the pavement; I clutched at Gary's sleeve, anxious for Charles to pull up, but he kept driving on. A gunshot wracked the frosty air. The panicked animals entangled themselves in their traces.

We ran toward the caisson, but the military police held us off. My strident pleas could not convince them to allow us to go to Charles, who lay slumped, bleeding from the abdomen, on the carriage seat. Our attention arrested by a nearby scuffling, we turned to see Frank Davis of the *Underground Stream*. As he attempted to capture a photograph, three MPs wrested away his camera. An ambulance arrived and whisked Charles off.

After two days of inquiries we learned that he had been taken to Walter Reed Hospital. He was in critical condition and unconscious; visitors were not allowed. Gary and I debated contacting his mother, but decided that Charles would prefer that she not be distressed. We were able to locate his sister Jackie, though, and called the hospital every day. After a week his condition had improved. He was off the ventilator and had regained consciousness. They finally allowed us to visit, though two gruff MPs patted us down carefully before ushering us into the room.

"Chuck," Gary said as we stood at Charles's bedside, "I don't know about this one, man."

"They must have changed the guard on me," Charles groaned, shifting painfully in his bed.

"What guard?"

"At the Pentagon. I'd gotten to know those guys, you know, hanging around the area so much. We were pretty tight—at least I thought we were. I told them I was coming on Valentines Day and not to do anything messed up. Maybe they didn't get what I was saying. Or they lost their cool and freaked out . . ."

"They probably thought that casket was loaded with high explosives," Gary said.

"They should have known I wouldn't do anything like that. I leave that kind of action to the boys in the E-ring. I just wanted to deliver a message. Signed, sealed—you know, messages, that's what I'm about, right?" He managed a stilted grin.

We spoke about the war. The ground invasion had begun, and American troops were making quick work of remaining Iraqi units. Charles labored heroically to allay my concerns about Bob with assurances of American tactical superiority. Gesturing to a newspaper on his nightstand, he lamented the carnage on the infamous "Highway of Death," where Iraqi troops fleeing Kuwait City were bombarded until there was no sign of life.

"Chalk up another one for the history books," he said. "Humankind, with all our vast potential, solves yet another problem the good old Neanderthal way."

We sat in silence for a moment, and Charles inquired about the Gathering. Gary said that the couriers were anxious to visit, but that he had held them off until he could determine whether Charles was ready to have company. After assuring us that he would be delighted to see them, Charles propped himself on his elbows. Peering into Gary's eyes, his face grew somber.

"What about Clark?" he said. "Still no news?"

"I'm afraid not."

"Bro, I wouldn't delay. You don't want to be living with regrets, you know. Thinking you might have done something . . ."

"I've been prepping to go down," Gary said. "I just wanted to wait until you were on your feet again."

"Don't worry about me," Charles said. "Jackie's around."

"And me," I said.

"Yeah, and the kids," Charles added. He took me by the hand.

"What about the biz?" Gary asked. "Who's going to take care of things in Dispatch, and bookkeeping, and—"

"They're big boys and girls," Charles said. "Hey, they'll figure it out. I'm right here if they have any questions, and Randy's always there to chaperone." He started to laugh but, wincing, wrapped an arm around his mid-section and sucked in his breath. He remained still for a long moment, and then cautiously exhaled. "Actually," he said, "it looks like they're starting to take some real initiative. This'll be good for them."

Gary nodded his agreement.

"Listen," Charles said to Gary, "make sure you see me before you go." He pulled him close enough to whisper. "There are some survival skills I want to go over with you."

THE WAR was soon over. Bob called from overseas to let my mother know that he was safe—physically, at least. He told her that he had arranged to stop by Washington on his way home.

The campaign was considered a wonderful triumph, as there were few American casualties. The cost to the Iraqis was never precisely calculated, though later estimates placed their dead at one hundred thousand and more. In spite of all the television coverage, the Pentagon's skillful press management prevented the public from knowing much until after the guns quieted and unfiltered information began to emerge. It was only then that we learned, among other unspeakable things, how thousands of Iraqi boys were buried alive in desert dunes by American earth-moving machines at the start of the ground invasion.

Gary made his preparations for Guatemala with calm deliberation. I stood with him at Dulles, holding the lapels of his jacket, my forehead resting on his breast. There were few words. But I prayed inwardly to all the gods and goddesses I could think of, all avatars and benevolent forces, to bring him back to me in one piece.

He has been away now for the better part of a year and his letters, always lacking a return address, have been infrequent; he has been understandably careful about drawing attention to himself. I've spent my time writing this report and working at my loom. As you can see, the report is almost finished, as is the tapestry I had so much trouble beginning last year. Though I would not by any means call it perfect, I am content. It does not, of course, rise to the level of the Barbara Greenfield piece that so moved me at Textile House last autumn, but it encourages me to keep trying. The colors mesh in ways I had hardly imagined when I conceived of the project. The deep red, which became a stumbling block last fall, ceased to be a problem when I let it be the blood of war as well as the joyous cherries of my childhood. The green of lawns likewise eddies into camouflage and army fatigue, and with the open blue sky I was able to suggest, quite to my satisfaction, the kind eyes of my father. In lieu of my solitary bird in the piece that once hung at the clinic, an interlacing flight of multi-colored swallows represents the indissoluble bonds that keep us tied to one another in warmth and spirit.

Another Christmas is now approaching, and I have received a present of immeasurable value. The well-dressed gentleman who delivered the letter in person said only that he is a friend.

Gary is coming home:

Darling,

I was able to get this to someone at the embassy I know I can trust. I didn't want to put it through the mails.

I have wonderful news. My inquiries have led me to this little town in Guatemala's highlands. I've been here for two months, turning over stones, getting to know people and gaining their trust. Today at dawn a brief but pointed note was delivered me by a veiled woman who promptly departed without a word. It's from the man himself. I here copy the relevant portion:

My investigations are nearly complete. The only problem is how to get out of here without blowing my cover. Fortunately, there is every reason to believe that large sums of cash placed in the proper hands can facilitate my departure. This is where you come in, Bro. I need you to get back stateside and talk to my folks. They'll supply the ten thousand. The woman who brought you this letter, or one of her associates, will provide you further details on how to get the funds to me. They have an extensive web of contacts, so you won't need to come into the back country again. They'll meet you in XXXXX. I look forward to catching up with you when I'm back home. By the way, I have tons of material for my book.

I'll be leaving within the next couple of days [Gary resumed]. After a visit to Clark's parents, and back to XXXXX, I'll be home. There's something I want to discuss with you, by the way, when I return. I'll just give you the bare details here. There's a little boy I've gotten to know. He's an orphan, like too many children in this battered country. He's kept alive by the church, and the sporadic largesse of the community, but there's really no place he can call home. He used to beg from me when I would stroll in the plaza, and later he started to come to the place where I'm staying. I play stick ball with him, help him with his letters, and feed him. He's actually helped me to make some crucial contacts. To make a long story short, the kid needs a home. He's very clever, and polite, and I don't think he'd cause any problems. I wish you could have seen the delight in his eyes when he unwrapped his Christmas present—a real soccer ball! (The kids here play their street fútbol with a bundle of old rags.) What do you think? Maybe you and I could be his Mom and Dad? I don't know all the legal details, but I think we could find some way to adopt him. We'd probably need to get married. I guess that's a proposal. Think about it.

Yours ever . . .

There wasn't much to think about regarding Gary's proposal: even phrased, as it was, in a manner befitting one born in the year of the horse ("needs absolute freedom of maneuver"). When he gets back to Washington, in fact, I'll have a proposition of my own; and Howie, you can consider this my formal resignation. There has been a great deal of time to reflect during my sabbatical, about many things, including my work at the clinic, and I've come to the conviction that my career as a therapist is at its end. I don't regret one minute I've spent working with traumatized veterans, but I now feel certain that it is time to move on. My experiences in the desert, weaving at Sarah Tilly's studio, have been ever-present in my mind. I long to start anew, far from where decisions are made to use powerful engines to maim and kill.

Gary also speaks of being at the end of an era, and I still have some savings. If we're ever to make a break, now is as good a time as any. I'm encouraged by my own Chinese horoscope (it assures me that we goats make good artisans). I see myself at my loom, sun-sparkled desert all around, with Gary in his study nearby working on his *magnum opus*. I sense we'll find some way to get by. I'm concerned about my mother, naturally, but she truly seems freer these days. She's back in the gardening club, and continues with the volunteer work she started during the war. I sense that she'll be all right. It's only a four-hour flight, after all.

With great appreciation for all you've done, and warm affection,

Marj Llewellyn

P.S. My regards to all at the clinic . . .

Epilogue: Arturo Llewellyn-Devers to Caroline Curtis, literary agent

Ms. Curtis:

I was thinking you might want to know what happened after Dad returned to Washington. From what they've told me, he and Mom just packed up and came out to New Mexico. After that Dad made a few more trips to Guatemala. On one of those trips he showed me a picture of Mom and asked me if I wanted to come to America and be their son. It seemed pretty scary to leave my town, but at the same time like an exciting adventure. After all, people always said that everyone in America was incredibly rich, and that they lived in huge palaces with everything their hearts desired. (I was so young and naive, I actually believed it!) But I liked playing soccer with Dad and the way he helped me with my lessons. I also thought Mom was pretty, and also nice-looking, in the photographs that he showed me.

My kid sister Alicia was born the year after Mom and Dad adopted me. We've always gotten along pretty good. She's in her last year of high school and plans to study veterinary science at UNM.

After continuing her training with Sarah Tilly, Mom became a master weaver. Her tapestries command a good price in the Santa Fe galleries. Dad spends a lot of time in his study writing. He's still working on his *magnum opus*, as he and Mom jokingly call it. He swears it will be ready for publication soon. Maybe he'll contact you. It's over one thousand pages long, and it skillfully demolishes all the theories used to justify war since the beginning of human history. In the last chapter he offers a plan to completely eliminate weapons from the globe. He knows about treaties and international law from when he worked in the United States Foreign Service. Sometimes he writes an article for one of those stuffy journals about world affairs. When he's not writing, he works on the sheep ranches. He says he likes to get some fresh air and exercise now and then.

Every spring Uncle Chuck (that's what me and Alicia call him, anyway) comes out with Aunt Cynthia. It sounds like he's about to retire from the courier business where Dad used to work. In the summer we usually travel to San Francisco, where my dad's old foreign service pal Clark is president of a non-profit about peace in my native land, Guatemala. At Thanksgiving we always drive up to Ohio to visit Uncle Bob and Aunt Gloria, and my cousins Drew, Tommy, and Kathy. Uncle Bob quit the reserves a few years back. Thank God it was before the latest Iraq war, Mom says. Most Christmases Aunt Cheryl and Uncle Dan come out to the desert with my honorary cousins Julian and Emily. We young people have a great time together, and Mom's always psyched to see her best friend (except my dad, of course). My grandma lives right down the road in a nice, new assisted living center. I go over there and hang with her whenever I get the chance.

As for me, I'm not sure about my next move. I majored in ecology, and I really love the desert. I'm thinking about applying to the U.S. Geological Survey. One thing I know for sure, I'm not about to go into the army.

Mom would kill me.

Yours,

Arturo Llewellyn-Devers

&

Kim Phuc Phan Thi
(from the papers of Gary Devers)

Kim Phuc Phan Thi, you're only nine,
Your nakedness should not an eyebrow raise,
It's understood you hadn't time,
To clothe yourself again once being braised.

It's hot! It's hot! they say you cried,
And on your face I see the frozen pain,
In four degrees your flesh was fired,
Such clever use of naphthalene!

An image works a thousand words,
The billowed smoke and sobbing child attest,
Is war a glorious grinning game?
Ask Kim Phuc Phan Thi—she'd know best.